A Popular Murder

by

Simon Hall

authorHOUSE™

1663 LIBERTY DRIVE, SUITE 200
BLOOMINGTON, INDIANA 47403
(800) 839-8640
WWW.AUTHORHOUSE.COM

This book is a work of fiction. People, places, events, and situations are the product of the author's imagination. Any resemblance to actual persons, living or dead, or historical events, is purely coincidental.

© 2006 Simon Hall. All Rights Reserved.

No part of this book may be reproduced, stored in a retrieval system, or transmitted by any means without the written permission of the author.

First published by AuthorHouse 12/30/05

ISBN: 1-4259-0452-1 (sc)

Printed in the United States of America
Bloomington, Indiana

This book is printed on acid-free paper.

Cover design by Mark Hannon

*To Jess, for all your love,
support and patience*

Thanks to Darin for all your hard work and encouragement, Mark for your excellent artwork and Brian and Jane for medical advice and characterisation.

Prologue

It was only a short wait, but it felt like a long, long time. Murder did that. It stretched the minutes.

The darkness was thick and heavy, the only light the dancing chinks and circles of white from the speeding line of headlamps that penetrated the trees dividing the lay by from the main road. Every car that could have been him, could have slowed, but didn't, roared on, kept driving. Would he come? It was almost time now, almost.

So much could have gone wrong, could still go wrong. Someone could have been in the lay by, a broken down car, a lovers' meet, even a policeman sipping from a flask of tea, sneaking a break in his patrol car. But no one was there; it was deserted, as it almost always was. And then there was the rest of the day, a long day, a nervous day. But it had all gone smoothly too, all according to the plan. It was nearly time now. Would he come?

The shotgun lay in the boot, hidden under a blanket and some newspapers, its twin barrels loaded, primed. It was just a question of pulling the trigger now. Just a gentle finger on that little crescent of smooth metal, just that final act now, just pulling the trigger now..

The rain was drumming on the car's roof, the trees, the tarmac, the misty spray colouring the speeding headlights with rainbows. The glowing clock turned. It was time now.

An engine growled then slowed, the amber blinking of a careful indicator, hard white beams sliding across the shining tarmac. He was here.

Chapter one

He knew he shouldn't have paid those two prostitutes. He could feel trouble coming when he'd done it.

Ok, so it wasn't much money, just 30 quid each, the going rate they'd called it. They'd made that up surely, they couldn't often be asked for what he wanted. But they'd said they'd only do it if he paid them, so he went to the bank and got the money out. He'd kept the cashpoint receipt, it was the best he could manage to prove what he'd done. The girls didn't hand out receipts, certainly weren't VAT registered, and the expenses division always squealed for a VAT number so they could claw some money back. But he hadn't claimed for it yet, and didn't think he would be now, not given the simmering look on Lizzie's face.

'What the hell do you think you were doing?'

He'd been through all this. 'Well, as I said…'

'I know what you said.' She cut in, her three inch black stiletto heel grinding into the carpet. A bad sign. 'I asked you what the hell you thought you were doing?'

'I was doing what I always do. What I think's best to get the bloody story on air. That's what I was doing.'

Her head snapped up from the two pages spread over her desk, the MP's complaint that had brought him here, to her office, and the electric chair. There was a line of three soft and enticingly curved red armless seats, pushed together against the wall to make a genial sofa, and there was one battered plastic, grey, metal-legged chair.

It was jarringly out of place with the framed family snapshots on her desk and the vibrant seascapes, bright skies and smiling faces of the prints on the walls. Deliberately so. The chair was there to remind her staff who was in charge here, and it worked. The electric chair.

'By paying a couple of tarts good company money for their services?'

It's not company money, is it, he thought. It's mine. Or it was. Fat chance I'll get it back now with that irritating little MP sticking his nose in. 60 quid blown on a pair of hookers and nothing to show for it except a savaging from Lizzie. Good work.

He managed to stop himself saying it. 'I wasn't paying them for me, was I? You make it sound like I was having a damn good time with them. I was paying them for the bloody programme's sake, not mine.'

She shot him a warning glare, said nothing.

'Look Lizzie', another deep breath, fragile calm. 'I was just doing what I thought best. We needed the story for the programme. It was the lead splash. We couldn't do it without an interview with some of the pros and they won't do anything without being paid. So I paid them. What choice did I have?'

She sat silent, studying him. He'd been here enough times for a ritual going over, it was part of the job. You can't be a TV reporter without bending the rules, or as Lizzie joked in her lighter moments, just snapping them. This wasn't a lighter moment. The stiletto was still grinding the carpet.

But this time felt different. The others had been standard. He'd upset someone, they'd complained, she'd done her duty in gently mauling him, he'd left with the unspoken understanding that getting the story on air was what mattered. Everyone happy. Complaints happened, it was part of the job. But this felt different.

'So let me get this straight.' She sounded calmer now and he was glad of it. 'I've got to reply to this guy. You were covering the attack on that prostitute down at the docks?'

'Yeah. She was badly beaten, in hospital critical for a while, you remember?' A nod. 'There were a few people off sick that day and a couple of others on a course, so I volunteered to help out and do it.'

Another nod. The heel had stopped grinding the carpet.

'I interviewed the police and they appealed for witnesses and warned the other girls working there to take care. But to make the story work I had to interview some of them. And they won't do anything without being paid, so…'

'Ok, I know the rest, it's all down here.'

Her left eyebrow arched upwards and it heartened him. A fine looking, almost beautiful woman, she said she was in her late 30s, although the average guess was more early 40s. She was slim, the product of Plymouth's most expensive gym, and habitually wore black trouser suits with black shoes so highly and sharply heeled they took her to nearer six feet. The shoes were a useful clue to her mood. High heels were a danger warning.

Her raven hair was cut sharply into a chin length bob, but it was her nose and lips that blunted any real beauty. They were thin, the nose a sharp taper, the lips reddened lines, and the combination could make her look cruel. Her eyebrows were over plucked into sharp lines, and when she was amused, the left one would arch involuntarily. The shift was shallow, but unmistakeable. He relaxed a little and shifted in the clammy chair.

'This is real trouble.' The eyebrow flattened again, a heel working the carpet. What was going on? 'Alan Jones has got to hear about it. It's a nasty complaint.' She flicked at the letter. 'He says it's disgraceful that we're funding illegal earnings. So what have you got to say about that?' A tilt of the head, a change of tone. 'Bearing in mind that ITV are currently negotiating with the government for the renewal of our licence to broadcast and we're supposed to be squeaky clean at the moment?' She let the words linger and he shifted awkwardly in his seat again. 'You haven't exactly managed that, have you?'

Alan Jones, irritating little man, full of himself, Labour MP for Plymouth Devonport, overpowering ministerial ambitions. A serial complainer after the story of him being near the top of the league for claiming parliamentary expenses, but second from bottom for attendance at the House of Commons. A gently mocking report on South West Tonight had labelled him 'poor value for money, must do better.' He'd never forgotten, let alone forgiven.

'The first thing I'd like to know is how he's so in with Plymouth's prostitutes?'

Another glare said that wasn't the right answer. He felt his temper bubbling again. Big mistake Mr Jones, breaking cover. Now I know my target and I nurture grudges lovingly. I'll get you, and I know exactly how. I know someone who'll be very interested to hear about your closeness to the city's pros. Very interested indeed, will make excellent use of it I'm sure. Mental note; tomorrow, a quick call to set up Mr Jones.

'Look, I did what I did because it was an important story. I couldn't do it without talking to the girls. We needed to hear about the risks they face and what they could do to try to prevent attacks. They wouldn't talk without being paid, so I paid them. That's it, I paid them, big bloody deal.'

He was sure the eyebrow arched again, briefly, then flattened.

'Well, that certainly explains the complaint', she said slowly, carefully. 'And it's all true, so I've no choice. I'm going to have to take action.'

'What? What?!'

Dan looked down and took a disguised breath as his mind flew, panicked. The last time he'd felt such a shock was when the grill caught fire in his flat. It was a spinning sickening in the stomach. Within a second, he'd seen the beautiful Victorian house burn down, his beloved dog die, howling in the flames, his CDs, clothes, furniture, paintings, all incinerated, all that, instantaneously played out in his mind.

Another series of disasters unfolded in front of him now. Goodbye beloved job, career, comfortable lifestyle, hello to a grotty room in a shared house and flipping burgers at some fast food stall. The electric chair's plastic grip tightened.

What was going on? He'd been here before and for worse, much worse. He'd been prepared for an amused telling off, been ready to make a light-hearted apology. That was the way it had always been. He and Lizzie understood each other didn't they? Get the story on air, that's what counts. She'd been a reporter herself and had played the game. Get it on and make it good, and if you have to pull a trick or two, I'll pick you up on it afterwards. But get it on.

'What?' It was all he could manage. 'What are you talking about?' The anger was venting, he couldn't hold it. 'Take some jumped up little MP's whinge and use it to do me over? I didn't even have to be doing the bloody story. I volunteered to help out and now you're using it against me. Thanks. Thanks very much. I won't make that mistake again. That's the last time I..'

'That's enough.' Sharp, but no anger. What was going on? He'd expected a screamed retaliation. 'I'm not talking anything drastic. You're not being sacked.' How big of you he thought, how very large. But he felt his chest heave, couldn't hide the relief.

'I'm moving you. You'll be doing Crime in future, not Environment.'

'What? What?!'

Why did he suddenly feel like he was 21 again, and the day the woman he had fallen hopelessly in love with told him they had no future and she was leaving? Thomasin. A moment when you think you've found what you want in life, and suddenly it's taken away from you. He loved the Environment Correspondent job. For five years now he'd enjoyed every day. He'd never been able to say that about anything else.

'Come on, it's sexy.' Cajoling, persuading, she knew he was lost, wasn't listening. 'The best of the correspondents' jobs. All the big stories. Murder, arson, rape, police, courts judges, all that sort of thing.'

But Dan was on Dartmoor, high up Hay Tor, looking south through the racing clouds to the shimmering sea at Torbay, then turning north towards Exmoor, feeling the relentless pummelling of the angry wind, staring up at the scowling grey rock of the mighty Tor, unbowed by millions of years of snarling rain, and thousands more pairs of clambering shoes. He was telling a camera about the dangers of erosion, the difficult balance of encouraging access to Dartmoor without damaging its fragile fabric. Now he was outside the imposing white stone of Exeter Crown Court, one of a babbling pack of reporters, telling a camera about the life sentence handed down to a teenager for the murder of a baby..

'What? What?! For Christ's sake! I've got environment taped. I know the stories inside out. I know all the people. We get all the big news first.' I love it, he could have added, it's a precious part of my life, please don't take it from me.. 'I don't want to move. I don't see why I should be victimised for trying to do the job well..'

'Tough. I'm moving you and that's that.' Lizzie stared into him, her heel grinding the carpet again. 'And don't give me any more of your bleating. I've heard enough.' Her voice sharpened, a fingernail jabbed at him. 'You've landed me with an evil complaint and I've now got to take this guy out for lunch and suck up to him in the hope it'll calm him down. So let me set you straight on this. It's Crime or you'll be covering vicars opening village fetes for the next God knows how long.' The words hung between them. 'Your choice.'

'Some bloody choice', he grunted, and stomped out of the office, slamming the door as hard as he could. Behind him Lizzie waited, pursed her lips until she was sure he was gone, then slowly released the laughter she'd been holding back. She dabbed at her eyes with a tissue, then, still chuckling, reached in a drawer for the newly published annual viewer's performance survey.

It was open on the page; 'Subjects Viewers Like / Want more.' Top of the list was Crime. She picked up her fountain pen, crossed it out twice, and started chuckling again. The thought of Dan paying prostitutes for an interview wouldn't leave her. It was one of his best yet. She hoped one day she could tell him so. One day when she wasn't his editor.

～

It was almost seven o'clock that evening when a leaden Dan Groves trooped out of the studios, glared back at the lights in the old Victorian part of the building where Lizzie's office was, swore loudly, stuck two fingers up at her window, then climbed slowly into his standard issue, ITV Peugeot and drove the half mile back to his flat.

There was beer in his cupboards, and beer was his simple plan for the evening. But other people had other plans that night, murderous ones, which would suck him into the first story of his new job and deny him the alcoholic oblivion he desired.

～

A woman finished the details of the greying highlights in the hair on a portrait of the man she loved. She worked under the natural daylight bulbs of the second bedroom that doubled as her studio. She stood back to admire the image. She stood still, rigid, almost at attention, her arms by her sides as she studied the features she'd reproduced. She stretched out a hand to stroke the canvas, on the mouth, where it was dry, but stopped herself. It was, she thought, as close as she had come to the intimacy she craved, perhaps as close as she would ever come. Unless..

A man stood outside his house, staring up at the sky, his clothes quickly soaking. He didn't mind at all. It was a perfect steady rain, just perfect. His mind slid back to last week, surfing the Internet, checking the Met Office site. Five days ahead, it warned, that was the earliest the weather could be predicted with any real accuracy. Just five days. The preparations needed time and the forecast had been wrong once before when everything was ready. Monday was due to be wet and miserable, classic English autumn weather and exactly what was needed. This time the forecast was right. A perfect rain.

Another man looked out of the window of his cold, one-bedroom ground floor flat, towards the house where his wife and son lived. His breath fogged the glass, casting halos around the streetlights outside. He couldn't see the house, there were rows and lines of Victorian terraces in the way, but he could feel it. He could feel Tom sleeping on his side as he always did, his blonde hair tussled on his pillow, and Annie reading one of her celebrity gossip magazines and blowing on a steaming cup of jasmine tea. He could feel the warmth of the real flame gas fire on his face, and the comfortably worn sofa beneath his back. He longed to go to them. Then he forced Sarah back into his mind, her beaten, bloodied face, almost unrecognisable, her strangled, anguished sobs. He nodded to himself and stayed.

An older man watched a modern war film. The computer generated white blazes of tracer bullets flashed across the room, and machine gun fire boomed and bounced around the television's stereo speakers. He sat still, his feet in threadbare burgundy slippers suspended on a brown leather pouf. The film played as a distraction but he saw none of it. He was trying not to think of what he had done to make his only son hate him so much.

A younger man sat in one of the bedrooms of his house and played with the money. He hadn't counted it for a few weeks now, didn't need to anymore, but he knew there were tens of thousands of pounds at least. The familiar purples and browns of the 10 and 20 pound notes were softened by the opaque plastic of the bags they filled, and they rustled delightfully as he shifted them from the bed and back to their hiding place. It was time to go and make some more.

Another man saw the neighbour's curtains twitch as he walked quickly up the path. And it wasn't the first time either. Damn! He'd tried leaving the van around the corner, but there was nowhere you could really hide it. He didn't need to knock, the door swung open and he slid in to the welcoming light, but he knew the damage was done, that he'd been seen. It dampened his pleasure at the squeezing hug that awaited him. This couldn't go on.

A woman was deleting emails in a darkened office. She couldn't remember how to remove them in blocks, so she guided the cursor through the intray, one by one. They were almost all gone now, almost, but she'd check back at the end to make sure. As each disappeared, she felt a gentle nudge of relief. The reflection of her face in the screen showed it. She couldn't believe she'd really considered doing what they discussed.

A man lay on his bed, wrestling with his mind. He knew he shouldn't do it. But the urge was so strong now. He'd held it back for days, weeks, into months, but it was still there, still growing. It hadn't waned, as he'd been promised it would. It had grown. And now it was becoming irresistible. He could feel the pull of surrender; see the young boy's face in front of him, the hand reaching up to take his. He could resist it no longer.

∼

Dan lay on his favourite of the two great blue four-seater sofas in his living room. He was going back over the day. He'd done it so many times now and was determined this would be the last.

He went through his pep talk again. Point one; I'm healthy and lucky. Yes I am, come on now; believe me when I tell you. I'm six feet tall, and with a fairly athletic build, this great brute of an Alsatian keeps me fit enough. He reached out and ran his hand over the dog's head, raising an appreciative whining yawn. Ok, so the hair's receding a bit on the top, but then I'm 34 now, so I suppose you'd expect that. And it's a good burnt brown colour, like freshly ground coffee that's only suffered a dash of milk. Some people pay for such tints.

The nose is a little fat perhaps, but not too bad. The cheekbones are passable; the lips full, perhaps even too full, and on balance, I'd say the eyes are the best feature. Sky blue, according to those interior design catalogues. It's an unusual combination with the hair, but it seems to work ok. There are a couple of women who are interested in me at the moment, even if the same old hang up means I'm not particularly interested in them.

I've got good friends, and enough of them, some who want to drink with me, some who want to look after me, some who want to set me up with a potential wife, and some who want to do all three. I've got this faithful companion of a soppy dog lying on the floor next to the sofa, snoozing but keeping one half open eye on me as ever he does. Thanks Rutherford, my wonderful friend.

I've got this elegant flat, the ground floor and one of four in a mid-Victorian semi. The ceiling is high, some 12 feet up there I'd guess, with white plaster cornicing.

The fireplace is charred black stone and original, framed by ornate white marble. The bay window takes up most of one wall, and looks south onto the amber glow of nighttime Plymouth. There's no road out there, no houses overlooking, and it's quiet, peaceful in fact.

So, as far as I can tell, I've got all a man could possibly need. But I can still feel the pull of the swamp. Churchill used to call it the black dog, but not me, not with this beautiful and loyal creature lying beside me. For me it's a swamp, an irresistible, bottomless, dark sucking pit.

I hate the swamp because it's so vindictive. I can have everything in life. The world is running for me, and I can be so outwardly happy, but that's the most dangerous time of all. When you start to think you're safe from the swamp, that's when it really wants you. All you can do is try to fight it, with friends, and drinks, and walks and work, but it just sits back and waits. It's patient and it's cunning. It knows you can't escape. It only leaves you when it's ready and it returns on a whim.

Sometimes – like today - there are triggers. Something changed today. A job I've been doing and delighting in for more than 5 years has been taken away. No wonder I can feel the depression, back again, lurking at the edge of my mind, like a mugger in the darkness at the end of a street.

The cupboard was open and the beer beckoned. Enough. Time to succumb to its brief release.

He pulled himself up from the sofa, leaned over, and gave the dog a cuddle, then headed for the kitchen. His mobile warbled its cicada ring tone. The duty journalist, no good evening, no small talk, just babbled urgency. A man's body, freshly dead, sprawled in a rain soaked lay by, most of his chest blown away. Rumours of it being someone well known. He reached automatically for the car keys. The flush of the adrenalin was as good as alcohol for fending off the swamp. For now.

Chapter two

The rain was gentler than earlier, but it didn't improve his mood. It beat on the windscreen and made the darkness denser. Monday night, 8.50, weather cold, wet and miserable, and a scramble call to a story. Bad days built up a momentum; once trouble started it rarely stopped, just grew.

He tried to come up with a plan for when he got to the scene. It was the first story of the new job he didn't want. His colleagues, his bosses, they'd be watching it closely. What would he write? He knew he had no idea. He felt unprepared and vulnerable, just like he did as a nervous trainee, first walking into a newsroom years ago.

And then there was the pressure. File a report for the 10 o'clock bulletin, Chris, the night producer had said. Send back some pictures and a voice track, 45 seconds worth. We'll order a despatch rider to come get it.

8.55 now, it was 10 minutes back to base on a bike. He'd have to give them 20 mins for a rushed edit, so he had about half an hour to find out what was going on and write something. He felt a surge of adrenalin and was glad of it. It helped to clear his head.

He hadn't asked exactly where the murder scene was, it was more important to get there, but he didn't need to. Ahead, on the A 38, the dual carriageway linking Plymouth to Exeter, he could see the ranks of blue flashing lights painting the grey night sky. He slowed, pulled off the main road into the lay by and parked next to a line of police cars.

Half a dozen uniformed officers were milling about, patrolling the cordon of familiar fluttering blue and white police tape. The detectives would be the other side of that, along with the victim. An ambulance crew stood around chatting, stealing time for a cigarette, red ends smouldering through the rain. There was no urgency, no apparent hope for the man who's been shot. A few locals had also gathered and were pointing, gawping and gossiping from beneath coats and umbrellas. This is the future now, he thought, and tried to contain a rising distaste. Violent death, police, ghoulish sightseers, and me, bringing it all to the thousands of fascinated others who can't be here in person. How delightful.

He took a breath, got out of the car, pulled on his coat and walked up to one of the constables in what he hoped was an assured way.

'Good evening officer. Dan Groves, ITV News. Can you tell me what's going on please?'

The policeman was young, looked flushed and excited, possibly new and getting his first taste of the type of police work he'd seen so often on TV. He looked oddly satisfied. Well, it had to be better than pounding the beat in the downtrodden parts of Plymouth, being abused and spat at from every other window of the graffiti-coated, decaying tower blocks.

'Sorry sir, we're can't say anything at the moment. All I can tell you is there's been an incident.'

No, really? He thought, thanks a lot. 'Any hint about what type of incident?'

'No, sir, sorry.'

'How many of your lads here?'

'Can't say sir, sorry.'

'What time were you called out?'

The policeman shook his head. 'Detective Chief Inspector Adam Breen is in charge. He's over there, behind the cordon, but he did say he would be coming out later to have a word with the press. If you wouldn't mind just waiting here, I'm sure he won't be long.'

Great, no info yet, just 25 mins to deadline.

Another car drew up, an old and battered Ford Fiesta. One headlight was on dipped beam, the other full, and the smell of oil laden exhaust smoke choked the air. The handbrake screeched and the engine spluttered to a halt. Out lumbered Ellis Hughes, a freelance photographer known locally as Dirty El. A tussled mop of unruly black hair sat above his chubby, freckled and permanently grinning face.

Dirty El's nickname was well earned. He took the pictures no one else could. Last month he'd got the snap of the mayor of Plymouth, an upright moralist of a man, emerging from his mistress's flat in a half dressed state by setting off the fire alarms in the exclusive harbour front block in which she lived. The city had enjoyed his shamefaced hypocrisy.

In the weeks before that, El had broken through a police cordon around a double fatal shooting by donning a black suit and tie, borrowing a large black estate car, and telling the gullible officer on sentry duty he was the undertaker come to discuss burial arrangements. There were many other such tales.

'Hi El.' At least that's one ally here. They always looked after each other. 'So you picked this one up too eh? Know anything much? The cops aren't saying a thing.'

El's grin widened. He tapped one of the many sagging pockets on his ragged body warmer and nodded knowingly at the bulge there.

'Got a scanner.' He checked around to make sure there were no police to overhear him. 'Tapping in to the cops' frequencies'. He looked pleased with himself. 'The body was found about 6 after a tip off. Gunshot wounds. One hundred per cent dead. A pathologist's been called, along with all available detectives. Some cop on the radio said it was a local businessman, but didn't say who.'

How did they know that so quickly, wondered Dan, writing it all down. 'Someone well known then, maybe? This could be an interesting one.'

'Yeah, and they won't let us through this cordon to get some shots of the scene.' Dan could imagine the pound notes floating tantalisingly in front of El's eyes. 'So I'm off for a little circuit, see if I can get around the back somehow and get a snap.'

'El, just before you go. I've got an idea for you, could be a lucrative one. I was going to call you, but as you're here..'

He knew he shouldn't, but what the hell. The cold thought of revenge warmed him.

'Alan Jones MP seems to know the pros by the docks a bit too well. Could be worth staking out.' El nodded, smiled, stroked the long lens of his camera lovingly and disappeared into the darkness.

⁓

He'd seen enough bodies before, cold and blue on the mortuary slab, slumped in kitchens or hallways, patterns of congealed blood pumped out around them, in alleyways, knives protruding like unnatural limbs or dumped in fields, decaying, ligatures still choking long dead necks, but this one made him flinch, turn away.

It was the savagery of the gaping chest wound, right where the heart would once have been, a stack of white, blood flecked ribs, cracked and caved in, their defences viciously breached, inside shades of sickening human colour, scarlet and port, shredded hints of soft organs and sinewy arteries exposed to the rain and air they should never have known.

He took a couple of quick, deep breaths, turned back, aware of the eyes on him, the other detectives, doctor, pathologist, peered closer. Christ, the wound was the size of a saucer. And was that steam coming from it?

One of the younger detectives, full of keen bravado had seen it too. 'Guess it's only to be expected sir, warm in there, cold air getting in..'

A wave silenced him. Enough of the body, the medics could bring him what detail they could of that tomorrow. Enough of the banter too, natural of course to deal with the horrors of what they had to see, but the dead deserved respect, and it was turning his stomach.

'Weapon?'

'Shotgun.' The pathologist's voice was muffled under the hood of his coat. 'Not sawn off, judging by the wound. It's relatively compact and well defined, but deep. Looks like a standard 24-inch barrel gun. Fired from close range I'd say, probably a couple of yards. Angled upwards, suggesting the killer wasn't tall. Clinical, right into the heart, the plug of shot concentrated at that distance, so causing massive trauma. Death would have been instantaneous.'

'No sign of the gun?'

'No Mr Breen.' The young detective again, quieter, more respectful this time. 'Although we've only done a basic search so far.'

'Footprints?'

'No sir.'

'Tyre tracks?'

'No sir, not after this rain.'

'Any hint of a motive?'

'Probably not robbery. His wallet's still on the dashboard and doesn't look like it's been touched. There's obviously plenty of cash in it. That's about all we've established so far.'

'Ok, get the area sanitised. Only those that really need to be allowed inside the cordon from now on. I want a register of everyone who's been here and the prints of their shoes taken so we can eliminate them. I want a list of all their clothes as well in case we pick up any fibres. All vehicles noted too, and their tyres.'

The body was sprawled just a couple of feet from the Range Rover, its door open, the light inside still on. The rain had diluted the seeping blood, creating a vague aura around the corpse. He closed his eyes for a moment; let his mind run over what had happened here. Victim pulls up, turns engine and lights off, opens door, gets out, eyes adjusting to the darkness, killer's waiting, emerges from the gloom and bang..

'Full forensic check of the jeep please, I want to know if the killer could have been riding in there with him.' He knew they wouldn't, but had to check. 'And the victim too, particularly fingernails and what's left of his clothing. Could he have struggled with the killer? Was any of his skin clawed off and left under the victim's nails? Is there any trace of fibres or DNA on the victim's clothes that could have come from the attacker?'

It had to be done, but again he knew there wouldn't be. This killer meant to leave no clues.

It was a fair guess the victim knew his attacker and had arranged to meet them here. Why else would two people, one armed with a shotgun, be in this desolate lay by on a miserable autumn night? That meant a planned killing. The lack of tyre tracks or footprints backs up the theory. And if this man, lying dead at his feet was who they suspected he was, he was going to have plenty of suspects to talk to. Someone short? A woman perhaps? Maybe, but killers were getting cleverer, more aware of what forensics and science could do. It could easily be someone taller who kept the gun low to give them a false lead.

He knew he shouldn't think it, had a job to do here, but couldn't help himself. A major investigation, a careful killing, the case would become his life unless they were very lucky and the murderer had been careless. From what he'd seen, he didn't hold out much hope of that. The shot to the heart suggested calm ruthlessness, the culmination of a detailed plan, not someone who'd panic and leave precious evidence behind. And why the heart? Most of the other shootings he'd dealt with had been to the head, tended to be where a killer went for to ensure the job was done. Could this murderer have had a special reason for going for the heart? Some kind of statement they wanted to make?

He plunged his hands into his pockets, fiddled with some coins, nodded at a vision of long, frustrating days and weeks ahead, hunting the killer. So much for his careful timetable for reconciliation with Annie and Tom in time for the coming Christmas.

∼

Another car pulled into the lay by, a green Renault estate, a car Dan knew well from the thousands of miles he'd sat in the passenger seat, writing scripts and making the endless calls to interviewees, outside broadcast engineers, researchers and producers. The nervous loneliness he felt from being the new kid in the class at these crime stories lifted a little. His cameraman and friend, Nigel Stein.

'Evening Nigel.'
'Evening. All change eh?'
'What?'

'All change.' He sounded tetchy. 'Those lovely days of meeting up by a riverbank at a civilised hour to film some leaping salmon have gone now eh? Now it's nighttime meets at dodgy dives to film dead bodies. I think I preferred it how it was.'

Dan felt a jolt of anger. *As if I didn't too..*

'Look mate, I didn't apply for this job. As you know, it was dumped on me. Still, we continue to work and get paid, so we'd better make the best of it. They want something for the late bulletin so we've got 20 mins.'

Nigel said nothing. He was hauling his camera, tripod and microphone from the back of the car and checking them. In his early 50s, he'd worked with Dan for most of his 5 years. Initially a quiet and shy man, with time the extraordinary spectrum of his experience had emerged. He'd managed the sound on T-Rex tours in the 70s, got bored with that, and moved on to doing the lighting with David Bowie.

After his rock and roll days, he'd taken up camerawork, travelled the world filming news for the BBC and ITV for 15 years before deciding it was time to slow down, and settled back in his native Devon to marry and bring up two sons. It was only a few months after they'd begun working together that Nigel's wife had been diagnosed with breast cancer. She died five months later. The thought still brought a tingling to the back of Dan's eyes.

Nigel kept working – Jayne had insisted on that – which meant their days were often punctuated by breaks for intense emotional unloading, and tears, so many tears. Dan had spent evenings looking after the boys, James who was 6, and 7 year old Andrew, whilst

Nigel and Jayne made the most of their remaining time together.

When she'd died, he'd helped arrange the funeral. He hadn't known the family long enough to feel a real part of the service, and had watched from the back of the church while his black suited friend held the hands of the two young boys as they tried to understand the sorrow around them, the pity in the eyes of everyone who spoke to them. It was Dan's first experience of bereavement, and he'd discovered that watching people he cared about suffering was worse than hurting himself.

A quiet and thoughtful man, Nigel had a touching humility and a delightful way of finding much of what the world had to offer comical. About five feet 10, he had untidy grey to silver hair and was prone to fits of the giggles.

Dan occasionally teased him as someone who should be in the SAS of newsgathering. Nothing stopped Nigel. Dan had followed as he barged his way through impenetrable scrums of people to get pictures and interviews at celebrity photocalls, and sat next to him, eyes screwed shut as he drove for two miles on the wrong side of the road past a queue of cars to get to a train crash. He'd even seen Nigel climb 20 feet up a precarious tree to film Prince Charles as he fed the birds at Dorset's Abbotsbury Swannery. His determination was a wonderful contrast to his affability.

'What's happening then?' asked Nigel, mustering a cheerful tone that said his protest had passed. His moods never lasted long and Dan was thankful for it. It made them compatible. His own sulks could linger for days.

'Beyond that police cordon there is apparently a well-known local businessman lying dead of shotgun wounds. A detective is due to grace us with an address about what's happened at a time of his choosing and convenience. Aside from that, we know nothing. I'm going to try to knock together a sensible script for the report. If you could pick up some shots of the police activity and cordon, I'll give you a shout when the offending Inspector arrives.'

Nigel hoisted the camera up on his shoulder and started filming. The pictures would be the mainstay of their report. Wide shots of the police cars and cordon, tighter ones of the officers guarding the scene and the onlookers, close ups of the police tape fluttering. Dan stood beside and slightly behind him, the standard position for a good reporter. Watch your cameraman's back, that had been drilled into him early. He can't tell what's going on around him while he's looking down the viewfinder. Look after him and he'll look after you.

The pack was gathering, more journalists arriving in their various cars. There were now three camera crews, themselves, Spotlight, the local BBC news programme and Sky News. Some newspaper reporters were clustered together, hunched against the rain, comparing speculation on what was going on. Several photographers lit the night with their flashes, taking pictures of the line of police cars and cordon. Nigel swung the camera and filmed the snappers, always useful for Dan to talk about the media frenzy around a story. A couple of reporters detached themselves to go and talk to the gawping public. Dan shuffled over to keep an ear on the conversations. Part of the pack mentality was to make sure you didn't miss anything.

It was all the usual clichés, 'what a shock, terrible, who'd have thought it would happen here.' He didn't bother getting Nigel to film it, didn't have the time. 10 minutes to deadline. They'd better record the words he'd jotted down. Nigel handed him the long fluffy microphone. 'I've got enough pictures to cover 45 seconds of report', he said. 'We'll stick the voice track on the end of this tape'.

They climbed into the back of the Renault, the best they could do for soundproofing from the road and clamour of the hacks and photographers.

'Recording', said Nigel.

'Cue is as follows; a murder investigation's underway after the discovery of a man's body by a main road outside Plymouth. It's thought he's been killed by a shotgun. Our Crime correspondent Dan Groves reports from the scene.'

'Voice level fine, sounding good and clear', said Nigel. 'Go ahead with the report'.

Dan took a deep breath. 'The police have called all available detectives to the lay by on the A38 just to the east of Plymouth. A major investigation is beginning here tonight. A man's body was discovered at about six o'clock this evening. It's thought he has shotgun wounds. The area's been cordoned off while police officers examine the scene. The attack has already caused great interest in the media, with reporters from radio, TV and newspapers gathering here, amidst talk that the victim is a well-known local person. The police have released no more details as yet, but are due to do so in the next hour. This is Dan Groves, on the A38 outside Plymouth, for South West Tonight'.

Nigel gave a thumbs up. 'About 40 seconds worth'. Close enough.

'For the picture editor', said Dan, 'use shots of the police cordon, officers on guard, hacks and sightseers looking on. There should be plenty on the tape. End of despatch.'

Nigel stopped recording, ejected the tape from the camera, handed it to Dan. He scribbled 'Murder, Dan/Nigel, A38 Plymouth' on it, strode over to waiting Despatch Rider and handed it to him. 'Go!' he shouted over the growling bike.

Dan let out a sigh of relief. First deadline met, albeit with minimal information and a bit of padding out. But it would do for a start. Now to try to find out what was really going on.

El materialised silently back at his side and tugged him away from the other hacks. That was the other thing about the pack; if you got a sniff of something tasty you had to lose them to keep it your own.

'Did you get anything?'

'Nah. Think they've got wise to my tricks now. There's a cordon all the way around the site with coppers guarding it. They've got big lights up, but they've put up a tent over the body so I couldn't see anything. I did get one juicy bit of info though'. El couldn't disguise his glee. 'As I was coming back along the lay by, I saw this shiny big new Range Rover parked up by the tent. And guess what? Its door was open and it's got a personalised plate. And guess what it is?'

'No idea.'

'EAB 1'

'And?'

'Don't you recognise it?'

'Nope. Funnily enough, I don't make a habit of memorising number plates.'

El look surprised. 'EAB 1 is the personal plate of Edward Arthur Bray's jeep. Bray who owns a quarter of Plymouth. Bray who shoved his Dad aside to take over the empire. Bray who bankrupted some of Plymouth's other big fish and took over their territory. Bray who's got even more enemies than business interests. In short, as he used to be known, Bray the bastard.' El paused, shook his head and the grin dimmed. 'That was until he got involved in saving the hospice and we had to start calling him 'The Angel of St Jude's'. Weird guy, confusing. One minute a bastard, the next an Angel. And we never did suss why.'

Dan nodded thoughtfully. Bray was infamous in Plymouth. All the journalists he knew had tried to get an interview with him to find out why he'd saved St Jude's, but he'd never spoken about it. Never spoken about anything come to that. Requests for interviews were politely declined by most people; they generally said 'no comment'. Bray told you to piss off. If it was him, this was going to be a hell of a story to kick off his new job with.

A stirring amongst the other journalists and camera crews interrupted them. Striding silhouetted figures approached from inside the cordon. They radiated authority. Even in the dark detectives stick out. A couple of 'about bloody time too' comments rumbled from the soaking pack. He pushed his way past a radio reporter, then a photographer who was fumbling with his lens and got a shove of retaliation back. He ignored it. Positioning was all in a media scrum.

The tallest of the group held up his hand for calm as the journalists formed a semi circle around them. The unspoken hierarchy was at work, camera crews and photographers in the middle of the line, reporters fanned out to their sides. Dan often thought of it as like a firing squad, and for some of their interviewees, that was exactly what it was. Execution by the media.

There was more jostling in the line, and a mumbled oath as a couple of flashes flared. The man blinked hard as he was flooded with the stark white light from the spot lamps fixed to the top of the TV cameras.

'Ladies and gentlemen, thanks for coming out here. I'm Detective Chief Inspector Adam Breen, the senior investigating officer. You'll want to know what's happened here of course, but I'm afraid we're in the very early stages of our investigation and there's only a limited amount I can tell you. However, what I can say is this. Police officers arrived here at about 6 o'clock this evening after a tip off from a member of the public. We found a man's body. Our initial investigations indicate the cause of death is a shotgun wound to the chest. He's in his late 30s, and is believed to be local. All available detectives have been mobilised to investigate, and a major incident room has been set up at Charles Cross police station in Plymouth. That's about all I can say for now, except to appeal for anyone who may have witnessed what happened here to come forward. We'd particularly like to talk again to the person who called us. They didn't leave a name or contact number. Thank you.'

There was a burst of shouted questions: 'who is he? Any ideas who did it?' but like politicians, the detectives had said all they wanted to, ducked back under the police tape and were returning to the crime scene. The camera lights flicked off and the line broke as reporters began phoning their news desks, to moan about the lack of information and file what copy they could for the morning.

He and Nigel retreated to the shelter of the Renault to decide what to do next. He'd have to write something for the breakfast news, and it'd have to be different from what went out tonight. Fresh copy, new angles, keep the audience interested, the constant demands.

First dilemma, do I say it might be Bray? Easy one, of course I can't, not on the basis of it being his jeep. Anyone could have borrowed it. I'll look a right idiot if I say he's thought to be dead and he rings in to complain. Not the time to make a fool of myself, not after the prostitutes and with Jones on my tail. But now Jones has got El on his tail..

The thought warmed him. 'Come on then Nigel. I've got a piece to camera in mind, then we can go home. Or rather, you can go home, I'll go back to the office and write it up.'

In his younger days, Dan had been taught that the address to the camera was the reporter's way of building up their profile and stamping their authority on a story. He'd believed it too, until an older hack had laughed in his face. Forget the professional spin boy, he'd said; it's your slice of glory too. What's the point of working in television if you don't appear on the thing?

In his environmental work, when he knew what he was talking about, he used his appearances to interpret and analyse. Fat chance of that here, he thought, I know just about nothing, so he stuck to the safety of the facts. Police appeals for witnesses were a terrible cliché, they did it all the time, it was too safe and easy. But this time they were asking for whoever phoned the report of the body in to come forward. That was more mysterious and interesting, so he used it as his fresh line for the morning. It sounded dramatic enough.

He said goodnight to Nigel and drove wearily back to the studios to leave the second tape and his script for the morning, when it would be edited together by the early news team.

He got back to the flat just after midnight, and was greeted by a pained look from Rutherford. I need a wee, it said. Where have you been? The Alsatian rushed gratefully past him, through the open door, and down the steps to the garden. 'Hi honey, I'm home' Dan called after him.

So that was it, my first story as Crime Correspondent. Or to be fair, the first chapter of it. If El was right about the man who was lying dead in that lay by, there'll be plenty more of it to come. How did the first one go?

He didn't know. He'd done what he thought he should, stuck to the basic facts, told the viewers what was going on, and that was about it. He didn't have any experience of similar stories to measure it by. All he could hope was that his work was adequate. It'd do for now. He could aim higher in the months to come, when

– if – he knew what he was talking about. The feeling of loneliness and vulnerability was back and the swamp was lingering at the edge of his mind. Time to think about something else.

Women, that was a good distraction. He was due to go out for a drink with Kerry later this week. He'd met her at Mike and Jo's house – his surrogate parents he thought of them - over supper. 'Dinner with new friends', they'd called it. He'd known just what that meant. They'd befriended some poor single female and decided he should be introduced in the hope of finally easing him into a decent relationship. He wasn't struck but she was ok, worth seeing again certainly. Or did he mean probably?

He meant to pick out a decent shirt and put it in the wash ready, just in case he felt the need to impress. He scanned the rack, but found he was looking but not seeing and left it. I've had enough for one day, he thought. I can do it tomorrow. And what is a decent relationship anyway? Longer than one or two nights he supposed. He hadn't done very well at that lately.

He set the alarm for 6.30; get up, take the dog for a couple of miles run and get in to the newsroom by eight, ready for more on the murder. He wanted to look up some of the old stories they'd done on Bray. As El had said, they were highly colourful. Record numbers of enforced bankruptcies, plenty of threats and then saving the hospice, quite a collection as he recalled. And he had an idea to sell to Lizzie too.

It was an odd one, but it was buzzing in his brain and would make for a great story if it worked out. It'd be fascinating too, and would give him an excellent and badly needed insight into police work. And it would certainly be exciting, and probably even fun. He checked himself. Was he starting to get into this new job?

Chapter three

The police withhold the names of people who've been killed until their families have been told, to spare them the shock of learning about their loss from the media. In this case, it was one of the detectives' simplest tasks. The victim's name was released on the Devon and Cornwall Constabulary's Internet media site the next morning.

The dead man had only a father, and didn't like him. There was no wife, no children, no friends, only what are politely called acquaintances, and deliberately so. The investigation team was later to find that one of his favourite sayings was 'A friend in need is a pain indeed.' They didn't find any similar sayings for women, probably because he'd never been known to have any time for them.

Dirty El was right. The victim was Edward Bray.

The stories about him were extraordinary, Dan thought. It was ten past eight and he was sitting in the studios' News Library, checking through what they'd run on Bray before his murder. The log of the Plymouth

Herald's reports was interesting too. They told similar tales.

'16 people were bankrupted today in Plymouth County Court' said the newsreader in the recording of a South West Tonight from just over a year ago. 'It's believed to be a record, and all enforced by the same local businessman, Edward Bray. From the court, Kate Heever reports.'

It started with pictures of a man and his wife sitting on a sofa in their home. There were Christmas decorations on the walls. He was introduced as Andrew Hicks and told the reporter his story. 'I'd lost my job at the dockyard, they hadn't got a contract for a ship refit they were depending on, so they laid a few of us off. This house is rented from Bray, it's not a bad place at all.' He gestured around him. It looked cosy enough. 'We like it, don't we love?'

The woman sitting next to him in the shot nodded but said nothing. She was holding his hand tightly. 'I told him we'd struggle a bit to pay the rent, but I'd applied for lots of other jobs and thought it wouldn't be long before I got one. Well, the rent was due in a few days, and he just told me if it wasn't paid, we'd be out. That was despite us living here for six years without giving him a single problem. Of course I couldn't pay it, so he took us to court and now we're being evicted.'

Tears began to roll down the woman's face and he turned to her. 'There there love, we'll be ok. Something'll come up.' She cuddled into him, hiding her face. Just what the reporter would have wanted, Dan thought. I certainly would. Tears make great TV.

'I tried to ask him for a chance', Hicks went on, anger rising in his voice. 'I said to him, 'come on Mr Bray, it's Christmas time'. And do you know what he said?' Hicks glared at the camera, his face taught. 'He said 'I don't believe in Father Christmas.' The reporter let the silence run, good work, it was tense, powerful. 'I could have punched him, strangled him even. I couldn't believe anyone could be so brutal', Hicks added.

There were pictures of the court while the reporter explained the record number of bankruptcies, then a shot of Edward Bray striding from the building. 'He wouldn't be interviewed', went the commentary, 'but made his feelings clear'. The report ended with Bray sticking a middle finger up from the window of a taxi as it pulled away from the court.

Dan stopped the tape and leant back on his chair, trying not to feel some grudging respect for the man.

The second report came from a couple of months later. Plymouth Cats Home had run out of money and was closing, that was unless someone came forward with the funding to renovate the run down building. It was in a prime site, an old Victorian place in Hartley, one of Plymouth's more upmarket areas. Edward Bray had put in a bid to buy it, wanted to turn it into flats the newsreader said, and the home's owners had asked him if he could instead donate some money to keep them going. It was their last hope.

They'd be so grateful, an old woman, the manageress told the interviewer, so very grateful. So bloody naïve, thought Dan. Surely Mr Bray would realise what fine work they did and help them out? Everyone loved cats didn't they? And the home had been going for more than 40 years. The camera panned across ginger and tortoiseshell, black and white cats mewing and purring, rubbing themselves against the mesh of their cages. They might have to be put down if the place closed. They were confident such an upstanding local businessman as Mr Bray would help.

The shot changed to an office, the reporter talking about Mr Bray not wanting to comment. Dan wondered what he'd really said; nothing so polite no doubt. Then the glass doors flew open and out he strode, straight towards the camera. It tilted to the sky, a dazzle of sun, then came back down and a hand blocked the lens. 'Get off my property' he could be heard shouting, 'get off or I'll call the police', and the camera wobbled backwards towards the pavement. There was a succession of electronic bleeps, covering up the tirade of abuse Bray had shouted about the cats.

Then something strange. He turned back to his office and knelt down by a sapling planted in the earth beds alongside the shining glass doors. It was no more than a stick sprouting a few buds, encased in a protective metal mesh. He ran a gentle hand over it. 'And touch my apple tree', he shouted back at the camera, 'and I'll have you flogged.' Dan replayed that part, puzzled. What did an apple tree have to do with anything?

The report finished with the news the home was to be closed and converted into flats, although the cats had been found new owners. Bray had received hate mail, which the police were investigating. The ITV report didn't use it, broadcasting tended to be more polite, but the banner headline in the Herald ran 'Bray the Bastard'.

Then just a month later in the log came the surprise. St Jude's hospice needed a complete refit to bring it up to date with new safety regulations. It would cost tens of thousands of pounds and the money wasn't there. Closure was threatened. There were a couple of days of reports on how important it was for Plymouth, the care it provided for terminally ill people, interviews with them. He remembered it well, a real tearjerker, great story, the kind journalists live for.

Then there was a gap of a few days before the next mention. 'More bad news for St Jude's today', went the brief report. 'Ruthless local businessman Edward Bray has been seen in the hospice. He's been holding meetings with the management. Staff and patients fear the worst, the closure of the home and it's redevelopment.'

On the next day's programme came the twist. A live report from outside the hospice.

'Breaking news. This extraordinary statement', the reporter said holding up a piece of paper, 'tells us St Jude's has been saved by what is referred to as a 'sizeable donation' from local businessman Edward Bray. It doesn't detail how much, but we know tens of thousands of pounds at the very least were needed. This is a major surprise.' To say the least thought Dan. 'Mr Bray has a reputation for ruthlessness, and when he was seen here yesterday the worst was feared. Now it seems St Jude's has been saved. The statement is brief, but it says the donation was just that, no strings attached, no share in the buildings, nothing, a simple gesture of generosity and humanity.' Dan shook his head in disbelief. 'It goes on to say that by request of Mr Bray, no one from the hospice will be commenting.

We approached Mr Bray himself for an interview, but he declined to talk to us.'

They had managed to get one interview though, with the family of a woman who was staying at the hospice. Gladys Everard was her name, and the reporter had grabbed a few seconds with her son and daughter-in-law as they came out from a visit.

'I know people have said terrible things about Mr Bray', the man said defiantly, 'but he's an angel to us. A bloody angel. He saved the hospice and the quality of what's left of my mum's life with it. He saved her dignity too. He came to her rescue as she was dying and that makes him an angel in my book. She loves it in there; they look after her so well. It would have killed her if it was shut and she had to move out. We've nothing but thanks for him.' The woman next to him nodded and the man turned, stared straight into the camera. 'If you're watching Mr Bray, thanks. You're an angel.'

Dan checked what the Herald had to say about the story. The details were the same, and they'd lifted some of the interview with Mrs Everard's family from the TV coverage. They quoted an unnamed source at the hospice saying Bray had stood for an hour in the freezing cold in the garden, gazing at the buildings with tears in his eyes and had been prepared to give them anything they needed to keep going. But there was still no explanation why. Their headline was 'The Angel of St Jude's'.

After that there were no more stories in the South West Tonight programme log, but the Herald had another couple. 'Normal service resumed', muttered Dan to himself.

One was about Bray evicting more people from their homes. None would speak out, were still hoping for a reprieve and didn't want to anger him. But they carried an interview with Andrew Hicks, now living in a flat, alone. The stress of being forced out from Bray's house had made him and his fiancée split up. He told the reporter all about it, good quotes. 'Don't give me that angel stuff', it said underneath Hicks' photo scowling out from the paper's front page. He looked older now than in the TV coverage. 'He was more like the devil with me. The bloke didn't have a heart. He enjoyed watching people suffer. He destroyed my life. I'll always hate him for it.'

The last story in the Herald was that Bray had turned down a plea for help from the Rainbow Trust, a local charity that arranged holidays for terminally ill children. It had been forced to close. There was an interview with one of the trustees. 'Why won't he help us when he saved the Hospice?' the woman asked. 'And all we needed was a few thousands to tide us over and we'd have been able to keep up our wonderful work. We just got a letter from him saying no, he didn't like kids and he was starting to wish he'd never saved the Hospice. He said too many people were scrounging for his money now.' There was a photo of her holding Bray's letter, looking tearful.

The changes in Bray must have taxed the paper's headline writers, but they'd found a solution. He'd become 'Plymouth's Jeckyl and Hyde'. Clever. Dan shook his head again, logged out of the computer and made for the newsroom. It wasn't his imagination. He could feel a growing fascination with the case and a sense of starting to enjoy himself.

∼

Lizzie was in already and buzzing with an editor's relish of a big story. He tried to duck back out of the newsroom's wooden swing door, but she was tense and alert and spotted him.

'It's great. It's got everything.' She was fizzing, talking in headlines. 'Big local businessman brutally murdered. It could be a contract killing, a conspiracy of his enemies, anything.'

Dan felt his enthusiasm wane. He looked ruefully out of the window at the angry rain. The thunder from last night's storm had moved off east, out across Devon, riding on the prevailing wind, but it had left behind a downpour. He looked down at his boots and the holes in their seams. Another day of wet feet. There was no chance of getting into town for some new footwear, or to Sainsbury's for some much needed food for him and Rutherford. He was running out of deodorant too. It looked like there'd be no time this week for anything but work the way Lizzie was planning.

'And what a start for you in your new job eh? This is going to be one of the stories of the year.' The row about the prostitutes had been forgotten. Lizzie was working herself up into a crescendo. 'The investigation will keep us going for days. Then there's the trial to look forward to, that's if the police catch anyone. Let's hope they don't get them too quickly. I can see this being the lead story all week.'

The best way to deal with Lizzie in this mood was to avoid her. He started edging towards the door. 'I'd better get going and get started then', he said.

'Hang on, hang on.' He waited. 'We need a full obit on him, warts and all', she continued. 'Mainly warts in fact. Let's go to the library and get a montage of all the headlines he's made with his business dealings. Let's put together everything his enemies have said about him. Let's go see some of his tenants and find out what they have to say about him. Let's get the police into the studio to explain how their investigation is going. Does Bray have any family who'll speak to us? Didn't his Dad used to run the business? How about him? And we need pictures of Bray, from his schooldays to now. Let's see if we can dig up any old school friends.'

Dan had begun dutifully writing her thoughts down in his A4 notepad, but the words had petered out into a series of doodles of M shaped birds over lumpy hills. He was waiting for the chance to spring his idea on her. Timing was all with Lizzie. She'd stopped for a rare breath, so he took his chance.

'I was thinking about the new job last night, and I wanted to run something by you.'

'Sure, go ahead. Particularly if it helps with the Bray case.'

'It might well.'

'Go on.'

'You know you thought I was a pretty decent Environment Correspondent? Lots of good exclusives, knew my stuff, that sort of thing.'

'Agreed', she said slowly, wary, wondering where this was leading.

'Well, the secret was good contacts. It was knowing the people in power in the region, getting them to trust me and tell me things they probably shouldn't.'

'Sure. Cost me a few quid in expenses for the lunches you took them out for, but worthwhile.'

'Well I'd like to try something similar with the police.'

'Good idea. Fine by me. So long as it's not too expensive.' Her shoe was grinding into the carpet tiling again. She wanted to get on with the story. The heels were unusually low today, probably only an inch and a half, perhaps two.

'I'd like to take it a bit further', added Dan, as persuasively as he could.

'How?'

'Well, the trouble is I know just about nothing about police work at the moment. I don't know how they go about their investigations or anything like that. And I don't know any detectives at all, let alone enough for them to trust me with any juicy info.'

'So?'

'So, I need to get in with them.'

'So?'

'So I've got a proposal for you.'

'Which is?'

'You have those quarterly meetings with the police hierarchy don't you?'

'Yep, afraid so. Dull but necessary. Just regular liaison things to keep the working relationship sweet.' She frowned, looked puzzled. 'You don't want to come in on those do you? I wouldn't recommend it. Bloody tedious.'

Dan lowered himself onto the edge of her desk. 'No, it's nothing like that', he said. He hated meetings, too much talk, too little action. 'But I do remember you saying the police were concerned they didn't get the press they deserved, that all the hard work they put into many cases gets overlooked?'

'That was part of the reason we wanted you to move to Crime, to get better coverage of things like that.'

Dan saw his chance.

'Right. So here's what I'd like to do. How about you using your contacts with the police to get me in to shadow their investigation into the Bray case? It'll give me a great insight into police work and get us some brilliant stories. I know the detectives will have concerns about prejudicing their investigation. You can tell them we won't broadcast anything until whoever they catch has been convicted. It could be great PR for them, and good for us too.'

The eyebrow arched. 'You've been thinking about this, haven't you?' She stared into him. 'Ok, deal. You're right, it could be good. I'll have a word with the Deputy Chief Constable later. It's one he'll have to approve. I'll let you know.'

Dan hid a smile. His theory about the best time to approach Lizzie had worked again. Lower heels, always the way.

∼

He headed north, out to the edge of the city and the teacher training College of St Mark and St John, known locally as Marjons. Nigel was waiting for him in the car park. It was a standard meeting place. Mercifully the rain had thinned, replaced instead by a steady, petulant drizzle. 'Good morning my friend', said Dan cheerily. 'How are you doing?'

Nigel was chomping on a Danish pastry and mumbled an indistinct reply, so Dan outlined his plan.

'You won't be surprised to know we're on the Bray case all day. We're off to his house first to see if we can get any reaction from his neighbours.' Nigel gave a thumbs up, still chewing. 'The newsroom is trying to get in touch with his parents so we can interview them. We're doing an outside broadcast at the lay by for lunch. Any questions?'

The Danish still wasn't finished, so there were none. Nigel followed him the half mile to Tretower Close and they found the house.

Bray lived in a newly built place, a model of mock Tudor bad taste, detached, with five bedrooms. There was a long gravel drive and, most conspicuously, a security fence, powerful motion sensitive lights and what looked like a keen modern alarm system.

His neighbours were mostly senior managers and consultants from the nearby Derriford Hospital, the south west's biggest. Dan knew fellow journalists who'd tried to stand up a story about some moving away and property prices there falling because of Bray's arrival, but no one would speak out against him.

The black wrought iron gates were shut. There was no sign of any activity. They parked, got out of their cars and Nigel unpacked the camera and put it on the boot of his Renault in what he called his standby mode. He watched as Dan began knocking on the doors of the neighbouring houses.

A Popular Murder

It was the journalist's task he hated most. It reminded him of a terrible month between his first and second year at university, when, desperate for money he'd taken a job selling aerial photos of towns to people in the south east of England. It was pure cold calling. He'd managed to sell less than a dozen pictures, and those only to people who took pity on him, although he had learned some interesting new obscenities.

First and second houses, no answer. He wasn't surprised; most people who lived round here would be at work. Third house, a familiar response. 'Hello, I'm Dan Groves from ITV News.' Door slammed.

Fourth house, no answer. Fifth a quick chat with a middle aged man, but no comment, he didn't know Bray. Sixth another familiar response.

'What are you doing at my door?' An older woman.

'I just wanted to have a chat with you about Mr Bray. You know what happened..?'

'Of course I know', she cut in. 'It's shocking'.

'Ah, well, I was wondering if we might just do an interview..'

'And I think you're shocking too. You people are like vultures'. Her voice rose. 'Vultures circling a corpse. Disgusting'. He wasn't taking that, had heard it too many times before. Hypocrisy.

'So you don't watch TV news then?'

'What?' She seemed puzzled.

'Don't buy any newspapers?'

'What?'

'How do you think we find out the things you want to hear about? Get the interviews? It's by knocking doors like I'm doing now. So bear that in mind next time a journalist comes calling eh?'

She stared at him, then huffed and found her voice. 'That's completely different'.

'Of course it is', he said over his shoulder, 'it always is.'

'Now get off my property before I call the police', she shouted, but he was already trudging down her drive, taking satisfaction in her deflation and the gnomes surrounding the pond in the front garden. It's not so bad being abused by someone with such awful taste he thought, but he couldn't bring himself to do any more door knocking. He'd rather have no interviews than more doors being slammed in his face.

He returned to the cars to find Nigel still in standby mode, but now talking to Dirty El who was munching a doughnut.

'Hi Dan', said El, swallowing. 'You doing the door knocking bit? Get anything?'

Dan shook his head. 'No. It's a bloody thankless task. Nothing to put in whatever report I come up with.' He was wondering what that might be. 'What are you up to?'

El was polishing his lens on a dirty coat sleeve.

'Just come out to get a couple of shots of his house. Some of the national tabloids are interested.'

Nigel stirred dutifully. 'I suppose you want some shots of the house and area?'

'Yes please', said Dan. It wasn't great but at least he'd have some pictures to write about.

'El, can we borrow you for a mo?' asked Nigel. 'I can film the house, but it's dull on its own. If you wouldn't mind standing there and pretending to take some snaps of it, that'd liven the shot up. Then Dan can script some lovely words around it being 'the centre of attention' that sort of thing, in his inimitably elegant style.'

El grinned. 'To you, no charge. It'd be good for my profile to appear on the TV. But only on the condition I can do a shot of you filming the house too.'

'Ok El, no problem' said Dan. 'Any news on that little job we discussed yesterday?'

El winked. 'Probably tonight. I might go and have a little look through Mr Jones' bins. You never know what treats you can find in someone's rubbish.'

His mobile rang. 'Dan, it's Lizzie.' She was still fizzing. 'We've managed to get through to Bray's dad and he will speak to you. He's keen to talk in fact. It should make a corking interview. He's got to go out this afternoon, so I said you'd get up there as soon as possible. Where are you now?'

'Derriford.'

'Perfect. He's just up the road, at Meavy, on the edge of Dartmoor. Get going and you can get it on the lunchtime news.'

'How does he sound? How carefully do we have to play it?'

'He sounded a little fragile, but mostly ok. But be gentle.' She could smell the power of the interview, sounded anything but gentle. 'And it must be our day. The police have been on to me too. They've agreed to let you shadow the investigation. Detective Chief Inspector Adam Breen will call you later about when to start and where. You'd better bear that in mind when you do the interview. Arthur Bray will be important in helping the police with information about their son's background, so don't upset him. It could annoy the detectives and make them think twice about helping us. I don't want to lose this exclusive angle.'

Don't upset him, thought Dan with a swell of irritation. What is she talking about? Easy for her, sat there in the office, not so much when you're looking the man in the eye. And no pressure of course. Ten minutes to prepare to interview someone who's just lost his son in a brutal killing and I've got to ask him that dreaded old hack's question, how does it feel? Or what effect has it had on you and the family, or how are you coping, or some equally pathetic attempt to soften it, none of which ever work.

And that wasn't the end of it either. He'd also want to find out why Edward Bray was such a ruthless businessman and why then had he suddenly decided to save a hospice? And hadn't one of those Herald stories said that Bray's business had been inherited – or stolen as many claimed – from his Dad? So how am I supposed to ask him all that without upsetting him? And aren't his tears what we want anyway?

Chapter four

Arthur Bray was determinedly containing his grief, but Dan could feel it just below the surface. Its sharpness was like a reef of rocks, ready to break free when the disguise of their cover ebbed, as surely it would. He was from the generation, now dismissed as 'old fashioned' that had been expected to guard their feelings. However much the shrinks might say it was wrong, that suppression made the suffering worse, Dan preferred it to the modern wailings and outpourings that those who suffered today were encouraged to vent. He, the media, television, were mostly responsible he knew. They'd indoctrinated the viewers in the expected reaction to grief. Scream it loud and long.

The heavy knotted wood and black iron studded door of the detached converted farmhouse growled open as Dan and Nigel were getting out of their cars and an upright man in his mid 60s strode out to meet them. He was just less than six feet tall, slim, dressed in light chinos with a dark cardigan, under which was an impeccably ironed Oxford blue shirt and blue and white diagonally striped tie. The years had taken the hair from a perfect circle on the crown of his head, but a tightly trimmed fringe still surrounded it, like well-kempt silver grass around an oasis.

He greeted them with an efficient 'Good morning!'

'Mr Bray, I'm Dan, Dan Groves the reporter.'

'Yes, yes indeed, I've seen you on the television many times. I always watch South West Tonight. It's good to meet you.'

'And this is Nigel, the cameraman.'

'A pleasure to meet you too. Please, call me Arthur. Do come in.'

They walked into a short and dimly lit hallway with well-worn shiny grey flagstones, and were ushered to the far end, an open door from which daylight streamed. They emerged into a lounge overlooking a pristine rose bounded lawn, backed by the open expanse of the Vale of Meavy.

'I thought we could do the interview in here. It's a lovely view'. He gazed at it fondly. Dan and Nigel followed his look and made the expected appreciative noises. 'I know how you cameramen types like a good view', he continued to Nigel. 'I'll probably spoil it by being in the foreground no doubt, but at least the viewers will have something pleasant to look at in the picture.'

Dan was unsure how to handle Arthur Bray. He'd prepared himself for a meeting heavy with grief, slow and laboured movements, tears and sighs. He thought they were there, somewhere, but the man was covering them well. He tried not to think how much better it would be if they were exposed; more emotion, more power, gripping television.

'Mr Bray, I'm sorry, Arthur', said Dan. 'Thanks very much for agreeing to see us at what must be a difficult time for you.'

'Well, it's not easy of course, but life must go on eh?' said Arthur Bray brusquely. 'I've never been one for wallowing in grief.'

'Arthur, we've asked to talk to you because we think it could help the police. By reporting on what happened to Edward it may bring witnesses forward.' Dan didn't mention it made a great story too. 'Please don't think me rude if I say we don't have much time. We want to get this onto our lunchtime news, so we can reach as many people as possible. That means we've only got about half an hour to interview you. Is that ok?'

'It's fine yes, fine, of course. I know you people are always up against deadlines. It's rather an exciting life I've always thought. Just say what you want to do and we'll do it.'

Ok then, easy so far. Arthur Bray was handling it well. 'The first thing we'll need is a couple of pictures of Edward. The viewers relate much more to someone if they can see them. That way they get a sense of the person rather than just hearing about them.'

Arthur Bray closed his eyes, as if thinking hard. 'Well, that's possible, but it'll take a few minutes. I know there are some in the cupboards upstairs.'

Dan realised what had been bothering him about the house. There were no photographs of Edward Bray the baby, the toddler, the adolescent, the young man, the businessman. There were no family holidays, no school pictures, no graduation, no family photos at all. There was no pride on show.

'I'm sorry, the cupboards? Upstairs?'

'Yes.' A pause, more thoughtful now. 'Perhaps I should make one thing clear before we go any further.'

Now Dan felt the emotional shield start to crumble. It hadn't taken long. The old man paused again and looked out of the window before taking a deep breath and continuing.

'This may come as a shock, but I didn't like my son.' The words were much slower now, the efficiency and strength faltering. 'I didn't like him at all.' Another pause. 'I wouldn't say I hated him, that would be too strong. He is my son after all. But I certainly didn't like him.'

Dan didn't know what to say. His father was the greatest influence in his life. His warmest memories started with his Dad taking him for walks in the park and playing football with him and Sam, the Alsatian dog he had grown up with. He sometimes wondered if his desire to buy the puppy that grew into Rutherford was an attempt to recapture those carefree childhood years. They seemed a long way off now.

His Dad had always supported Dan with love and understanding, even through the rebellious throes of hateful adolescence, which had seen him suspended from school and hitting out at everyone around him. Dan knew he could never pay him back for all that he had given. The nearest he had come was when he'd seen the pride shine in the man's face at his graduation ceremony, and, even brighter, when he had watched his son on the television after he joined ITV. There was no such pride in this house, not in pictures, nor mementos and certainly not in Edward Bray's dad.

'Arthur, this will be difficult, but it might help me to understand better.' Gentle, easy, take it slow. Do you mind me asking why?'

'There were a couple of reasons', said Arthur Bray, in a matter of fact way, as though any emotion had long since faded. 'Firstly, he took my business away from me.' The old man looked down at the floor, then back up. So the report had been right. 'I wanted to hand it on to him of course, most of the reason I built it up was for him. But I also wanted to stay involved. It was my life and I thought I could help him. So we discussed it and he was keen to take over, but he said he thought we ought to do it properly and make it legal, to protect his future in case anything happened to me. We went to a solicitor, and I handed it over to him, fully and legally. I trusted him when he said he would run it together with me, as a partnership, and that the change was just a legal move to cover us. But once it was in his name, that was it.' Arthur Bray shook his head gently. 'I was sidelined. He didn't want me involved. He just pushed me aside and wouldn't listen to anything I had to say. He just did what he wanted, when he wanted. After a while I gave up trying to have any influence at all.'

'I see'. Again Dan didn't know what to say. 'That must have been very difficult for you', he managed. It sounded lame.

The upset had overtaken Arthur Bray now. The momentum he'd worked up for their visit had left him, and he'd become a lonely old man. He looked out at the view, stared wistfully for what the deadline conscious Dan felt was at least a minute, and sighed, a deep and resonant sigh. No one wanted to break the silence. There was the first hint of tears as he continued, a watery shine in his eyes.

'Now where was I? Ah yes, there were two reasons. When he'd taken over the business and pushed me aside, he treated people in the most appalling way. We had tenants who'd been with us for years and he just threw them out of their homes so he could get others in who'd pay more rent. One chap whose wife had just had a baby had some complications. He had to take time off to be with her and got behind with his rent. Edward just had him evicted. The poor man came to see me but there was nothing I could do.'

Arthur Bray faltered, had to gather himself to carry on.

'I wanted nothing much to do with him after that, and he had no time for what he called a sentimental old fool like me. Business and feelings don't mix he used to say.' His voice rose and his hands tightened into fists. 'Well I did fine in business for 40 years, and I always looked after people. Yes I could drive a tough bargain along with the best of them. Yes I could make money, and yes I could talk tough. But I was always a decent human being first and a businessman second.' The voice fell again, to little more than a whisper. 'I'm afraid my son didn't follow my example.'

Arthur Bray lapsed into silence. He seemed to retreat into himself. The shine in his eyes had become a soft, single track of tears.

Dan had lost count of the number of upsetting stories he'd reported on in his career. He'd spoken to distraught people who had vented screaming, furious, anguished, emotion at him. But never had he been so moved by the depth of the quiet pain in the old man now sitting hunched in the chair in front of him. There is, he thought, a unique sadness in the estrangement of a father and son.

Nigel was looking out of the window, his back turned. He knew his friend was thinking of Arthur and Edward Bray, the destruction of the precious bond between them, and of his own two sons and what the future would hold for them.

He let the silence run, while Arthur Bray stared unseeing out of the window, lost in the misery of his mind. The deadline nagged at him, wouldn't quieten, and he knew he'd have to say something, force the pace, but he had no idea what or how. It was the old man who broke the silence. He needed to speak, to finish his story.

'You might be wondering what happened to his mother. She died when he was young, just eight in fact. It was cancer. The sort of thing that happens every day to other people, but never to you of course. I don't think Edward ever got over it.'

His hands were knotting into fists again. 'After that, I threw myself into work. I built up the business to make sure Edward would always be provided for. It wasn't easy. I worked long hours and didn't see him as much as I should.'

Arthur Bray's voice caught again on his words, and he struggled to go on. He raised a hand to the lump in his throat, and the silvery tracks on his cheeks.

'And that was what he said to me, on the last time we really talked. He said I wasn't there for him when he was growing up. He said he felt like an orphan and that I couldn't have loved him. He said the business came first for me, and him second, a long way second. I tried to explain that I worked so hard for him because I loved him, to make sure he would be all right.' The tears were sliding slowly down over the creases of pain on the old man's face. 'But he said all he'd learnt from me was that business was life, and that was what he was going to do.'

Arthur Bray stifled a cry. 'I got it all wrong Dan', he choked. 'All wrong. I loved him too much, and didn't see what it was doing. I wasn't there for him. I loved him too much, and this is what happens. I turned him into something he should never have been. And now he's dead...'

Arthur Bray's words faded into sobbing. Dan looked on helplessly at the hunched figure in his chair. The interview, he had to get the interview done, but how? He was still struggling with the story of the disintegration of a family.

Look for something to say. He could think of nothing. What about a distraction; anything. Kerry, would he see her later today? Tomorrow? Would they get it together? No good, not powerful enough. How about the view? Dartmoor was at its best today, the glowering grey of the weather giving the rugged Tors a magnificent moodiness. He stared out at it, the lunchtime deadline back, nagging at his mind, knowing he had to get on with the interview but also acutely aware of the anguish of the old man sitting opposite him. He tried to phrase his next question as gently as he could. But how could it be gentle?

'Arthur, do you mind me asking why you wanted to talk to us, given what you've just said?'

Arthur Bray exhaled, a deep breath from within. 'No, of course not, I understand. I know it's your job.' He drew himself up in his chair. 'It may sound old fashioned to you, but I think it's my duty. I may not have liked my son. Some may even say he got what he deserved.' A father talking like this about his only child, his son, Dan was still struggling to believe it. 'But what has happened is wrong, and I've always prided myself on living a law abiding and decent life. If I can help the police I will. And if you say that me being interviewed may help bring witnesses forward and catch the person who killed him, then I think I should do it.'

Duty, the rallying call of his time had given Arthur Bray strength. He straightened and sat up in his chair.

'And hadn't we better be getting on with the interview now?'

'Yes, yes of course', said Dan, relieved the tension had been punctured and that he hadn't had to do it himself. 'Are you ready Nigel?'

A nod from the ashen-faced cameraman. Thank God for that thought Dan, who wanted to get this done and get out. He wasn't sure how much more he could take. But Arthur Bray hadn't quite finished.

'Don't worry, I won't come out with all that in the interview. I'll find something more appropriate to say.

I may have thought my son a most unpleasant man, but no one else needs to know all that family strife stuff, do they? It's best kept to ourselves I think.'

Dan hid his relief. It was hardly what the viewers would expect from the interview. Not to mention Lizzie.

'I just told you because, well, I imagine you're going to dig deeper into Edward's life and so you're going to find out anyway. And it's also I think because I feel I almost know you.' The old man managed a forced smile. 'I see you in my living room most nights. You're roughly the same age Edward was too.' He looked at Dan in a way that made him feel uncomfortable. A father in search of a lost son? 'Now then, I've held you up enough with my ramblings. The interview.'

But Dan had something he had to ask first. He wouldn't be doing his job otherwise, but it was more than that. He wanted the exclusive yes, of course, but really he wanted his own fascination satisfied.

'Just one more thing Arthur, if you don't mind me asking?'

'Of course.'

'I was looking back at some of Edward's', he stumbled for the word, '.. err, career, and saw how he saved St Jude's'. He was sure Arthur Bray stiffened at the name, pursed his lips. 'There was no explanation though, he didn't give interviews. Do you know why he did it?'

'As I've said, family business.' His voice was as hard as it had been and Dan felt the warning. 'There's no sense bringing all that stuff out. It's not really relevant here, is it?'

Dan shook his head, wanted to push it but couldn't risk losing the interview. But I will find out, he thought, somehow.

～

Nigel was still pale and quiet as they packed up the camera and tripod outside Arthur Bray's house.

'It makes you wonder what goes on inside families, doesn't it? When he was talking in there, I was thinking of James and Andrew. I was wondering what they'd grow up to be. Edward Bray was like them once. You know what I mean. They're full of wonder about life, wanting to explore and learn, all laughter and happiness, full of love. I'd hate the thought of my boys growing up to become anything like he was. I promised myself in there I'd never make the mistakes he did.'

And how, thought Dan, can you ever believe that, when the decisions you make for the best at the time have consequences such as you can never imagine? Nothing would have made him tell Nigel so. It was the difference between them. For Nigel, the glass was always half full and he loved the man for it. For him, ever conscious of the pull of the swamp, it was not only half empty, but some days dirty and cracked too.

As they drove the 20 minutes back down to Plymouth, then turned off eastwards on the A 38 towards the lay by where Edward Bray's body had been found, Dan kept looking down at the two photos on his passenger seat. They hadn't had time to film them at the house. Nigel could record them as he sat in the outside broadcast truck and edited the lunchtime news report.

In one, Edward Bray was wearing a suit and tie, and was surrounded by several men and women who were also smartly dressed. Dan guessed it must have been a wedding. Some of the people had their arms around each other, or on a friend's shoulder. Bray stood alone, slightly apart from the group. In the other photo it was just him against a background of parked cars. He was wearing a grey T-shirt and seemed to be at a summertime sports event.

In both pictures he was looking directly at the camera, and in both he had a slight scowl. He was a handsome man in a sullen way, with thick black hair, kept short and slightly spiky, a tanned complexion, brown eyes, thin nose, and ears which were just a little too large. Dan thought he looked angry and disillusioned, but that could have been his imagination projecting the character he'd heard about onto the image

They got to the lay by at just after 12.30. Not comfortable for time, but not too pressured either. Picking the best bits from the interview with Arthur Bray was worth taking a few minutes over. It was powerful stuff.

The white Mercedes transit van with ITV South West News emblazoned on the side, and an oversized satellite dish on its roof was awaiting them. The door was open and the engineer and picture editor Jim Stone stuck his head out.

In his mid 50s, he was fat, brown haired and bearded. Beards were almost a uniform amongst engineers, and the more unkempt the better. Bespectacled and nearing retirement, Jim was noted in the newsroom for two things; his bizarre taste in loud Hawaiian shirts which he wore however spiteful the weather, and his unshakeably grumpy demeanour. Today's shirt was a vintage example. It was more colourful than the TV test card, with green and brown turtles crawling across a sandy beach, towards a deep blue sea and orange sky.

In a fit of irritation with his colleague on one particularly long day working together, Dan had christened Jim 'Loud and Furrow Browed'. Nigel had enjoyed the rant, passed the story around and the name had stuck.

'I've run a cable out to a camera position for you, although that's not my job of course', said Jim grumpily. He exchanged a brief look of the fellow sufferer with Nigel. To Loud, journalists were the enemy and anyone who had to work with them an ally by default.

He gestured towards a blue cable which ran from the back of the van up to a point about 10 yards from the police tape marking the edge of the cordon. A patrol car was parked next to it, with a fluorescent yellow-coated constable standing uninterestedly alongside. It was as good a backdrop as any.

'Thanks Jim. I'll pop in', said Dan, who knew the best technique for handling the engineer was to jolly him along. 'We've got an edit to do, a minute and a half piece, with a live introduction and interview to follow.'

Loud looked pointedly at his watch.

'A minute and a half piece? And a live? For lunchtime? There goes another of my arteries.'

Dan slid into the van. 'Don't worry Jim. Most of the report will be interview. We just need to add a couple of bits of my commentary, a few pictures of the scene here and a couple of photos of the victim. Nigel's doing those now. It's a 45 minute job, if that.'

The beard twitched as Loud considered this. He looked suspicious. Dan tried to adopt a relaxed air, but wasn't sure he succeeded.

'I've heard that too many times before' grunted Loud. 'Well come on then, let's get on with it.' He fumbled a piece of paper from his pocket. 'Oh, and there's a message for you from the newsroom. Some Adam Bream will be here at 1.15; they want you to interview him live. They said you'd understand.'

Dan didn't bother to correct him. The fishy detective was an appealing idea. 'Fine, let's do it then', he said.

There wasn't much room in the van with Jim, so Dan shuffled his chair as close to the wall as he could and began work. He picked up the portable microphone, scribbled a few words onto his notepad and put on his best authoritative broadcast voice. Loud recorded it onto the tape and edited the pictures to match whilst Dan wrote the rest of the script.

The report began with the photographs of Edward Bray, Dan talking of him being a well-known local businessman, his property empire worth millions of pounds. Then it went into a long section of his father speaking about what an appalling crime it was, how shocked he was, how no one deserved to meet such a vicious and violent end, and how he hoped anyone who could help the police catch the killer would come forward. The report ended with some of last night's pictures of the lay by, with Dan recapping on where and when the body had been discovered.

It was simple and effective. Arthur Bray had been true to his word, leaving the viewers with a strong feeling of his pain and the need to bring the killer to justice, without fogging the story with the sad details of his relationship with his son. As Loud put the last shot down there was the kind of banging on the van door that comes from a hand practised in officious knocking.

Dan leaned over, opened it, and was greeted by a smartly suited purposeful looking man he recognised from last night. A less well kempt woman stood beside him.

'Daniel Groves?'

It sounded like his words would be followed by 'I arrest you, for the crime..'

'Afternoon' said Dan, wondering how it was that police officers could always make you feel like a criminal. He rose from his chair, squeezed his way past Loud and stepped down from the van.

'Detective Chief Inspector Breen I take it? It's good to meet you.'

'And you.' He wasn't at all sure the detective meant it. 'And this is Detective Sergeant Suzanne Stewart'

They all shook hands. DCI Breen gave Dan the kind of look he could imagine the detective intimidating suspects with. It said 'I know exactly what you've done, don't think I don't.' He seemed amused.

'Actually, I don't know whether to say good to meet you, or welcome to the force.'

Dan shuffled slightly despite himself.

'Ah, you've heard.'

'Yes, I've heard', said DCI Breen levelly. His voice had a slight tang of the Devon burr. 'The Deputy

Chief Constable has been on the phone. It's not often I'm honoured with such calls, so I guessed something was going on. I'm always looking for extra staffing, particularly for a major investigation like this, but I have to say it's not quite what I expected.'

'It's not exactly what I expected either, but I hope I can help out. I hope we can help each other.'

The detective seemed resigned to his fate.

'So do I', he said. 'Now, the press office tell me you want to do a live interview for your 1.30 news. That's good for me. We need some witnesses, and so far we've got none. What do you want to cover?'

Sharp and straightforward, just the way I like it, thought Dan, warming to the man. Good, especially if I'm going to be working with him. 'It's probably best if you watch the report I've just cut. Our interview will follow that. So have a look, then we can discuss the questions.'

The two detectives turned, looked into the outside broadcast van, and wisely decided not to try to squeeze in beside Loud's bulk. They watched from the door as he played them the report. Dan stood outside and manipulated into his left ear the soft moulded plastic earpiece that would allow him to hear the studio. He picked up the microphone, which Loud had left out for him, and used the 90 seconds of the report to study the detectives.

He was surprised at how young Adam Breen was. Dan put him in his late 30s, just a little older than himself. He was about five feet 10, thinly built, with dark, almost, but not quite black hair, the sides of which were flecked with subtle grey splashes. It was only lunchtime, yet he had a darkening shadow of beard. His nose was slightly crooked at the bridge, and Dan wondered if it was a memorial to earlier days of breaking up fights on the beat. His eyes were dark brown but with the brightness of a sharp intelligence. His suit was black and double breasted. Dan had bought a similar jacket for himself – the trousers wouldn't fit - from a shop in Brighton, second hand, a year ago. It was Armani, and he'd christened it his funerals and disasters jacket. He guessed Adam Breen's was Armani too, but somehow he didn't think he'd bought it second hand.

DCI Breen also had an aura, he thought, a presence that's often described as 'that certain something'. It's a feeling of honesty and strength, depth and dependability, instantly reassuring. Dan could imagine him calming hysterics just by his arrival at a crime scene. Had he been an actor, Dan would have cast him as a detective. Like his suit, he was made to measure.

Suzanne Stewart was more of a mystery. As Adam Breen looked like a detective, she didn't, instead more of a schoolmistress. She too wore a suit, but it was of the kind that teachers favour, at least several years out of date, and worn and shiny from daily use.

She wore her bobbed blonde hair on her shoulders. The ends were unruly and looked in need of a cut. She was shorter, perhaps five feet five, but her fuller figure made her seem shorter still. Proud and self-conscious women avoided that with their choice of clothes, but she had not. Her lips were pale and thin, her eyes an indistinct watery blue. Dan noticed she wore no make up or jewellery and flat, air soled black shoes.

Everything about her was designed for practicality. If there were any running after suspects to be done he thought, it would be Suzanne Stewart who did it. Adam Breen would be the one in the office, the one with the vision, anticipating the getaway routes and directing the chasing pack.

They turned from the van. 'That's a good report.' DCI Breen looked pleased. 'It's very good in fact. That interview with his father really makes it. It should help people realise what a horrific murder this was.' He tightened his tie and studied Dan. 'How did you get so much out of him? It can't have been easy.'

'I just treated him decently and honestly', said Dan, but he knew it was more than that. 'And people do tend to want to talk to me.' He'd never understood it. 'I don't know why. Maybe it's because they're used to seeing me on the TV and think they know me, but people I've spoken to have often confided in me and told me their innermost secrets.'

Adam Breen studied him. 'Funny', he said. 'I seem to have the opposite effect.'

I'm not surprised when they're being questioned about murders, thought Dan. 'Have you met Arthur Bray yet?' He glanced at his watch. Time to get back to the story. It was only minutes from the broadcast. 'Very touching he was, and an interesting tale he tells.'

'No, not yet' he said. 'We've had a few other things to do first, checking the crime scene, establishing timings, that sort of thing. We're due to see him later this afternoon.'

Dan was interrupted by a voice in his ear. It was Loud, talking to him from the van via the radio link.

'Testing testing. One two. One two.' He broke into a tuneless dirge; his standard way of checking the link was working. To the tune of 'In the Bleak Midwinter' he sang flatly; 'One One was a racehorse, Two Two was one too. One One won one race one day and Two Two won one too.'

'Ok, thanks, got that Jim. Hearing you loud and clear'.

'What?' said Adam Breen.

This could get confusing he thought. And it's no time to screw up. Maybe in the old days when we're reporting on Dartmoor ponies it was forgivable. This is about murder.

'I was talking to the man in the van' he said. 'We're checking the studio back at base can hear me.'

'What?' said Loud in his ear. So the man did have a sense of humour after all, even if it wasn't well developed.

Another voice warbled into the mix in his ear, this time Emma, the lunchtime news director.

'Hi Dan. Emma in the Plymouth studios gallery here, just checking you can hear us.'

'Hi Emma, yes, we hear you.'

'Good. We're 6 minutes to on air, so can you ask Nigel to give us a picture please.'

Nigel was linked to the van and studio via a pair of bulbous headphones. They made him look like Mickey Mouse. They still had red sparkling tinsel wrapped around the plastic band which ran over the top of his head, an early Christmas gift from his sons. He hoisted the camera up onto his shoulder and pointed it at Dan.

'Thanks OB team' said Emma. '5 to on air. You're the top story. Next time we talk to you, it'll be for real.'

'What?' came the voice from the van again, followed by a low chuckling. Dan glared at the camera, and the giggle tailed off.

'Mr Breen, we're only 5 minutes from on air, can you come and join me here please?'

Adam Breen walked over to Dan, and he went through the briefing he'd done many time before.

'Here's what'll happen. The presenter in the studio will read an introduction to the story. I'll then pick up live with what they call a scene set, saying a few words along the lines of 'It was here, in the lay by, that the body was found, that sort of thing'. Then they'll play my report, the one you've just seen. That goes on for a minute and a half. When that's finished, I'll introduce you, and interview you for a minute and a half. We'll probably have time for three questions. Does that sound ok?'

DCI Breen looked entirely unruffled. Most people Dan interviewed live had confessed to being nervous. Those who insisted they weren't gave themselves away with a twisting of the feet, a need to scratch a recurring itch, or a jingling of the change in the pocket. Adam Breen simply stood there, hands together behind his back, looking at the camera like a man examining shrubs at a garden centre.

'Fine', he said smoothly. 'What are you going to ask me?'

'I'll want to know how the investigation's going, and whether you have any leads. And you were saying you needed the public's help?'

'Yes please.'

'Then I'll ask you if there's any way people watching this can help you. And you can appeal for witnesses.'

'Fine. And I look at you the whole time do I? Not the camera?'

'Yes please. Now standby, two minutes to air.'

As ever, broadcast time passed faster than any other Dan had known. It was faster than the blur of funfair trips in his childhood years, faster than the first Tenerife holidays in his late teens, faster even than the few months he'd spent with Thomasin, the woman he'd loved more than anything he'd ever known, and had failed to love anything like since.

The newsreader spoke sombrely of the vicious killing of a prominent local businessman, and our correspondent Dan Groves being at the scene outside Plymouth where his body was found. Dan talked of the shocking discovery here, last night, at this lay by. His report rolled. Adam Breen told the viewers it was early days in the investigation, progress was being made, he was confident they would find the killer, and the public could help by calling in if they thought they'd witnessed anything that could be useful to the police.

The gallery gave them an all clear to de-rig. Dan popped the earpiece out and thanked the detective.

'It worked well that, thanks for your time. I know you've got more important things to be doing. We appreciate it.'

'It's no problem; I could do with the help. It's witnesses to what went on here that we need. Forensics will tell me if he was killed here, and we'll get a rough time of death, but that's about it. I could do with someone saying they saw him come in here, or even better, they saw someone else here with him. That'd be lovely. Particularly if they could give me a description, and a number plate. That'd be even better. We could all go home early then.'

'So no suspects?'

'Oh no, I've plenty of suspects. Loads of suspects. More suspects that I've ever known in a murder case in fact. We're not 24 hours in, and I've already got hordes of suspects.'

As so often with his interviewees, Dan was intrigued by the difference between the face they wanted to show the viewers and the real person. It was as though television transported them to a world of politeness and formality, when the reality was usually far removed.

'How come?'

'When I said to you in our interview that we were at an early stage in our inquiries, that was quite true. So far, we've only done the superficial bits, talking to people who knew him and trying to find out if there was anyone obvious who might want him dead.'

'And what did you find?'

Suzanne Stewart had been lingering beside them as they talked. Now she reached out and gently and deferentially pulled at Adam Breen's sleeve.

'It's ok Suzanne. Dan's going to be so close to the investigation that what I'm telling him now won't be in the least bit sensitive. It's unorthodox I know, but you'd better get used to that. It's the way it's going to be.' He looked sidelong at Dan and smiled wryly. 'Deputy Chief Constable's orders.'

Dan nodded. He hadn't expected his plan to work so well.

'What we've found so far is more people who'd want him dead than alive,' Adam went on. 'I don't think I'd be exaggerating when I say he was a man who almost no one seemed to have a good word to say about. And that's just for a start. I dread to think what we'll find when we dig deeper.'

Dan pulled his coat tighter around him to hide a shiver. He suddenly felt part of the kind of murder investigation he'd thought only existed in Agatha Christie's imagination. A motorbike screamed past on the dual carriageway and Adam Breen watched its passage thoughtfully.

'Mr Breen, forgive me asking this, but do I get the feeling you're being a bit less discreet than I'd usually expect from a detective?'

'I wasn't being discreet at all as far as I could tell. There's no point. Should I let you know what the Deputy Chief Constable said to me?'

Dan opened his arms in a gesture that said go ahead, but he did wonder what he was about to hear.

'He said he'd struck a deal with the local ITV which could be of great benefit to them and us. He said that would mean a journalist working alongside me on this investigation, and I was to treat him like I would a new detective constable. And you know what that means?'

'What?'

'It means you get the lot. You get to come with me, see what I see and work through with me as I try to collar the crims. It's no holds barred, you see it just the way it is. You happy with that?'

'I'm very happy with that.' To their side, Suzanne Stewart was shaking her head, but he ignored it. 'It's exactly what I need. I've only just started this new crime reporting job and I know almost nothing about police work. It'll be a crash course, and it'll be ideal.'

'That's the deal then. There's just one thing though.' Adam's tone took on a warning. 'Don't expect it to be all glamour, action and excitement. There is some of that, yes. But most police work is routine. It's about finding out who was where and when, and what they were doing. It's about checking and cross checking what people say, and spotting the lies. It's all about connections. Connections between people explain their actions. Find the connections and you solve the crime. That's mostly what we'll be doing.'

Dan resisted the temptation to get out his notebook and write some quotes down. It was clearly a speech DCI Breen had given many times before, perhaps learnt from a mentor, and probably passed on to other officers.

'We've got to be off now, to go and see Arthur Bray. You beat us to that one.' Adam smiled again. 'But you can start with me tomorrow morning. We'll begin working through all the people Edward Bray's crossed. And I warn you; it's a long list. Meet me at Charles Cross police station at nine?'

'Fine', said Dan. Was he starting to feel a real enthusiasm for his new job? 'I'll see you there.'

∼

That afternoon, he sat with a picture editor and cut a longer version of the report, just over 2 minutes worth for the evening edition of South West Tonight. The job only took half an hour. Lizzie had liked what she'd seen at lunchtime, so it was just a question of adding a little more of Arthur Bray's interview, and a clip of what Adam Breen had said about needing witnesses to come forward. He was finished by four.

He found Lizzie in her office, knocked and was beckoned to the sofa. The electric chair stood empty in the corner. He must be back in favour. He told her he was starting with the police tomorrow, and she may not see him around the newsroom for a few days. She agreed and allowed him to go home, a reward for working late last night.

The usual ball of furry, bouncing yelping joy that was Rutherford greeted him at the flat. After a pat, stroke and cuddle, the dog disappeared down into the garden. His bowl of water in the kitchen was hardly touched. There was a key with the downstairs neighbours in case Dan had to be away for the night, or was going to be back late, but Rutherford had developed his own way of coping when his master was out for the day. Whatever people may say about the intelligence of dogs, he wasn't stupid.

Rutherford bounded back up the concrete steps, and yelped with uncontrolled joy when he saw Dan had got his lead out of the cupboard. He bowed his head obediently to receive the chain, and they set off, up the slight rise out of Hartley Avenue and to Hartley Park.

The fruits of long hours of training in his comical gambolling puppy months, Rutherford was at least capable of walking to heel when he wanted to be, but only when he wanted. And like all dogs, that didn't stop him from sniffing ecstatically at every possible place where the spray of a fellow might be. Dan had learnt to factor that into calculations of the time needed to go anywhere with his dog. It meant the walk to the park took them five minutes when it would take two on his own. He was a journalist, so it was a habit to measure time precisely. He even did it on holiday, to the annoyance of whoever he was with.

They walked up the tree-lined path into the park, and Dan freed Rutherford from the lead. He sprinted away across the expanse of grass, skidded to a halt to sniff the base of a sapling, then sprinted back. Dan hadn't brought a ball. With Rutherford you didn't need to, the simple delights of grass, trees and an open space could entertain him for hours.

Dan watched as he ran up the steep slope which hid the underground reservoir, turned to look at him from the top, then sprinted back down again, lost his footing, slid, tumbled and rolled, before righting himself and re-joining his amused master, his coat flecked with coppery leaves. Dan stepped onto the grass and felt the first leak of water into his battered boots.

He climbed the slope to the top of the bank while Rutherford sprinted circles around him. It was the changing hour between night and day on a mild and damp autumn evening. The air was still, the low clouds painted amber by the city's glow. This was one of Plymouth's highest points, a place that always made him feel reflective. He looked down at the lines of shuffling red lights as commuters headed ritually home, and the countless dabs of white of the household windows and doors that would welcome them.

Overhead a plane droned as it headed into Plymouth airport, a dark javelin in the sky, its silhouette tipped by winking green and red lights, its whining jets blending into the bass background rumble of traffic. In the far corner of the park, in the play zone which Rutherford knew from painful experience was strictly out of bounds, a man pushed a young girl on a swing whilst talking into a mobile phone.

Rutherford had found a stick, and Dan knew that meant he had to play the parent. With them, there were three stages to the game. First he had to grab the stick and wrestle the dog for control. Only when he'd lost and given up to Rutherford's satisfaction would he lay the stick down at Dan's feet. The next stage was the simplest, and consisted of Dan repeatedly throwing the stick in a variety of directions, whilst Rutherford sprinted after it, then jogged back. Finally, when both had their fill, Dan had to throw the stick over a wall, or get it stuck up a tree, anywhere to make it irretrievable so they could both leave the field of play with honour intact.

When they got back to the flat, Rutherford still had leaves and grass interlaced with his fur, so Dan got the brush out of the cupboard. Already dizzy with pleasure from the walk and stick game, the dog gazed at his wonderfully generous master, his head tilted to one side, his eyes bright with adoration. Two old ladies waddled past and stared at them, mumbling to each other. When he'd freed a full Sainsbury's plastic shopping bag of fur, they pushed open the door into the flat's welcoming warmth.

Chapter five

Dan turned into the car park of Plymouth's Charles Cross police station at ten to nine the next morning. He pressed the buzzer beside the white metal gate.

'Hello?' A tinny female voice from a small grid of a speaker.

'Hello. Dan Groves from ITV News. I'm here to meet Chief Inspector Breen.'

There was a muffled metallic chuckle, which seemed to find echoes in the background. He thought he heard the words 'the glamour boy's here'. The barrier ground upwards and he drove in and parked beside a police van that was taking up two of the three visitors spaces. Adam Breen emerged from a door across the courtyard and greeted him.

'Morning Detective Constable Groves', he said with a smile.

Dan looked up at the grey four-storied building. At least a dozen of the windows were filled with grinning faces looking down at him. There was a bit of pointing going on too. His attachment to the force was causing some amusement.

'Morning Chief', he said. There was no point fighting it. He was here on their terms, play along and tough it out. But he stuck two fingers up at the faces as he followed the detective through the door into the station.

'Not a good idea Dan, don't upset the uniforms, you might need them one day', came Adam's voice over his shoulder. How the hell had he seen it? 'They're cannon fodder, but the odd one's smart and will rise up the ranks. They can be your boss in a few years, or mine anyway. So don't annoy them.'

'How did you..?'

'And it might save you a speeding ticket one day too'.

Dan followed along a gloomy corridor. 'How did you see?' He tried not to sound impressed, or embarrassed.

'I'm a detective mate, don't forget that either. Don't think you'll get away with anything with me. You're not in your hack pack now'. A very different Adam Breen from the man he'd interviewed yesterday, more relaxed on his own territory, laying down the law? He didn't sound angry, just amused. 'And it was the door's glass. Reflections are a detective's friend. Good lesson for you'.

Dan followed in silence, feeling stupid and angry with himself. Great start to your time with the police he thought.

'Cheer up', echoed Adam's voice. 'We all make mistakes, especially journalists eh?' Dan didn't take the bait, said nothing. 'And if it's any consolation, we've already got our first suspect for Bray's murder.

If you don't abuse any more fellow cops you'll get to see me turn him over in a while.' Adam sounded buoyant, looking forward to the confrontation. 'Sounds like a nasty guy, a hard little builder with previous convictions too. He's been into Bray's office several times to threaten him apparently. Could be a valuable customer for us.'

It was another typical day of the transition from Autumn to Winter, the kind of weather Dan likened to a sulky teenager. Not wanting to do one thing or another, it was just hanging around. The sky was grey, there was a hint of dampness and the wind persisted in its absence.

He'd rummaged in his wardrobe, but hadn't managed to find any shoes even vaguely like Adam Breen's. They were the smart, shining black and businesslike leather footwear so much more befitting of a detective. For him it was another day of leaking and weather-beaten boots.

He had made the effort of dressing them up with his best sand coloured chinos, a royal blue shirt, a dark blue blazer, and a yellow and blue diagonally striped tie. He was dealing with a murder and wanted to look respectfully smart. DCI Breen was wearing a similar suit to yesterday's, but this time a shade of dark bottle green. Dan suspected it was by Hugo Boss. He wondered how many other designers the detective's wardrobe held.

Adam Breen led him up three flights of stairs. He took them two at a time, walked briskly down a dark corridor and pushed through the last of a series of swing doors. Dan struggled to keep up. The door opened into a room a little bigger than a typical classroom. There were scrawl-covered whiteboards around the sides, a dozen large desks, all with phones and computers, and at the front of the room a series of green felt screens with a picture of Edward Bray in the centre. One middle-aged woman with glasses tapped at a keyboard at the back of the room, but otherwise it was deserted.

'The Murder Room', said Adam with a wave of the arm, as if introducing an old friend. 'I've got 50 detectives working on the case with more to come if needed. They're all out interviewing people who knew Bray. It's the start of the inquiry, so we're putting together a picture of his life, who he knew, who he did business with, what he did in his spare time, every detail of the day he was killed, basically as much information as possible. You never know what tiny little bit of info will lead you to the killer. It's bog standard detective work. Most importantly, we want to know about his enemies, anyone he crossed, anyone who could have wanted him dead. As I said to you yesterday, that's already a long list and it's growing.'

Dan seated himself on the edge of a desk at the side of the room by the window, looking down on the city centre. The police station was named after Charles Church and the roundabout that now surrounded it. A ruin, the church was Plymouth's most poignant reminder of the Blitz, when hundreds of years of history were levelled to rubble in a few short and viciously destructive weeks of bombardment. Built in Gothic style in the mid 17th century, it now stands hollow, only its stone walls surviving the blasts and fires of the incendiaries and explosives. But Dan always felt it radiated defiance, as if its body may have been taken but its soul would always remain.

Around the church spur three of the city's main roads. Anyone who lives in, or visits Plymouth can't avoid it. It's a ghost that the turning of time means the city can now live alongside, but which will never be exorcised. It remains a cold reminder of the losses of the past.

DCI Breen stood by the felt screen, like a teacher before a class. 'Are you ready?'

Dan looked at him, didn't know what he meant. 'For what?'

'For real murder'. He let the words hang. 'Not the films and books you've seen and read, but true hatred that leads to killing. Real killing. A finger on a trigger, a spray of blood, the taking of a life.'

Dan said nothing but felt a shudder. Was Adam Breen enjoying trying to unsettle him? Testing him to see if he could handle it? If he was worth bringing along on the case?

'We're about to pick apart a man's life to find something that led someone to want to murder him. I can guarantee you one thing. It won't be pretty. Everyone's got their nasty little secrets, everyone.' Dan sat silent, thought of a few of his own, waking up with that woman at the weekend, the one he'd known for approximately three hours. He held Adam's unblinking gaze, wondered what his secrets were. 'You ready for that then?' he asked. Dan nodded.

'So, first off, you want to hear the voice of the killer?'

Assistant Chief Constable (Operations) Alan Hawes had returned from holiday in a rank mood. Spain had been wonderful, warm, relaxing, such a contrast to England in the Autumn. Even the kids had behaved, for most of the holiday anyway. Not for the first time he was wondering if they could afford a second home out there, or if he could get the time off to make it worthwhile.

Devon and Cornwall Police Headquarters, Exeter, a grey sprawling complex on the brightest of days felt even colder in the dull drizzle. And there was so much to get through, a pile of papers, agendas, reports, an intray of emails. This one needed immediate action; he didn't like the look of it at all.

'Are you sure about this sir?' He put as much doubt into his voice as he dared. Deputy Chief Constable Brian Flood wasn't known for his patience. 'This man Groves, he's caused us problems in the past. In the foot and mouth epidemic he kept dodging our cordons to get to infected farms and the culls. We arrested him but we didn't have anything concrete and ITV sent a barrister to get him out. The bastards really embarrassed us, showed us up as acting outside of our powers. It caused havoc for a while, there were hacks running everywhere.'

The Deputy Chief Constable wasn't having a good morning either. The Home Office had been on the phone three times already wanting details about the force's policy on tackling drunken violence. A general election was looming and policing, as ever, was going to be a major issue. He didn't have time for this.

'Alan, it's simple.' He kept his voice calm, but the tone said there'd be no further discussion. 'The government want us to build more links with the media and show the good work we're doing to tackle crime. It's become a political priority. This is a high profile case. It was too good an opportunity to miss.'

There was a knock at the door. 'Not yet', he shouted.

'But sir..'

'No buts, it's happening.'

Alan Hawes nodded, teeth clenched, turned to leave. He was a good man, reliable, worked hard, the DCC thought. Remember your management strategy, plans for promotion; give him something to keep him on side.

'But if you're so worried about him, let's watch him carefully. Get the press office to tape every report he does. If there's any hint of anything coming out we don't like, we'll throw him off the case.'

～

Adam Breen walked over to a hi-fi system in the corner of the room and pressed play on the DVD. A muffled voice crackled from the speakers. It was a man, but he was deliberately slurring his speech. It was muffled too, like he was talking through thick drape curtains.

'Dead body. Lay by. A 38. Eastbound. 3 miles east of Plymouth.'

He played it again. Dan felt a shudder run across his back. 'The killer?'

DCI Breen nodded. 'Most likely, or their accomplice. The voice is obviously very disguised. Call received at 5.45 on Monday afternoon. The number is a mobile. We've already traced it. It's a pay as you go phone, came from a shop in Exeter. Cash paid, no ID required to buy it, so it's untraceable, a favourite trick with criminals. No description from the staff, no one could remember selling it, no CCTV in the shop to see the person who bought it. So no leads there.'

He paused, looked at Dan expectantly. 'It does raise some questions though', Adam continued. 'If it is the killer, or their accomplice, why call it in? Why not just let someone else find the body in time?'

'And the answer is?'

'We don't know yet. But it's something we'll certainly be looking at carefully.'

Dan nodded, felt tempted to write all this down. It'd make a great story, but, he kept reminding himself, he was here on trust. Shame..

'Ok then, here's what we do know', said Adam, straightening his tie. 'The victim was Edward Bray, a 37 year old, well known but - to put it mildly - not well liked local businessman. He was killed by a single shotgun blast to the chest. His body was found in a lay by to the east of Plymouth. Forensics show he was killed there, there's a blood spray pattern by his body consistent with being shot just after he got out of his jeep.' It was a bullet point list of facts, reeled off without the need for notes. 'We got that tip off, then the first officers got to the lay by at 6.01. Bray was dead when they arrived. The medics put the time of death anything up to an hour or so before we arrived, so the window for the shooting is between 4.45 and 5.45 on Monday evening. My initial thought is that he was killed about 5.15. He had an appointment to meet someone there at that time, and we're told he was obsessively punctual. That's useful. Obviously finding the person who he was supposed to be meeting is one of the first priorities of the inquiry. There was no sign of any theft from the jeep or Bray himself.'

Dan nodded, but didn't say anything.

'So far we have no reports of anyone seeing him there, but then I wouldn't expect to.' Adam Breen gestured to Bray's picture on the felt board. 'It's a grotty lay by; you'd only stop if you needed the loo, and then you'd have to be desperate. It was also dark and a rainy night, as you'll remember. There are no houses or paths close by. Equally, so far we have no reports of anyone hearing a shot, but again, unless we were very lucky, I wouldn't expect to. As you know, the lay by is just off the A 38, cars belt along there at a hell of a rate, and they'll drown out most noise. There's no forensic evidence either, no DNA or fibres on Bray that might have come from the killer. We didn't find any fibres or traces of the attacker anywhere in the lay by. And we didn't find any tyre tracks or footprints there either, the rain saw to all that. There is one potential clue in that the shotgun was fired upwards into Bray's chest, which could suggest the killer was short, but might equally indicate they fired from the hip area, so it's not a great deal of use.

As for motive, well, it doesn't look like robbery, nothing appears to have been stolen. So my guess is hate or revenge. It's unusual in these cases to see a shot to the heart. Most killers go for the head. I wonder if shooting Bray in the heart had some symbolic meaning for the killer, almost as if they wanted to take out the very essence of his existence. And as for suspects, as I said to you, we've got plenty. Edward Bray was by no means a well-liked man. And that is about it.'

Adam Breen looked at him, seemed to be waiting for something. It was a good briefing, Dan thought, but there was something missing. He sensed he was being tested. He'd done it with younger journalists who'd been sent to shadow him. See if they've got some spirit, if they're up to the job. Ok then, you want to play..

'Not quite universally disliked though, was he?' Adam raised his eyebrows, said nothing. 'Any idea why he saved the hospice?'

The detective was used to hiding his feelings, trained in it, experienced. But Dan knew he'd hit something; saw a slight turn of the polished black shoe on the carpeted floor, a shift of his body, a hint of a reaction. Just enough.

'Go on?'

'He wasn't black and white'. Who is, he thought? But keep going.. 'Did you know he saved St Jude's from closure?' A shake of the head and a flash of interest in the eyes. 'I checked it in the log of stories we'd done on Bray. There were a few that you'd expect, bankrupting people, evicting them, that sort of thing. But then there was something strange, a story about him saving the hospice, totally out of context with everything else about him.' Adam nodded slowly. 'But nothing about why. Not a thing.'

A pneumatic drill began a dull hammering outside. Adam turned to look. 'Any guesses?' He said.

Now you're asking, Dan thought. Maybe I'm getting in too deep here. Trying too hard?

'Only guesses. I asked Arthur Bray about it, but he clammed up, wouldn't say anything at all. I thought the question hurt him. So I reckon from that it's something personal, in the family.' A memory from his interview with the man. 'Didn't Edward's mum die of cancer? Some link there?'

Adam nodded again. 'Worth looking at certainly.' He studied Dan. 'We'll check it out. Good idea'.

Another pause as the two men looked at each other. Dan had a bizarre feeling like he was in a job interview, trying to impress an employer. The idea rankled. He was a senior TV News Correspondent, not some kid on work experience. Was that how they thought of him here?

'Any other suggestions?' said Adam, breaking the silence. Dan wondered if he was being sarcastic, but he didn't sound it. You're the detective here he thought, you come up with something. I'm just busking it. But what the hell, I don't mind bluffing, it's worked for me so far.

'Ok, you've given me the facts. But what's really going on?' Adam Breen looked at him quizzically but said nothing. 'Look', he said thinking fast. 'My job as a reporter is about interpreting facts, to fit them into a pattern or trend. I'd guess in that respect it's no different to yours. So what do you make of them?'

Adam Breen gave Dan a long look that made him think – hope perhaps? - he was reappraising his new colleague. He straightened his already impeccable tie again and looked out of the window at the church, then turned back, a slight smile creasing his face.

'You're quite right. I often think of what I know in an investigation as those bits of an iceberg that you can see.' The lecturer was back. 'They're interesting in themselves, but more so because they hint at what you can't see. Down there below the water is the real story. In this case it's what made someone hate Edward Bray so much they fantasised about killing him, then researched it, then actually pulled the trigger. I think it's a hate crime because of all the people who had reasons to dislike him, and because the killer shot him in the heart. That looks coldly deliberate and very personal to me, as though they wanted to destroy the very core of his existence. Most shootings are in the head. So, the tip of the iceberg is our murder. It's what we're seeing at the moment. Below lurks the reason why, and there with it, our killer.'

'You said researched it', said Dan, who was thinking like a journalist, and wondering if that wasn't so different from a detective. 'You think this was all planned?'

'Oh yes. Yes indeed. It's already clear to me that whoever shot Bray is clever. Possibly very clever. They knew him, and used that knowledge to lure him to that lay by with something he couldn't resist. Otherwise why else would he be in such a Godforsaken place at that time? Then they had the gun ready to shoot him. He was found by his jeep with the door wide open. I think he was shot a few seconds after he got out of it. Whoever did it researched and planned the killing carefully and left us with what I suspect will be no forensic evidence. Possibly no evidence at all.'

'How come?' Dan was surprised. He'd seen the wonders of criminal science celebrated many times in the press.

'They used a shotgun. Do you know anything about forensics?'

'Only what I've seen on the TV.'

'Right. Well, forget that. In fact, forget all that stuff you see on TV, it's rubbish. We don't solve murders in two hours, half of which is spent in a pub chatting about the case, more's the pity. We solve them by hard work. It's as simple as that.'

'Ok', said Dan impatiently. 'I had suspected that.'

Adam ignored the sarcasm. 'Forensics are useful, but they're just a tool, and not one you can always rely on. This case is a point in fact. You see, from a detective's viewpoint, shooting someone with a shotgun is not helpful. If someone uses a pistol, there are always flaws, tiny lumps, imperfections, rifling on the inside of the barrel that you can match any marks on the bullet with. So you know what gun fired it. But with a shotgun you can't tell. A ballistics expert might give you an opinion on a gun, and say it could be this one, or one like it that fired the shot, but nothing conclusive enough to sway a jury. So that's probably a waste of time, although we'll try of course, if we can find the gun, that is. We're way behind the killer and they've no doubt got rid of it, and the clothes they were wearing. So no blood spray evidence from the shot to find there either. And you know the other problem with shotguns?'

'What?'

'Come on Dan, you're in Devon. Just about everyone in the countryside's got one, and perfectly legally too. His Dad, Arthur Bray for example. He's got two. He showed me them quite proudly. He uses them for shooting rabbits. I didn't ask if he'd used them for shooting his son. Not at that point anyway, I was taking it gently, but I'll doubtless have to at some stage.'

The image of the old man, hunched in his armchair, his eyes filled with pain filled Dan's head.

'He's a suspect?' He couldn't hide the surprise.

The smile returned to Adam Breen's face, but this time it was cold. He looked like a teacher about to give a naive pupil a hard learned lesson of life.

'Get used to it Dan. You're moving into a world of suspicion. That's what happens when you join the police. You become so used to being lied to that you assume everyone's doing it. Why do you think most police marriages never last?'

Did he blink there, wince at his own words? What was that about? 'It's no basis for a way of life', Adam continued quickly, not letting the words settle, covering up what he was thinking, Dan wondered? 'But that's what happens. Institutionalised is the word some people use. It's sad I know, but there you go, you wanted to know all about it and that's part of it.' He seemed to relax a little. 'Mind you, to be fair – and I know it's a cliché, but it's one your TV detectives do have right – everybody is a suspect at the moment, and that includes Arthur Bray. So don't let it trouble you too much. Not yet at least. Not until we have to ask him that question.'

Dan looked out of the window at the stooping cranes slowly piling up the great concrete blocks that was the start of their task of rebuilding the northern quarter of the city centre. It was long overdue. What was supposed to be a temporary city built up quickly and defiantly after the war had lasted for almost 60 years and was showing its age. He looked hopefully across at the five stories of the Dingles department store, rebuilt 20 years ago after a fire started by animal rights' activists. The ground floor boasted a fine selection of shoes, and he wondered if he might have the chance to get away for half an hour to buy some new boots. He was fed up with suffering damp socks.

'Then there's the mobile. I'm assuming that was bought specifically to call us with. And another thing tells me it was well planned.'

There was little chance of that, he thought.

'What?'

'It's a lay by. What do you know about mud and dirt?'

'Very little', said Dan. 'It's good for growing veg'. What answer did he expect? 'My dog always comes home covered in it after a walk. That's about it. '

Adam Breen shook his head. 'Forensically, lay bys are no good for detectives either. Most mud is distinctive, you can tell to within a few hundred feet where it came from. So if there's some on a suspect, you can match it to a crime scene. But a lay by killing means there's no mud on the killer or their tyres, assuming they got there by car. And they usually do. And no tyre tracks either, the rain saw to that. A dark lay by, on a wet Autumn night, next to Devon's busiest road. It's an assassin's dream. There's minimal chance of witnesses or evidence, hence a well planned killing. It's going to be an interesting case. You've picked a good one to join us on.'

I hope so, thought Dan. For giving me the time to go following it, Lizzie is going to expect a decent reward. He looked down at his watch. It said 9.15, which meant it was about 9.20 or maybe even later. It was a Rolex he'd bought second hand for a very reasonable price from a back street jeweller in Brighton. It didn't take long to discover why. No matter how much he wound it, the watch ran an average of five minutes slow. He could buy a new one, but it looked good, even if it didn't tell the time very well. Plus he'd grown attached to it, and he'd got used to adding on the missing minutes. A new watch would confuse him for weeks.

'9.21' said Adam Breen, who'd been watching him. His own watch was small and silver with classical Roman numerals and a black leather strap. Like its owner, it was precise.

'So what do you do now?'

'We Dan, we. Start thinking of yourself as part of this. You want to know about police work, then think yourself part of the case. From now on, it takes over your life. That's the way it is with detectives and major investigations. It's all you do until it's solved.' He saw Dan's look. 'I'm serious.'

'Ok then, what do we do now?'

'We go find some suspects. Or rather, given there's no shortage, we try to put together a league table of them and work out who'd want him dead the most. Then we find out what they were doing on Monday evening between five and six. Then we cross check that, to make sure they're not lying. And if they're in the clear, we work our way down the list until we find something suspicious, and we worry away at it until we get a result, or not, as the case may be. And we repeat the process until we find the killer, although that will obviously be subject to approval by a jury.' His tone left no doubt he considered that part unnecessary. 'We've got one suspect already, a good one. So, are you ready to go play at being detectives?'

DCI Breen was grinning again. He had the first hints of a shadow of a beard already. Dan wondered which he was enjoying more, the case, or teasing his new assistant.

'I'm ready', he said. He hoped his voice sounded convincing.

'Then let's go. You can drive. I might as well take advantage of your company. Follow me back down to the yard. Our first stop isn't far, just Moretonhampstead. Half an hour or so if I know how you hacks drive.'

Adam Breen made for the door, then turned and looked Dan straight in the eye. He almost jumped, but just managed to stop himself. The detective had clearly planned the last words of his briefing.

'One final thing. You're in this on trust. If you should broadcast anything you hear without my say so, it could scupper the investigation into a vicious murder. If you do, Devon and Cornwall police will never help you again and we could even look at prosecuting you. Understood?'

Dan felt a shot of excitement and nervousness. He nodded.

Chapter six

Dan's sweet vision of bullying his way through the traffic as other motorists respectfully gave way to the blue lamped, fluorescent striped police car vanished as they climbed into a grimy, dark blue, four year old Vauxhall Astra. The ashtrays were full of cigarette butts and long discarded plastic petrol station sandwich wrappings littered the back seats. The car smelt of stale smoke, damp and mould. He flinched, and it wasn't lost on Adam Breen.

'No flash new cop cars for the CID Dan' he mused. 'We like to be inconspicuous, blend into the background. And you can't do much better for blending in than this old heap.' He patted the dashboard kindly. 'Mind you, we have made a few modifications and she can shift all right if you need her to, but let's just take it easy for now. You know the way?'

Dan set off east along the A38. He knew Moretonhampstead well from his days in environment. One of Dartmoor's biggest towns, he'd covered many stories there. Most were about farming, but the most recent was a major water pollution, a slurry leak into the river from a farmer's tank, thousands of fish dead, suffocated. They were piled up on the banks in silvery heaps, shining in the summer sunshine, roach, chub, carp, salmon and trout too. White overalled Environment Agency staff pumped chemicals into the river to try to revive its life. His dominant memory was the stench of rotting fish.

He expected to feel a sting of nostalgia for his old job, but it didn't come. This new world of murder and intrigue was drawing him in.

They passed the lay by where Edward Bray had been killed. It was deserted, the cordon gone, no hint anything had happened there. Adam, who'd been reading silently from his notes, looked up.

'What's unusual about this case is the lack of evidence', he said slowly. 'We've done all the forensics, fingertip searches, the usual stuff. We've found exactly nothing, which I believe is evidence in itself. We are dealing with a clever killer, who's up to speed with police techniques and evidence gathering, and has planned well to give us nothing.' He turned to watch the lay by drift past them. 'So we'll have to do this the old fashioned way, with good interrogations, detailed investigating, and plenty of thought. That starts here. We're off to carry out the first big interview of the case. Get this right and it could all be solved by tonight.'

Really? Thought Dan, but he'd already learned not to rise to Adam's baits. He kept driving.

'Tony Rye', the detective continued, checking his notes. 'A builder, working on the swimming pool refit. When we talk to you hacks to put out our little appeals, he's what we politely call 'someone we need to eliminate from our inquiries'. In plain speak that means he's a suspect and usually the hot one.' Dan nodded. 'We've got info from Bray's secretary that Rye used to go into the office regularly to make threats. There were quite a few shouting matches.' Another check of the notes. 'It was something to do with a big building contract they'd had a dispute about.'

Dan couldn't help but hope the case wasn't solved so fast. Forget the interests of justice, this was much more interesting than the standard grind of being in the newsroom. Come on, he thought, be honest. You're getting into it, aren't you? Damn her for it, but Lizzie was right. It's sexy stuff. We're about to see a man who might be a murderer. I've never met one before.

'Just one other thing you should be aware of', said Adam. His voice dropped conspiratorially, and Dan had to struggle to hear. 'Suzanne did a check of his past. He's got previous convictions for burglary and robbery. He held up a petrol station with a knife.'

The swimming pool is on the western side of Moretonhampstead, and as always with builders, it was obvious they were at work. There was a line of four dusty, scraped and scratched and untidily parked lorries, a small pile of scaffolding tubes another larger pile of bricks topped with earth from which forlorn fronds of grass hung and an off white portacabin. A distant radio provided a thumping background beat. An occasional metallic hammering echoed across the site, mixed with tuneless whistling and the odd shouted oath. The whole area was covered with squelching brown mud.

They walked over to the portacabin, up a concrete block of a step, and into the open door. On one end of the room was a table with a plastic kettle, an industrial size tin of unbranded coffee and some tea bags, a six pint plastic container of milk, a kilogram pack of sugar and a dozen chipped and cracked mugs.

At the other end of the room were two tables pushed together to make a square, and standing at them, looking over a blueprint bent a small and balding man. Adam coughed loudly and he looked up.

'Cops', he said sullenly and without surprise. 'You can tell 'em a mile off'. His voice had old echoes of London, not quite lost in years of Devon life.

'Mr Rye?' said Adam, with a patient tone that said he'd heard the routine many times before.

'Yeah', said Tony Rye. 'I'd ask you to come in, but you already have. Do you want a tea?'

The offer surprised Dan. Their welcome hadn't exactly been friendly. He wondered whether to accept. Adam looked at the mugs with undisguised distaste.

'No thanks', he said. 'I'm Detective Chief Inspector Adam Breen. This is my colleague Dan Groves.'

'I'd say pleased to meet you, but I'm not.' He looked them up and down. 'I've had trouble with the police before. I've got this swimming pool to get sorted and we're already way behind schedule. So how can I help you?'

'What's your role here?' asked Adam calmly.

'I'm what they used to call the foreman. That was in the good old days.'

Dan never heard the phrase without a desire to ask if sending children up chimneys, or burning witches, or badger baiting were good features of the old days too.

'I'm called the site manager now', he continued proudly. 'It's up to me to get the job done right, safely and on time. But I don't expect that's what you've come to ask me about, is it?'

'No Mr Rye, it's not.' Adam's voice sounded ominous. He took a couple of steps towards Tony Rye and leaned against the side of the table, then looked down at the dust on it and stood up again. 'I'd like to know about Edward Bray.'

Tony Rye looked unsurprised. 'Yeah, thought so', he muttered. 'Well get on with it then. And if I've got to stop and talk to you, I might as well have a cuppa.'

He walked past Adam and over to the tea table. His shoulder thudded into the detective's arm. Neither man said anything.

He was a small man, about five feet four Dan thought. He wasn't fat or thin, but stocky and muscular, from years of carrying bricks and pipes perhaps? He'd suffered the same hair loss as so many men, with a shining bare strip running from his temples, over the crown of his head, down to a tightly shaved dark fringe at the back and sides. There was enough stubble on his face to say he hadn't shaved that day. One ear was pierced with a dull gold stud. His face was oddly flat, the ears sticking out and his eyes small and peering. He had a flat and red nose, mottled with tiny blue broken veins. Dan guessed he was in his late 40s. He wore the builders' uniform of black, paint spattered steel toe capped boots, faded and threadbare jeans, also flecked with paint, and a thick lumberjack shirt with a T shirt beneath. As he made his tea, Dan saw his hands were cracked and blackened. There were letters tattooed on his knuckles, but too faint and covered in dirt for Dan to read. A woman's name?

'So then, Edward Bray', said Adam with a determined tone as the kettle began to rumble and steam.

'What about him?' grunted Tony Rye, heaping three spoonfuls of sugar into his mug and stirring it with a pen he'd taken from the breast pocket of his shirt. Dan was glad he hadn't taken up the offer of tea.

'You knew him?'

'Yeah I knew him. A right arsehole.'

'In what way Mr Rye?'

Tony Rye sipped the scalding tea and looked suspicious. 'You know in what way. You haven't come to see me for no reason.'

'I'd prefer it if you just told me how you knew him Mr Rye. It'd be much quicker and easier, then we can leave you alone to finish your pool.'

Tony Rye leant back against the portacabin wall. 'I used to work for him. Well, the company did. We did lots of work for him. Standard stuff, refits, extensions, new bathrooms, kitchens, that sort of thing.'

'But you fell out?'

'Yeah, we fell out', said Tony Rye his voice heavy with sarcasm. 'He cancelled our contract. My contract.'

'What contract was that Mr Rye?'

The Building Site Manager slurped the rest of his tea and glared at Adam, and then Dan too.

A Popular Murder

'New houses. Out near Ivybridge. Big contract. I'd done shit loads of work on it.'

'You say your contract? Was it yours or the company's?'

'The company's, but I did all the work on it. I got it for us.'

'And you would have done well out of it?'

'Yeah, me and the company.'

'Good bonus for you? Promotion?'

'Yeah, maybe', said Tony Rye, looking even more suspicious now. Dan wondered how intelligent he was. The trap of the pit beneath him looked yawning. Adam was scarcely even having the decency to camouflage it a little. The case could be over by tonight at this rate. Well, at least he'd have a good exclusive to offer Lizzie then, but all the same..

'So what went wrong?' the detective continued smoothly.

'He pulled out', snarled Tony Rye. 'Cancelled the contract. Said he didn't have confidence in the design anymore. Gave the work to another firm. But I know what it really was. They undercut us.' He shook his head angrily. 'After we'd got the job they came along and undercut us. Wankers, them and him.'

His hands had clenched into fists. Dan wondered if Adam had seen it, if he should say something? Have faith, of course he had, he'd seen the two fingers up to the cops hadn't he?

'And what happened then?'

'He wanted the money he'd given us back.' Gritted teeth. 'We said bollocks to you. We'd spent thousands on the planning and turned down other work to do the job. The bastard said it was tough, that business was like that, and took us to court. We're too small to fight him so we gave in and gave him his stinking money back. Wanker.'

'Right. I see', said Adam. Dan had a feeling the punch line was coming. 'And I understand you went to see him last week.'

If Adam had expected a denial it didn't come. 'It wasn't the first time.' Tony Rye pulled himself up to his full height proudly. 'I have to go past his place quite often. When I do and I've got time, I go in and see him. I wanted him to know he wasn't going to get away with what he'd done. So I told him so.'

'You had a row?'

'Yeah.'

'And then?'

'Came out here and got on with the pool.'

'What did you mean when you said he wouldn't get away with what he'd done?'

Tony Rye looked down at his knuckles as though imagining them planted in Edward Bray's face. 'I just wanted him to know I hadn't forgotten. Wanted to make him worry a bit I suppose.'

'And nothing else? Just talk?'

Tony Rye scowled. 'Yeah, if you wanna put it that way. I just wanted him to know I hadn't forgotten.'

Adam was looking down, scribbling on his notepad. Dan felt an urge to ask a question, then stopped himself. He was an amateur here, just an observer; this man could be a killer. Leave it to the professionals. But then he'd never been good at keeping quiet, had he? And he was enjoying this confrontation. It was – what do they call it – real life drama? And is Adam expecting me to chip in? Leaving a space to see if I can do something with it? Another test? Oh, what the hell..

'Mr Rye, you're aware of what happened to Edward Bray?' Dan tried to control his voice but he was sure it was shaking. Adam glanced up at him but his expression was fixed, unreadable.

'Oh, the monkey talks as well as the organ grinder eh?', said Tony Rye, turning to face him. 'Yeah, saw it on the news', he continued. 'What a shame eh? What a terrible shame.' He smiled slowly, a blackened tooth exposed. 'Shame, shame, fucking terrible shame.'

Dan imagined him dancing at the news. 'How well did you know him?'

The smile faded. 'Too well. Wish I never knew him at all. Wanker.'

'Do you know anything about why he saved St Jude's Hospice?'

Tony Rye shook his head. 'Not a clue mate. Aren't you supposed to be the bloody detectives?'

Ok big man, thought Dan, you want to play nasty, I'll join in. 'Where were you on Monday afternoon?'

Adam gave him a sideways glance. He'd expected a scowl, but wasn't there the hint of a smile? Tony Rye looked uncomfortable. He fiddled with his earring.

'I was here.'

'Here on the site?'

'Yeah, for most of the time.'

'Most of the time?'

'Yeah.'

'Where else were you?' It felt like the interviews where he'd tried to pin down a slippery politician.

'I went into town for a while to get some shopping, and I went over to a yard in Ivybridge to pick up some tiles for the pool.'

'And can you remember what time you were here and what time you were away?' Was he doing this right? No help from Adam.

'Not exactly.' More fiddling with the earring. 'I went to get the tiles mid afternoon ish, then brought them back. I went into town later, when it was dark, probably just before closing time.'

'And did anyone see you?'

'Couple of shopkeepers, no one I know.'

'Could you tell us which shops?'

'If I have to.'

'Right. Thank you Mr Rye.' That's enough for now he thought, enough. It's gone ok. Do that thing you never got the hang of and quit while you're ahead.

Adam was watching Tony Rye carefully. 'Just a couple more things Mr Rye, for now at least. Do you own a shotgun?'

'No', said Tony Rye quickly.

'Does anyone you know own one?'

'No', he repeated. 'Why?'

'Mr Bray was killed with a shotgun', said Adam levelly.

'So fucking what? You trying to fit me up?' His fists were tight again.

'I wouldn't dream of it Mr Rye.' Adam paused, looked down at his mud edged shoes, then back up again, straight into the builder's eyes. Timing, thought Dan admiringly, beautiful timing. 'It's just that you have been known to use a weapon in the past, haven't you?'

There was a crash as Tony Rye threw down his mug. It hit the wall, spattering it with drops of tea, but didn't break. His face red, he jabbed his fist out towards Adam. Dan thought he was going to try to hit him, but he just pointed, his hand poking at Adam's chest, his face screwed tight.

The detective remained impassive. Dan wondered how many times he'd been in this situation. He had a feeling Adam had engineered it to see if he could provoke Tony Rye into a mistake.

'I did not kill Bray', he said, spitting and spelling out each word. 'I hated him. I admit that. Yeah, I hated him. But that ain't a crime. The bloody jails would be full if it was. And yeah, in the past I've done some stupid things. But I'm all right now. I've got a wife and a house and a decent job and I don't do that stuff anymore. I'm straight. So you can fuck off out of here.'

Dan's heart was beating fast. He realised his body had been preparing him for a fight. Adam looked as calm as ever. Dan wondered what it would take to unsettle him.

'Thank you Mr Rye', said Adam pleasantly, as if accepting a piece of cake to go with some tea. 'We've no more questions for now, although we will need to speak to you again.'

'Shite you will' mumbled Tony Rye, clenching and unclenching his fists as he glared at them.

'Are you going to bawl me out then or what?' asked Dan as he drove the Astra west over Dartmoor and back towards Plymouth; next appointment, Bray's secretary, Penelope Ramsden.

He'd been expecting Adam to say something as soon as they'd left the swimming pool, but all he'd done was read through his notes, scribble down the odd thought and straighten his tie a couple of times.

'For what?'

'For sticking my oar into that interview'. No reply, more scribbling. 'I don't know, for impertinence, getting ahead of myself, that sort of thing. Getting in your way.' Still no reply. Come on, say something! 'For thinking I can help out instead of just watch, like I'm supposed to.'

Adam looked up. Dan glanced across at him, expecting a scowl, irritation, resentment. Instead he got a smile, a genuine one, the first he'd seen on Adam's face. He looked younger, and just for a moment not like a detective. 'Do you really want to know?' Dan wasn't sure he did, but Adam continued anyway.

'Well, it's like this. When my bosses told me you were going to join us, I wasn't best pleased to say the least. In fact I was distinctly narked.' His face showed it, a grimace. 'I thought you'd get in the way and couldn't be trusted. You're a journalist after all and cops learn quickly not to trust you lot. And I don't like carrying passengers. Everyone on my team's here because they deserve to be. It's a murder inquiry and we haven't got the luxury of time to mess around.'

Dan looked over again. Stirring he thought, but I can still feel the kick coming.

'Well, now I have to say I think you can be trusted. I've given you plenty of inside information about the case which I know would make a great story for you, and you've made no attempt to try to get it on air. It wasn't exactly a test, but I did wonder if I'd be watching the TV, or listening to the radio and hearing an exclusive report on the inside workings of the Bray case. Nothing like that's happened. So you have my trust, on that level at least.'

Dan felt oddly touched. He managed a low 'thanks'. Few people know how to accept praise, however faint, and Dan wasn't amongst them.

'As for you getting in the way, well you haven't done that either. I was wondering how you'd handle that interview and I think you got it just right. You let me get on with it. I've seen plenty of new detectives make a right hash of their first interviews with suspects or witnesses because they think they're so clever, or powerful, or they want to make a mark and impress the senior officer who's with them.'

A shake of the head, painful experiences relived. 'They end up getting no info at best and, at worst, totally misled. The way to learn is from someone who knows what they're doing. I'm not saying I know it all, hell no, but I've picked up a few useful things over the years, enough to usually find out what I need. That was just an opener in there, testing Rye out, to see if it was obviously him or if we can push him into a mistake. No go yet, but we'll have to come back and see him again, test out his alibi. It's enough to get us started.'

Dan felt his trepidation lift. He was reminded of something Conan Doyle had written.

'You sound like Sherlock Holmes', he said. 'He always used to tell Watson he was the ideal companion because he understood the gift of silence.'

'I wouldn't quite put myself in his league', said Adam, sounding amused. 'And I wouldn't have put you down as the quiet type who's content to be my foil either.' He tightened his tie again. 'But here's a funny thing', he added.

'What's that?' asked Dan. He was feeling a little uncomfortable that Adam seemed to have such a good insight into him already.

'I actually welcomed your input into that interview. Detectives normally go out in pairs because it works best that way. If one cop has a line of questioning, the other can watch the reaction of the person to see if they look evasive, or their body language is odd, or even if there are any obvious lies or inconsistencies. But it also helps that if one officer wants a few seconds to think about an answer that's been given, the other can chip in with a question to keep the suspect talking. That way you don't give them time to think up excuses or alibis.'

That explains why all those TV detective shows are duets thought Dan. At least there's some grounding of truth then.

'You're an experienced interviewer', Adam continued. 'Perhaps not in exactly the same way that I am, but our jobs aren't that different. We both need to get information and get to the bottom of what's going on, get past the lies and spin and find the truth. And you're also experienced at dealing with people who are upset. I think your input could be useful. So feel free to chip in with questions or thoughts. Obviously be sensitive to me if I'm going through a line of inquiry with someone, but when you feel it's right do put some questions in.' It sounded like a challenge. 'I'll be interested to see what you think is important.'

Dan was going to thank Adam, but the detective had only taken a pause for breath.

'In fact', he said heartily, 'it's damned pleasant to have someone around who's intelligent, with a good insight into people and a fresh perspective.'

It was one of the kinder things anyone had said to him for weeks, and Dan was surprised to find himself taken aback, unable to find any words in return.

'And please, forget all this police formality stuff in future and just call me Adam', he added.

'Ok Adam', said Dan, feeling like he'd just been accepted into a new and exclusive club.

⁓

He could never drive across Dartmoor without the urge to walk on one of its wild and remote Tors, but he knew there'd be no time this week. The investigation had already begun to dominate his thoughts, just as Adam had said it would. He went back over the interview with Tony Rye. Could he have been the killer? He reacted violently to the suggestion, but that could have been an act. He wasn't stupid and he had a violent past, wasn't form the word the police used? And his alibi looked thin.. He checked himself. He was starting to think like a detective already.

Then there was his day job - Lizzie - to satisfy. He could see himself in her office, her three-inch heels grinding into the long-suffering carpet. When was his next report coming? Would it be an exclusive? He'd have to find a story at some point. But not now, not yet, not just as Adam was beginning to trust him, not as the investigation was getting interesting. And he'd said he'd take Kerry out this week too. His mind wandered back to the dinner party that Mike and Jo had hosted. They'd called it a party, but it was just the four of them, matchmaking at its most obvious.

Kerry was naturally tall, about five feet ten, and she'd dressed to impress. Her shoes were striking; red, open toed and layered in sparkling sequins. She walked with that self-consciousness and care that told Dan they were new. She was slim, very slim, but still had the curves of chest, hips and thighs that many women lost in their quest for a model's shape. She wore a knee length red dress; figure tight at the top, with a slight flaring as it sloped down below her waist. It was cut back off her shoulders with a gentle parabola down onto her chest. He suspected this too was new; it had that starched look of clothes, which have yet to be softened by the washing machine. There was a thin plain silver necklace, which hugged her skin, matched by two-inch stalactite silver earrings. It was a pleasant memory.

Her hair was blonde, probably shoulder length, he guessed, but she was wearing it up. Having finally grown wise to a woman's way of highlighting her strengths, Dan thought that was probably to emphasise her cheekbones. They were sharp and fine. Her eyes were blue, her lips a little thin, and she'd used the standard ruse of red lipstick to make them look fuller.

It'd be too strong to say he'd been dreading the evening's introduction, but it'd been a tiring few days and he wasn't looking forward to putting in the effort politeness required. He'd felt lacklustre and short of charm. And there was always the spectre of Thomasin with him, ready to scare off any woman. But suddenly, surprisingly, somehow, that changed. He'd felt a wave of unexpected enthusiasm. He had a vision of her naked and tried to push it from his mind, pleasant though it was. Would he never change?

He'd enjoyed the evening despite himself, they'd swapped mobile phone numbers and he'd promised to take her out this week. He didn't think there'd be time now, but how about a Dartmoor walk at the weekend instead? It was an original idea for a date and he'd enjoy it, as would Rutherford. At least that way, if they didn't get on so well without the lubrication of wine, it wouldn't be a waste of time. He decided to send her a text later to see if she fancied it.

∼

The Astra's engine growled in protest as he dropped a gear to hold the car back as they descended from the moor's uplands to the outskirts of Plymouth.

'Edward Bray's secretary is a woman called Penelope Ramsden' said Adam who'd emerged from his quiet thinking. 'She was distraught when Suzanne spoke to her on the phone yesterday. She managed to tell us a bit about Bray's movements and gave us that tip about Tony Rye, but then she dissolved into tears so I said I'd put off seeing her until today.'

That's a relief thought Dan. At least someone's sad he's dead. But why his secretary, when not his family? 'What do we expect from her?'

'Just information I think. I've no reason to believe she's a suspect, not yet at least. I want to find out more about Bray, how he managed the business and if there was anyone he had a particular feud with. It's not really anything specific; I'm just trying to get a feel for the man. Secretaries often know more about their bosses than anyone else, so if there are any little secrets that might have led to murder, it's here we could well find them.'

Dan turned into a car park surrounding a modern red brick two-storey office block in the Crownhill area in the north of Plymouth. Lights were on behind the silvered glass downstairs, but not above. It looked new and he suspected not all the building had been let yet. They parked, got out of the car, and walked over to the glass entrance doors.

There were a series of bronzed plaques and accompanying buzzers on the door. Adam ignored them and strode in. A man was walking down the corridor towards them.

'Bray Associates?' asked the detective simply.

'He's dead', mumbled the man, followed by 'shame eh?' and hurried outside. He sounded anything but mournful.

They walked through another glass door into a large open plan office. Four young men were working at computer terminals, their desks arranged in two squares. Only one looked up and then quickly returned to his work. A glass door at the far end was closed and sealed with police tape. Edward Bray's personal office? Two banner-sized signs dominated the walls. They read 'NO SMOKING' in angry red letters. By the window was a much grander desk with rows of files on the shelves about it, and along the walls to the side. A woman slowly swivelled her chair round to them and stood up with a laborious effort.

Dan tried not to look surprised, but wondered how well he succeeded. She was simply ugly. Layers of fat hung off her, seeming to drag her down and making her almost comically triangular. Her hair was mousy brown and dangled greasily onto her shoulders in limp fronds, lank and lifeless, moving as reluctantly as heavy curtains. Her complexion was mottled and sweaty, her nose, mouth and eyes all too small for her bulk. Her clothes were loose fitting, a faded ankle length flowery skirt, a baggy black jumper with a once white blouse underneath. Dan imagined her schooldays, and the inevitable nickname piggy. He guessed she was in her mid to late 40s, but as with many people who'd lost self-discipline and respect, ageing her accurately was impossible.

She'd been crying and had made little attempt to cover her tears. She wore no make up, and her eyes were swollen and darkly ringed.

'Ms Ramsden? Enquired Adam in a neutral tone. She nodded. 'I'm Detective Chief Inspector Adam Breen. This is my colleague Dan Groves.'

Dan was trying not to stare. Penelope Ramsden nodded again. 'Thanks for seeing us', he continued. 'I know it can't be easy for you.'

For a third time she nodded, although now a little harder. More tears began to form in her eyes. Dan wondered how useful this interview was going to be. So far Penelope Ramsden hadn't managed a single word.

'Don't be too nervous' said Adam, trying to make his voice light and draw some precious conversation from her. 'We're just here to see if we can get a better idea about Mr Bray and what he was like. We'd also like to know about his diary on Monday, who he may have seen, that sort of thing.'

She nodded, and the movement freed the tears to trickle down her cheeks. She stared at the grey carpet tiles on the floor. Then, with an apparent effort she lifted her head and broke her silence in a strangled but sharp voice.

'He was a good man!'

Adam looked surprised. 'I'm sure he was Ms Ramsden', he said soothingly.

'You're not', she spat, her face creasing. 'I bet you think he deserved to die. I bet everyone has been telling you he was evil. Well I don't care what they say.' She only just managed to get the words out. 'He was always good to me.'

All four men had now looked up from their screens. She turned on them and her voice rose to a screech.

'Get on with your work! Just because he's not here anymore, that doesn't mean things are going to be any different. You want paying, you work for it.'

The words, Dan thought, of her boss, repeated so often it had become a mantra here. Penelope Ramsden pushed past them, through the door, out into the corridor and disappeared. Adam followed hastily. Dan had no idea what to do, so he followed too. They found themselves waiting outside the ladies' toilet. The two men looked at each other.

'Is police work always like this?' asked Dan, who was wondering if he preferred the confrontation with Tony Rye. At least he understood anger and knew how to handle it.

'No, this is one of the more straightforward jobs', replied Adam levelly. 'She's upset, give her a chance.'

Dan studied the battered posters in the corridor while they waited. Neighbourhood watch, reflexology, pilates, a local kids' club wanted more parents to help. There was the odd muffled sob from the toilet. Surely they wouldn't have to go in and get her? He didn't fancy that. After 10 minutes, the door opened slowly and Penelope Ramsden waddled out. She glared at them sullenly. The tears had been wiped away, but the eyes were even more swollen and resentful than before.

'He was a good man', she said again, softly this time.

Adam tried an understanding smile, reached out an arm and rested it on her shoulder. It wasn't rebuffed.

'Ms Ramsden, I know this is difficult for you.' His best beside manner, Dan thought, I wonder how many bereaved people have heard it. 'But if we can have just a few minutes of your time, it may help us find whoever did this to Mr Bray. Your help could be vital. You want to help us, don't you?'

She nodded again. It was like drawing a story from an unwilling child. 'Do you have his diary for Monday?'

She nodded. 'Can I see it please? Can you photocopy it for us? Monday and the couple of months leading up to it?'

She nodded again. 'Is there anything you can think of that was out of the ordinary that happened on Monday? Anything at all unusual?'

She shook her head. The tears were gathering again. 'What about in the days before Monday?' persisted Adam in an encouraging tone, still the teacher with the child. 'You've told us about the threats from Tony Rye, but were there any other strange calls or visits? Anything unusual at all?'

She nodded her head, gulped a breath and with an effort, managed a word, just one. 'Yes.'

Dan could feel Adam stiffen. 'Yes to which part Ms Ramsden? Help us please, it's important. To visits? Calls? Threats?'

She gulped. 'Calls.'

'What happened? Can you remember?'

The offence of his question stung her into speech. 'Of course I can remember. A call. A call a week before...' Her voice tailed off and the tears flowed again.

Adam's hand was back on her shoulder. 'I know you're upset Ms Ramsden, but I'm going to find the person who did this.' She nodded, a tear dropping from her chin. 'But to do that I need your help. I know it's not easy, but please try.' The hand held her shoulder tighter. 'You can do that for me, can't you?'

She screwed up her eyes, nodded. 'Now take your time', said Adam. Dan fished a handkerchief from his pocket and passed it to her. Thankfully it was fairly clean. 'Tell me about the call.'

She dabbed the droplets away and looked up at Adam, a trusting look. 'A call. Last week.' A half swallowed sob. 'A man, didn't know him. Said he'd have to cancel the meeting for tomorrow.'

'What day was this Ms Ramsden?' No answer, more dabbing. 'What day?'

'Monday. It was Monday.' Another muffled sob. 'The meeting was Tuesday. At the lay by.'

'And what did he say?' No answer again, a shake of the head. 'Ms Ramsden, this is very important.' Adam leaned down to her to emphasise the point. 'What did he say?'

'Cancel. He said he'd have to cancel. Something else came up.' A deep breath, a big effort. 'Said he'd call back later in the week or next week to rearrange.' Another breath, one final effort. 'He called on Friday. It was the man who made the appointment for Monday.' Her voice dropped to a moan. 'Monday.' A gulp, more sobbing. 'Monday, the day...'

Adam cut in, didn't want her going back there. 'Thank you Ms Ramsden, thank you. We've upset you enough. That's almost it for now.' She looked up again at him, a pathetic, pleading look Dan thought. 'I know it hasn't been easy for you, so I'll leave you alone in a minute. I've got just a couple more questions.'

Adam's voice was insistent, trying to drag the words out of her.

'What was he like to work with Ms Ramsden? Was he punctual or usually late? Did he have any habits? Were there any clubs or societies he was a member of?

Was there anyone he was particularly friendly with who we should speak to? Anywhere he went?'

She shook her head.

'No to which part Ms Ramsden?'

'All.'

'All?'

'All!' The word came like a shot, the change in her startling. 'You want me to tell you lots of horrible things about him don't you? Like the others have? Well I wouldn't even if they were there to tell. He was a good man.' Her hand was slapping into the wall now. 'He was always on time. There weren't any people he was friendly with and no clubs. This business was his life.' One more big breath, one final effort. 'All right?'

'Thank you Ms Ramsden.' Adam sounded relieved. Dan wondered if he been afraid they'd learn nothing from her. 'I think that's all we need to know at the moment. If we can just take a photocopy of Mr Bray's diary, we won't bother you any longer, but I will need to come back again in a couple of days.'

She nodded. The sobs had calmed and the silence returned. But she had one more thing to say before they left. She sounded like she'd been rehearsing it.

'He was a good man. He was always good to me. I know I'm nothing to look at. I'm fat and old and ugly. I'm not young and thin and pretty like those other secretaries you see. I'm not clever like some of them. But he gave me a chance and he was always good to me.' She was losing it again at the memories. 'He was a good man.'

They stayed in the corridor while Penelope Ramsden walked slowly back into her office to photocopy the diary for them.

'That', said Dan, who was relieved the interview was over, 'is the first tribute we've heard to the late Edward Bray. It's almost a shock to hear a good word said about him. What a strange set up this is.'

'Meaning?' said Adam, who was adjusting the knot of his tie. Dan could see him thinking about that cancelled and rearranged appointment. Could the voice on the phone have been Tony Rye's?

'Meaning four young men doing most of the work of the business, ruled over by a secretary who's clearly been brainwashed by her boss.'

'Odd perhaps, but I've seen stranger. What's your point?'

I must be getting into this detective work thought Dan. Here we go again. 'My guess is that Mr Bray didn't like women much. For him, loyalty was by far the most important quality. The only woman here is no looker, and that has to be unusual for a youngish boss who's single. Most men in his position would at least in part be influenced by looks. It might add up if she was brilliant at her job, but by her own admission she's not. I think he chose her because he didn't really see her as a woman. No complications that way. And maybe because she would be grateful for the job and so very loyal.'

Adam Breen considered. 'Mmm', he mused. 'Interesting. And the men?'

'Well, the fact that they are men, and not women, which backs up my point. I think they're just cannon fodder. They're menials to do the phoning, the chasing up, the filing. They're motivated by fear. Did you see how only one looked up when we came in, and then not for long? They've been conditioned not to. Probably every time one did, he got a rollocking from Bray. And that little saying, learnt by heart "you want paying, you work for it." Nice set up.'

Adam nodded thoughtfully, and seemed about to say something when Penelope Ramsden pushed slowly through the door and held out a sheaf of photocopies.

'Just a couple of things before you go Ms Ramsden', said Dan. She looked at him, closed her eyes as if in pain. 'They are only very quick questions.' She nodded.

'Why the big no smoking signs? Was that Mr Bray's doing?'

She nodded again. 'Yes. He hated smoking. Hated it.'

'And the apple tree planted outside?'

She showed no surprise at the question. 'He planted it himself. He loved it. Watered and fed it. I had to do it if he was away. He insisted.'

She gave a final nod, and turned and slowly walked back into her office. The two men made their way back to the car, Dan enjoying the freshness of the air after the dark oppression of the atmosphere in Edward Bray's office.

'Where to now chief?' said Dan, from the comfort of the driver's seat.

'Nowhere for a minute. I want to have a think. And you can help.' Adam looked at him. 'You've interviewed lots of emotional people in your time as a reporter.'

That's right, it's all I do, thought Dan resentfully, but didn't bother trying to correct him. It was a common view of journalists. 'What did you make of her?'

Dan considered for a moment, drummed a couple of fingers on the steering wheel.

'I thought she was genuine. I'd trust what she said. Why? Don't you think so?'

Adam reached out a hand to turn down the car's heater. It wasn't on. 'Most of me does, yes. But there's just a little bit inside which says a show of grief like that is a hell of a convenient way of stopping the police from asking you too many awkward questions. I've seen something like it before on another case and it nearly caught me.'

Dan was surprised. Whatever he may have thought of Penelope Ramsden, the place she worked or the man she worked for, he'd still felt for her.

'Well I'm no expert, but I thought she was completely honest'. He debated his next question, but then let it go anyway. Adam hadn't pulled any punches with him. 'Don't you think you're being overly cynical?' He saw a brief flash of surprise in the detective's eyes. Good, he thought, keep going, this relationship isn't a one-way street.

'Look at her. The way she dresses it's clear there's no man in her life. No make up, no smart clothes, no one to make an effort for. There was nothing on her desk, no pictures, nothing which said she had a family or any real interests to dedicate herself to. So I think work was her life, or to be more exact, working for Edward Bray was. And now he's gone, and so has most of her life with him.'

Adam Breen looked back at the office where Penelope Ramsden was probably either crying or shouting at the four young men.

'Ah, you're probably right. Maybe it's just me doing what I warned you about and suspecting everyone. That cancelled meeting's a strong lead though. It sounds like it's the killer. That may be the way into solving the case and it's something we'll have to focus on. Why would the killer put off the murder for a week?'

Adam sat, silently, thinking. 'No idea at the moment, but we'll look at it', he said. 'Ok then, that's enough here for now. Let's get going. You're in for another good one. Someone else with a grudge against Bray, said he wasn't surprised he'd been murdered.' He looked down at his notes. 'Just one more thing first', he added with a slight frown. 'What were those questions about the smoking and apple tree to do with anything?'

Dan tried not to sound pleased with himself, but wasn't sure he succeeded. 'I think I'm getting an idea why he might have saved the Hospice.'

Adam looked at him, interested. 'Go on then, I'd..'

He was interrupted by a squawk from the radio. 'Child missing, believed abducted. Plymouth, all available officers to attend.'

'Go!' said Adam urgently. 'Go!! Charles Cross, now! Go!!!'

Chapter seven

Adam called it the emergency police officers dreaded most. Dan knew it was the kind of story journalists love, but he didn't say so. The radio kept repeating the message. 'Child missing, believed abducted, Plymouth, Devonport area. All available officers to attend.'

'Shit', said Dan. 'I don't know what to do.' He knew exactly what he wanted to do and his mobile was in his pocket. 'That's a big story but I'm bound by what we've agreed not to report anything we do unless you give me the go ahead.' He took a sideways look at Adam.

'If they've got any sense, they've put it out to the media already, but I bet they haven't', he replied. 'Pull in.' Dan did, so fast the car behind them had to swerve. Adam took the wheel. 'The first few minutes after a kid's snatched are vital. We want as many people as possible on the lookout. Call your newsroom.'

Dan phoned the details in and heard a satisfactory panic at the end of the line. Nigel would pick him up at Charles Cross in a couple of minutes.

'Keep this to yourself please', Adam added calmly as he screeched the car into the police station car park.

There were uniformed officers running into a line of police vans, a sergeant shouting instructions at them. 'We're not supposed to give the media stuff like this without going through the press office. I did it because they'll take ages and time is vital. Just say you got it from some contact if anyone asks. And make sure you get a description of the lad and the car on the news. That's what's most important in trying to find him. I'll probably see you down there anyway.'

'Ok', said Dan, scrambling out of the car. He could see Nigel drawing up outside. 'And thanks. For what it's worth, I think you did the right thing.'

It took them just a few minutes to reach Devonport, but they were overtaken by a couple of police cars, sirens screaming on the way. Dan felt a surge of excitement. In the park, by the naval dockyard, the search was being coordinated. A uniformed police inspector was addressing a crowd of more than a hundred people from the back of a police van.

Dan marvelled at the community spirit. It was one of Plymouth's poorest areas, yet bonded closer than many middle class communities. Nigel grabbed his camera and got some pictures of the gathering, then the people dispersed, groups walking quickly off in different directions, all clutching hastily photocopied sheets with a picture of the boy on. Dan noticed he was smiling. He felt an involuntary shiver.

He moved towards the Inspector but his mobile rang.

'I want something on the one thirty news.' It was Lizzie. 'We'll take a bit of you on the phone. I don't mind not having any pictures, it's such a big story.'

'Ok.' He'd expected that, checked his watch. Ten past one it said, so it must be getting on for twenty past. Not long to get some details and work out something sensible to say. Another surge of adrenalin. 'Call me back just as you're about to go on air and I'll have something ready.'

'Fine'. The line went dead. Not for the first time, Dan was thankful Lizzie had been a reporter herself. No time wasted in pointless discussion.

He pushed his way through a crowd of constables and several traffic wardens. 'Inspector, Dan Groves, ITV News.' The policeman looked glad to see him. That didn't happen very often. 'We want to help you find Ben by getting this on the lunchtime TV news. Is there anything you can tell me? And as fast as possible please, I've only got a couple of minutes before we're on air.'

The man consulted his clipboard. 'Ben Dixon, 7 years old. About four feet six tall, short blonde hair, blue eyes, wearing jeans, white trainers and a green and white striped Plymouth Argyle football shirt.' Dan nodded, writing quickly. 'He was playing in the park with some friends. They say a man came up to him, had a chat, then took him by the hand and led him to the car, a red Vauxhall Cavalier.' Dan nodded again, still scribbling on his notepad. 'That's about all we know. All available officers are coming here to help in the search. We'd ask any members of the public to call 999 if they see him or the car.'

Dan's mobile rang again. 'You ready? We're 2 mins to on air.' It was Monica, the day's news producer. 'Yep, ready when you are.'

He scribbled a couple of notes on his pad and for the first time noticed his heart thumping. Remember the golden rule, he calmed himself. Keep it short and simple. What do I want to say here? What's the key point? That a boy's missing, probably abducted, and this is the description of him and the car. That's all we need, what's most likely to help in finding him.

The opening music of the lunchtime news played, the newsreader told the viewers of the abduction and Dan came on and said what he'd planned to say. He repeated the part Adam had told him, about how the first few minutes were vital in an abduction, but that was ok he thought, it needed emphasising. He was thanked and they were onto the next story. He breathed out heavily.

'What next?' asked Nigel, who'd been keeping people away while he was on air. They'd known some try to have a chat whilst they were broadcasting in the past. It was one of the perils of being on television.

'Let's go film some of the cops talking to people and knocking on doors', he said, pointing to a block of flats where a pair of officers stood talking with some residents, showing them the photocopied pictures. 'Then I think we just hang around here and see what happens.'

He tried an interview with a couple of the people who the police had been talking to and got the response he'd expected, the standard 'oh, it's terrible, shocking, who'd have thought something like that would happen around here.'

It was useful for a bit of colour, to fill a few extra seconds, but it didn't say much. Any journalist would have heard it many times at the scene of any killing, robbery, abduction or even car crash. It was what the people had seen others say on the TV when they'd been in similar situations. They subconsciously regurgitated it. Dan and Nigel followed the two policemen as they walked around talking to other people, showing them Ben's picture.

They were walking back to the park when they heard a spontaneous cheer go up from the crowd of people milling about there. Even the police officers joined in and a couple clasped hands in the air. They hurried on and were grabbed by two middle-aged women at the edge of the crowd. 'He's been found', they said, laughing. 'Found, safe and well!' One hugged Dan, Nigel filming it.

'Inspector?' shouted Dan, shaking himself gently free of the embrace. 'Yes Mr Groves', said the smiling man, who took off his cap to reveal a shock of silver hair. 'Ben's been found, safe and well. He was at a supermarket on the edge of the city, buying sweets with a man. You'll appreciate I can't go into too much detail as this is a criminal investigation now, but I can say Ben was found after a call from a member of the public who heard about his disappearance on ITV.'

Adam had been about to join the search for Ben Dixon when the news came through. The police station's narrow corridors echoed with shouts of triumph. He didn't have to go, an officer of his rank with a murder case to work on, it wasn't expected. But it was an unwritten rule of police work in a case like this. You went.

A man had been arrested and was being brought back here to Charles Cross for questioning. Ben was coming here too, in a separate car, for interview and a medical examination. He was said to be unharmed but you never could tell. Already there was talk in the corridors of retribution, and Adam didn't like to think of what awaited the man here. The days of the police meting out their own justice to offenders were largely gone, but there were exceptions.

He'd known a couple of suspects accidentally fall down the stairs. Attacks on police officers and children were the crimes that usually goaded tempers beyond control. He would have nothing to do with it and didn't condone it, but he did understand. With a son of that age, of course he did. He knew exactly what he would do to anyone who harmed Tom. He tried to blot out the question of whether he, himself, his father had harmed him with the way he'd brought him up, or the time they'd managed to spent together. The lack of time as Annie had called it in their last conversation.

Enough. He had a crime to solve. He looked around the murder room. It was empty, all the other officers out looking for Ben. They'd be filtering back soon, full of cheer for a rare success in the hunt for a missing person. It was harsh but true. You usually found a corpse in cases like this.

~

'I hate to be hard hearted about this', said Lizzie. 'But what a shame they found him so quickly.' A couple of sharp intakes of breath punctuated the quiet of the afternoon news meeting. 'I'm not saying it would have been better if he was dead', she added hastily, grinding a stiletto into the newsroom carpet. Dan was surprised. Lizzie on the defensive was a rare sight. 'I'm delighted they found him safely'. She looked around the newsroom, challenging anyone to defy her. 'It would just have made a better story if they hadn't found him until tomorrow say, or even the next day. Much more drama.'

Not for the first time, Dan wondered about the ruthlessness of news editors. Stories are what they're interested in, and that's all they're interested in. 'I still think we've got a decent splash', he said. 'We've got pictures of the search for him, reaction in the area to him being found and because we were there first, none of the other media have got that. Plus we helped to find him. Let's not overlook that. We've done some real good here, and it's not often we can say that.'

Lizzie gave him a long look, and he wondered if she was debating whether to agree or maul him. Finally she nodded and her heel ground into the carpet again. 'Agreed', she said sharply. 'Use that as your angle.'

The meeting broke up and Dan walked quickly to the edit suites to put the story together. He wanted to get it done fast, to re-join Adam for the interview they were supposed to be doing this afternoon. Hadn't the man said he wasn't surprised Bray had been murdered? He didn't want to miss that. Editing the report shouldn't take long he thought, probably an hour or so. Then he could get back to the case. He tried not to think that his day job was getting in the way.

This time Adam picked him up. 'Thanks are in order', he said. 'It's mainly down to you that we saved the kid. We owe you.'

They headed for Ermington, a village just a few miles outside of Plymouth. 'Nice one this', Adam said. 'Guy called in with info about Bray and said he was a right bastard and worse.' Dan stifled a yawn. It'd been a long day already, and it was still only four o'clock. 'After this it's a de-brief back at base, then a beer if you're up for it? I'm buying. Call it payback for the kid.'

Ermington is one of those villages that have grown up close enough to a city for its urban incomers to create a small town. It's 20 minutes east of Plymouth, in the classic gentle Devon countryside of the South Hams. It's popular with the middle classes who work in the city but don't care to live there.

There's a line of small shops, a general store, a butchers, a newsagent, a hairdressers and a tiny granite blocked 14th century church of the type so much in demand from marrying couples. Its spire leans drunkenly with the kind of look most often described as quaint. Around the church is a core of thatched cottages, which are surrounded by more modern houses, unsuccessfully designed to try to mimic their older neighbours.

The two pubs, the Crooked Spire and the First and Last both serve food fine enough to be listed in various tourist guides. It's a sign of how well off the people who've come to live in the village are. Locals have long since been priced out, a common problem in Devon and Cornwall.

A Popular Murder

Ermington Business Park was on the outskirts of the village, and pure marketing spin for what was just a dozen one storey corrugated roof sheds, joined together in two rows of six, facing onto a yard. Unit two had 'Erme Internet Design' in a Technicolor futuristic type on a sign next to the uPVC door. They knocked, and when there was no answer tried the door and walked in.

A young woman at a desk was talking into a small microphone, which ran down from the headset she wore. She looked no more than 20. A triangular sign on her desk said Ellie Jones in the same type as the sign outside. She waved, smiled and motioned them to a blue and new looking sofa. They sat down. Dan had looked at sofas for his flat only a couple of months ago, and thought he recognised it from one of Plymouth's cheaper stores.

The walls were covered with colourful silver-framed posters of computers and artists' visions of light flashes zipping down an imaginary information superhighway. A Yucca plant leaned lazily towards the only window. A pile of computing magazines was arranged tidily on a spotless glass coffee table. Dan picked one up, and then put it down again when he saw its main story was about a new and super fast processor chip. He'd had a Sinclair ZX Spectrum 16k when he was young and had never got the hang of that.

The woman had finished her conversation and greeted them without getting up.

'You're the two gentlemen from the police?' They nodded, Dan supposing his was justified. 'Mr Clarke won't be a minute, he's on a conference call.' She looked towards the closed door of the office behind her. 'Can I get you a coffee?'

'No thanks' said Adam politely. 'How long have you been here?' he asked.

'I've been working for Mr Clarke for about a month now' she said proudly and put her hand out, still without rising. They got up and shook it.

She didn't introduce herself, but continued. 'The company's been going for just under a year. It's getting so busy he had to take me on. Mr Clarke's going to teach me all about the net and web design.'

Dan tried, but failed not to suspect that wasn't all he planned to teach his young assistant. Then again, he wasn't sure he blamed the man. She was very pretty. Seeing Kerry wouldn't be a bad idea at all. He wondered if they'd end up in bed together and what it would be like if they did. Enough, concentrate on the job in hand.

Ellie was the perfect contrast to Penelope Ramsden. She must have been a size eight thought Dan, and all her clothes were chosen to show off her figure. She wore a black fitted trouser suit, with a wide collared purple blouse. Her hair was blonde and cascaded half way down her back, yet was still in shining condition. He knew from an ex girlfriend of a couple of months endurance – one of his longer relationships, he thought, uncomfortably - that wasn't an easy trick. She wore full make up, but not in distracting quantities. Her eyes were green, she had a small and cute nose.

'I was lucky' she said. 'I'd just got to the end of my computing course at college when Mr Clarke came in looking for someone to work with him. He said he knew straightaway I'd be right for the job.'

I bet he did, thought Dan, but at least had the grace to wonder if he was judging others by his own standards. Next to him Adam stood flicking through one of the computing magazines with what looked like genuine interest. He seemed impervious to Ellie's charm.

The door at the back of the room opened and a tall and smartly suited man stepped out.

'Gentlemen, I'm sorry to keep you.' A deep and resonant voice, full of authority. 'A call I couldn't get out of. I'm Gordon Clarke.' Dan knew he'd meant to keep them waiting. He'd seen it before in interviewees, particularly those in business or senior positions in organisations. They thought it gave them an added importance, an edge in the power games they played every day.

They shook hands. 'Adam Breen, Detective Chief Inspector. And this is my colleague Dan Groves'.

They went through to the office. It was dominated by a desk on which a computer and racks of silver CDs took up most of the space. There were more framed computer posters on the walls. They sat down.

Gordon Clarke had that brisk air that said his time was precious and you were lucky to enjoy any of it. He wore a dark blue suit with a chalk pinstripe and was just over six feet tall. His hair was the shade of ginger that women who have it like to call strawberry blonde. His face was fatter than fitted his height, a classic chubby cheeks baby who'd never quite grown out of it. His eyes were blue and steady and he held the men's gaze as they talked.

'So how can I help you gentlemen?'

'Mr Clarke, can I first of all thank you for calling us'. Adam leafed through his notes and found the sheet he was looking for. 'We're at the initial stages of our investigation and we need to build up a picture of Edward Bray. Anything you can tell us would be helpful. Anything at all, what kind of a man he was, what he liked to do, the people he knew.'

Gordon Clarke smiled coldly. 'Yes, I think I can help you with that Inspector. The man was a bastard, pure and simple.'

An understudy for the role of prime suspect thought Dan. Adam will be pleased.

'He was one of the most unpleasant men I've ever had the misfortune to have dealings with. A cold, hard bastard', Gordon Clarke's face creased into a scowl and he leaned forward over the desk. 'Interested in only three things was Bray. Himself, money and power. Nasty through and through. I probably shouldn't say this, but the world's better off without him. You won't find many shedding a tear for Edward Bray. The number of people he's ruined, the celebrations will probably go on for weeks. I bet his funeral attracts hundreds, but they won't be mourners, oh no. They'll be revellers.'

Dan glanced at Adam. He looked unruffled by the man's venom. He was studying Gordon Clarke closely. 'You'd say he got what he deserved then?' the detective asked calmly.

Gordon Clarke sensed a trap opening up. He paused and calmed. Some of the flush of colour left his face. He was no Tony Rye, too clever for that.

'No. No I wouldn't say he got what he deserved', he said, more quietly now. 'Being gunned down in a lay by, well, I can't imagine anyone deserving that. And I knew his Dad. He was a fine man, and this will have been terrible for him. No, I wouldn't say he deserved to die. Suffer a bit, yes, go bankrupt like he forced others to, but no, not die. I'm sorry if I went overboard, but I didn't like the man at all.'

'That's alright Mr Clarke', continued Adam, still looking into him. 'I can imagine it's been a shock, and that can sometimes make us react in ways we don't expect. And to be fair to you, you're not the first to tell us he wasn't a pleasant or popular man.'

Gordon Clarke was looking embarrassed now, fiddling with a gold cuff link. The adrenalin had ebbed and his face was a salmon pink. Dan wondered if he was a drinker, if that desk of his had a special section in the bottom drawer to help him through the day.

'Yes, thank you officer.' Calm now. 'It was a shock. I'm sorry.'

'Well Mr Clarke, all we really need to hear from you is how you knew Mr Bray and what you knew of his life?'

'Yes, yes of course. Well, I knew him because I used to rent one of his buildings. It was in Peverell, in Plymouth, a shop with a flat above. I've always loved computers and I used it to start up a computer business. Not an internet company like this, but designing and building computers for people's specific needs. You know, whether they needed one for accounting, or emails, or internet use, or a combination of things.

They'd say what they wanted and I'd design and build it.' His face relaxed as he relived a favourite memory.

'And how did the business go?' asked Adam, encouragingly.

'At first fine. Good in fact. Business was brisk and I turned in some decent profits. In fact I was even thinking of expanding. But then everyone started doing it.' His dry smile faded quickly. 'I was being undercut by these people who sell their services online. They don't have the overheads of an office, so they're cheaper.' Adam nodded, understanding. 'The business started to go downhill. I thought I could still make it work, so I took out a loan. But things didn't get any better and I really struggled. I started to get into arrears with the rent. Bray was ok for a while, but after only a month or so he said if I didn't get him the money I'd be out and he'd take me to court as well. I didn't have the money to pay him, so he gave me notice and threw me out.'

Gordon Clarke's voice and colour were rising again, his face tightening.

'I had to move back in with my parents. Imagine the embarrassment of that, back with your parents at 40 years old. Then he chased me through the courts for the money I owed him. He was going to make me bankrupt, and that would have finished me as a businessman. That's always been my thing, business.' He reached out and rolled the computer mouse over his desk. 'It was only my parents giving me some of their savings that stopped him. Can you believe that? As I said officer, he was an absolute bastard. Not content with ruining me, he waned to humiliate me as well.'

There was a silence. Adam was busily scribbling notes and looking thoughtful. Dan felt he was starting to understand the detective, that it was time for him to ask a question. But he still felt self-conscious. This was a clever and resourceful man. What if he saw through him? Come on he thought, come on. You've done this many times as a journalist. What's the difference?

'Mr Clarke, you said you knew Edward Bray's father. How?' He thought he managed to hide his nervousness.

The businessman shifted in his chair, turned to Dan.

'It was him I originally rented the building from. He was very kind, the complete opposite of his son. Isn't that extraordinary?' Gordon Clarke's voice softened. He was back in happier times. 'There were a couple of things about the shop which weren't ideal. The layout wasn't great and I needed some extra phone lines for the computers' internet links, and for taking calls from customers at the same time. Most landlords would have let me make the changes if I paid for them myself. Arthur – he always insisted you called him Arthur – wouldn't hear of it. He said he wanted me to be happy and comfortable there and it was in his interests the business thrived, so he arranged and paid for the work himself. He was a real gentleman. You don't get them like that any more. His son certainly wasn't like that.'

'So what happened? What went wrong?' asked Dan, thinking he was getting into his stride.

'Arthur retired. Well, I say retired and I couldn't prove this, but there's been plenty of talk that Edward forced him out. Probably told him he was getting too old and soft for the business and took it over himself. Anyway, he became my landlord just as things were taking a turn for the worse. The rest you know.'

Adam was still scribbling and didn't seem to want to intervene. Some help would be welcome thought Dan, but he didn't see any choice except to continue. Was he being tested again? It was getting irritating.

'Do you know anything else about Mr Bray that could help us? Anything about his personal life?'

'Nothing much.' Gordon Clarke looked thoughtful, and brushed his hand over his mouse again. It was a fond gesture, like a father might ruffle a son's hair. 'I remember he didn't have any family. He used to say that women and kids only caused pain and trouble. He told me that when I was talking to him about the end of a relationship I'd been having. I think he thought it would help, I really do. We were sitting in my office, talking about business, and I told him I wasn't focused at the moment because of my problems with Amy. It was the only time I ever saw him laugh, but it wasn't a pleasant laugh.'

He frowned, hesitated. 'He said something very strange that day too. I'll never forget it, I think it was the only time I saw him let himself go a bit. He said the one woman he'd ever been involved he had no choice about, and she'd broken his heart. It was weird the way he said it, really bitter. I never understood what he meant.'

Dan thought he did. Only one woman, and no choice about her. Maybe that ties in with him saving the hospice..

"Emotions and business don't mix', Bray told me, and that was it, he just carried on asking about my profit projections', Gordon Clarke continued. 'That was all he was interested in. Business was his life. I can't even remember him having any friends. He just wasn't the type who formed bonds with anyone. There was the hospice of course, but I don't know much about that. It was the only human thing he ever talked about.' He clearly thought he was giving Edward Bray too much credit. 'I reckon he only did it so he could boast about it', he added. 'He was always on about how he was going to shake it up.'

Adam still wasn't offering any help. Dan decided this question would be his last; he was here to learn, not take the lead. 'Do you know anyone else he upset? Anyone with a grudge against him? Anyone who may have argued with him, or threatened him?'

Gordon Clarke snorted, an unpleasant spluttering. 'How long have you got? I don't think a day went by without him upsetting someone. He's had more rows and threats than you could count. I know I'm not the only one he's thrown out of one of his places or chased through the courts. He was notorious for it. I met some others the day I was up in court.'

There was another pause while Dan wondered if he was missing anything. Adam stopped scribbling and looked up. About time, Dan thought. The detective smiled, but it wasn't the look Dan had seen when they talked in the car earlier. It was a smile without feeling, a professional smile.

'Mr Clarke', he said. 'Please don't think this anything other than a routine question, but would you mind telling me where you were on Monday afternoon and evening?'

Gordon Clarke returned the smile, with what seemed to Dan genuine humour.

'It's quite all right Inspector. I've read the books. I know you have to 'eliminate me from your inquiries'. Isn't that the phrase?' Adam nodded but his face stayed set. 'I was expecting you to ask.' He reached into a drawer in his desk and pulled out a black leather pocket diary. It had the company's logo on the front. 'I was in Bristol. I went to an information technology fair, which turned out to be a disappointment and I didn't want to waste the day, so I spent the afternoon shopping. I wanted a new suit. Bristol's so much better than here for clothes shops, don't you think?'

Neither Dan nor Adam took up the invitation to conversation, and Gordon Clarke continued. 'I got the train from Plymouth about eight in the morning and got back home about seven that night.'

'And can anyone verify that Mr Clarke?' asked Adam. 'Did you see anyone you know?'

'I'm afraid I didn't inspector. As I said, the fair was disappointing so I didn't stay long. I had a sandwich and coffee in a café, then went into the city centre.'

'Did you buy anything?'

Gordon Clarke seemed puzzled by the question.

'It can't have been my day. I'm afraid all I bought was a tie, quite a nice one but nothing stunning. Why the interest in my wardrobe Inspector?'

'It's just that if you'd used a card sir, that would have done nicely to verify your whereabouts.'

A Popular Murder

'I see. I'm afraid it was only twenty pounds, so I paid cash. Am I really a suspect?'

Gordon Clarke didn't sound surprised, just interested. 'I called you as I remember.'

And if you've read the same books I have, you'll know that makes you a good bet for the murderer, thought Dan. 'As I said Mr Clarke, it's simply routine', continued Adam. 'But it always helps to be able to eliminate people from the investigation as soon as possible. It saves time and means I'm not wasting valuable resources.'

Dan thought there was an odd game of mental sparring going on, but he couldn't see why. He glanced at Adam, but his face was still set. He got the feeling he didn't like this man.

'Well Mr Clarke, did you perhaps use a cash point whilst in Bristol?'

'Not in the city itself Inspector, but I did get some money out at Temple Meads station just before I got on my train home. I fancied a glass of wine and a sandwich en route. Will that take me off your suspects list?'

'That should do nicely sir, thank you.'

There was another silence while Adam Breen and Gordon Clarke studied each other.

'Oh, and another thing Inspector', said the businessman. 'I had my mobile with me when I was in Bristol. I'm never without it. You never know when you'll be needed in business, much like your profession I expect?' He tried a smile, but it wasn't returned. 'I seem to recall from reading of some court case in the papers that you can trace where a mobile is from its signal. Will that help? I've no objection to you checking with Orange if you want. I think I even sent a text message while I was on the train. I was in one of those quiet carriages where they don't allow mobile use, and I had to check with Ellie about a deal we're working on.'

Adam nodded and made to get up. 'We'll do that sir. Thank you for your time.'

～

It was dark now, evening time, trails of cars filling the streets outside Charles Cross police station, people rushing along the pavements, all heading for home. The Murder Room provided a fine view over Plymouth, the rainbow of neon shop and sodium streetlights of the city centre in the foreground, the floodlights of the Hoe and coastline behind, the white dots and lines of household windows in the surrounds.

This was the daily de-brief, Adam had told him, an important part of the investigation's routine. The detectives would get together to discuss what they'd found that day, anything important that would become a focus for the days to come. The room was full, about 30 detectives there, mostly men but also a handful of women.

Suzanne Stewart had joined them. She was dressed in another trouser suit, this time grey, but equally well worn. She still wasn't wearing any make up. Dan thought she was making an effort to ignore him, leaning against a desk on the opposite side of the room, her eyes only for the Detective Chief Inspector.

Adam had been manoeuvring some cards on one of the felt boards and stood back to admire his work. It was a collage of connections, thought Dan.

In the middle was the photograph of Edward Bray. Arranged around it were cards with the names of people who he'd known or had business dealings with. Computers were great for logging information on and pinging up suggestions when you were searching for links, Adam had said, but to really visualise the web around someone, you had to see it. Sometimes the old ways were the best.

'Ok everyone, listen up please. Here's what we know so far.' The background conversations died away, and Adam pointed to a card below Bray's. 'This is Penelope Ramsden, who I don't suspect of anything yet, except perhaps excessive loyalty to her boss. I did wonder if she was trying to put us off a scent, or lay a false trail, but I can't see what that would be or why. She doesn't benefit at all from Bray's death, does she Suzanne?'

Suzanne Stewart stopped leaning on the desk and stood up straight. Like a child reacting to teacher, thought Dan.

'No, not in any way that we can find sir. There's no provision for her. Bray didn't have a will, so a chunk will go to the taxman and the rest to his next of kin. That's his Dad.'

'The return of the stolen empire', mused Dan, a little too loudly.

Adam looked at him sharply. 'We're detectives here Dan, not journalists. I could just see that line in one of your reports. Not yet though please.'

Dan felt his face reddening under the gazes and grins of the other detectives. He looked away, out of the window to the ruined church.

'So she's got no financial motive', Adam continued. 'I can't see any envy or jealousy unless she's hiding it well. She actually seemed to like him. She had access to his diary, and could have sent him to that lay by, but I can't see why she would. I can only see her losing from her boss's death.' There was a murmur of agreement. 'We'll have a bit more of a look into her background just in case, but I don't consider her a suspect, although that could always change of course.'

He looked around the room. 'There is one very interesting thing she's given us.' Adam explained about the cancelled appointment. 'Keep that in mind team, it could be a very useful clue. It looks like whoever killed Edward Bray was planning to do it almost a week before, but couldn't for some reason. So why? Why would that be?' He let the words linger. 'Keep an eye out for that when you follow up leads and interview possible suspects. Did something happen unexpectedly in their lives last week that could force them to change their plans?'

Adam waited while the detectives digested that. 'Another question to keep in mind; was it the killer, or perhaps their accomplice, that called 999 to tip us off about the body? If so, why?' He stared around the room, challenging for an answer. 'Why? Could it be to make sure we quickly had an accurate time of death? And could that be to ensure an alibi they'd prepared beforehand – perhaps got someone to provide – took them out of the frame for the murder? Keep that in mind too team when you're talking to possible suspects. Might their alibi depend on timings?'

Suzanne was taking notes, so Dan thought he'd better do the same, then stopped himself. How pathetic, like two child rivals competing for a friend's favour.

'Next, Gordon Clarke', continued Adam, pointing to another of the white cards. 'There's a nice clear motive here. Bray humiliated and almost bankrupted him. I could see the anger in him today. It was cold but powerful.' A couple of the detectives leaned forward, as if they could smell a scent. 'So the question is; could it have been powerful enough to prompt murder?' Again he looked around, but the room was quiet. 'Our problem is his dispute with Bray was a year ago, and he's got a good alibi for Monday. So again, more checks into his background please Suzanne, and his alibi. He's a big possible' – he jabbed at the cards with his index finger – 'but I don't think he's our prime suspect.'

More notes from Suzanne. Adam moved onto to another piece of card, and this time he smiled, his cold, professional smile. He tapped it.

'This man however I want us all over. Tony Rye. He hated Bray with a passion, and that's as good a motive as you'll get.' More murmurs of agreement. 'Also he's got form, and he hasn't got much of an alibi, so let's see if we can demolish what there is.' A couple of light laughs from the room. 'Suzanne, your priority is to pin down his movements on Monday afternoon. Get to the tile shop in Ivybridge he says he went to and find out if he was there, and if so, when, how long for, and what he did. Did he look agitated? Like he was killing time? In a hurry? Anything that gives us a hint he might have been up to something. Then check in the shops in Moretonhampstead to see if anyone in them saw Rye, and at what time. That's tomorrow's work, first thing please.'

Adam paused whilst Suzanne finished her note taking. He tightened the knot on his tie again. Dan smiled, and turned to look out of the window to hide it from the room. He wondered what habits he had and how other people saw him. Detective work made you look hard into people and it wasn't so comfortable when you turned it back in on yourself.

'So then, your turn.' Adam addressed Suzanne, his voice encouraging, almost patronising. 'What did you find out today?'

Suzanne Stewart looked as though she was happy to talk from where she stood, but Adam beckoned her up to the board. She walked reluctantly forward, not making eye contact with anyone in the room.

'We've been looking through his accounts and we've been to see a couple of people today.' Her voice was thin. 'Both painted a similar picture of Bray. They hated him too.'

Adam nodded encouragingly.

'Andrew Hicks lost the home he rented from Bray after he got into arrears with his rent. A nice touch on this one was that it was just before Christmas. He said he begged Bray to let him stay at least until January, but Bray seemed to take a delight in throwing him out. Hicks said he remembered Bray saying he didn't believe in Father Christmas.'

Dan nodded; it was the story he'd seen in the log back at the studios. There were a couple of puffs of breath

A Popular Murder

and murmurs from the audience. Even the hardened detectives thought it harsh. 'Yes, he remembered that very well. Bray also took him to court for the arrears. He seemed to like doing that.'

'What's Hicks like Suzanne?' asked Adam. 'How did he strike you?'

She considered for a moment, as if she was giving evidence to a jury and had to be true to her oath.

'He's a big man, physically powerful and I got the impression he's capable of violence. I checked his record, and there are a couple of minor convictions. One was for using cannabis and the other for assault, fighting in fact. But it's a long way from making him a murderer of course. And he lost his home about a year ago too. It's quite a wait to kill someone.'

'Yes, indeed', said Adam, nodding. 'Alibi?'

'He was fishing on the River Plym. He was having a week off work and is a keen fisherman. He spends most of his spare time fishing apparently.'

'Any corroboration?' asked Adam.

'Yes, oddly from the other suspect we went to see, James Stead. He's another keen fisherman. They were out together.' She checked her notes. 'He also rented a home from Bray, and he too was kicked out. It was nothing to do with getting into arrears with the rent this time. His wife was due to have a baby and Bray got to hear about it. Now he can't prove this, but Stead says Bray threw him out because of the baby. His houses have a no pets agreement apparently, and the word is he'd like to say no children too, but the law won't let him. So he just tries to pick tenants without families. And if they look like they are going to have kids..'

Even Adam drew in a whistling breath at that.

'Stead went to court to try to keep his home, but he didn't have a chance. You know how it is, if a landlord wants to get someone out, they can. They just have to give notice, they don't have to give reasons.'

Adam nodded. 'What's he like?'

'Mr Average really', she replied. 'Doesn't talk much. Neither fat nor thin. He's got brown hair, receding a little, about five feet eight tall. There's nothing remarkable about him at all. No criminal record of any kind. I didn't get any feeling that he could be the violent type.'

Adam turned to the board and pointed to the two cards with the men's names on.

'I don't like two possible suspects giving each other alibis. Is there any corroboration?'

She nodded. 'Yes, I worried about that too, but there is. They said they finished fishing about five, and popped into a shop to get some cigarettes, milk, and a copy of the Evening Herald before going home. The old lady there remembers them because Stead broke a milk bottle. It slipped through his hands as he took it out of the fridge. She remembers because she said they were gentlemen, the kind of customers she doesn't see much of nowadays. They insisted on cleaning up the mess, and they paid for the bottle too. She knows it was five exactly because the BBC Radio Devon news came on, followed by the travel report. She always listens then to see if there are any hold ups on her way home. I checked with Radio Devon and she was right, the news goes on at five for seven minutes. Their timings are precise to within a few seconds. Hicks and Stead say

A Popular Murder

they caught the bus home together after they'd been in the shop.'

'Mmm, ok', said Adam. 'If that's so, it would probably rule them out then, unless they got to the lay by very fast indeed.' He considered. 'How do Hicks and Stead know each other?'

'Funnily enough, through Edward Bray. They met in court. Apparently there were a few of his old tenants and debtors in court at the same time. It's the way the small claims court works. Cases with common participants are listed together for efficiency.'

And that would explain the record number of bankruptcies on one day story, thought Dan. The hospice reports he'd seen were echoing in his head. He wanted to say something, but the room was intimidating, lots of experienced detectives and one keen amateur. He caught himself by surprise. Was that really how he was thinking, that he was a keen amateur here? Anyway, was what he knew relevant? Could it have had anything to do with Bray's murder?

'Interesting', said Adam, but it wasn't clear whether he was talking about the workings of the court, or the friendship of Andrew Hicks and James Stead. 'Check if those two have cars, and if so, could they have been using one to get around when they were fishing? What if they didn't take the bus? And if they did have a car, could they have got to the lay by in time to kill Bray? If they don't own cars, what about hire cars? Or friends' cars?' Again he waited, looked around the room to make sure the team had taken that in. 'Ok, anything else before we break?'

There were a few shrugs and mumbled 'no's'. Adam looked around the room and caught his eye. Had he forgotten their discussion about the hospice? Was it another test? Oh, what the hell.

'Mr Breen?' Did he really say Mr Breen? What was the matter with him?

'Yes Dan?' Heads snapped round to him, some surprised looks, some amused. There was the hint of a smile on Adam's face too.

'I'm sure you're aware of this, but I thought I'd mention it anyway.' He kept his voice level. Adam nodded, but he noticed Suzanne Stewart had pursed her lips and folded her arms. 'I don't know if it's relevant, but I thought I should just say. You know that Bray saved St Jude's Hospice, don't you?'

There were a couple of mutters of surprise and interest. 'So?' A hard voice, Suzanne Stewart's. The room quietened again.

Dan capped a spike of annoyance. 'So', he said as calmly as he could, 'so, it was totally out of character with everything else he's done in his life. So, that means there's more to him than just a ruthless businessman that everyone hated. So, there could be something there worth looking at.' Still she was glaring at him. 'So we – sorry you – should at least be aware of it.'

Another pause, heads turned to Suzanne Stewart. Detectives could sense tension, loved it.

'Are you suggesting it could be a reason why he was killed?' Her voice was softer now, but mocking. 'He might have been murdered because he decided to be nice for once.' She shook her head. 'Don't know many murder cases where someone's been killed for being nice.'

There was a ripple of laughter around the room. Heads turned back to him. He hoped he wasn't turning red, giving away his anger. He glanced at Adam, but he was standing calm and relaxed, one arm on the felt board, watching the exchange. Ok then, he could fight this one on his own, he'd taken on bigger people that a sarcastic detective.

'All I'm saying is there's another side to him we should be aware of, and it's a mystery. I've checked all the news reports on Bray, and there's nothing about why he saved the hospice. There could just be something in there.' There were a few nods from around the room, a mumble of agreement. Heads turned back to Suzanne Stewart, but Dan hadn't finished, had a trump card to play. 'And I've got a feeling I might know why he did it.'

Her lips were a thin line now, arms folded tight. Adam stepped forward, Dan was sure he was holding down a smile. 'You're both right. There may be something in there, there may not. Either way, let's be aware of it and have a look at it tomorrow. What's your thought about the possible reason Dan?'

Now, with all the detectives looking at him expectantly, listening to him, he wasn't so sure.

'Well, it's just a guess. But there were huge No Smoking signs in his office. And his mum died of cancer when he was young. Maybe she smoked and got it from that. Maybe he was very attached to her. What if she was cared for in St Jude's, and he remembers it well and appreciated the work they did? Perhaps that's why he saved it. And what if something to do with that caused someone to want to kill him? I don't know, something like a deal with the hospice that wasn't made public at the time, or maybe even him threatening to withdraw his support and ask for his money back?' It sounded thin to him now, but he couldn't think of anything else to say.

'Ok, we'll take a look at it', said Adam. Discussion closed.

After a few more minutes on the details of who else needed to be seen tomorrow, the meeting broke up. Tired looking detectives trailed out of the door. Suzanne Stewart walked over and had a brief and whispered conversation with Adam. She glanced occasionally over at Dan. Her lips were still tightly pursed.

He could feel a lingering anger, but at least it was waning. He wondered what he should do. He checked his watch. It said 6.20, which meant it was nearer half past. Rutherford would be waiting, expecting a release to the garden and some food. The dog's company would be welcome. He'd done his bit, he'd had enough of waiting on detectives. He walked towards the door, trying to catch Adam's eye to say goodnight.

'Hold on a minute Dan, I'd like a word before we go', said Adam. 'I won't be a minute.'

He sat back down, picked up a discarded copy of the Daily Telegraph, and scanned the front page. More parliamentary deliberations about a ban on smoking in public was the main story. Just get on with it, he thought. No one has the right to inflict their anti-social habit on those around them. Whenever he went to a pub or restaurant, he made an issue of asking for the non-smoking section, and if there wasn't one, he would usually leave. The only exception was when his passion for good beer got the better of his principles. It was an unfair fight.

'Sorry about that', Adam was at his shoulder, the door closing on Suzanne Stewart as she left. 'Good detective Suzanne, very thorough, but lacking confidence. She always needs to be reassured she's doing well or following the right lines in an investigation. She always is, but she needs to be told. It's an odd insecurity for someone who's been in the job for years.' Spoken like a man who doesn't have any such paranoia thought Dan. Adam gave a wry smile. 'Perhaps you could bear that in mind?'

No wonder she was upset at a new boy barging his way in and sharing her boss's affections then, he thought. Not even a professional new boy either. He couldn't help but think he'd won that little joust over the hospice though, hadn't he? He felt himself relax and a memory of an earlier conversation surfaced.

'I was just wondering, well, what we did now?' said Dan. 'It seems like the end of the day. Aren't detectives all supposed to go off to the pub together and have half a dozen pints?'

'You've been watching too much of 'The Sweeney''. Adam looked amused. 'Maybe in the old days, yes. Now we just tend to go home and come back tomorrow morning.' He looked at his elegant watch. 'However, if you fancy a pint, I've got an hour to spare. I'd hate to disillusion you about the glamour of police work.'

Dan thought Rutherford was disciplined enough to wait a little longer for his master's return. 'Fine', he said. 'Where?'

~

They went to the Minerva, Plymouth's oldest pub. It's oddly long and thin, never more than 18 feet wide, but with a fine snug at the back, threadbare but soft sofas circling a glowing log fire. It stands on the outskirts of Plymouth's historic Barbican, the old port and fishing centre, a convenient 5 minutes walk from Charles Cross.

The choice was Doom Bar, Bass or 6X. Adam asked for a recommendation, so Dan gestured to the left hand pump and they sat in the vacant snug with the two pints of Doom Bar.

'Very nice', said Adam, sipping quickly.

'Yes, but be careful. It's not called Doom Bar for nothing. It slips down more easily than you realise.' Dan held the beer up to the light in appreciation. 'It's named after a spit of sand in the Camel estuary off Padstow, and the beer's been known to do an equally proficient wrecking job on people as the spit did on ships.'

They sat quietly sipping and surveyed the surroundings. There was a score of Brian Pollard prints on the walls, a Plymouth GP and self-taught artist some critics had called a modern Lowry. They were his earlier works, with less detail in the people, landscapes and skies, but they added flashes of vibrant colour to a dark but cosy room.

Dan had a couple of originals on his walls at home, one of Plymouth Hoe on a starry night, one of the eclipse of 1999 over St Michael's Mount in Cornwall. It was the favourite painting of his collection, not least because Dr Pollard had kindly added him, talking to a camera amongst the crowd enjoying the spectacle.

A couple of regulars propped up the bar next door, but otherwise they were alone. The angles they were leaning at and the loudness of their conversation made Dan suspect they'd been in the pub most of the afternoon. He tried not to feel envious. It was one of his favourite ways of spending a day off.

'What do you make of police work so far then?' asked Adam. His body language had relaxed from the commanding detective at the felt boards, the leader of men. He sat back with his legs crossed at the ankles, one arm laid over the sofa, the other on his pint. It was as if he'd shed the skin his job demanded.

'It's certainly interesting, although not quite as action packed as I'd imagined. You were quite right, there is a lot of routine stuff to go through. But it has exciting moments.'

Dan sipped his pint and thought back on the day. 'That bit with Tony Rye was tense. I really thought he was going to go for you. Were you winding him up on purpose?'

'Yes indeed', Adam nodded. 'You noticed then. It's a standard trick. People often get stupid when they're angry. The adrenalin swamps the brain.'

'Funny, you find that in journalism too. The most provocative question often gets the best answer.' He'd often wondered why that was. Because it stirs a passion that can be hidden by nerves, diplomacy or modesty?

'As I said to you at the start, I reckon there are plenty of similarities between our jobs. And you learn fast.' Adam shook his head. 'I nearly laughed out loud when you asked Tony Rye what he was doing on Monday afternoon.'

He chuckled into his beer, which was depleting fast.

'Another?' said Dan. 'Just a half?' he added, remembering he was talking to a Chief Inspector.

'Not for me, I've got to be off.'

'Family?' Dan asked automatically, then just as quickly regretted it as he saw Adam flinch.

'What have you heard?' The voice was instantly angry. 'What have they told you?'

'What?' asked Dan, startled. 'Who told me? Told me what?'

Adam stared into him, unblinking. 'About me.' He leaned forwards. 'What have they told you about me?'

Dan struggled to get the words out. The detective's change of mood was unnerving.

'Nothing.' He almost stammered it. 'Nothing', he said, regaining his composure. 'No one's told me anything about you. I don't know what you mean.'

Adam Breen continued to stare at him, then reached for his glass and drained the remains of his pint.

'Listen', he said. Dan thought his voice was softer, but he couldn't be sure. 'We're doing a professional job. I'm helping you out because I've been told to and because I think you can help us. It's interesting having you around. You're shrewd and you bring a new perspective to it. But it's work, ok? Our private lives are something else, and I don't share mine with anyone. Tell someone about yourself in this job and the next minute it's written on the bog wall in the nick. Whatever gossip you might have heard, forget it. Ok?'

'I haven't heard any gossip', protested Dan, confused. 'I really don't.. '

'Ok then, forget it', cut in Adam, getting up and taking his coat from the back of the chair. 'But I have got to be off now. Cheers for the drink.'

He turned and walked quickly out of the pub, the door banging shut behind him.

Dan let him go. He didn't know what else to do. He finished his pint, went home and made a lavish fuss of Rutherford, even puzzling the dog by grabbing him for a hug. The last time that had happened was 2 years ago when his grandfather had died of a stroke.

He sent a couple of texts, one to Dirty El and got a cryptic reply he thought he understood. 'Bin day tomorrow, am helping the recycling later. Politically important work. El.'

The other was to Kerry, apologising for not being in touch this week, making the usual excuses about work, but asking if she fancied a Dartmoor walk at the weekend? He half expected a cold reply, or none at all, but it was quick and warm. 'Walk would be lovely! See you Saturday, looking forward to it already. x'.

At least he had a couple of things to look forward to then. He could feel the pull of the swamp on the edge of his consciousness again, and they'd help to fight it, for a while at least.

He spent the rest of the evening lying on his great blue sofa, gazing at the passing clouds lit white by the night's luminous half moon, listening to Bob Dylan and trying to read a book. But mostly he thought about Adam Breen and wondered what had happened in his life to make him react so angrily to an innocent question when he thought they were on the verge of becoming friends.

Chapter eight

The next morning, Dan was woken at quarter past seven by Rutherford's wet and insistent nuzzle in his face. Alarm clocks are redundant when you've got an Alsatian who wants a walk. He put on his old lazing around jogging bottoms and a sweatshirt over his bedtime Inter Milan canary yellow T-shirt. He caught sight of himself in the mirror and thought how obvious it was he didn't have a partner. His nightclothes weren't the sexiest.

Rutherford watched, impatiently pawing at the floor as Dan rummaged in the hallway cupboard for his trainers. He opened the front door and the dog bounded out and skidded round the corner of the building towards the garden. He used the reprieve to tie his shoes, and when the happier looking dog returned they set off for their jog.

Rutherford's favourite was their countryside walks, but a run through the streets came a close second. Years of amateur football had battered Dan's knees into a state that meant they couldn't stand up to more than a couple of miles. But it was 20 minutes of exercise, more than enough with a day's work to follow.

Dan estimated the dog roughly doubled the distance he ran with his technique. He'd dash on ahead at a sprint, then canter back to his master, then dash a hundred yards behind him in search of an overlooked scent, then canter back again. Pedestrians would either attempt to pat him, or leap out of the way, both usually with little success. Rutherford was not a graceful, elegant, or easily slowed creature. Throughout the run, his mouth would hang open and his tongue dangle down in a way Dan always thought of as a smile.

They ran down Eggbuckland Road and along to the Deer Park, in fact just a run down 1970s estate surrounded by a few trees. He always found it comical how the roughest neighbourhoods were given the most alluring names.

They carried on in a loop, heading gently downhill to Lower Compton. It was the most challenging of Dan's routes, the way back up to Hartley Avenue a daunting hill. As so often, his good intentions faded in the chill of reality, and the last half-mile slowed to a walk. Rutherford continued to bound around him. Dan thought the dog looked both amused and scornful at his master's lack of stamina.

He got into the newsroom at half past eight and called Adam. The phone rang but switched to the answer machine. He left a message and then went downstairs to the canteen for some breakfast.

Multicoloured rows of grease glistened sausage, bacon, hash browns, eggs and tomatoes greeted him. Tempting yes, but the morning run had made him feel virtuous. He chose some grilled tomato halves on wholemeal toast and didn't even bother with butter. When the early shift of journalists, presenter, director, picture editor and engineer hurried hungrily into the canteen and loaded their plates with fried food he tried not to look smug. His mobile rang.

'Hi, Dan Groves.'

'Hi Dan, Adam here.'

Why did he suddenly feel nervous? 'Morning Adam, how are you doing?'

'Fine thanks, fine. I'm just sorting out what to do today.'

'I've just got into the office myself. I was wondering whether I'd be with you today, or whether you needed to be doing other things.'

A slight pause. 'You're welcome to come join me of course, but I'm not sure if it'll be very interesting or worthwhile for you.'

Dan felt crestfallen. He'd rung Adam with trepidation. It was, he thought, oddly similar to calling a woman after going out on a date, liking her, and wondering if she'd want to see him again. They'd got on well, then, well, what then? He didn't know, except that he'd hit a trigger sensitive enough to turn the cool and authoritative detective into an angry and defensive man. Dan wondered if he was embarrassed.

'Really?' He tried not to sound disappointed. 'Well, it's your call of course, it's your investigation. What are you planning?'

'To be honest with you Dan, I think I'm going to be here in the office for the next couple of days. I saw the people I wanted to see in person yesterday. Now I need to go through what they said and get some of the team to check it out. We've also got background checks to do, and we've got to start going through the details of Bray's business dealings. It's not a job for me. I should be here to take an overview and guide the team. I also want to have a look at Bray's diary, to see if there are any clues in it and do some work on that cancelled appointment. That could be very important. All that's going to mean a lot of boring sitting around and going through paperwork. I don't think you'd benefit from it.'

Dan wondered why he felt jilted.

'Fine, no worries. I quite understand', he lied, trying not to sound deflated. 'I'm sure there's plenty to do here. I've got lots of other stories to work on'

'Ok Dan, thanks. Do give me a call if I can help you with anything you're doing.'

He had to ask. It was a question he'd posed several times in the past, but in very different circumstances.

'Adam, about last night?'

'Yes?' He sounded wary. A familiar response.

'I'm sorry if anything I said upset or annoyed you. All I can say is that I hadn't heard any gossip of any kind. As far as I'm concerned, we were just having a chat.' He decided to risk some humour. 'And nothing you tell me will ever end up written on the toilet wall.'

There was silence at the end of the phone. The line hummed.

'I'm sorry if I snapped at you.' Adam sounded genuine. 'It's just I've got a lot going on at the moment.' There was another pause. 'I'll tell you about it the next time we have a beer. Look, I've got to go now, but do you want to come to Charles Cross first thing on Monday? I'll know where the investigation's going then and we can get on to some more interesting bits.'

'That's great, thanks. Good luck with it. I'll see you on Monday'.

He finished his breakfast, then plodded through a routine morning. He answered some emails and made a series of calls about potential stories for the future. Lizzie stopped at his desk during one of her whirlwind sweeps through the newsroom.

'What are you doing in here then?' She was in a brisk mood. 'I thought you were out solving a murder. I didn't expect to see you back for a few days.'

'There's a lull in the investigation. The Chief Inspector is having a couple of days checking alibis and doing paperwork. It's not interesting or useful for me, so I thought I'd come back here and catch up on a few other things.'

Lizzie sat down at a spare desk next to Dan's. Experience told him that wasn't a good sign.

'This is proving worthwhile, isn't it?' She looked him in the eye. 'I don't want to lose one of my most experienced correspondents for days if there's nothing in it for us.'

Dan noted she described him as experienced rather than talented. He must be out of favour again.

'I think it is. I'm getting a much better insight into how the police work. I'm also making some good contacts.' Lizzie still looked dubious. He had to do better than that. 'And I've got some corking material for a story.'

The eyebrow arched and her face lightened with it. 'That's alright then. I'm glad to hear it. When are you back with the police?'

'Monday morning I think.'

'So we've got the pleasure of your services for a couple of days eh? That's good, I've got an idea you might be needed this afternoon.'

'I am at your disposal as ever.' It was Thursday, almost the weekend and it had been a busy week already. He fancied a day in the office catching up, but what else was there to say?

Lizzie smiled. He thought it was genuine, but you could never tell with her.

'You'll be glad to know I straightened that prostitutes business out too. Jones has accepted my action in moving you and is dropping the formal complaint.'

I bet he wouldn't if he knew what El was up to last night, thought Dan. But that was nothing to do with me, was it? Just a freelance earning a living, doing what they do.

~

'I suppose there's still no chance of me getting that 60 quid back on expenses then is there?' Lizzie's look was answer enough.

He returned to his emails. They were always a baffling array. One viewer wanted details of a new bird feeder he'd interviewed the Devon Wildlife Trust about. Another warned him of a countrywide conspiracy to set up mobile phone masts in church steeples, and demanded to know why he wasn't covering it. Another was a severe weather warning from the Met Office.

Floods were imminent. He looked down at his leaky boots and thought the afternoon would be a very good time to replace them. Sneaking off after lunch was his best bet. Wander round the newsroom for a bit, talk loudly to a few people about stories that were coming up, let them know he was here, then quietly disappear.

Monica arrived at his desk. He was popular today, he thought ruefully.

'It was that I wanted to talk to you about', she said, pointing at the flood warning flickering ominously on his screen.

'Yeees?' said Dan warily. He knew trouble when he saw it.

'You did environment for years.'

'Yeeees', said Dan again. He could feel an unwelcome invitation to go out and get soaked coming.

'Any guesses where might get flooded? Only I want to send the outside broadcast truck to somewhere that might go under and do a live report.'

'Yeeeees?' he repeated, wishing she'd get to the point, but suspecting he already knew it.

'Lizzie mentioned you were free, and so...'

'Yeeees?' he said for what he knew would be the final time. He didn't have to make it easy for her, did he?

'Can you go out and do it?'

His instinct was right. She wanted him to go and stand in a flood. Wonderful. At least now it wouldn't matter that his boots leaked. Not a great consolation though.

'Where did you have in mind?' he asked, resignedly.

'That was what I wanted to discuss with you. Any ideas would be welcome.'

He looked back at the email. High tide was at 6.35 tonight. She was right; it was perfect for going live on the programme. It was a spring tide, much higher than normal. The atmospheric pressure was low, so the waters would rise even higher and there was a strong southeasterly wind forecast. It was an unholy trinity. The region's ports were all built to defend against westerlies coming in from the Atlantic.

'Looe', he pronounced after a moment's reflection.

'What?' said Monica.

'Looe, southeast Cornwall. It's low lying around the river. The wind will drive the water right up into the town, over the quay, and quite probably do some real damage. I'd go to Looe.'

'Looe it is then. Call Nigel, he's free. And Loud's on the OB truck. Can you let him know?'

A Hawaiian shirt in a flood, thought Dan. That should impress the locals.

'Will do', he said. 'We'll set off after lunch.'

He found Nigel in the canteen, where he was picking suspiciously at what was supposed to be a shepherd's pie.

'Trouble?' he asked, knowing it was.

'Indeed', said Dan, joining him at the table. 'Have you got your wellies with you?'

'No, I haven't today. I was supposed to be covering a court case, but it was postponed. Why?'

'How unfortunate.' Dan tried not to smile. It was good to have someone to share his suffering. 'We're off to Looe this afternoon to see if it floods. From the forecast it could get quite nasty. We've got to do a live bit into South West Tonight.'

Nigel relaxed. 'We should be ok then. Whenever we're there ready, it never happens', he said, with the wisdom of experience. 'It only floods when we don't expect it.'

And that's one of the basic rules of television thought Dan. I can't remember the number of times I've got to a location, and someone's said to me 'You should have been here an hour ago. You wouldn't believe what happened..'

~

They left the office in mid afternoon and took the A 38 west towards Cornwall. A persistent blattering rain began as soon as they got into Nigel's car. An ill omen, thought Dan. He'd started to look forward to the excitement of reporting from the middle of a flood, now he was feeling the pull of the swamp again. Mood swings he thought, beware the mood swings, a very bad sign.

When they got to the bridge over the Tamar, there was a cocoon of mist marring the view up and down the great river that marks the boundary between Devon and Cornwall. On a clear day you could see grey multi gunned warships manoeuvring carefully in the river's mouth as they prepared to put into Devonport docks. Yachts and pleasure boats headed up the meandering river through its waving golden reed beds to the waterside village of Calstock and its welcoming jetty and Inns. Today there were no green sheep speckled fields drawing back from the shining waters, just a dark and dank fug.

Dan had seen flooding in Looe before and had directed Loud to the west of the town, by the fire station. It was one of the lowest lying parts, next to the river, and surrounded by cafes, pubs, shops and houses. If there was flooding, it would be here, and if it came, this was where it would cause the most damage. It would be bad for the locals but good for dramatic television.

They pulled up next to the van and banged on the door. It rolled back and Loud's head stuck out. He was grinning, an unusual and worrying sign.

'Have you seen it?' he asked, pointing at the quayside, some 30 feet away.

They had as soon as they'd parked. It was aggressive and unmistakeable. Waves were riding angrily up the river towards them and the seawater was already slopping over the quay. It was only half past four, still two hours from high tide.

'It's going to flood', said Loud gleefully. He loved bad news. The engineer leaned further out of the truck to get a better view of the sloshing water and the whistling wind ruffled his beard. Today's shirt was subdued by his standards, creamy white with red and blue flowers flourishing under an unseen sun.

Loud noticed Dan's look. 'Court case, the one he was supposed to be doing', he said, conscious of his reputation and now pointing at Nigel. 'It was a murder, so I thought I'd better show some respect and tone it down a bit.'

'Ah', said Dan, trying not to laugh at his idea of tact.

'I wish I'd brought my wellies now', said Nigel, looking ruefully at his fine brown brogues and the ever-rising tide. He'd dressed for court too.

By quarter past six, the wellies Dan had gratefully donned earlier were proving a handicap. The water had risen up to his waist, and each boot was filled with its cold dead weight. Nigel was swearing quietly to himself from behind his camera. A little shorter than Dan, he was suffering waters lapping nearer to his chest, and wasn't enjoying it.

'Nice shot boys', came Monica's voice in his ear. 'It was a good call to go to Looe Dan, it looks great. We all feel jealous of you, being stuck here in the boredom of our warm and dry newsroom.'

Dan stuck two fingers up to the camera and was rewarded with a chorus of laughter from the studio.

'What are you going to do?' shouted Nigel grumpily from behind the camera, the wind whipping his words away.

'They want me to describe what it's like here, so I'll do a little wade through the water, point to the river, then over to the pub, cafes and houses, and ad lib a bit around that, then hand back to the studio. I'm not exactly sure. It depends how much wading I can do, and what I see around me when I do it. Just follow me through.' Another whistling swirl of wind. 'We'll make it up as we go', he yelled.

'In the traditional manner. Ok, fine', shouted Nigel.

10 miserable minutes to broadcast, thought Dan. The water was freezing and stank of a mix of sea salt and diesel oil leaking from the fishing boats being

battered in the harbour. The flood had extinguished some of the orange and white streetlights, casting much of the quayside into darkness. Waves were still riding up the river towards them, but the quay was dampening their anger so they were washing at Dan rather than pummelling him. He could see at least a dozen houses with water sloshing into their doors. Some owners stood outside, hopelessly trying to bail the water out, or build temporary barriers of clothes, planks of wood and bags of soil. Some just looked on in resignation. Dan couldn't help but think they were the wiser ones. Nature's power was irresistible.

Worst affected was the Jolly Sailor pub, the nearest building to the quay. The wooden doors had been pinned open by the force of the flood, and water poured into the front and out of the back. Regulars in rolled up trousers drank pints whilst standing on the wall of the beer garden, surveying the rising waters. Next-door, white plastic tables bobbed inside the glass windows of the Café on the Corner.

A crowd of about a hundred interested onlookers stood further up the hill that rose steeply from the quay. Safe and comfortably dry, they were pointing at the flood, and taking photographs of him and Nigel as they stood in its midst. A fire engine, it's blue lights flashing across the black water drove slowly past, washing a wave that made Dan struggle to stay upright. It stopped and half a dozen firemen piled untidily out.

'What are you up to?' shouted Dan.

'We were going to try to pump some of the water out', bellowed a fireman pointing at the café and pub, 'but I think there's no point until the tide turns.' He looked at Dan as though he were a prize fool. 'What are you doing in the water?'

'My stupid job', Dan said, managing a rueful smile.

Another dark figure was clambering clumsily down from the fire engine's cab. It steadied, seemed to fumble at its midriff, and there was a series of blinding white flashes.

'Shit', yelled Dan, dancing blurs of light fogging his vision.

'Alright mate', yelled a familiar voice.

'El! You nearly blinded me!' Dan blinked to rid his eyes of the lingering flares. 'What are you up to?'

'The same as you mate. The nationals love flooding, so I've come to get some pics to flog them. A TV reporter and his cameraman up to their waists in it could be a classic image. And lucrative.'

'Thanks mate, I appreciate that. I'd love to look a bloody idiot for the entire nation. What're you doing on the fire engine?'

El started to wade over, then thought better of it. 'The cops have cordoned off the road down here. They wouldn't let me in. So I flagged down these boys to get a lift and hid in the cab. The cops just wave them through.'

'A low trick El. Not your worst, but low.' Nice one though, I must remember it, he thought. Officious constables were the bane of a journalist's life. 'Do let me know if my picture gets in the papers.'

'Will do mate. Good luck with the broadcast. Got something to tell you about last night when we get a mo.'

El waved and slid off to take some pictures of a group of teenagers trying to skateboard through the flood.

'Two minutes to air Dan, standby', came Emma, the director's voice in his ear. He gave a thumbs up to the camera. 'You ok Nigel?' he shouted. 'You ready?'

'As I'll ever be', came the sullen response.

'Tonight, floods are battering the region' came the newsreader's cue. 'The south coast is worst affected. Our correspondent Dan Groves is in the Cornish fishing port of Looe, Dan..'

'You join us just minutes before high tide' shouted Dan above the now howling wind. 'And you can see the effect it's having'. He gestured to the waters. Nigel panned the camera off onto the street behind him, where cars stood with water up to their bonnets, and houses with waves beating against their walls. 'About four feet of floodwater has swept into the town', said Dan, pointing to his soaked waist as the camera came back to him. 'I've counted at least 20 houses now which have suffered flooding.' He began to wade through the water towards the pub, where a cheer went up from the regulars in the beer garden, 'and over here, the pub and café are being inundated.' Nigel followed him round. A middle aged and stout woman moved forward to meet him, wearing a soaked 'Jolly Sailor' tee shirt. A wet T-shirt joke surfaced in his mind, but he ignored it, kept going.

'You're the landlady here madam?' She nodded miserably. 'It must be awful watching it happen. Is there anything you can do to stop it?' he asked. He thought she was going to remain painfully mute as she shook her head, but the she wailed pitifully.

'Nothing, nothing at all. We've just had it all refitted, all done up, then this happens. It's horrible. I can hardly bear to watch it. We tried to keep it out, but it's hopeless. It's all ruined in there, all ruined.' She broke off into tears and was comforted by cuddles from the regulars. Dan felt sorry for her, but only a little. Her outburst would make compelling television.

'30 seconds', he heard in his ear. Time to wind up.

'So that's the picture here in Looe, and it's not a pleasant one', he ad libbed. 'It's too early to say exactly how much damage has been caused here of course, but even at this early stage, with all these homes and businesses flooded, it's clearly going to run into tens of thousands of pounds. And that's just the financial loss, the emotional upset, as we've just seen, will be far worse. With that, back to you in Plymouth.'

'Thanks team, great stuff, really strong. That's a clear', came Emma's voice in his ear when the next report was being played.

'Thank Christ for that', grumbled a cold and miserable Nigel from behind the camera. 'I've had enough'.

They waded back to the van, which Loud had carefully parked just up the hill where the locals had told him the water wouldn't touch. He was dry and warm and looked out contentedly at the waves lapping just a few feet from the truck's wheels.

'Good broadcast that', he said begrudgingly. 'The pictures looked great and that woman really made you feel what it was like.'

Dan was taken aback. 'Thanks', he said, not knowing quite what else to add. He hadn't experienced a compliment from Loud before. It must have looked good.

He sat on the step of the van and emptied two bootfuls of water onto the street.

'You ready?' said Nigel. 'I'm soaked and freezing and I'd like to get back to see the boys before they go to bed. Dot's looking after them, and you know what that means.'

Dan did. Dot was Nigel's mother in law. She'd lost her husband just after he and Jayne were married and had moved down to Plymouth to be near her grandchildren. She was wonderfully supportive of Nigel and looked after James and Andrew whilst he worked. He appreciated it, but they had completely opposite outlooks and he didn't like her having too much influence on the boys.

Nigel had an uplifting appreciation of life, an ability to always see the good in anyone or anything. Dot was unrelentingly negative. If she won 10 million pounds on the lottery, she'd complain it wasn't 12. A cure for cancer would have her worrying about the effect on the local undertakers. Nigel always did his best to see the boys for a while at least before bedtime, so he could tell them of the fun and interesting things he'd seen and done that day, and find out about theirs. It was a redressing of the balance, and Dan always tried to make sure he could, whatever the demands of their work. It was one of the few ways he could help.

'Sure', said Dan, taking the plastic sheeting Nigel was offering. They each put some down on the seats of the Renault and climbed in.

'Cheers Jim, thanks for your help', Dan shouted as they drove off. Loud waved back, and his shirt faded into the night as they followed the road up the hill and out of Looe.

'How are the young gentlemen?' asked Dan as they drove back.

'Good, yes', said Nigel, fiddling with some buttons on the dashboard as he tried to activate the CD player. The stereo had been fitted at his sons' insistence and he'd never got the hang of it.

'I don't understand how someone so good with the world of high tech camerawork can struggle with a car stereo', said Dan, revisiting a conversation they'd had many times before.

'Yeah, but I have to do that for a living. This is just something that's useful rather than necessary. I always struggle with things like that.'

Which makes no sense to me at all, thought Dan. 'Here, let me', he added, seeing the car drift towards the middle of the road as Nigel continued to fumble.

David Bowie's greatest hits began drifting from the expensive surround sound of the car's speakers. 'Ground control to Major Tom..'

'Yes, they're fine', continued Nigel. 'Great man Bowie you know. Used to be off his head when he did stuff like this, but still managed to create masterpieces.'

'So you've said. Wild days eh?' Nigel nodded slowly, said nothing. Dan wondered if he was back in the past. He understood. It could overtake him like that too, a warm and pleasant land. But his always went back to Thomasin. Thomasin.. Enough, the swamp was too close as it was, although the excitement of the flood had helped keep it at bay.

'So what do they want for Christmas?'

He'd become a surrogate uncle to James and Andrew and was proud of it. Apart from Rutherford, they were the only real responsibilities he had. The boys looked up to him as someone who worked with Dad and so deserved respect, but with whom they still had more leeway for mischief. Despite his initial doubts that he wasn't a role model anyone should think about following, he'd grown to enjoy it. Nigel had encouraged him, particularly as the boys got older. There'll be things they'll want to talk about, he'd told Dan, but which they can't with their Dad. So over to you mate, on the proviso you tell me if there's anything I really need to know. The usual stuff about girls and sex and drink you can handle. He was quietly looking forward to it.

Now that time had passed and Nigel had felt the pain of losing Jayne subside, Dan had babysitted the boys on the couple of nights his friend had gone out on dates. They'd been hectic, with games of hide and seek, and X-box battles with aliens, before he'd finally managed to cajole them into bed. Even then, there was just a couple of hours respite. Nigel would return, slightly the worse for a few drinks, and want to go through the intricacies of the evening and an analysis of the woman he'd taken out. It was like being teenagers again. That would always be followed by a need to seek reassurance he wasn't insulting Jayne's memory.

He was flattered by the trust Nigel had put in him. There was no greater compliment he could pay than giving Dan a role in his sons' lives. It was one of the very few things he took seriously.

'They want the usual stuff', said Nigel 'They're talking about bikes now, but I'm not sure they're quite old enough yet. Probably next year for that one I think.' Dan thought not. His friend found it hard to say no to his sons. 'They're starting to get interested in clothes too. I couldn't possibly get the fashion right, so I'll probably give them some gift vouchers, or take them into town for the sales.'

'Clothes eh? Watch out my friend', teased Dan with a grin. 'As far as I can recall that's the prelude to girls and that means trouble's on the horizon.'

'Don't I just know it. I don't know whether to look forward to it or dread it. I remember what I was like.'

'You and me both. Don't worry, we'll make sure they're ok'. Dan tried not to think of the multitude of hang-ups his broken relationships had brought. A smiling Thomasin drifted into his mind again, wearing that yellow dress of the first night he met her. A magical night. But he'd paid for it since, many times over. Enough, enough.

~

'Is there anything Uncle Dan can help with for Christmas?'

'Yes, possibly an X Box game each? Then you can play them when you come round. They'd like that.'

'Fine, games it is then.' He enjoyed the X box nights. They reminded him of when he was growing up and piling coins into Space Invaders machines on youth club evenings. 'Let me know what they want and I'll go shopping.'

He turned his mobile on only after he'd got back to his flat, given Rutherford some fuss and food, put his soaking and stinking clothes into the washing machine, had a cheese and ham toasted sandwich and lowered himself into a hot bath with a tin of Bass. He turned the light off in the bathroom, but left the hallway lamp on. The half-light was mellowing. Rutherford nosed open the door and rested his head on the side of the bath. Dan flicked some bubbles at him and he gave his master a contemptuous look, then yawned and lay down by the side of the bath.

He had two texts and an answer machine message. His personal rule was that for every three messages that arrived, one would be good news, one bad and one intermediate.

The answer machine held Lizzie's voice. She buzzed about the OB in Looe and said he could have tomorrow off as he'd already worked his hours this week, but he'd better wash his clothes before he came in on Monday. They were already on spin cycle. He relaxed further into the bath and decided that meant he could have another couple of tins of beer. This one seemed to be disappearing indecently fast. Cans and bottles of beer and wine grew smaller as you got older.

The first text was a pleasant surprise. It was from Adam; 'Nice report, since when were you swimming correspondent?! Investigation making interesting progress, will update you on Monday. Look forward to it. AB.'

He felt his spirits lift and had to stop himself from calling the detective. It was a disguised apology of the sort we men specialise in, he thought. It must be my night. A long weekend, then back on the case on Monday. Ideal. He flicked some more foam at Rutherford. 'I'm really getting into this detective stuff hound.'

He lay back in the bath and almost dropped the phone in the water, but just managed to catch it. He pressed the read button. Two good messages meant this one must be bad news.

'What nasty people, making you stand in a flood! Look forward to seeing you when you've dried. K. x'

Kerry. Intermediate, he thought harshly.

Chapter nine

They were known in the force as the Eggheads and Square Eyes division, but it was a nickname given in respect. The detectives wouldn't have known where to start with their work and the information they uncovered was often invaluable. They were teased wherever they went, but they were sought after too. The late Edward Bray had been the latest to suffer their scrutiny and he had come out surprisingly well. Disappointingly would be a better word, thought Adam, as he listened to the debrief on Bray's affairs. He had hoped the motive for the murder would be in there.

'He didn't go much on modern technology.' Zac Phillips, known as 'The Doc', obviously found that hard to believe. He patted the small silver rectangle fixed to his belt. An electric blue light winked slowly as it circled a track around its edge. It was the latest model. Zac always had the latest mobile phone.

His doctorate was in computer science, although the exact research he'd carried out had been something more to do with ultra high temperature superconductors. He had tried to explain to one detective he thought might understand, but he didn't make the same mistake again. It was a foreign language to CID and one they weren't interested in learning. Now he just told them he'd studied computer chips and that suited them fine. They didn't care how he knew the things he did, just what he could tell them. Computers and mobile phones were the Doc's speciality in Devon and Cornwall police's techno crime – Square Eyes - division.

'He's unusual in that his mobile didn't have an address list.' He thought for a second. 'Well, it did, but he didn't really use it'. Painful experience had taught him to check if the officer he was talking to understood and he gave a questioning look.

Adam nodded indulgently. 'All the numbers you use frequently in the phone's memory, friends, family, work, that sort of thing.'

'That's it', said Zac, looking back down at the lists of A4 paper in front of him. He'd worked with DCI Breen before and thought he was one of the brighter officers, although he told his small circle of friends that was a very relative concept in the police.

They were standing in the murder room at Charles Cross, him, Adam and Jim Fowler. All the other detectives were out following up leads and checking alibis. Adam liked to see an empty office. It meant he could at least tell himself they were making progress, but he wasn't sure he believed it. He could sum up the state of the investigation in a few words; leads some, suspects quite a few, evidence, none. And that meant the bottom line for a detective read; chances of a conviction, zero. His headache thumped again at the thought.

'Well, I say didn't use it, what I mean is there were only four there.' Zac began his short list. 'Office – self-explanatory. Hospice – St Jude's I assume?' Adam nodded. 'Pen, a mobile number – don't know that one.'

'His secretary, Penelope', said Adam. She'd told them Bray would occasionally text her if he was in a meeting and wanted something arranged but couldn't speak.

'Ok. Last is home – his own house. For calling the family no doubt.' No doubt, but wrong, thought Adam. So why then? 'That's it. Bizarre.' Zac shook his head and the slightly permed dark hair shuffled over his shoulders. It was the current fashion and the word was Zac had it styled to try to dent his geeky image. It hadn't worked. Perceptions stick, thought Adam, particularly in a set up as conservative at the police. He made a note to check why Bray would have his own home number on his mobile. He lived alone and didn't have a partner or family, as far as they knew anyway.

'I've done the mobile cell analysis for you', continued Zac. 'He arrived at the lay by at just a few seconds before 5.15. His mobile's an Orange. They've got a base relay above the A38 and it switched to that for its signal.'

Adam nodded. 'That fits. He was renowned for punctuality. Anything else Doc?'

Zac's eyes narrowed. He hated the nickname but had learnt not to object as that only made them use it more. Detectives were a bloody-minded bunch. He loved his job, it was exciting to be involved in crime, but he wasn't at all sure about the people he had to work with.

'I've checked his calls for you. They were all to the office, home or the hospice. No surprises in them. The only texts were to the Pen number, his secretary.'

Adam nodded again. 'That fits too. He used to get the office to do all his arrangements for him and did his business face to face. I don't think he liked phones much.'

Zac couldn't hide his surprise. Mobile phones, computers, they were a world of excitement to him. 'So what about his computer?' asked Adam.

'Nothing there either. There wasn't one at home. I went through his office one and they're all business emails. I checked all the web sites visited too and they're equally dull, finance and business research stuff. Nothing you'd be interested in.'

Adam made another note and tried not to think of last night and what Annie had said to him. But it kept coming back, repeating, echoing around his head. 'Ok, thanks Zac.' He turned to the other man who was chewing hard on a pen. 'So, Jim, what have you got for me?'

The chewing stopped. 'Not much better chief.'

Jim Fowler had been in the force long enough to get the hang of addressing senior officers. In his mid 40s, he was tall and thin with balding dark hair, brushed over to hide the emerging skull. Every time he saw Jim, Adam wondered why men did it. Surely that old footage of Bobby Charlton sprinting across a football pitch with a flap of hair trailing behind should be warning enough. He ran a hand over his own hair. Reassuringly thick and full. At least that was one thing to be glad about.

The smart suits of Fowler's days as an accountant had long gone, and now he wore jeans, trainers and chunky woollen jumpers. He'd been called in to help Devon and Cornwall police on a fraud case 15 years ago, had got a taste for it and had never left. He was now deputy head of the Financial Crime – or Eggheads – division. The top man was retiring soon and Jim was favourite for the job. Useful that, thought Adam. It meant any little extras, any overtime he needed wouldn't be turned down. Not that he had much to set them loose on, not much at all. Nothing in fact. He stifled a groan. His head was throbbing again. He hadn't slept much last night.

'We've been through the business accounts and put together a profile. Prepare yourself for a shock.' Adam looked up from his notes in expectation. Or was it hope? 'He was clean', said Fowler with obvious surprise. 'I couldn't find anything dodgy at all. With most businesses I expect to find something a bit off, not necessarily illegal, but dubious or creative in the accounting process or tax declarations. But as far as I can see, Bray was totally straight.'

'And what about any big movements of cash?' Annie was back in his head and he blinked hard, but it didn't clear the thought. He couldn't escape those words. 'You're not coming back in this house until it's resolved. I love you, of course I do, but I'm not going through all that again, and nor is Tom.' Why the hell did he go to see her? No wonder he hadn't slept.

'You ok chief?' He realised he hadn't heard what Fowler was saying. Sloppy.

'Yeah, sorry, just thinking about a possible lead.' He didn't like lying, he was a senior police officer, but he certainly wasn't going into the truth. 'Tell me again.'

'I said there's nothing odd I could see. All the money that's moving about is to places you'd expect. It's tax accounts, salaries, building and property maintenance, that sort of thing. No suspicious payments of any size in or out. Nothing that suggests anything criminal.'

The two men left together and Adam stared out of the window at the ruined church. He tried not to see it as a reflection of his life.

Concentrate, focus, calm, he thought. Personal issues to one side, I can deal with them later. Maybe. Maybe I can't deal with them at all. He shook his head again. Leave it. Later. The quiet of the Murder Room was giving him too much space for unwanted thoughts. There's a killer out there to catch. Remember what happened to Sarah. He didn't have to remember, it never left him. So where are we in the investigation? Concentrate. Focus. Calm.

So then, where are we? He tried to push the word nowhere out of his head. That wasn't fair. The question about why the murderer or their accomplice would call 999 so we would find Bray's body was a good lead. It might indicate the killer trying to ensure the time of death was pinned down quickly, so they could use an alibi they'd got someone to provide. We've got to keep that in mind while investigating suspects and their movements.

We've got a prime suspect in Tony Rye. Suzanne would be back later with news of what she'd found about his alibi. If that's not good enough we can put the pressure on. 'Invite' him in to the police station – he always enjoyed the ridiculous politeness of the phrase – to tell him they weren't satisfied with what he'd said and it was time for him to tell the truth. The case could be solved by next week. He shook his head again. He couldn't convince himself.

Rye didn't feel like their man, did he? Ok, so he was short, and that would be consistent with the angle of the shotgun wound. But apart from that.. there was no evidence at all against him. And was he the kind of man who could come up with such a well-planned murder? But if not him, who? No one else was looking like a good suspect and you usually got a feel for someone this far into a case.

What did Annie mean? The words were plain enough. 'You're not coming back in this house until it's resolved.' That she'd told him she loved him was no comfort. He'd imagined Tom upstairs, asleep in his bedroom while they argued in hushed tones on the doorstep, faces at the window next door. Why had he gone round there? He knew why. He couldn't take it, couldn't live with this, couldn't bear the thought of another night in that cold and lonely one bedroom flat while his wife and son were in the house they'd all shared just a mile away. He had to see them. To be with them. But then what about Sarah and what had happened to her? How could he betray her?

Let it go, stop torturing yourself. Later was the time for this. Home time, personal time. Not now, this was professional time. Later.

So what about Gordon Clarke? I didn't like him and didn't trust him, but so what? His alibi checks out.

The mobile analysis puts him in Bristol when he said he was, and he sent a text message to his secretary on the train back to Plymouth. She said it was definitely him, asked if there'd been a call about a contract they'd been working on, signed it G and added a kiss too. Couldn't be anyone else. He always did that. She didn't like it, that was the implication, but she said it was just his way. His cash card was used at Bristol Temple Meads station, just as he said it was. There's CCTV of him getting out of a taxi and going into Plymouth station in the morning, then coming out and getting a cab in the evening, more CCTV of him at the station in Bristol. Neither set of pictures show him going into or out of the two stations at any other time, so he can't have doubled back to carry out the killing.

How am I going to resolve it as Annie wants? What can I do? I want her and Tom but I need my job too. I'd betray Sarah otherwise, and how could I live with that? I've got to stop others suffering in the way she did. How can I do that without going out and hunting these people down? How can I be a husband and father without spending the time with my family that I know I should? Adam leaned on the window overlooking the bustling city, rested his head on a hand.

What about Hicks and Stead? Their alibis are good too. They'd have to really shift to get from that shop to the lay by in time to kill Bray. It'd take a car or motorbike or taxi, but only Stead's got a car and his wife was using it, there's CCTV of it parked at the factory where she works, not leaving until 5.45. They always get the bus by all accounts, or walk. There are no records of taxis or cars being hired by either of those two, or anyone who fits the descriptions. We'd better check their mobiles too, see where they were and when, but it's thin isn't it? Thin hopes.

What about the force's much trumpeted policies on being a family friendly employer? They talk a good game, but where's the action? Could that help me? He thought of Tom's smiling face as he took him for that last kick about in Central Park, and Annie's mock anger as they returned home, caked in mud.

Then he remembered the laughter which echoed around the CID office after that Family Friendly poster went up. One Detective Sergeant had pencilled an asterisk next to the words and added 'does not apply to detectives' under it.

Uniform had it easy with their rotas. Scheduled hours meant nothing in CID, and in truth that was part of the attraction. He could go back to uniform of course, but.. But what? It was an easier life. It was also a dull one. He couldn't go back to breaking up fights and arresting shoplifters. He'd worked to become a detective, done it for a reason. Not a reason he'd ever told anyone in the force. If they knew, he wouldn't be here, would be kicked out as a vigilante. He couldn't turn his back on that, on Sarah. He'd rather.. Rather what? Lose his family?

What about Arthur Bray? Could he have killed his son? He had a motive, but I can't see it. Can I? The old man was in anguish when we interviewed him, and unless he's one of the best actors I've ever seen that was genuine. But then, he's got no alibi and he owns two shotguns. Forensics were going over them now. But it was thin again, thin.

Penelope Ramsden was being seen again, John was doing that one on Monday. She'd been some help, but there must be more she could tell them. John was going to her home, getting her out of the office where the memories of her boss surrounded her. Good idea that, good man John, rock solid Detective Inspector and second in command. He wanted time to think about that oddity in Bray's diary too, the cancelled appointment. Maybe that'd be the breakthrough. But still nothing from it yet, no reason for anyone connected with Bray – any possible killer – to change their plans suddenly.

And what about the hospice? Good piece of work that, by an amateur too. Clever man Dan, and perceptive. Funny with it. Made you want to talk to him. No wonder he was a good hack. Wouldn't make a bad detective either. We'd have got it of course, it'd just have taken longer. John was doing that one as well, on Monday when the hospice's Chief Exec was back from some business trip. She was the only one who really knew Bray. He'd never been in there, only knew it by reputation, a good reputation too, if any place so associated with death could be described that way.

So what would he do about Annie and Tom? His wife, his son. 'I'm not going through all that again', Annie had said. Could he give up this job he needed to be with them? No more missed parents' evenings and birthday parties. He closed his eyes. No more catching murderers, rapists, robbers. Arresting shoplifters and breaking up fights instead. Sarah haunting his mind for it. Wouldn't I just end up resenting them and wouldn't that destroy us anyway?

A gentle mist had enveloped the ruined church and fine tracks of drizzle were grazing the windows of the police station. A bus had broken down on the roundabout and a trail of traffic was tailing back towards the University. There was the odd blare of a frustrated horn, but most of the motorists suffered in resigned silence. Adam looked across the city towards the house he and Annie and Tom had shared, then turned quickly away.

I want to see Bray's house, he thought. I need to get a better feeling of the man. I'll do that in a minute. There are a couple of detectives and a forensics officer up there at the moment. I'll go and see how they're doing. It's not far and I need to get out of the office, do something to stifle these thoughts taunting my mind.

∽

Dan suffered a frustrating afternoon too. One of the city centre's shoe shops had no Timberland boots bigger than a size nine. Another had only a black pair in size 12, and he wanted tan. As a last resort, he walked into Dingles, more expensive but usually reliable. 11 was the biggest size they had, and try as he might he couldn't convince himself they'd stretch. The drizzle began to fall as he left the store. He glared at the leaden sky and walked down to Royal Parade to catch a number 44 bus home. By the time he got back to Hartley Avenue, the familiar dampness was spreading through his socks.

∽

In a darkened room, a surfer was scanning the ITV internet site. A click of the mouse selected the south west news page. Council tax in Cornwall was going up by 11 per cent, more than four times the rate of inflation. A pair of dolphins had been caught in fishermen's nets and their carcasses washed up on a beach at Falmouth, and Torquay United had signed a new and highly promising young goalkeeper. There was no word of any progress in the Edward Bray murder investigation. Satisfied, the surfer nodded, sipped at a mug of tea and moved onto the evening's TV prospects.

～

Dirty El shifted in his tree and fished the mobile from his pocket. 'Dan mate, can I call you back a bit later?' He listened to the reply. 'It's just I'm a bit busy at the mo.' Another reply. 'I'm up a tree. Yeah, a tree. In the city centre. I'll call you later.'

From the windows of the first floor of Plymouth Crown Court, the former scoutmaster saw the cameramen and photographers had finally given up their wait. He bounded down the stairs, pushed through the swing door and walked gratefully onto the concrete plaza for a much-needed cigarette. It was ridiculous, the court being a non-smoking building. His nerves needed calming. It was a long running and now infamous child sex abuse trial and he'd seen enough of the inside of that court building for a lifetime. Seen enough of bloody journalists, photographers and cameramen too. Vultures. The tabloids had nicknamed the case the Packs of Prey. The main defendant hated them, took the cigarette out of his mouth and spat in distaste. They had no idea what they were talking about.

15 minutes, the judge had said, then the case would resume. He stood on the concrete plaza and puffed

deeply. It was his first chance of the day to escape the trial. He was determined his picture wouldn't be in the papers. He'd arrived at court with a scarf covering his mouth and nose, big dark sunglasses and a baseball pulled down to his eyes. No chance for the vultures he thought, and smiled. He knew the photographers would leave to do other jobs eventually. His fellows had tipped him off about that. They couldn't wait there forever they'd told him, had a living to earn, and they were right. They looked after each other, his little network of special friends. Good friends.

So what if he'd had some fun with a couple of kids? More than a couple if the truth was told. They'd enjoyed it, he was sure of it, although he wouldn't be telling the court that. Oh no. Calm denial was the way. Shock at the accusations. Hurt too. Plausible in refuting them. Look at me jury, just look at me. A respectable man, no stain on his character, someone who's devoted much of his life to helping youngsters, brought before you as the victim of vindictive juvenile imagination because I told a couple of them off, wouldn't let them go on an expedition. It was a sadly familiar story in modern life. And what evidence was there against him anyway?

In a few days he'd walk free from the court, his head held high, and there was no way some low life paparazzo was peddling a picture of him to the papers. Mud stuck and he'd want the freedom to go back to working with kids again. When all this fuss had died down that was. He knew it would. It always did. He took a last puff on the stub of his cigarette and felt good for the nicotine hit. Maybe a beer tonight he thought, maybe even a bottle of wine. The trial was almost done now and they'd got nothing on him. Not a thing. His barrister was good. He could tell the jury believed him, nodded with some of the points he made. They'd be sent out to consider their verdict and come back within an hour he reckoned, a resounding not guilty. Yes, maybe a bottle of wine tonight, and a decent one too. Why not?

He was oblivious to the soft whirring of the camera motor, the long lens sticking out from the leaves of the tree a hundred yards across the concourse, and the victorious grin of Dirty El as he sat on the branch he'd clambered up to with the help of a stepladder borrowed from the city council offices. Gotcha you pervy bastard, the photographer chuckled to himself. That's my bit for society done for today, and a few hundred quid in my pocket too. Gotcha.

~

Edward Bray's house was sterile, thought Adam as he looked around. It was big enough for a family with three or four children, yet Bray lived here alone. Why? Did he want to make an impression? If so, on who? Did he plan a family one day? Did he have nothing else to spend his money on? Did he just like it? Did any of that help the investigation at all?

He started in the kitchen, the order – or disorder – there so often an insight into a person. He'd never known a murderer who was a keen cook, although several victims had been. It was clean, perhaps surprisingly clean for a man living alone. He thought of the state of his small and rented flat, then tried to push the image from his mind. He was here to stop thinking about his own troubles.

The work surfaces were white and pristine, not a hint of any serious cooking. The tiles surrounding them were also a shining white, no cracks, no grease, no marks, no stains. There were gadgets, plenty of gadgets, a microwave, food mixer, blender, coffee maker, toaster, fridge freezer, all expensive, all in virgin white.

He opened the fridge. Milk, two small plastic bags of salad, out of date orange juice, packet soups, olive oil spread, low fat yoghurts, some ham and cheddar cheese. The cupboards were mostly empty but one held pasta, tins of tomatoes, some herbs and spices, tomato sauce and baked beans. Another held a small collection of pots and pans. A stale wholemeal loaf sat on a wooden breadboard. The only colour in the room came from a line of takeaway menus stuck to the fridge; pizza, Chinese, Indian, Thai. The bin was full of metal foil containers. He recognised the lifestyle. His own flat wasn't so different.

In the hallway was a central heating timer connected to the telephone beneath it. That explains the calls to home, another line of inquiry gone. Nice idea, call when you're coming home to make sure the house is warm. Much better than my freezing flat. On the wall was a framed Monet print of Rouen Cathedral. The carpet was cream, thick and expensive, the walls an apple white.

A black leather sofa dominated the lounge, facing on to a wide screen television, with DVD, satellite TV, expensive hi fi and an X box system. A few games were piled up next to it, all military shoot to kill types. He picked up one and put it down again. 'As much killing as you can handle' it boasted. Tom would never play such games. Enough of that.

A big No Smoking sign, red letters, on the wall. Who was it warning? He couldn't imagine any visitors here. Maybe Dan was onto something there; maybe it was tied in with his mum's death and the hospice. A real flame gas fire was the only other feature. Adam slowly shook his head again. He felt a sense of loneliness in the house, a man trying to forget his solitary existence.

The downstairs bathroom was also white but looked unused. A shower hung above a bath, the cabinets were empty. Upstairs, only two of the five bedrooms showed signs of life. Both had chrome double beds. One was clearly Edward Bray's, the duvet thrown back, suggesting someone getting up in a hurry. There were built in cupboards of shoes and suits, all expensive but not what he thought in good taste, too businesslike, too many stripes and checks. In the next-door room, the bed was made up and pristine. Adam sat down on it. He got the feeling no one had ever slept here. Was it kept ready in the hope of a visit?

'Sir?' Detective Constable Ian Renals flushed face appeared around the door, disturbing Adam's thoughts. 'Something you should see.' His voice was excited, urgent. Adam got up and joined him in one of the other bedrooms. On the bed were three large transparent bags. The colours and shapes inside were distorted by the opaque plastic but still instantly recognisable. They were notes, 10, 20, 50 pound notes, hundreds of them.

'Where?' asked Adam. 'How much?'

A Popular Murder

'In the wardrobe sir, hidden behind a false partition, just sitting there.' DC Renals stared at the bags and drew in a whistling breath. 'There must be tens of thousands of pounds there. Must be.'

Adam nodded. Maybe even hundreds of thousands, he thought. Perhaps Bray's business wasn't as straight as the Eggheads had believed.

'And there's this sir. It was in there with them.' DC Renals handed him a folder, brown, A4, standard for filing office papers. 'The Apple Tree' was written on the front. Inside, it was full of pieces of paper. Adam took out the first one.

"Words not for me, but overheard,
A warm and cloudless summer's day,
All light with life, but dark with death,
Such sour regret, and choking sorrow,
Is this the way it always ends?"

He rifled through the papers, read another couple.

"Summer punctures secrecy,
Windows open, leaves to hide,
An apple tree, an innocent's refuge,
An eternal turning of the tide."

"Some words should never be heard,
Some words can never be escaped,
Some words echo everafter,
End the innocence,
And the life."

～

Tony Rye was trying to fend off his wife. A pair of detectives had been round, for a 'follow up chat', they'd called it. But they'd taken a formal statement too. That meant the lies were written down, in black and white.

She'd sat there quietly through that, but wouldn't join him on the sofa, leaving him to answer the questions alone. Now they'd left and her face was throbbing red and her arms were flailing at him.

'You bastard. You stupid bastard.' Her voice rose to a hysterical screech. 'I hate you. You're a stupid fucking bastard.'

He held out his hands, willing her to come to him. 'Just stick by me love, please, stick by me. You know I love you.' Insistent, trying to penetrate her anger. 'Please. Help me.'

Maureen Rye's voice rose again, now nails down a blackboard. 'If you fucking love me, why did you do it?' She sat down heavily on the sofa, dropped her head into her hands and sobbed, deep, wracking sobs. 'You bastard. After all we've worked for. I wish I'd listened to what they all said about you. I hate you. I hate you.' Her voice tailed off into her tears. Tony Rye looked on helplessly. He didn't dare try to put an arm around her.

∼

Lizzie Riley sat in the planning meeting in the conference suite at the end of the newsroom. The diary for Monday was looking thin. A press launch about some new wave power thing off the Cornish coast wasn't going to excite the viewers. She ground a three-inch heel into the carpet. 'Any ideas?' she asked forcefully and looked around expectantly at the dozen journalists gathered there. 'How about an update on the Bray murder?' said one of the more ambitious researchers. 'We've not gone back to it for a while.' Good idea she thought, noting it down in her diary. I know just the man. It's about time he did some work.

~

In the Murder Room at Charles Cross, Adam Breen and Suzanne Stewart were having a disagreement. Suzanne's respect for her boss meant she would never question him openly. But even this mild dispute was rare enough to see the couple of other detectives now back in the room furtively stop work at their terminals to listen in.

'So he's got absolutely no alibi for the time of the killing?' asked Adam.

'No, none at all', Suzanne replied. 'What he told us about getting the tiles was true. The man in the shop remembers him clearly. He often buys stuff there. He couldn't put an exact time on when he was in, but he said it was about 4. Luckily for us, they've had a robbery in the past so they've got CCTV. I checked the tape. He bought the tiles at 4.24 according to the clock on the recorder, which is right, give or take a minute. They took a few minutes loading the tiles onto his van, so I think he was away from Ivybridge by about 4.35.' She looked at her watch. '4.40 at the latest.'

Adam adjusted his tie. He realised Suzanne's story had pushed Annie and Tom and Sarah from his mind and he felt momentarily guilty about it. Wasn't that proof of what Annie had said to him, about his true priorities? But he was a detective, investigating a murder, and he could smell a lie.

'And how long to the lay by from there?'

'I timed it. Doing about 60, which I reckon is right for his van, it takes ten minutes to get to the lay by. But you have to go past it on the A38, then off at the next turning, then come back on yourself. It's about 15 minutes in all.'

'So he could be at the lay by at 4.55?'

'Yes.'

'Just as it was getting nicely dark. Just in time to lie in wait in case he was early.'

'Yes.'

'Just ready for Bray to turn up at 5.15. He pulls in, gets out of his car and bang! Then Rye scarpers, drives as fast as he can back to Moretonhampstead, gets rid of the gun somewhere on the way, drops the tiles off and goes home.'

Adam paused. He seemed taken with his theory.

'We'd never find the gun', he added thoughtfully. 'There are a thousand places you could dump it on that route. Woods, rivers, ditches, gullies. But you'd better get the Tactical Aid Group onto it anyway. Get them searching within a boundary of about thirty yards of the roads from the lay by to Moretonhampstead. It's a big area, but not impossible. Tell them they're after a shotgun, so it needn't be a fingertip search. And it'd better be from tomorrow too, regardless of the overtime.'

Suzanne nodded. She shared her boss's dislike of budgets. 'I reckon if he did kill Bray, he'd be back at Moretonhampstead by 5.40ish. And that's the only sighting we've got of him after the tile shop. One of his workmen, a welder saw him. He'd been doing some inside work, staying on a bit late, and he saw Rye at 5.45 in the portacabin office at the pool. He says he's sure it was 5.45 because he promised his wife he'd be home for tea at 6 and it's a 15 minute drive from there.'

'And no other sightings of him in the town? No one saw him shopping as he claimed?'

'None. No one at all. We've checked all the shops in the town. There are only about a dozen of them, and no one saw him.'

'Well', said Adam, leaning back against the window. 'It looks like Mr Rye has some explaining to do.'

He walked over to the felt boards at the front of the murder room, adjusted his tie again and then prodded the postcard with Tony Rye's name on it.

'It looks like you've got some explaining to do Mr Rye', he said menacingly to the card.

'So shall we go and pick him up?' asked Suzanne Stewart eagerly. The two watching detectives craned their necks to hear. Adam stood staring at the felt board.

'No. No, I don't think so', he said, turning round to face her.

'Why not?' Her voice had quietened, and had a query in it that was the closest she came to questioning her boss's judgement. If Adam sensed it, he didn't let it show.

'We're by no means there yet are we? Nowhere near in fact. We've got a motive and no alibi, but no real evidence. And that's the thing that's bothering me about this case. Unless we catch someone out, or somehow manage to get a confession, proving who killed Edward Bray is going to be almost impossible.'

He tapped the photo at the centre of the boards. 'We've no forensics, no witnesses even, in fact nothing to put in front of a jury. So far it's all circumstantial, and that's not going to get us a conviction. And then there's the issue of the call, tipping us off about the body. Was that Rye? And if so, why? What could he possible gain from doing it?' He paused again to glare at the card. 'I think we might learn more from Mr Rye if we leave him free for a while. He's not one for a confessional.'

'Well, that's your decision of course sir.' The voice was even quieter, the doubt unmistakeable. 'Don't you think we could crack this case this afternoon if we get him in? With respect sir, aren't you concerned he might disappear?'

With respect, as ever it had come to mean, with no respect. Again Adam rode the criticism.

'I don't think he's going anywhere Suzanne. But you're quite right, we shouldn't take the risk. I want someone tailing him this weekend. It's worth the chance that if he was the killer, he might lead us to the weapon or even go back to the lay by. You're right, he might even try to run. Then we'd have a case. If he does nothing over the weekend, then we've lost nothing, apart from a few quid from the Assistant Chief Constable's overtime budget.' The flicker of a smile said that was no concern. 'We can get him in on Monday and discuss matters with him then.'

∼

Dan took Rutherford for a run, then ordered a curry as a Friday night treat. He was feeling good so he went for a Vindaloo, about as ambitious as he got. It arrived after he'd showered, perfect timing, and by nine he was walking down to Mutley Plain to meet Dirty El who 'had some news for him, political stuff'. That meant Jones. El didn't like doing business on the phone, was paranoid about conversations being tapped, particularly when money was involved. Dan didn't bother arguing, didn't take any persuading to meet for a beer instead. It was Friday night after all.

He knew it was pointless trying to tempt El out of Wetherspoon's pubs, so he agreed to meet in the Mannamead. A converted bank, it was soulless in terms of atmosphere, but the beer was good and cheap, and beer was what he needed. The swamp was starting to tug again and he wanted to numb it. Sometimes it was the only way.

He walked in and spotted El in his customary shady corner opposite the bar. He made the gesture of lifting a glass to his mouth. El raised a thumb unsteadily. Dan thought the photographer's eyes were focusing several feet away. He bought two pints of Abbot Ale and joined him. The pub was quiet, usually was by this time, tended to be a place where people started the night.

'You ok El?'

'More than ok', the photographer slurred. 'I should have bought you that pint.' He slapped his palm on the table. 'You know the snap I took of you in the flood?'

'Yes?' said Dan warily.

'See The Telegraph tomorrow.' El started giggling and rocking on his chair. 'It made me quite a few quid.' And me a right fool, he thought, but he couldn't blame El for it. It was all part of the game.

'Come on then, tell me about Jones.' El straightened in his chair. 'Ah, Mr Jones.' His grin widened. 'The excellent Mr Jones. There lies the potential for more earnings.'

And revenge, thought Dan, but didn't say so. Even better, revenge without me being implicated.

'Mr Jones is a clever one. I had a little look through his bins. Not much there, not much at all. Only rubbish, lots of rubbish, no interesting little bits of paperwork, except..' El giggled again, but Dan knew not to interrupt. It would only prolong the wait. '..Except a couple of mobile numbers scribbled on the back of a constituency newsletter.'

'Jesus El!' Dan felt a wave of irritation, another tug of the swamp. 'You said you'd got something interesting to tell me and that's it? They could be anyone's numbers for anything.'

El shook his head, his grin widening. 'Hey, when's your old mate Dirty El let you down?' Dan didn't want to answer, just took a draw of beer. Anyway, why was he being angry with El? It was Friday and he'd come out for a drink, anything on Jones would be a bonus. Come on, relax.

'So I did a little more research', El continued, another big grin. 'A little more research, just a little more research.' It was almost a song. Dan wondered how much he'd had to drink. 'And I went to the phone boxes in the city centre to see what I could find. And guess what I did find?'

'What?' Dan was starting to unwind and enjoy the photographer's drunkenness. Maybe it was time he caught up. Hell, why not? All he was doing tomorrow was going for a walk with Kerry.

'I found some little business cards of Plymouth finest pros. And guess what?' An even broader grin. 'What?' said Dan, now smiling too. He couldn't help it. Mood swings, a lust to get pissed and blot the world out. They were danger signs but they felt good.

'The little numbers written on the newsletter matched a couple of the little numbers on the pros' cards.' El leant back on his chair happily and finished the remaining half of his beer in one go. 'So next week Dirty El's going to go out on a little night time expedition to the docks to see what he can see.'

'El, you're a genius. Sit there and let me get you another beer.' The photographer made no attempt to stop him. 'And how about a chaser too?' he called unsteadily from his seat as Dan walked up to the bar. Not a bad idea El, not a bad idea at all..

Chapter ten

He'd fallen asleep on the sofa last night, but at least the chicken kebab he'd picked up on the way home had helped sober him up, and he didn't feel too bad at all. Remarkably well in fact.

Kerry lived on the way out to Dartmoor, just off the A386 at Crownhill. It was a modern, red brick, semi-detached house with a little garden at the front, enclosed by a low white plastic picket fence. A neighbour's curtain twitched at the sight of a man struggling up the path with an excitable Alsatian. There were Neighbourhood Watch signs on the lampposts and the green in front of the rows of houses was unusually free of litter. A couple of children kicked a football back and forth quietly. It felt like a small and proudly ordered community.

She'd been waiting and the white double glazed door opened before he could knock. The sparkling sandals had given way to walking shoes, but even these looked conspicuously new. He suspected she'd bought them specially and wondered if a walk would have been her choice of a first date. She wore jeans, a fleece, and a denim jacket too. Her hair looked newly washed and flowed around her, but she had a hair band wrapped round her fingers ready for the assault of the Dartmoor wind.

She bounced out of the door and kissed him on the cheek with an effervescent 'Hi!' He returned the compliment, keeping the energetically curious dog at arms length until he could see how she reacted to him.

'And this must be Rutherford', she said, and went to bend down to him. So touchingly naïve, not a chance thought Dan as the dog leapt up and raked his damp paws down her jacket. She squealed.

'Sorry', he said. 'He gets a bit excited with new friends.'

If she was annoyed, she covered it well. 'No problem. I put on my old clothes. I thought it might be muddy. He's gorgeous', she added, tying up her hair and now being nuzzled between her legs.

'Sorry'. Dan was well used to apologising for his dog. 'He's very forward. I didn't teach him that.'

They headed up to Princetown, one of the moor's bigger villages, and parked at the back of the Plume of Feathers pub, then walked down the main road towards the Blackbrook. A couple of car swept past them but the moor was quiet. Sunday was busier, the traditional family walks day.

'Where are we going then?' she asked.

'I thought we'd do the Devonport Leat', he said pointing down the valley to the south. 'It's a good and varied walk. There's not too much rough ground and we can cut back towards the car anytime we feel hungry or cold. Rutherford loves it.' The dog turned and let out a resonant couple of barks at the mention of his name. 'There's lots of space to run around in, and plenty of water for a swim. He loves swimming. I thought I'd get us lunch in the Plume after as I've dragged you out here.'

'I don't feel dragged at all', she said and he believed it. 'It's a lovely idea. I've never been on a walk for a date before.' She looked at him to see if he'd react to the challenge. Was it a date? He let it pass. We'll see how it goes, he thought.

Just before the bridge over the Blackbrook, they left the road and picked up the leat, heading downstream, following its grassy bank. Dan thought it was time to show off his knowledge of Dartmoor.

'It was built in the 1790s to channel water to the docks at Devonport. In those days they were really booming'. He hoped he didn't sound too pompous. 'It doesn't make it that far any longer. It stops at Burrator Reservoir now.'

'You know the moor well then?'

'I had little choice but to know it. You can't be an Environment Correspondent here without spending plenty of your time on Dartmoor.' Dan took a deep and appreciative breath. 'I love it. It's only when you taste the fresh air here you realise how toxic the city's atmosphere is. And listen, listen to that.'

She listened. 'What?'

'Nothing. That's just it, nothing. Silence. Silence is something you very rarely hear in our modern lives. There are always mobiles going off, or cars roaring by, or planes in the sky, or music blaring out. People have almost forgotten how to be quiet, or how pleasant it is.'

She listened again. 'Yes', she said.

Rutherford had decided it was time for a swim. He was wavering on one of the pairs of granite blocks that lie opposite each other and jut out in the leat for sheep to leap across. He looked back at Dan, and in the absence of any warning shouts plunged into the water. It was just deep enough for him to swim. Dan whistled and he turned to them in mid-paddle. He had his smiling face on.

The dog bobbed downstream with the current, taking the odd bite at some dangling grass, then turned back on himself and swam furiously towards them, but made no headway. They burst into laughter and he paddled even harder, making the water around him froth. After a minute's straining exertion, he gave up the unequal struggle against the current and let it sweep him to the side of the leat. He clambered up the grass bank and ran over to them.

'Run!' Dan shouted.

'What?' she cried, but her hesitation made it too late. From the safety of the 20 feet separation zone experience told him was required, Dan watched as Rutherford shook himself into a blur of hair, spraying an explosion of water droplets all over her.

'Lovely', she said, brushing water from her face. 'Thanks dog.'

Dan tried desperately not to laugh, and she lunged at him, caught him, and rubbed her damp body against him. He didn't resist too hard, initially to humour her, then because he found himself enjoying it. He hadn't planned it, and didn't even think about whether he wanted to do it, but he leant down and kissed her on the lips. She responded, and they stood locked together by the leat, kissing, until the surging fear of commitment within him shrugged off the hold of his lust. He pulled away.

'Mmm, well, errm,' he said, wondering what he'd just done.

'Don't say a word'. She was smiling broadly. 'You don't have to.'

They carried on down the Leat, heading through a thin line of trees and turning west towards Fox Tor Mire. The grey of the sky shifted slowly to an ominous black and rain began to fall. A fog rose, as if steam from the earth, swallowing the proud granite pillars of Dartmoor's famous hill topping Tors. The rain grew harder, and he stopped to help her over a stile. He kept hold of her hand until she was on the grass, and they stayed linked together as they continued along the leat.

Dan felt an awkwardness and enjoyment combined.

'Are you enjoying the walk?' he asked lamely.

'Very much, despite the rain.'

'We don't have to go on much further. We'll do another mile or so, then turn back towards Princetown for some lunch.'

'That'll be lovely', she said, with gentle relief in her voice.

Rutherford had found one of the biggest sticks Dan had ever seen him attempt to lift. It looked like oak and extended fully three feet either side of his mouth, but being Rutherford he wouldn't let it go.

'What's he going to do with that?' asked Kerry incredulously. She hadn't taken long to realise the dog wasn't completely sane.

'He'll try to carry it proudly and resist all efforts to take it off him', said Dan, who had given up being embarrassed by Rutherford. 'The only way to get it off him is to find another stick and pretend to love it more than the one he's got. Then he'll drop it and come after yours.' He looked around. 'Watch.'

He found a more modest stick by the side of the leat, and held it up to the sky, whooping and shouting. Rutherford turned, dropped his caber, came bounding up and after a brief struggle, Dan let go and the dog ran off with his new prize. 'As discussed', he said.

The rain had grown dense and looked like it wouldn't be moving on without a struggle. The leat became a mass of splashes and ripples and a regular drumbeat grew from the downpour's pounding of the remaining brown leaves clinging to the trees that lined the watercourse. From 20 yards ahead, where he'd found a fascinating fox's scent in a bush, Rutherford turned and looked back in the direction they'd come. Dan knew the hint well. They turned off the leat and headed north, picking up the road that led to the old tin mines at Whiteworks and following it up the hill towards Princetown.

'Sorry about that', said Dan, as he settled a large white wine in front of Kerry and sat down at the closest slate table to one of the Plume's pair of woodburner stoves. 'That's the thing about the moor. It can be very bad tempered. It rains on you at the slightest opportunity.'

'It's fine, I really enjoyed the walk, honestly', she said. 'Look at him', she added, pointing to Rutherford who had crashed out in the best position to soak up the fire's waves of heat. Small puddles formed around his prone body.

'So, tell me more about yourself', she said. 'You didn't give that much away over dinner at Mike and Jo's.'

Ah, she noticed, thought Dan. 'Didn't I? Well maybe I was too interested in finding out about you.' He was surprised she'd seen it. Whenever he wanted to create a decent impression on someone he let them talk, about themselves, their hobby, friends, family, anything. Most people liked to talk, very few to listen and they'd come away thinking they'd had a good time. Most didn't notice it either.

She smiled, broadly again. 'You're a charmer', she said. 'Jo did warn me. But don't stop! A girl can't get too much attention, especially from a chap like you. But come on then, I want to know more about you. Are you a local lad?'

He went through his history, from birth, to school days, to college, to career, adding the odd anecdote to entertain her. A couple worked well enough that she laughed so loudly Rutherford hauled himself up and wandered over to them, unsure if the noise meant he was missing out on something important.

Lunch arrived, Stilton and Broccoli soup, with ham and cheese sandwiches. Rutherford appeared from under their table as he sniffed the food and was rewarded with some of Dan's ham.

'Another drink?' she asked as they finished eating. She ate quickly, not daintily, just as he did. He liked that.

'I'd better not', he said looking ruefully at his empty glass. 'I've got to drive us home.'

The rain was attacking with new vigour as they drove back. He took it slowly. Dartmoor ponies are fond of sheltering near roads and he didn't want to ruin the day by running one down. He'd found it unexpectedly enjoyable.

'I've had a really good day', she said as he pulled into her street. 'Thank you.'

'So have I', he said, trying not to sound as if it was a surprise.

'Would you like to come in for a coffee?' She looked over to the back seats. 'Rutherford is very welcome too of course, so long as he behaves.'

Would he like to go in? He didn't have long to decide. It sounded like the fast track to the start of a relationship he still wasn't sure he wanted. But he hadn't done this for a while and he had to admit she had grown on him. He'd enjoyed the kiss and, if he was honest, he was feeling a little excited. But there was the commitment thing to worry about..

It was a good thing she made the decision, he thought later. I could have sat in that car all day.

'Come on dog', she said, opening the Peugeot's back door and grabbing Rutherford's lead. 'We can go in and get warm, even if your master's going to sit here.'

A Popular Murder

He followed her in. They stood in the kitchen as the kettle boiled and Rutherford lapped at an old aluminium saucepan full of water. She leaned over past him to get to the tea bags from a cupboard, and planted a kiss on his cheek at she did so. He turned and caught her lips, and this time it was more passionate than out on the cold and windy moor. Then she pulled back and looked at him. He wondered what he'd done wrong.

'Are you cold?' she asked.

'I'm not warm, but I'm ok.'

'I'm freezing. I fancy a nice hot bath. Here..' She reached out and took his hand. 'Follow me', she said, leading him up the stairs, the tea forgotten.

Rutherford watched them disappear, waited for a moment, then lay down by the kitchen's radiator, yawned and closed his eyes to shut out the noises from upstairs.

Chapter eleven

It was just before 9 o'clock on Monday morning, and Dan's phone rang as he pulled in to the car park at Charles Cross. 'Lizzie mobile' flashed up on the display. He debated whether to answer, but knew he had little choice. You couldn't escape Lizzie for long. She was calling on her way to some community liaison meeting in Exeter. She hated them and it showed.

'A story', she said, 'we want a story. Remember those things you're paid for? Not playing detectives, but reporting stories.' Sarcasm was a favourite weapon. 'Would it be too much trouble to bother you to file a story? Just a little one would be nice.'

He'd risen to it, she knew how to get to him. 'Bloody hell Lizzie! You said I could go and find out about how the police work and make some good contacts. I'm doing that! It's hardly surprising I've not been filing stories then is it?'

'Not for the rest of your bloody career I didn't.' He could almost feel the stiletto grating into her car's footwell. 'You've got another day, two at the most, then I want to see something on the investigation. Got it? We pay you, not the constabulary. You're a hack remember, not a detective.'

He'd hung up, resisted the temptation to say anything else. Did she have a point? Had he got too involved, forgotten he was supposed to be a journalist? He didn't like the answer that nagged at him. And how was he going to file a story on the case when Adam had begun to trust him? He slammed the car door as he got out. Not a good start to the day.

This time there were no curious eyes at the windows. He used the pass Adam had given him to make his way to the Murder Room without attracting any more of the interest an exotic caged animal might suffer. The novelty of the TV detective had worn off.

'Morning Dan, how are you? Good weekend?' Adam looked pleased to see him. He had yet another sharp suit on, this time navy blue, three buttoned and single breasted. Dan wondered when he would see any of the detective's clothes twice. His own wardrobe wouldn't stand up to more than four days without an encore from a shirt, jacket or trousers.

'Yes, very good thanks', said Dan bashfully, feeling his cheeks redden and his irritation wane.

Adam's smile widened and Dan felt he was watching a replay of his memories of Saturday.

'Mental note. Further inquiry needed', said Adam, adjusting his bright red tie. 'For now though, to business.' Dan took his place over at the window whilst Adam addressed the crowd.

There were twenty detectives there, a couple sitting at the desks, but most standing or leaning against the walls. Dan had noticed CID didn't like sitting down.

Suzanne Stewart stood to Adam's side by the felt boards, like a prefect in class. She avoided looking at him.

'Come on then, listen up', called Adam. The background muttering faded. 'We're a week on from the murder. And where have we got?'

There was a general shuffling, looking around and down at notes. Just like a classroom, no one wanted to risk a wrong answer. Adam answered for them. 'Somewhere', he said. 'Somewhere and nowhere.'

He looked around the room in his most commanding way, like a general addressing his troops on the eve of battle. Was this really the same man that he'd seen brittle with anger in the Minerva? Relaxed and amused a few minutes ago? Now resolute in leadership and inspiration for a team of detectives in pursuit of a murderer?

'We're somewhere in that we have a prime suspect; Tony Rye'. Adam was pointing to the card with his name on it. 'And it's he who's going to be our focus today. We're going to pay him a little visit for a friendly chat.'

There was a ripple of laughter. The team knew exactly what that meant.

'But we've also got nowhere. Nowhere in that if he denies having anything to do with it, we're stuck. We've got no real evidence against him'. He paused and looked round the room again. 'So while Suzanne, Dan and I are having our chat, I want you lot going through his family and friends and anyone who knew him.'

Suzanne was coming? What was that about? Hadn't it worked well with just the two of them? He wasn't being jealous, was he? He felt his day darken further.

'I want to know anything about anyone who may have a shotgun. I want to know if Rye was interested in it, or even – please! – if he asked to borrow it. And I want to know what he talked about. Did he ever, however much in jest, or after a few beers, or whatever, did he ever say anything about wanting to get Edward Bray? And did he have a garage, or shed where he could store things? We've still got no murder weapon; the search teams didn't come up with anything over the weekend. So get cracking please team. Suzanne has a list of who's been assigned what.'

Adam turned to Dan whilst the other detectives clustered around the prefect.

'You're going to see what I believe you in the media call 'some action' today', he said grinning. He was obviously looking forward to it. 'I've got a warrant to arrest Mr Rye and go over his house. I'll ask him gently at first to account for his movements, but if he can't, or he gets tetchy, we'll bring him in. The search teams will be in place in half an hour so we'd better get over to the pool to lift him. He's there at the moment. We've had someone watching him all weekend.'

Dan sat in the back of the familiar Astra, whilst Suzanne Stewart drove them to Moretonhampstead. She'd insisted. From the passenger seat, Adam outlined his plan.

'As I've said, we've got no real evidence against Rye. But of course he doesn't know that. So I'll be bluffing a bit in the questioning to see how he reacts. Let me get on with that without interruptions please.'

'Yes sir', said Suzanne Stewart.

'But there is one thing he's given us, and it's very interesting. Very interesting indeed. I didn't mention it to the team in case it made them relax and think it was all over. But one of the surveillance squad reports that Rye went to the lay by where Bray was shot yesterday. He didn't get out of his van. He just drove very slowly through.'

'And isn't it the case that murderers often return to the scene of their crime?' asked Dan, who remembered it from a book.

'Yes indeed', said Adam adjusting his tie.

⁓

'That funny smell's back', said Tony Rye, looking up from his drawings as Adam walked into the portacabin, followed by Suzanne Stewart. 'Why don't you fuck off and leave me alone?' Dan had been warned to wait outside along with a couple of sizeable uniformed officers.

'Tony Rye, I arrest you on suspicion of the murder of Edward Bray', said Adam gravely. So that's 'taking it gently', thought Dan.

'You bastards!' bellowed Rye, and lunged towards Adam, his right fist tightly knotted and raised above his head. The detective ducked neatly inside the blow and twisted the flailing arm behind Rye's back. The uniformed officers rushed in and pinned him against a wall. One took the arm Adam held and cuffed it to Rye's other hand.

'Bastards! Wankers!' yelled Rye, his anger muffled by the pressure of the portacabin wall on his face.

'As I was saying', continued Adam smoothly to Rye's back. 'Tony Rye, I arrest you on suspicion of the murder of Edward Bray. You do not have to say anything, but it may harm your defence if you fail to mention something now you later rely on. Do you understand?' A muffled oath. 'I'll take that as a yes. Take him away please.'

The policemen bundled Tony Rye out of the portacabin and into their patrol car. 'Wankers! Wankers!' Rye spat back over his shoulder at the portacabin. 'I'll get you Breen', was the last they heard before the back door of the police car slammed.

'Well that all went smoothly', said Adam, adjusting his tie which had slid fractionally down his neck in the struggle. Suzanne Stewart nodded, jangled some keys from her pocket and headed back towards the car.

~

Penelope Ramsden's house was the last but one of a 1900's terrace in Higher Compton. It's one of Plymouth's 'wannabe' areas, almost Hartley and nearly Mannamead, but not quite either. The houses are more modest, 2 bedrooms, living room, kitchen and bathroom, and the gardens smaller than their noble high Victorian neighbours. The cars in the street told a story of enforced social mixing. By her house there was a new dark blue BMW parked next to a rusting Ford Fiesta, then a Lexus, then a 10-year-old mini.

It had been a respectable but unspectacular area of the city until the property boom made it desirable. It was almost an upmarket location but still affordable. Cheeky estate agents spotted the opportunity and marketed the area as Lower Hartley and it worked, probably because people wanted to believe it. The middle classes had moved here in numbers in the past three years. Penelope Ramsden had been here for almost fifteen.

Detective Inspector John Rose would have preferred to be in on the action of lifting Tony Rye, but that was the chief's prerogative. As Deputy Senior Investigating officer, he got the second most important job and that meant seeing Penelope Ramsden followed by Emma Paget, the Chief Executive of St Jude's hospice. He raised his fist to knock at the door, but it opened first.

He was ushered into a small sitting room and one of a pair of two seater sofas. Penelope Ramsden sat on the other. She was dressed for work and was already looking at her watch. He didn't know it, but her clothes were the ones she'd worn for Adam and Dan's visit, one of two sets, which alternated through the working week. An hour she'd said, that was all she could spare. The business wouldn't fail because of the death of Edward Bray, she owed him that. She didn't offer DI Rose tea or coffee, just an impatient stare.

He went through the questions he'd discussed with Adam and got answers he thought were satisfactory. He couldn't see any obvious evasions or lies, and you could usually tell. Usually. He wasn't sure he could with Penelope Ramsden though. The flood of emotion Adam had described had receded, there wasn't even the suggestion of upset now. She was flat and leaden, lifeless even. He'd seen it before in people who'd been bereaved. It was almost as if they ran out of tears, cried themselves out of pain. Understandable yes with a wife or husband, son or daughter he thought, but with your boss?

It was only later in the day, when he went through the interview with Adam that he thought how lucky he'd been. A chance remark, that was it, a polite comment on his way out of the door or he would have missed it. And it could be important. Perhaps he should have picked up on it sooner, it was right there in front of him, after all. But you wouldn't expect something like that, would you?

'Nice paintings Ms Ramsden', he'd said of the four portraits that hung on the walls of her living room. 'Your husband? A relative?'

She'd stared at him, first looking surprised, then amused, then starting to laugh. He was nonplussed at the change in her.

'Ms Ramsden?' He hadn't known what else to say. 'Is there a problem?'

When the laughter had subsided, she shook her head, pityingly he thought, and managed only two words. 'It's him. Him.'

'What?' He didn't understand. 'Who?'

She walked over to the biggest of the portraits, over the fireplace, stood beside it and touched its frame. Later, as wrote up his notes of the interview he decided reverent was the word to describe it.

'Him.' A soft voice, tender, a loving voice.

Suddenly he understood. 'Edward Bray?' He couldn't hide the astonishment. She nodded, smiling up at the face on the canvas. 'Mr Bray', she said, her voice lingering on the surname as if she didn't want to let it go.

He looked around at the other three portraits. He'd only really glanced over the photograph of Edward Bray in the murder room, he wasn't a missing person or criminal they were hunting after all, but now he saw the likeness. In each painting Bray stood against a different backdrop, one a coastline and blue sky, one an office full of shelves and computers. His own office? In another he leaned on a car, a Range Rover, and in the last he stood, arms folded, upright before a modern looking red brick building. In all he had that glowering, disillusioned look of the photo.

'Where did you get them?' His voice was still full of surprise.

She looked blank and shook her head. 'I didn't get them anywhere. I painted them.'

⁓

When they back got to Charles Cross, Dan expected to head straight for the interview rooms. Adam made for the canteen.

'Let's have an early lunch', he said. 'I'm peckish after all that work.'

'Good idea sir', said Suzanne Stewart. 'I'm hungry too.'

Yes sir, no sir, good idea sir. Dan had always disliked creeps. Could he file a story on Tony Rye's arrest? Of course not, he'd be chucked out of here the moment it hit the air. Food sounded a better idea. 'Fine by me', he said. He'd been too agitated by the arrest and worrying about getting a story out of the case to think of eating. He'd only just realised he was hungry. 'But what about Rye?'

'Let him sit and think for a while', said Adam. 'He can stare at the inside of an interview room. It might make him more inclined to tell us the truth.'

The police canteen was similar to the one back at the studios in its range of menu, which was limited, its prices, which were low, and Dan was subsequently to discover, its quality. He had a portion of chicken lasagne, Adam a cheese sandwich, and Suzanne Stewart the Oxtail soup and a bread roll, although Dan thought he'd seen her look longingly at the serving tray piled high with chips.

'I can't find much chicken in this lasagne', he complained. 'Is everyone else's food ok?'

'Perhaps you should try getting them under the Trades Descriptions Act', said Adam. 'Mind, I suspect you could even get them for describing themselves as a canteen. I play it safe these days and go for simple foods they're less likely to make a hash of.' He prodded the remains of his sandwich.

Suzanne Stewart paused in between her slurps of steaming soup. 'I think they do well given the number of people they have to feed. It's not easy you know.'

Dan wondered if she would disagree with everything he said. She hadn't looked at him all morning and the couple of efforts he'd made at conversation had been greeted with abrupt replies. The sympathy he'd felt after Adam's explanation of her insecurity had quickly worn off. Well, he'd tried. The memory of his victory over the hospice was still warm. He couldn't quite figure her out though. Her look at the chips but choice of soup had been interesting, but he didn't think he'd better ask why. A possible promotion bid perhaps? A new romance?

'Yes, they do pretty well Suzanne, all things considered', agreed Adam, ever the diplomat. 'We'd miss them if they weren't here. Are you enjoying the soup? It's not your usual choice.'

He'd noticed it too. Dan looked down at his lasagne to hide a smile. 'It's fine thanks sir.' Her tone said no further enquiries would be welcome.

'Ok then', said Adam. 'Let's go and see Mr Rye. He should have had plenty of time for a little think now.'

∼

The interview room was small, uncomfortable, cold and intimidating, no doubt by design thought Dan. The walls were whitewashed brick, the floor was concrete and the ceiling was low and also whitewashed. There were two fluorescent strip lights; one which had developed that almost imperceptible flickering and low buzz that said it had reached the end of its life. One tiny and grimy frosted thick glass window by the door let in some lame daylight. It was the basement of the building and felt like it.

Tony Rye was sitting on a black plastic chair by an old grey plastic topped table. He was hunched forwards, resting his head on it and didn't look up when they walked in. A uniformed policewoman stood by the door. They sat at the three chairs opposite Rye, Adam in the middle. Suzanne Stewart made a point of sitting on his right. Pathetic, thought Dan.

'Good afternoon Mr Rye', said Adam pleasantly.

'Good afternoon bollocks', said Tony Rye quietly, without raising his head.

Adam pressed a button on the tape recorder set into the wall by the table. It buzzed loudly. He introduced himself and the others in the room and gave the time, 12.30pm.

'Mr Rye, we'd like to ask you a few questions about Edward Bray', continued Adam.

'Bollocks', said Tony Rye again, but this time looking up at Adam. 'Whatever anyone's told you, or whatever you think, it's bollocks. I didn't kill him.'

'Ok then Mr Rye. But I'll be honest with you. You've made yourself a suspect by what you've said about Mr Bray, so if we're to be sure it wasn't you, you'll have to help us out.'

Tony Rye looked suspicious. 'How?' he asked.

'You'll have to tell us exactly what you were doing and we'll have to find someone who can verify your story.'

Tony Rye pushed himself violently backwards from the table. His chair scraped across the floor.

'I've told you what I was fucking doing all right. I've told you. I was doing my job. That's all I was doing. I never saw Bray. I never killed Bray. I never done nothing to Bray. Yes I hated the bastard. But loads of people hated him. Go and ask them if they killed him. It weren't me, alright?'

He got up angrily from his chair and stalked over to the wall, which he kicked out at with the sole of his boot. It left a crescent of dry mud. He turned round and glared at them, breathing hard. His face had turned puce.

'Ok Mr Rye, calm down please', said Adam. 'As I said, I'll try to help you. If we can find someone who can verify your movements last Monday, that'll be it. You'll be in the clear and we'll leave you alone.'

'Thank Christ for that', grunted Tony Rye.

'Now, please come back and sit down and take us through Monday afternoon again.'

The door opened behind them and a plain clothed man came in. 'Mr Breen, can I have a quick word please. It's important', he said. Adam got up and went outside, followed by Dan and Suzanne.

'Yes Jim?' said Adam.

'Preliminary results from the search of Rye's house sir. Not a thing. No guns, no weapons of any kind. No clothing with any suspicious marks. Nothing about Bray at all.'

'Great', said Adam. 'Not helpful.'

'The team did get a right ear bashing from Mrs Rye though', said the man. 'The boys said they've never heard language like it, and that's saying something. She followed them round the house screaming at them.'

'Right', said Adam. 'That makes sense. Mr Rye is a fan of colourful language too.'

Another man was walking hurriedly up the grey corridor towards them. He was panting.

'Mr Breen!'

'Yes Sam', said Adam patiently, turning to him.

'Something from the team who've been speaking to a couple of Rye's friends. He has used a shotgun sir. They've been out shooting rabbits a couple of times. They said he hasn't got a gun of his own. He borrows theirs apparently, but he hasn't for several months. We had a look at the gun and we've sent it to the labs, but it looks pretty obvious it hasn't been fired for weeks.'

'Right', said Adam again, looking thoughtful. He straightened his tie. 'That's useful, thanks.'

The two men walked off up the corridor.

'Where does that leave us?' asked Dan, who was getting fed up with trying to read Adam's thoughts. Suzanne Stewart glared at him.

'I'm not sure Dan. I was hoping we'd find something in Rye's house, but I didn't think we would. It could mean he's innocent of course. On the other hand, he's not stupid and it could just mean he's been very careful with his planning.'

'The shotgun thing's interesting though?' persisted Dan, ignoring another glare from his left.

'Interesting yes, but again not exactly hard evidence. He doesn't seem to have a shotgun of his own. We haven't found one and he's got no licence. That doesn't of course mean he couldn't just have bought one, used it to shoot Bray and then dumped it.' He turned back to the interview room door. 'It does help us that he's used one. It's something I think I'll drop into the interview in a while. Let's get on with it.'

They sat back down at the table. Tony Rye looked even more suspicious now.

'What've you been up to?'

'It's nothing for you to worry about Mr Rye', said Adam, more in the manner of a doctor at a bedside than a detective hunting a killer. 'Just routine police work.'

'Bollocks', said Tony Rye again, but this time sounding resigned.

'Ok Mr Rye', said Adam. 'I said I'll be honest with you. That conversation was with a police officer who's supervising a team searching your house.'

'You what?' shouted Tony Rye, jumping to his feet again, and sending his chair tipping over. He leered over them. 'Get those bastards out of my house!'

Dan felt ready to jump up himself. The tension in the room was stifling. Tony Rye stalked back over to the wall and pounded a clenched fist against it.

'Calm down Mr Rye', said Adam evenly. 'This isn't helping. As I explained to you, you're a suspect so we have to check. We have a search warrant. Nothing in your house will be damaged It'll be left exactly as we found it. But we have to check.'

From the wall, Tony Rye mumbled something Dan couldn't catch. Adam either had better hearing or just more experience of similar confrontations.

'As for what else we've been investigating Mr Rye, well, something interesting's come up. You like shooting, don't you? You like using a shotgun?'

'What?' said Tony Rye.

'Shooting. Rabbits. With a shotgun.'

There was a silence as Adam and Tony Rye stared at each other. He walked back over to the table and sat down. Dan felt Adam stiffen slightly beside him, but outwardly the detective was impassive.

'Who told you that?' said Tony Rye quietly.

'That's not important', said Adam. 'But it's true, isn't it?'

'So what if it is?'

'Edward Bray was killed with a shotgun.'

Dan tensed, expecting another explosion of anger but it seemed Tony Rye had tired of raging.

'And?' he said simply.

'You don't have a shotgun Mr Rye?'

'You know damn well I don't.'

'You borrowed a friend's when you went shooting?'

'Yeah.'

'And you haven't borrowed it recently?'

'Not for months.'

'And you haven't been shooting at all recently.'

'Not for months.'

Adam considered. 'Ok then. So let's go back over what you were doing on Monday afternoon.'

'I've already told you all this. I got some tiles, then went back to Moretonhampstead to do some shopping and drop them off at the pool.'

'Right. Well, we've checked all that and you'll be glad to know your story is backed up by the people in the shop and the CCTV they have.'

'It ain't my story. It's what happened.'

'Sorry, yes, of course.' Adam's tone was almost sarcastic. 'But you see there's still a problem Mr Rye. According to the CCTV you bought those tiles at 4.24. Then you loaded them up into your van, which I'd say was a ten-minute job. Then you left Ivybridge just after that.'

'And?'

'And you say you went back to Moretonhampstead to do some shopping.'

'Yeah, that's right.'

Softly now, baiting the trap. 'But here's a funny thing Mr Rye. We've checked in all the shops, and no one remembers seeing you. No one at all. And how many shops did you go into?

'Two or three.'

'And no one saw you.'

Adam let the words linger in the air. The sting was coming.

'Were you really there Mr Rye?'

'Yeah! Yeah, I was. What are you trying to say?'

'Well, it's just we think Mr Bray was killed at about 5.15 that evening.'

'And?'

'Well, perhaps it's my imagination, but run with it for a moment', said Adam. His tone had gone from friendly and confiding to cold. 'I'd say if you left Ivybridge at about 4.35, or 4.40, you'd be able to get to the lay by where Mr Bray was shot for about five. That'd be just happily in time to check that nice new shotgun you've bought over the internet. Just in time to lie in wait for Mr Bray. Just in time to shoot him dead when he pulled in to the lay by and got out of his car.'

'You bastard!' screamed Tony Rye, jumping to his feet. And this time Adam jumped up too and faced him over the table. The men's faces were inches apart. Neither flinched nor drew back. Dan held his breath.

'And then you can drive back, dump the gun in some nice stream or gully on Dartmoor and be home in time for tea eh?'

'You sick bastard', spat Tony Rye. 'I didn't kill him. I didn't kill him all right? He deserved it, but I didn't kill him.'

'You like that thought of him being shot though don't you Mr Rye? You like the idea of him lying on the ground, gasping for breath, screaming in pain, his cries unheard, his life blood pouring out of him onto the cold tarmac, him dying in the dark and rain, alone in a lay by, dying?'

'You're sick, fucking sick! You're supposed to be a copper, but you're sick!'

Tony Rye's face was throbbing red. Adam's was taught, the lines around his brow and mouth pronounced. He moved his eyes an inch closer to Tony Rye's. They were almost touching. Adam's voice fell to a whisper.

'Then why else did you go back to the lay by at the weekend Mr Rye?'

He paused to let his words sink in.

'You went to have a nice gloat didn't you, a nice gloat about your excellent handiwork in killing Edward Bray. Get off on it did you?'

'What?' said Tony Rye, his voice almost as quiet as Adam's.

'You went back to the lay by, didn't you? You drove through, nice and slowly. Savouring the moment were you? You just couldn't resist it could you? Did it give you a thrill? Don't bother denying it Mr Rye, a police officer was following you. We've got chapter and verse. You'd think killers would have learned by now not to go back to the scene, but they never do.'

'I didn't kill him!' screamed Tony Rye, his clenched fist crashing down on the table. 'I didn't!! You're trying to fit me up you bastards! All right, I went to the lay by and yes I enjoyed it. I fucking loved it. I wanted to see where the bastard died, and I loved it. But I didn't kill him, all right?!'

Adam took a breath and slowly sat down. Tony Rye seemed unsure what to do. He clenched his fists again and then also sat down. His chest was heaving.

'Thank you Mr Rye', said Adam, his usual calm restored. 'You can go now. I'll get an officer to drive you home.'

'What?' said Tony Rye, looking more surprised and suspicious than at any time during the interview.

'You can go home now. Thank you for your time.'

'That's it?'

'That's it', replied Adam. 'For now', he added ominously.

'You ain't going to charge me?'

'Do you think we should?'

'Fuck you', said Tony Rye bitterly.

~

John Rose didn't know whether to say he was suffering or enjoying a day of surprises. Emma Paget was not what he expected in a Chief Executive of a hospice, not at all. He knew he shouldn't allow himself preconceptions. It was a sure way to drop a balls, but he also knew it was human nature, even for detectives. You could be aware of it, guard against it, but it could still get you.

She was young, late 30s he reckoned, pretty, and very thin too. He liked that. Self-consciously his hands cradled his burgeoning stomach. Mrs Rose had commented on it more than a couple of times, and with Christmas coming too, he'd have to be careful. A diet beckoned, but it could wait until after the holiday. He liked his turkey and mince pies too much to start yet. Not to mention the whisky.

Her hair was dark, full and slightly wavy, and it brushed the tops of her shoulders with what DI Rose thought was an erotic touch. She had that olive skin that makes women the envy of others and is so often on magazine covers, a hint of some Mediterranean family perhaps? Her eyes were hazel, the eyebrows elegantly plucked to dark rainbows, and her nose was slender. Her suit was black to complement her hair, with a pearl white blouse. She wore no jewellery he noticed, particularly no wedding ring. He reminded himself he was married, and a Detective Inspector investigating a murder, although not necessarily in that order.

If he had any thoughts along the lines of the old 'what's a nice girl like you doing in a place like this', they were quickly neutered by her manner.

'I didn't like him, but we needed him.' Her voice was frank, disarming. 'That's the way it is in business. You don't have to be friends to be partners.'

DI Rose took hurried notes. He didn't want to spend all of this interview looking down at his book. 'What didn't you like about him?'

Emma Paget shuffled some papers on her desk, then found the one she was looking for. Her office was small and simple, just a desk, a computer, a couple of slightly padded wooden seats the other side. He sat on one, facing her. He feared his backside was spreading out onto the other chair and tucked his trousers around him. He hoped she hadn't noticed.

'My proposals', she quoted, 'are as follows'. She looked up. 'That's why Inspector. He wanted to run this place his way. He thought I wasn't up to the job and the hospice wasn't 'maximising its potential'. That's how he put it. 'Maximising its potential'. She dropped the paper and flicked at it angrily. DI Rose tried not to like the way she did it.

'I ask you Inspector! This is a hospice. The people in here are dying. They're not TVs, or circuit boards, or packets of bacon. You can't measure productivity in a hospice. We give them the loving care they need for as long as they need it. It's not a factory line. We don't give them 20 minutes and then turf them out.'

DI Rose was scribbling quickly. 'What were his proposals Ms Paget?'

'Please, call me Emma.'

He'd hoped she'd ask. 'Sorry, Emma.'

'I won't bore you with the details Inspector, unless you really want to know.' A nod and smile indicated he did. 'Very well then'. She sighed and picked up the discarded sheet. "Accommodation too generous. Smaller units equals more customers and throughput'. Did you hear that? Not patients, but customers. 'Reception areas also too generous, see above. Questionable overstaffing issue. Part of grounds prime for development.''

She looked up from the paper. 'In short Inspector, he wanted to take the place over and run it like a business. He seemed to think the fact that his mother was cared for here and he helped us with the donation and then fundraising and advice gave him free reign to take over the place.' So his mother was here, thought John Rose. That's one question answered.

She shook her head, sending her hair tussling across her shoulders. 'Well I put him straight on that anyway.' She smiled and her face warmed. 'In a nice way of course.'

DI Rose forced himself to stop thinking about her hair and concentrate on the case. 'So you had an uneasy relationship?' He regretted the cliché as soon as he'd said it.

She laughed, a gentle and elegant chuckle. It reminded him of a babbling brook.

'You could put it that way Inspector. Screaming rows would be more like it though. He used to phone or call in when he wanted and I had to make sure he felt welcome and valued for all he's done for us, but also make it clear we weren't going to carry out the changes he wanted.' She sighed. 'It wasn't an easy balance. He did save us with a very large financial gift, that is absolutely true, and we will always be grateful for it. But there are limits. That didn't mean he could take over the place. That's not how charity works, but business people don't always see it that way. He meant well Inspector, don't get me wrong and we are – sorry we were – grateful for his help. But he did only see things from a business perspective, and that's just not what you need when you're running a place where people come to ease their fear and escape the lingering threat of death.'

DI Rose shivered. He almost looked over his shoulder to see if the grim reaper was waiting there outside her office.

'Just one more thing, if you don't mind Emma?' He enjoyed using the name. She smiled and he wondered if she could tell. 'Did he ever say why he saved the hospice?'

She looked puzzled, shrugged. 'No, not really. Because his mum came here to die I assume? He never went into details. He wasn't that kind of person Inspector. He was only young when she passed away. I assume it was from gratitude for what the hospice did for her, but I couldn't tell you for sure.'

⁓

Back in the canteen they each had a coffee. Adam leaned back on his chair looking relaxed, Suzanne Stewart stirred a sweetener into her decaffeinated drink, and Dan fiddled with the edge of his polystyrene cup, unsure what to make of the confrontation. At least the canteen drinks were better than the food.

'We can't charge him on that sir,' said Suzanne Stewart.

Adam smiled. 'We can't even hold him on that Suzanne. We've still got basically nothing. But not to worry. I didn't expect a confession. We've ratcheted up the pressure on him and that sometimes pushes people into making mistakes. We'll keep the tail on him and see what he does.'

Another possible story gone, thought Dan. 'A man's been charged with the murder of the Plymouth businessman Edward Bray', he could imagine the newsreader saying. 'Tonight we have an exclusive report from our correspondent Dan Groves..' Lizzie nodding in the background, pleased. No chance of that now. So then, what could he do? Stick with the investigation and hope something comes up. What else was there?

They sipped at their drinks. He was caught between wanting to say something about Tony Rye and fearing the reaction of the two professional detectives.

'I, I erm..' he began, deterred by another glare from Suzanne, then annoyed with himself for being put off.

'Yes Dan?' said Adam. 'Come on, I told you at the start I wanted to hear what you thought. Try me.'

'This may just be my inexperience of these situations, but I believed him. I could see myself doing the same thing and going to have a look if there was someone I hated that much who was killed. I know it's morbid, but it's a kind of human nature thing. Not nice I know', continued Dan defensively in response to Adam's raised eyebrow, 'but sort of understandable. We have it all the time when we cover big stories. People come from miles around to visit the scene.'

Suzanne Stewart snorted. 'He's a born liar', she said. 'They all do it. Whatever you put to them, they invent some explanation. It's just like they're facing a jury in court. I've seen it so many times it's untrue. Born liars.'

'You may be right Suzanne', said Adam, finishing his coffee. 'There are lots of reasons why our man Tony Rye might be the killer. But there are also lots of reasons why he might not. Let's keep working on the case and come up with some real evidence that might get us a conviction. We'll keep the tail on him and do some more work on his background. In the meantime, let's have a look at the other possible suspects and see who we can rule in or out.'

'Yes sir', said Suzanne Stewart with no hint of dissent. She opened her notebook. Dan wasn't surprised to see a list of names, each in capitals with lines of neat writing below them. There were a couple of asterisks dotted around too.

'This is how it looks so far. James Stead and Andrew Hicks are out. They've both got good alibis from each other, and, more importantly, the woman in the shop. We've checked if there were any taxis or hire cars or anything like that which could have got them to the lay by in time to kill Bray and we came up with nothing. We're waiting for the analysis of their mobiles to confirm they weren't at the lay by, but I think they're very unlikely, bordering on out.'

'Ok', said Adam, jotting a line down in his notebook.

'We've checked on the bits Gordon Clarke told you too. He used his debit card to buy his ticket to Bristol at Plymouth station in the morning. He used his cash point card to get some money out at Bristol Temple Meads at about 5 o'clock and he sent a text on the train on the way home which his secretary confirms came from him. So I think he's out.'

'Ok', said Adam again, scribbling another note.

'Then there's Arthur Bray. He has no alibi at all for the time his son was killed. He says he was at home, but there's no one to verify that. Also, he has a couple of shotguns which forensics say have been fired recently, and as we know, he didn't like his son. So I think we have to consider him a suspect.'

'Yes', said Adam, not bothering to make a note this time. 'Agreed.'

Suzanne Stewart nodded. 'Then there's Tony Rye, who I think we still consider our chief suspect', she said, with a glance at Dan.

'Right', said Adam.

'So far, the theory about the 999 call that led us to Bray's body being from the killer or an accomplice to give them an alibi has come to nothing. We haven't got any joy from the cancelled appointment a week before the killing either. We haven't found anyone who would need the body found at a precise time to establish an alibi, nor anyone who had a sudden emergency, or something like that, the week before which might make it impossible for them to take part in the killing.

'Ok', said Adam. 'But make sure the team keep them in mind please, they're still good possibilities.'

'Yes sir. Finally, there are a few other people we need to talk to who might be suspects. There are some from the big crowd of people he's upset in his dealings, and a couple of business rivals too.'

'Ok then Suzanne, you get the team onto those', said Adam. 'I'm going back to the Murder Room to work through what we have. Dan, you can help me with another idea. It's time we made a bit more use of your inside track on the media. I need a big splash of publicity and you're the man to deliver it.'

A wave of relief hit him. Thank God for that, he thought. A story, a precious story. I knew one day I'd be lucky.

Chapter twelve

Dan's mobile rang as soon as he arrived at work the next morning. He glared at it, but thought he'd better answer. It was a Dartmoor number, Arthur Bray's, and he knew just what he wanted. He was the cause of it.

'Mr Groves? It's Arthur Bray here, Edward's father.'

'Hello Mr Bray, and do please call me Dan. Everyone else does, if not worse.' The joke went unnoticed. 'It's good to speak to you again. How can I help you?'

'I don't know what to do Dan I'm sorry to trouble you but you were so kind to me when we met, telling me I could call you if I needed to talk about anything. I've got no one else to talk to you see.'

Don't overdo it, that was in case you were useful for any more stories, he thought. It was always worth leaving a card, you never knew.

'Arthur, it's no trouble', he said, sitting down at his desk and starting the laborious process of logging into the computer system. It wanted him to choose a new password. He agonised about passwords. The golden combination of memorable, yet difficult for others to guess always eluded him.

'The police have called to ask me if I would come into Plymouth for a news conference they're holding later today. They want to do another appeal for witnesses, and they said it would be much more powerful if I was there. I told them I'd think about it overnight but I don't know if I can face it. Do you think I should? Was it of any use last time?'

Nice dilemma, thought Dan who had planned the news conference with Adam yesterday.

'Yes I do Arthur.' At least he could be honest, if not telling the whole truth. 'For all the police can sit there and talk to the media, nothing has the same impact as someone who knew Edward well. It often helps bring witnesses forward and sometimes they can give vital information. It's not for me to advise you to do it, but I can honestly tell you it could help.'

'Then I'll do it', said Arthur Bray resolutely. 'Thank you so much for your help.'

'Mr Bray, sorry, Arthur?' said Dan, before he rang off.

'Yes?'

'Don't be surprised if one of the journalists asking you questions is me. I'm sure we'll want to cover the press conference', said Dan, who'd arranged it with Lizzie last night.

'Of course Dan, that's no problem at all. I'll be delighted to see you again.'

Dan stared at the computer screen whilst a procession of words bounded through his head. They'd had a couple of attempted break ins to their computers recently and a memo had come round about choosing a password wisely. It had told him not to do exactly what he'd always done. The names of partners, pets, or simply the word 'sex' were banned. They were far too easily guessed.

He'd found it amusing as he often measured the success of his love life by his current password. If he was seeing a woman, it would generally be her name. When the affair came to an end, it would usually be Rutherford. The best passwords, he had been advised by the pompous memo, were misspelt words, combined with some punctuation and numbers.

He mixed the advice with a little of his tradition and came up with Kez,69, the year of his birth. He thought he would remember, but wrote it down in his diary anyway, in exactly the way the memo had said you never should.

He looked up to find Lizzie bearing down on him. Her hair was tied up and her heels were particularly high, a pair of danger warnings.

'It's 11, this presser?'

'Yes, 11 at Charles Cross. I reckon I'll have enough time to get it on the lunchtime news.'

'Good', she said. He thought she sounded like a sergeant major. 'Any family there?'

'His Dad.'

'The chap we interviewed before?'

'Yes.'

'Good. Liked him. He was very strong. Any idea what the cops are going to say?'

Dan had a very good idea as he'd spent a couple of hours of the previous afternoon going through the best way to get maximum media coverage with Adam. He wasn't going to tell Lizzie that. She wouldn't care for being set up. Best to let her think the contacts he'd been building had given him an exclusive insight into the police's strategy.

'They're going to take the line that they fear witnesses aren't coming forward because Edward Bray was not well liked.'

'So it'll be 'He might have been a bastard, but he didn't deserve to die?''

'Yes', said Dan, who had predicted exactly that headline to Adam.

An eyebrow rose. 'Excellent.' She turned to go, but then stopped and wheeled back. 'And we're going to keep quiet about your closeness to the investigation?'

'Yes. It's best for all concerned I think. I don't want the other journalists trying anything similar, and we don't want to put the police in an awkward position if anyone asks. I'll just report what happens as straight and honestly as ever.'

The eyebrow rose further into its customary arch and Lizzie walked purposefully away. She stopped at the sports desk and began a haranguing about the cliché-ridden coverage of the weekend's football. Dan felt glad he was on his way out of the newsroom.

~

The plan worked. When a police press officer escorted Dan and Nigel into the Murder Room just before 11, it was already full of journalists. There were also a couple of other camera crews and several photographers, Dirty El amongst them. Dan noticed he was sporting what looked like a new black eye. He sidled over as Nigel set up the camera.

'So then?' said Dan quietly into his ear.

'So then what?' El looked defiant.

'Your new eye make up?' He pointed at the shiner and El flinched back. 'A jealous husband of some unfortunate female you've been wooing?' asked Dan, safe in the knowledge that wouldn't be the reason.

'No way. It was some bloody drug dealer. I was outside the Crown Court trying to get a snap of him and he smacked my lens so the camera went right in my eye. Bastard. Mind you, I had the last laugh. The place was full of cops and they arrested him for assault.'

Dan couldn't hold back a chuckle. 'It's getting increasingly dangerous to be seen in public with you El, let alone out for a beer.'

'Occupational hazard mate', said El grinning. 'I got the snap, and it'll be worth a few quid for me when he goes down. I might even get some damages for the assault too.'

'Any news of that political job?'

El shook his head. 'Not yet, but should have some time later in the week. I've got a plan.' He stroked his camera lens lovingly.

A uniformed police press officer opened the door of the murder room at precisely 11 and Adam walked in, followed by Arthur Bray and Suzanne Stewart. Dan was relieved to see Adam wearing the same suit as the day they had first met, although the tie was new, dark blue, no doubt to match the sobriety of the occasion. So his wardrobe did have some limits.

Adam and Arthur Bray sat down at a table that had been put in front of the felt boards. Suzanne Stewart remained standing by the door. Dan noticed the names of the suspects and those connected with the case had been removed and replaced by Devon and Cornwall Police posters. They were all commitment to community beat officers, tackling yobbish behaviour and safer citizens. Smiling constables helped old ladies across roads and joined in football kick abouts with youngsters.

Adam surveyed the crowded room and gave Dan an almost imperceptible nod.

'Ladies and gentlemen, I'm Detective Chief Inspector Adam Breen', he began. 'I'm the senior officer investigating the murder of Edward Bray. This is Arthur Bray, Edward's father. I'll make a short statement to bring you up to date with the case. Then Mr Bray will say a few words, then we'll take your questions.'

Adam paused at the television cameras whirred into action. A series of photographers' flashes strobed across the room.

'We now think Edward Bray was killed at about 5.15 at a lay by on the A 38 just outside Plymouth last Monday', he intoned. 'The murder weapon was a shotgun. It has not been recovered.' Adam looked around the room. 'We need to find that gun. A total of 50 officers are now working on the case and we are determined to find the killer.' A pause. 'We will find the killer.'

Adam paused again as the journalists scribbled into their notebooks. Dan knew what was coming next – he'd written it - but he couldn't help admiring the drama of Adam's delivery. A Shakespearean actor would have been proud.

'This was a vicious and shocking attack, make no mistake about it. The victim was gunned down in cold blood as he got out of his car by a busy main road. It was clearly well planned. Some witnesses have come forward to help us, but not as many as I might hope for such a violent killing.' A pause, a look around the room, eye contact for all the hacks. 'My fear is this. Edward Bray was not a well-liked man. His business dealings could make him unpopular. Some people may have thought he got what was coming to him and so haven't come forward to give us any information that could help us. Edward Bray may not have been an angel in many people's eyes, but whoever killed him was ruthless and cold in the way they did it. I do not like the thought of that person being out there, free, walking the streets. So if you can help us, I would appeal to you, please do get in touch.'

Arthur Bray took the end of Adam's speech as his cue, and began to read from his prepared statement.

'What Mr Breen said about Edward was true. He wasn't always the easiest person to know. He had enemies. But I don't care about that. He was my son. He was my only child, and my son. Not a day goes past now without me thinking about the day when he first walked, or our first family holiday, or his graduation from University. They're happy memories, but now they've all been tainted by the agony of what happened to him.'

Arthur Bray's voice faltered and tears began to run down his cheeks. Dan thought he could scarcely have cued them better. He heard the motor of the camera whir as Nigel zoomed the picture in for the dramatic full screen close up of the old man's face.

'Whatever anyone may have thought of Edward, he was my son. He was my son and he didn't deserve to die. He didn't deserve to have someone blast him with a shotgun, and then leave him to die, alone, in the dark on a cold and wet road.'

Arthur Bray hunched forward, sobbing quietly into the table. Suzanne Stewart walked quickly over to him and took him by the arm. He stumbled up looking pitifully lost. He glanced forlornly around the room before she led him out of the door, his tears beginning to stain his beige jacket. For one of the very few times in his experience of the media, Dan looked around to see the room hushed by the old man's pain.

∼

Back at the studios, he sat with a picture editor and they put the story together for the lunchtime news. It was easy work, one of those rare reports where the person speaking was so powerful Dan had to add only a couple of bits of commentary, a quick recap on the murder. It made the lead report, and was followed by the Crimestoppers phone number for people to call if they had any information that could help the inquiry.

His computer terminal flashed up a message from Lizzie. 'Great stuff, real tearjerker. Top work. More please.'

She was never satisfied, he thought. The story was strong and the boss was happy, or at least as happy as Lizzie ever was. At least she was off his back for a while.

But he didn't feel any pleasure. He felt cheapened. Twice now he'd profited from Arthur Bray's distress. It was a feeling he'd known several times before and he welcomed the discomfort it brought. For him it was a sign he was a human being first and a journalist a long way second. May it remain ever thus.

A similar report was broadcast on South West Tonight, this time a little longer, with more of Adam's speech. Again it was the lead item, again with the accompanying phone number. That evening as he lay on his great blue sofa, listening to Paul Simon's 'Live in New York' CD, he called Adam. He dipped the sound of the track, 'She Moves On', a wonderful evocation of summer nights and lost love. It reminded him of Thomasin and university days. Happier days..

'Hi mate, Dan here', he said, as Adam answered. 'I just wanted to check with you how the appeal went?'

'Brilliantly Dan, it went brilliantly. You've done us proud. It was the lead story for you and the local BBC TV. It's been all over the radio stations all day, and I'm told it'll be one of the main items in the papers tomorrow. No one could miss it. It worked exactly as you said it would. I'm really grateful.'

'Thanks Adam, but you don't have to be. You've helped me enough by having me along, and with all you've shown me about how you investigate cases. I'm the one who should be grateful and I am.'

'It's been a pleasure Dan. I mean that.'

He felt oddly touched. 'So, most importantly then, did you get any new leads?'

'Aha! Ever the journalist, you ask the killer question.' Adam sounded buoyant. 'Well, Suzanne and some of the other detectives are going through the calls now, but she's already rung me to say we've got some very interesting stuff. A couple of people called naming suspects. Some of them are people we've already looked at, but some aren't. So we've got some new stuff to check there. One even says a couple of people were overheard talking about killing Bray in a pub. That's a priority. And a woman called saying it wasn't Tony Rye and she could prove it. Now that will be interesting too. We're going to go through them all in more detail tomorrow and start following them up. Do you want to come in on it?'

He remembered a favourite phrase of his dad's. Do bears shit in the woods?

'Yes, I'd very much like that. The usual time and place?'

'Yes, it's worked well so far. See you tomorrow.'

He ended the call and lay back on the sofa. He hadn't realised he'd been sitting up to talk to Adam. A sign of respect, or excitement about the case?

He tickled Rutherford's ears and decided it was time to do what he'd been debating all evening. 'Toilet hound', he said getting up and opening the front door. Rutherford disappeared around the corner of the flat and scrabbied down the concrete steps to the back garden.

Initially he'd thought it would have to be one or the other tonight, but now he didn't see why it couldn't be both. It was still early, and they'd both be pleased to see him.

Rutherford padded back into the flat. 'I'm off out, back later old fellow and maybe not alone, so look after the place'. He gave the dog a wink, picked his mobile up from the lounge table and typed a quick text message as he got into the Peugeot. Both the things he had in mind he was far less than sure he should be doing, but he was going to do them anyway.

Chapter thirteen

He awoke early despite not getting much sleep, and was startled by the whispery breathing next to him. It took him a few seconds to remember the night before and why he wasn't alone in his bed.

Kerry was lying on her side, facing away from him, her blonde hair played out in a halo on the pillow. Dan felt an instinctive desire to reach out and hold her, but he resisted it. She was sound asleep, and anyway, if he was honest, the morning always restored the defences the night's loneliness had weakened. He put a finger to his lips, whispered a 'shhh' at the stirring Rutherford and slid out of the bed.

He left a note in the kitchen in case she should wake and they ran for a couple of miles. Winter was pressing irresistibly on, and the first frost of the season sparkled on the car windscreens. The air was clear and the sky the virgin blue that only lasts an hour before the day's sullying reach. The sun was rising across to the east, over Dartmoor, but it had yet to stretch to the ragged skyline of the city's houses, flats and offices. Their breath left condensation clouds as they jogged along the pavements. The cold stabbed at Dan's lungs, and he decided they'd avoid Plymouth's hills today and keep their run as short and flat as possible.

When they got back to the flat she was still sleeping, so Dan put the kettle on and noisily made some tea. She was sitting up in bed when he brought the steaming mug in.

'Good morning', she said. 'What a sleep. You must have tired me out.'

Dan sat on the bed beside her, feeling awkward. Last night the sliding towards a relationship had seemed easy and natural. He'd enjoyed it. Not so now. This morning he felt he'd silently promised her something he couldn't - or, more likely, wouldn't - deliver.

'Are you ok?' she said, putting a hand on his leg.

'Fine yes, fine. I'm just a little puffed out by the run and preoccupied thinking of work today.' It was a time-honoured excuse, and she knew it.

'I know you're busy. I'll get up in a sec and be off. I've got to get to work too.'

'You don't have to.' He put on his best smile. 'There's no rush.'

'I know, I know. But we've both got lots to do, so I'd better be going. I'll have a shower at home', she said, pulling on her jeans.

He tried not to sound relieved. 'Sure, if you've got to get on, that's no problem.'

She slid a jumper over the T-shirt she'd borrowed from him. 'I'm keeping this for now though', she said playfully, gently poking his ribs. 'Call it a hostage to make sure you see me again.'

'You don't have to worry about that. Of course I will.' Was it a lie? He didn't know. He'd work that out later. The sex had been good though.

～

The Murder Room was the busiest Dan had seen it. There were about 40 people crowded in, mostly men, but at least half a dozen women. The room quietened a little when he walked in, but the background banter quickly resumed. Dan took it as a sign he was becoming accepted. Detectives adjusted fast. They had to.

He navigated his way through the crowd to his favourite part of the window and leaned against it. Adam stood before the boards at the front of the room, quietly discussing a piece of paper with Suzanne Stewart. The names of the suspects were back up, and more pieces of card had been added to the tapestry overnight.

'Ok everybody, let's make a start then.' Adam waited for the rumble of conversation to die away. 'We've got some good new leads, thanks to yesterday's media appeal.' Dan kept his eyes straight ahead but was aware of some looks cast his way. 'That's where we focus today. Suzanne will take you through them.'

Adam retreated to the side of the boards and Suzanne Stewart took his place. She looked at the piece of A4 paper she was holding, hesitated, then began, her voice faltering slightly as she tried to project it through the crowded room. Dan was surprised to feel some sympathy for her. She looked acutely nervous in the face of this gathering and kept picking at the sleeve of her grey suit jacket.

'Some very interesting information has come in overnight', she said, her voice gaining strength by the word. Adam nodded encouragingly. 'We have several new people we need to speak to. And we have some people we've seen before who we need to go back to and check new information with. These are the headlines.' She looked at Dan, but he couldn't read whether it was a deliberate gibe.

'Our chief suspect remains Tony Rye', she continued. 'But we've had an odd call from a woman. She wouldn't give her name, but she seemed very calm and plausible. She said it wasn't him. It was a brief call and she would give no other details apart from that she knew we suspected him, but she could prove he wasn't the killer.'

'What do we make of that then?' asked Adam, now standing at Suzanne Stewart's side.

'Could be a crank', said one of the women detectives from the back of the room. 'It sounds like a classic time waster. She's heard some gossip about us bringing him in and wants to put us off the scent.'

'Yes Claire, it could be that. We certainly have enough of them. Any other thoughts anyone?'

'What about a mistress?' asked an older, and balding man at the front. 'It could be she loves him and wants to clear him, but can't give us any more info because it would give her away to his wife. He might have been with her at the time.'

'Indeed Jack', said Adam. 'That's what I was thinking. Well there's only one person we can ask about that, and it's Mr Rye himself. I don't think he'd welcome another visit from me – funnily enough he doesn't seem to like me - so you can do that one. Take Claire with you please.'

'Yes sir', said the detective, looking pleased.

'Next', said Suzanne Stewart, consulting her piece of paper, 'is some information about Arthur Bray. A couple of people have called in to say he used to have blazing rows with his son and had even threatened to kill him if he came back to his house again. As we know, Mr Bray possesses two shotguns, both of which have recently been fired, although he says they were used for shooting rabbits. So we need to go and see him again.'

Dan looked down and tried to disguise the slow shaking of his head. After last night he knew Arthur Bray hadn't killed his son and that he could prove it. He also now understood why Edward Bray had saved St Jude's, and it had been a surprise, not what he suspected at all. Families, you never knew what went on in them.

He hated the thought of the old man breaking down in front of a suspicious and unsympathetic police officer. He was sure they wouldn't understand, even if Arthur told them his story. A very big if. He'd probably just cry again and he'd cried too much these last few days, most recently in the hard eyes of the media. That was enough. He thought about speaking up about what he'd found out but knew he couldn't. He was still just an amateur here. What he had to say would be better done quietly, in person with Adam. He wasn't quite sure how the Detective Chief Inspector would react to him conducting his own personal investigations either.

'Suzanne, I'd like you to do that one. I think something as difficult as that needs your experience', said Adam. She nodded, also looking pleased.

'Great', he muttered under his breath. That's going to make telling Adam even harder, but I'll have to, before Suzanne Stewart gets to Arthur Bray and makes a fool of herself. Look at her, proud at being chosen for the job. She'll love me for this, just love me.

'Then we have a call saying Andrew Hicks and James Stead had been overhead in their local pub talking about killing Edward Bray', continued Suzanne Stewart, gaining in confidence now and making eye contact with detectives all around the room. 'We've already checked them out as you know, and their alibis are strong, but we need to go back to them to double check, and to see whether they could even have had some part in someone else killing Bray.'

'I'm going to do that one', said Adam, raising a few surprised looks around the room. 'I know it scarcely looks like the most important inquiry, but I haven't spoken to those two yet, and I'd like to meet them.' Dan caught his look and guessed that would be his task too.

'We have a couple of very interesting calls about Gordon Clarke', said Suzanne Stewart with an air of coming to the end of her list. 'Both are anonymous, but their information tallies. They say he was having a relationship with a woman who's an interior designer Edward Bray employed on some of his more upmarket flat conversion jobs.' She looked down at her notes. 'Her name is Kate Moore. Now here's the interesting bit. Bray was suing her for some of the work she'd done. He said it was shoddy, didn't have the appeal she'd promised, and it was putting people off renting the places. We know how litigious he was and the courts have confirmed he had issued a writ. He also cancelled another big contract she was due to get. So there's a motive there for both of them. We need to see her and find out what she was doing last Monday. And we need to see him again. He's got a strong alibi. As we know, he was in Bristol. But again, that's not to say he couldn't have had a hand in some plot to kill Bray, with someone else doing the actual killing.'

'Again with that one I think it's better if someone other than myself sees Mr Clarke, and finds Ms Moore.' Adam gestured towards two detectives standing at the back of the room. 'So Bill and Trevor, that's yours.'

Suzanne Stewart scribbled a note on her piece of paper and adjusted her plain silver necklace as she waited for Adam to finish. It was the first jewellery Dan had seen her wear. He thought back to the canteen and her choice of soup. Must be a new man. You don't wear necklaces to help a promotion bid, do you?

'Lastly', she said, 'a couple more bits have come up which name other people as having possible motives, or having at some time said something about wanting to see Edward Bray dead. These are probably less likely, but we have to go through them. That's what the rest of you will be doing.'

Adam moved back to his general's position at the centre of the boards. Suzanne dutifully stood aside. 'There are a couple of final matters, concerning Penelope Ramsden and the hospice, but again, I want to have a look at those myself.' He looked around the room. 'So, any questions?'

There was a general rumble of 'no'.

'Right', said Adam, straightening his tie. 'Go find the killer. That's all I can say. Go get them. But before you do, don't forget that we may have plenty of suspects, but we still have no real evidence for a conviction. And I don't think we'll get it. So cracking this one's going to come down to good police work. Hunt out the inconsistencies, sniff out the evasions and try to sense the murderer. Then ask the right questions, put on the pressure and let's see if we can get someone to give themselves away. That's our best hope. Good luck to you all.'

Stirring, almost Churchillian, thought Dan admiringly. He could see from how quickly the roomful of detectives clustered around Suzanne Stewart for details of their assignments that the speech had done its job.

Adam walked over to him. 'With me again this morning then, if that's ok with you?' he asked.

'That's fine by me boss. We shall catch them in the fields, on the beaches etc. etc. eh?'

Adam smiled wryly. 'I wouldn't put myself in quite the same league, but sometimes a bit of rhetoric helps the team along.'

'Yes sir!' said Dan, also smiling. 'Lets go get them then.' He ignored a glare from Suzanne Stewart. Right, that's it he thought, I'm not going to tell you, important though it is. It's over to you. Let's see if you get it.

∼

They were in luck. A call to Andrew Hicks' mobile revealed both he and James Stead were spending another day fishing, but this time from the small harbour by the Waterfront pub on Plymouth's West Hoe.

Adam offered to drive, said he had something Dan needed to read and handed over the folder from Edward Bray's house.

'Have a look at that mate. I can't make much of it.' He smiled wryly. 'You're the man of words here, and you do the psychoanalysis thing. See what you think.'

Dan read a couple of the poems from the folder, leaned back in his seat and closed his eyes to tame the growing pity he felt for Edward Bray. He could see it in his mind, what had happened and why. So that's why he'd stood, tearful, for so long in the garden of St Jude's, why he planted the sapling.

'The Apple Tree', he said slowly. 'I think it makes sense. Remember the tree outside his office, the one I asked Penelope Ramsden about?'

'Yeah?' Adam didn't sound impressed. 'So he liked gardening. So what?'

Dan hid a smile. Adam liked straightforward, no nonsense detective work. Whodunit was his thing, not why.

'I think it's a bit more than that. I remember a story we did about St Jude's a couple of years ago. They've got part of an ancient orchard in their grounds. There aren't many left in Britain so we did a little feature on it. Pretty blossom, nice pictures, emotional interviews with the patients who enjoy walking in it. Good TV.'

'And?'

Dan looked down at the folder, flicked through it. There must be several hundred poems in there, all, as far as he could see, on the same two themes.

'In a report from our log Bray gently tends that sapling outside his office. Penelope Ramsden confirms he loved it. We know his mum went to St Jude's to die.'

Dan paused. Should he tell Adam about his visit to Arthur Bray? They were almost at the Waterfront, and Suzanne Stewart was on her way to interview him. No, it could wait. She hadn't given him any help, quite the opposite in fact. Why help her?

'So Edward went to St Jude's to visit her', Dan continued. 'Now those poems are full of anger and remorse. They're basically saying that what happened there tainted his life. Look at them.

"Some words should never be heard
Some words can never be escaped,
Some words echo everafter,
End the innocence,
And the life."'

Adam shook his head, said nothing. 'It sounds to me like Arthur Bray and his wife wanted to have a conversation without Edward there', continued Dan slowly. 'A husband and wife saying goodbye. Not something he should hear, so they sent him out into the garden to play. It's summer and the windows are open. He's a kid and curious, so he climbs an apple tree close enough to the window to listen to what they're saying. I can only guess what he heard, but I'm sure there were lots of tears and maybe even recriminations about things that had happened between them in the past. It stayed with him. Ends the innocence and the life, as he puts it.'

Adam indicated and turned into the Waterfront's car park.

'Are you trying to tell me that what happened to him there made him the way he is? The cold and ruthless businessman that someone wanted to murder?'

'Almost, but not quite.' Dan leafed through another of the poems. 'Listen to this one.

"You tried to make amends,
But sometimes there is no way back,
And your amends were more wounds.
Where were you when I fell off the bike?
When I sobbed with the wasp's sting?
When the bullies blackened my eye?
Making money,
For me,
So now I make money,
For me,
Just for me."

And this one', said Dan, finding another piece of paper. 'I think this might even be a reaction to a headline I saw the Herald ran on him.

"They call me the bastard,
But wrong, so wrong,
Not in the usual way,
The ordinary perversion of words,
That I'm vicious, twisted, vindictive, evil,
True that, maybe.
But what of the true way?
A man without a father,
I had a father,

In the ordinary way,
But not the true way.'"

Adam opened the door and got out of the car. 'And?' he said.

No poetry fan you, thought Dan. 'When I interviewed Arthur Bray, he told me that after his wife's death, he threw himself into his business to try to drown his grief and to make sure Edward was provided for. He said he wasn't around enough when his son was growing up, and that poem bears it out from Edward's perspective. I think you've got the death of his mum, the tears and recriminations between mum and dad in the hospice, then dad spending all his time building up the business for Edward, and him resenting it.'

Adam looked out to the sea, then turned back. 'Do you really think things like that can shape people?'

Dan thought of Rutherford, how he'd bought the puppy to have a friend who would always love him unconditionally, who would be there for him whatever, who he could love safe in the knowledge that he wouldn't one day decide their relationship was over and walk off. Unlike Thomasin..

'Yes', he said quietly. 'Oh yes.'

Adam sensed the feeling and nodded slowly. 'An interesting analysis', he said, his voice warmer. 'And an insight into our victim. But does it help us with the case at all?'

Dan shrugged. 'Probably not.'

'Then let's go get on with something that might.'

The Waterfront has probably the best view of any of Plymouth's pubs. It's well named, just feet above the steely waters of Plymouth Sound. The building is a bookend type edge of a small concrete breakwater and harbour built into the black slate rock, and is a favourite haunt of boat owners and divers.

The harbour is permanently watched over by a row of fishermen dangling their lines in the water, as if on a rota. It's always busy and on a summer's day it's packed. People sit clustered around its wooden tables and gaze out across the shimmering Sound to the brief green spike of land that is Drake's Island, further to the breakwater, and sometimes, on a clear day, the Eddystone lighthouse.

Silent grey battleships slide smooth and menacing through the sparkling waters as they head for the docks at Devonport, and a thousand yachts, pleasure boats and gin palaces jockey for space like bees seeking the sweetest flowers. Dan enjoyed it for a drink and the view, but like so many places with great natural gifts, the service was poor and the prices were steep. The staff thought they didn't have to make an effort to attract customers and the owners thought they had a right to charge you for the spectacle. People complained, but still they came. It was the English way.

It was another grey day, mild, calm, and damp. A lorry was delivering vegetables to the pub, a high-pitched beeping filling the air as it reversed. A couple of fishermen turned to give it angry glares.

There was the usual line of anglers, so Adam started at the end closest to him. The man he questioned pointed silently to the far side of the pier, then returned his concentration to the orange float sitting impassively in the water. If there were any fish around, they weren't feeling peckish.

They walked along the line. 'Mr Hicks?' said Adam to the tall and well built man, his considerable figure further inflated by several layers of clothing and a yellow waterproof jacket.

'Yes, I'm Andrew Hicks', he said, his voice deep and strong.

He held out his hand and Adam shook it. He looked thinner than in the old South West Tonight report Dan had seen, but then TV did add a few pounds to your figure, much to the annoyance of many of his vainer colleagues.

'This is James, James Stead', he said, introducing his companion. He looked more nervous, and his handshake and 'hello' were weak.

'This is Dan Groves', said Adam.

'Aren't you that bloke on the TV?' asked Andrew Hicks immediately. 'I know you because I like all the environment stuff you do.'

Dan had wondered how to answer this question, which he knew would inevitably come up.

'Yes, I am, or rather I was.' The men looked puzzled. 'I've just switched jobs', he explained. 'I'm doing Crime now. That's why I'm here with Mr Breen. I'm seeing how the police investigate big cases like the Edward Bray murder. I'll be doing a report on it later.'

'Right', said Andrew Hicks. 'It's a shame you're not doing the countryside stuff any more. I used to enjoy your reports.'

'So did I', said Dan with some feeling.

'Mr Hicks, we're sorry to bother you and Mr Stead again, but there's just one matter that's come up I'd like to ask you about?' Adam had had enough of the media small talk.

'Sure', said Andrew Hicks looking entirely unconcerned. Dan noticed that James Stead was fidgeting though, fiddling with the ends of his woollen gloves where several of the fingers were wearing through.

'Please don't take this the wrong way', said Adam, 'but you'll understand when information comes in, we have to check it out.'

'Sure', said Andrew Hicks again. James Stead was now pulling at each of the glove's fingers in turn.

'We received a call saying the two of you had been overheard in a pub talking about killing Edward Bray.'

Adam looked Andrew Hicks in the eye, waiting for a reaction. The man returned his gaze without flinching, and then began to laugh, great deep bellows.

'Mr Hicks, it's hardly a laughing matter, discussing killing someone', said Adam when the laughter had subsided.

'Yes, yes, you're right of course.' Andrew Hicks wiped tears from his eyes. 'Tell me, where and when were we overheard plotting our murder?'

'Well, you'll appreciate I can't reveal that Mr Hicks', said Adam, who Dan thought for once was looking annoyed.

'Sure, sure', said Andrew Hicks, still chuckling. 'I don't think I need to ask anyway. It was one of the gossips from the Red Lion, wasn't it?'

'Mr Hicks, that's really not important. What matters is what you were saying and why.'

'I'll take that as a yes then', said Andrew Hicks, who seemed to have regained control of himself. Dan noticed that James Stead had stopped fiddling with his gloves and was now staring intently at Adam. 'Yes, yes, we've discussed it many times. It's one of our favourite topics. A couple of beers down the Lion and we inevitably get onto the 'Kill Edward Bray' game.'

'Then you admit it sir?'

'Freely and openly, and with great pleasure!' Andrew Hicks started to chuckle again. 'I don't think I'm boasting if I say I'm the winner so far.' He glanced at James Stead, who nodded. He looked embarrassed. 'My bid was that he should be slowly simmered in boiling oil, just for a little suffering you understand, then fished out and publicly stoned. There are plenty of people who'd enjoy having a go at that. I thought we might charge a pound a go and give the money to charity.' His smile broadened. 'Then I thought he should be hung, drawn and quartered, before finally being dissected and his remains buried under one of those bloody houses he loves so much.'

Adam's voice was cold, menacing. 'Are you sure this is the sort of thing you should be saying to a police officer sir?'

'Of course! You wanted the truth didn't you? There it is. The 'Kill Edward Bray' game is a great favourite at the Lion. What was your idea Jim? You wanted to drive a steamroller over him didn't you? Slowly of course.'

James Stead nodded again, looking even more ashamed.

'Did you kill Edward Bray Mr Hicks?' asked Adam slowly.

'No, no I'm afraid I didn't officer', said Andrew Hicks between continuing chuckles. 'But good luck to whoever did I say, although I wish they'd have done it a bit more creatively. Perhaps they should have joined in our game. It might have given them a few ideas.'

'Do you have any idea who did kill him?'

'I'm afraid not officer. But do let me know if you find him. I'd love to shake his hand.'

Adam turned his glare to the other fisherman.

'And you Mr Stead? Did you have anything to do with killing Edward Bray?'

James Stead shook his head again, and managed a low 'No.'

'Thank you both for your time then', said Adam sharply. 'We may need to speak to you again.'

'Good luck with the fishing', added Dan, feeling he should at least say something.

Adam turned and stalked back to the car, Dan struggling to keep up. 'Arseholes!' he growled with uncharacteristic anger as they lowered themselves into their seats.

Chapter fourteen

Suzanne Stewart kept reminding herself of the need for diplomacy and tact as Detective Constable Ian Reed drove her to Arthur Bray's house. She'd chosen him as he was new and the quietest of all the CID officers. He could be relied on not to interrupt while she was going through the questions she was now rehearsing. He would watch and learn, and that suited her fine. This was her show. True to form, he hadn't said a word on the journey, save for a request for directions. Perfect.

She thought back on her training. It was limited yes, but rightly so. A detective can only really learn on the job they'd told her, and she knew that was right. Anyway, what had been emphasised time and again – drilled in really – was the golden rule. Never approach anything with preconceptions. Never assume. Always ask your questions and come to a view based on the evidence. Never let prejudices warp your judgement. That wasn't easy, she knew. Who doesn't see the world through a coloured filter of their own views? But that was how it should be. How it must be.

Her careful and methodical approach had served her well. She prided herself on it. It wasn't easy being a woman in the CID, even in these supposedly more enlightened days. Supposedly was the right word, one hundred per cent.

It was rubbish. Any of the women detectives would tell you that. It was a man's game, and they made the rules. The office was still dominated by men, and she knew what a few of them thought about her, what she'd even overheard said. Lezzer was the word they'd used, looking over at her in that sly way.

She'd ignored it. What else can you do? She was a lezzer because she didn't wear tight tops and make up and didn't want to flirt with them. She wanted to get on with the job and do it right. She didn't have time for their pathetic games. Well, she wasn't a 'lezzer', but blokes like that made you understand what was appealing about it.

Most of them thought a woman didn't have the ruthlessness and drive a detective needed. Well she could be ruthless, and she'd shown her drive. She'd been promoted to sergeant, but she could be more than that, she thought. Perhaps not all the way up the CID ladder, but certainly Chief Inspector. Why not? That way she could manage and lead cases, but still not be so far up the ranks that she couldn't be involved in investigating them. She had the talents for that she thought, and a few women detectives in more senior positions would do the police a great deal of good. It would soften the service, and my God it needed it.

She knew her faults. It hurt to think it, but if she was honest, her main problem was a lack of feeling. She couldn't empathise with the victims or suspects. They were the raw materials of the job to her and she was never moved by the many tears she saw cried.

She wasn't naturally cold. Ok, she had no partner, no husband - was it that which started the talk of 'lezzer?' But then the job never allowed time to meet people, let alone start a relationship with them. And she'd much rather be alone than trapped in the tormented marriages of some of her colleagues. Come to work bitching about what the bloody wife had done last night or at the weekend, dread going home to them. The thought made her shudder.

She had friends outside of her job, but when she was working she became almost numb. Perhaps it was a way of coping with the suffering she so often had to deal with. It was as if the humanity switch clicked off inside her when she walked into the police station. It was something other officers did too, a shield, a way of coping. She must try to avoid that with Arthur Bray. He'd respond much better to sympathy than hard and cold questioning.

Insecurity was the other problem, she thought. No matter how thorough in her investigations, or how much thought went into a plan, she could never truly believe it was right unless she checked it with a senior officer. Perhaps it was just the police's way that had become ingrained in her. Always cover your back by getting your boss's approval. Never go out on a limb and leave yourself vulnerable. It was understandable, of course it was. But it did erode your self-respect. Your self-confidence.

But on the whole, she reassured herself, she did a good job. She didn't go barging in and throwing her weight around like some of her male colleagues. The macho idiots quickly alienated witnesses and suspects alike, making their job far more difficult. She could win people over by calm dependable reason, not upset them with aggression, bluster and threats. It was a better way and all the more effective for not being what people often expected from the police. They could do with more of it.

Adam Breen wasn't like most of them though. He was the most unusual detective she'd ever met. He had a way of being all things to all people, a charmer, like a successful politician.

He could be tough when he needed to be and subtle when that was called for too. She'd learnt a lot from him. Everyone she knew wanted to do their best for Adam Breen. He inspired them. She loved working for him. She didn't see him looking down at her and wondering what she was doing in CID. 'Two teas and a coffee please love', was what one of the detectives had said when she first walked into the office. Mr Breen had torn him apart for that and it had never been repeated.

He treated her as an equal and a professional. She was sure he'd had a say in her promotion and she intended to pay him back by helping to solve this case, the most difficult she'd known in her career so far. He'd said the same himself. Most killings were mundane, domestic arguments, which festered until an explosion of anger brought a violent end, or petty rows, which escalated, usually under the influence of drink. They were sad, but simple for a detective. This case was much more, a coldly planned killing he'd said, and by a clever murderer too. It was like something from a book.

His words echoed in her head. Good police work will solve this. Spot the inconsistencies and expose the evasions. In the absence of evidence, we're just going to have to use our brains more. It's down to you team, you, your good police work and your instincts. Go and sniff out who did this. She intended to do just that.

Suzanne couldn't hide her pride in being chosen to see Arthur Bray. Mr Breen had singled her out for the job. Her experience, he said, was vital for such a difficult task. She wondered if he suspected it was Bray who'd killed his son, just as she did. She checked herself. What had she said about preconceptions?

Perhaps Mr Breen thought she might be the best person to get the truth from him. He certainly had no alibi, but he did have a clear motive and with his shotguns, plenty of means. If she came away with a confession this afternoon, the case would be solved and she would be the one who'd cracked it. She could see his smile now as he welcomed her back to Charles Cross and congratulated her. She could also see the look on that reporter's face. He'd have a story then and she'd be the cause of it. That would be case closed and him off it, and quite right too. There was no room for amateurs in a murder inquiry. She knew just what she'd say if he tried to interview her.

'Turn right here maaam?'

She was dragged back to reality and the car. They were in Meavy and almost at Arthur Bray's house. A tractor was slowing them down, but you couldn't drive onto Dartmoor without meeting a tractor somewhere. Never mind, her timings allowed for such delays. She was a good planner, always built in contingencies. She studied the directions Adam had given her.

'Yes, right here.'

So how to handle it? Well, tact was the order of the day. It had to be. They had no evidence this man killed his son. She would start off gently and ask about how he was coping. Only then, when he'd relaxed a little, then they'd move on to the call that had come in about his rows with Edward. Yes, that was the way to play it. She was almost looking forward to it.

Arthur Bray showed them to the same room Dan and Adam had sat in. They sat down and accepted the china cups of tea he offered.

'Thank you sir. I can't go into details of course, but we wanted to let you know your appeal has brought us in some interesting new information.' He nodded. 'How are you coping?'

'It's not getting any better', sighed Arthur Bray, gazing out at the view of Dartmoor. 'You wake up thinking about it, you go to sleep thinking about it, and much of the day it's on your mind too. I can't see it getting any better, not for the foreseeable future anyway.'

Suzanne tried to feel sympathy, but failed. Her mind was full of the lack of an alibi, his shotguns and the rows with his son. Arthur Bray looked expectantly at her.

'So how can I help you today officer? Have you some important news for me about the hunt for Edward's killer?' He sounded pitiful, pleading.

'No sir, I'm afraid not.' She hadn't anticipated the question and was momentarily caught. 'That's not to say we're not making progress of course', she added hastily. 'We have many leads to follow up and we're investigating carefully.'

Arthur Bray seemed to sink further into his chair. 'Yes, yes of course officer', he said lifelessly, and then lapsed into a dense silence.

The easy notion of a pleasant and ice breaking chat before slipping in the question was hopelessly lost. The atmosphere was cold, no hint of a rapport. There was no easy way to ask. She did her best to soften the blow, but her suspicions made it hollow.

'Mr Bray, you asked me how you could help us. It's some of the new information your appeal brought in that I'd like to ask you about.'

'Of course officer', he said heavily.

'You may find this upsetting Mr Bray, but I have to ask. We had someone calling in last night to say you had some very fierce rows with your son.' His head snapped up. She could feel the anger and it took her aback, but she had to continue. 'We were even told you threatened to shoot him. Is that true?'

His eyes blazed. 'Get out.' The words came in a gasp. 'Get out of my house'.

'Mr Bray, please..'

'Out!' he roared, with an unexpected power. 'Out!!' he shouted again, pulling himself to his feet. 'How dare you? How dare you?! I do all I can to help you and you as good as come in here and accuse me of murdering my own son. Get out!!'

'Mr Bray..'

'Out I said!! Yes, we had rows, yes I even threatened to shoot him. But I didn't. Shoot my son? How could I? They were just rows. Every family has them.' He was trembling. 'Just rows! Get out!! Get out now!!'

Suzanne Stewart rose to her feet, shaken by the violence of the old man's outburst.

'Mr Bray, please..'

'Out!!!!' He roared, and she couldn't stand his screwed up face, twitching mouth, and bulging, raging eyes. She broke his gaze, turned and walked quickly over to the door, making for the sanctuary of the car, an ashen-faced Detective Constable Reed close behind.

~

Bill Wickens and Trevor King, both Detective Constables, were shown into Gordon Clarke's office by the beautiful Ellie and admired her even more obviously than Dan had done.

Both had been detectives for more than 15 years, and both had made no progress whatsoever in rising up the ranks. Bill Wickens was once asked if he was interested in applying to become a sergeant, but that was by a temporary Inspector who'd been covering for sickness. When DI Rose returned to work, the idea was quietly dropped.

They were usually teamed together as they suited each other. They were perfectly competent detectives who knew what questions to ask and did so methodically. But Adam Breen had once told another senior officer that what escaped them – what they'd never have and never understand - was the detective's greatest natural asset, the ability to feel hidden links between apparently unconnected facts. So they remained the plodding foot soldiers, mechanically gathering the information which the generals would fit into a pattern and form a prosecution.

Both were in their mid 40's, both about five feet ten and slightly overweight, and both wore the weather-beaten suits of the lower ranking detective. DC Wickens' hair was black and unruly, and his complexion was reddened from a fondness for whisky. DC King's was brown and cut short, and he had pale skin and a bulbous nose from which the first tufts of hair were sprouting.

They both called themselves old style CID. They got stuck in, solved the case, then celebrated over a few beers later. A few beers, then a few more whiskies in truth. They were a well matched pairing, and known quietly at Charles Cross as 'Double Jeopardy'.

'So how can I help you gentlemen?' asked Gordon Clarke, trying to prise their attentions away from Ellie's retreating figure.

'Some more information about the Edward Bray killing came in which concerned you', said Trevor King. They weren't deliberately blunt, but long days of dealing with unsophisticated criminals had long worn away any subtlety.

'Oh yes?' said Gordon Clarke warily.

'You were having a relationship with a woman he was in a dispute with. A woman by the name of', Trevor King referred to his notes 'Kate Moore', he said eventually with satisfaction.

'Ah, Kate.' Gordon Clarke looked thoughtful. 'Well, not having a relationship, unfortunately.'

'Then you do know her sir?' chipped in Bill Wickens, who was regarded as marginally the smarter of the pair, and was carefully taking notes.

'Oh yes, I know her. I wish I knew her rather better!' Gordon Clarke offered them a winning and knowing smile.

The two detectives stared flatly back at him.

'I met her through a friend', he continued hurriedly. 'We seemed to have a lot in common. A dislike of Edward Bray was just one thing. He was suing her, saying some work she'd done wasn't up to scratch.' He shook his head. 'It was an outrageous case and I can't see how he could have won, but she was worried about it. Anyway, that's by and by. I wasn't having a relationship with her. I'd have liked to, but she wasn't interested.'

There was a pause whilst Bill Wickens wrote all this down painstakingly, in longhand. Then he looked up.

'Ms Moore says it's a bit more than that sir. She says you were very keen indeed. Kept sending her flowers and chocolates and calling her. She says you wouldn't accept she wasn't interested.'

Gordon Clarke looked down at his desk and rolled his hand over the computer mouse.

'Yes, I was keen on her'. His voice was slow and heavy. He looked back up. 'Perhaps I was a little too insistent, you might be right. You don't meet women like her very often and I was quite taken. I was hoping a little persuasion might change her mind.' He sighed.

'But I did get the message in the end officers. I did give up.'

The telephone rang in the office next door, and Ellie's muffled tones answered it. Bill Wickens looked over towards the sound, but the blinds on the door stopped him seeing her. He turned back to Gordon Clarke.

'So both Ms Moore and you would have been quite happy to see some harm come to Mr Bray?' he asked.

'I can see what you're getting at officer', said Gordon Clarke, the indulgent smile returning. 'And I suppose put like that, you're right. But as you know, I was in Bristol when Edward Bray was shot.'

'And Ms Moore?' asked Trevor King.

'I don't know officer. You'll have to ask her that. As I said to you, we're not exactly as close as I would have liked.'

Bill Wickens noted all this down and then looked up again.

'You don't know of any plot, or plan to attack Mr Bray do you sir?'

'Really officer!' Gordon Clarke looked irritated. 'Are you suggesting Kate Moore and I conspired to kill Edward Bray because we both happened to dislike the man?'

The response came easily from familiarity. 'I wasn't suggesting anything sir. I was just asking a question.'

'Well in that case I shall just answer it. No, I don't know of any plot or plan. I was shopping in Bristol when Bray was killed. The first I heard of it was on the news when I got back. I am not in a relationship with Kate Moore unfortunately, and we didn't work together to bump off Edward Bray! Now is there anything else you'd like to ask, or can I get back to work?'

The two detectives got up and were shown out. They lingered in the reception area, they said to discuss the best route for their drive back to Plymouth but in reality to maximise the view of Ellie. It was one of the perks of the job.

~

Tony Rye looked up from his charts at the sound of an overloud cough to see a ruffled looking man and a smartly dressed woman in the doorway of the portacabin.

'Oh for Christ's sake, what do you lot want this time?' he groaned.

'Mr Rye? We're detectives', said the woman.

'No shit', said Tony Rye bitterly. 'What now?'

'Calm down Mr Rye', said the man. 'It's just a few questions we've got to ask you.'

'Just a few more questions you mean. It's bloody harassment. Oh get on with it then', said Tony Rye resignedly.

The detectives stepped up into the portacabin. The man pulled out a plastic chair, which the woman sat down on. He remained standing. In his late 40s, he was chubby, but not quite fat. He spread his legs slightly to distribute his weight. His suit was dark blue and double breasted in the way which had been the fashion a couple of years ago. His shirt had probably once been a pure white, but had long lost its shine. A light blue acrylic tie hung loosely well short of his neck. A ring of dark hair circled a small bald patch on the top of his head. If he'd occasionally smiled, people would have described him as jolly, but he never did.

The woman was also wearing a suit, but one which was clearly this year's selection. It was a dark grey and slightly bobbled. Her blouse was as immaculately white as her colleague's once was, long ago. Her hair was brown with blonde highlights and tied up in a short ponytail, which said she was more interested in her work than her appearance. She was probably in her late 30s, but could have been younger. Her features were warmer and kinder than the man's, but her eyes were cold blue and hard. She introduced them.

'I'm Detective Constable Claire Reynolds and this is Detective Sergeant Jack Retallick.'

'Delighted to meet you', said Tony Rye acidly. 'Now what do you want?'

'Mr Rye, we need to ask you about what you were doing last Monday afternoon', said Sergeant Retallick pleasantly.

'That'll make a nice change.'

He ignored the sarcasm. 'You've already told other officers you were buying tiles, then came back here to do some shopping and drop them off.'

'Yep'.

'Well, some new information has come in to us Mr Rye. We think you're not telling us the truth.'

'You can think what you like mate, but that's what I was doing', said Tony Rye defiantly, his neck starting to redden.

'Come on now Mr Rye', said Claire Reynolds soothingly. 'We're trying to help you.'

'That'd be a first.'

'Mr Rye, this is a serious matter', she continued. 'It's a murder inquiry. It's a murder inquiry and you're a suspect. Unless we know what you were doing on Monday afternoon, you're going to remain a suspect. The prime suspect in fact.'

Tony Rye considered this quietly. He stared at the plans laid out before him.

'Mr Rye', said John Retallick, after a minute to let him think. 'Don't you want to know what it is we've been told about you?'

Tony Rye shrugged.

'Ok Mr Rye', said Claire Reynolds. 'I think I'd better tell you anyway. We got a phone call from a woman saying it wasn't you who killed Edward Bray. She said it couldn't have been. She said she could prove it. Now how could she do that Mr Rye?'

Tony Rye shrugged again.

'Bollocks to you', he said quietly.

'I'm sorry Mr Rye?' said Jack Retallick.

'I said 'Bollocks to you!'' he shouted, jumping up. 'When are you bastards going to leave me alone?! I've told you enough times. I didn't kill Bray. Now fuck off and leave me alone!!'

He stayed standing, but neither detective moved. He pushed past Jack Retallick and strode over to the plastic kettle, flicked its switch on.

'Mr Rye', said Claire Reynolds gently and calmly to his turned back. 'That woman was your mistress, wasn't she? You were with her on Monday afternoon, weren't you? I can quite understand why you don't want to tell us, but if you come clean with us now, and we can have a quick word with her to verify it, we'll leave you alone.

That'll be it. No one else need know. You'll be in the clear and we'll leave you alone.'

Tony Rye turned on them, and Jack Retallick tensed, ready to deflect the attack, but it didn't come. The builder took a series of deep breaths, his lips pursed together, stared at them, then said quietly 'get the fuck out of my office.'

'Mr Rye!' said Claire Reynolds, sharply, making him stare at her. 'Perhaps you don't realise how serious this is. If we don't find a way to clear you, you could end up being charged with murder and spending the rest of your life in prison.'

Tony Rye was shaking his head. 'Fuck you', he mumbled, but he sounded defeated.

'Mr Rye!' Sharp again, sensing the weakness. 'I don't think you killed Edward Bray'.

Jack Retallick shot her a look. What was she doing? Did she think sympathy would work on this man? He went to interrupt but she got in first.

'In fact, I'm sure of it', she went on, more softly now. Tony Rye stared at her, still shaking his head. 'But if I'm going to prove it, you'll have to help me. I know it was your mistress Tony, I can see it in you. I know she phoned us to clear you and I understand why you think you can't say anything. Just tell us about it now, we'll check it with her, and that'll be it, we'll leave you alone.'

Still Tony Rye stared at her, breathing deeply. 'You're bastards. You're all bastards.'

'Come on now Mr Rye.' She stood up, put out a hand to his shoulder. He didn't move. Kindly again.

'Come on Tony. Let's get this over with and we can leave you alone.'

He looked down at the kettle, then back up at her. 'I'm coming with you.'

'What?'

'I'm coming with you.'

Claire Reynolds drove, Tony Rye in the back with Jack Retallick. He'd insisted the child locks were kept on in the car, was watching Rye carefully. He could be taking them anywhere, about to do a runner. Claire was clever, a good officer, would go far, often got results with her sympathy and kindness act, but it could be dangerous too. She didn't always know when it might get her into trouble. But Rye showed no sign of wanting to get away, just sat there silently, looking down at his blackened, tattooed hands, picking chips of dirt off them.

25 minutes in the car and they pulled up at the address he'd given them on the outskirts of Newton Abbot. Tony Rye got out, Sergeant Retallick at his shoulder. He led them up a neatly paved path to a semi-detached house. It was a dull yellow, primrose was the word, thought Jack Retallick. Nice little place really, a few kids playing up the street, all the houses and gardens looked well cared for. He was surprised Rye would have a woman in a place like this. He'd been expecting a flat on a council estate.

Still Rye said nothing, fished a key from his pocket, put it in the lock, turned it, pushed the door open. Jack Retallick held back for a second before following. You never knew what was waiting for you. But it was all quiet, just a radio playing, muffled, in another room.

Claire followed them in. The house was clean and tidy and smelt of pine.

A door swung open in front of them. Sergeant Retallick tensed, but it was a woman, small, dyed blonde hair, mid 40s, frowning. She looked at Tony Rye, then the two detectives. Still Rye said nothing, just stood there looking at her. Then she stepped forwards, making both Claire Reynolds and Jack Retallick stiffen. What would she do? She hesitated, glared at them, then reached out and put her arms around Tony Rye.

'He's a stupid bastard, but I love him', she said slowly, staring at them through narrowed eyes. Claire Reynolds noticed she wore a gold wedding ring. 'A real stupid bastard. Aren't you?'

Still Tony Rye said nothing, just cuddled into the woman. 'And I've forgiven him', the woman said. 'I haven't exactly been a saint in my life either, so I've forgiven him. We're going to be ok, aren't we love?'

She turned back to the two detectives and her voice hardened. 'So you two can fuck off out of here and leave us alone. I know why you're here. It was me who called you, me, his bloody wife. I've suspected for a while now, so I had it out with him. I'm not going through it all with you bastards, you've stuck your noses into our business enough, but it's sorted now. So you can fuck off and leave us alone.'

Neither detective knew what to say. 'You can have her name and address and check it out with her and her bloody gossiping neighbours, like you bastards always do' Mrs Rye went on, 'then you can fuck off and leave us alone.'

They pulled out of the Waterfront car park and headed back towards Charles Cross. Dan stopped at the back of a queue of cars waiting to get through some road works. He glanced over at Adam who was scribbling at his notes.

'It's ok, you can talk again', he said, looking up. 'I've calmed down now, but they were a real pair of idiots those two. I ask you! The 'Kill Edward Bray game."

Good, thought Dan, now I can tell you what I've been meaning to, about Arthur Bray and his alibi. He wasn't looking forward to the reception he'd get. He was wondering how to begin when Adam's mobile rang.

'Hello, DCI Breen. Hello Mike. No, it's no problem. What? What?! When? You've got it there? What do forensics say? Brilliant! Ok, I'll be down in a min.'

'Back to the station Dan, as fast as you can. A farmer's found a shotgun in a ditch a few miles from the lay by. No fingerprints, but forensics say it looks like it's got some fibres attached to it.'

He paused, calmed himself. 'I'm sorry Dan, but I can't let you come in on this one. I'm going to a scene where all access will have to be strictly controlled so we can go over it with a fingertip search. We can't risk contaminating any evidence.' Adam's hand clenched into a fist, held it in front of him. 'It looks like we might finally have got our break.'

'Ok Adam, I understand.' What else could he say? 'But I'd better call in to the newsroom, we'll want to get a camera there.'

'Not this time Dan.'

A Popular Murder

'What?' What would Lizzie say if they didn't report it? He didn't like to think. 'But it's a big story..'

'And if you put it out, we'll have ghouls coming to have a look, tramping around and destroying any evidence. I can't risk that.'

'My editor will go mad.' And I'll look a fool, he thought. What happened to my good contacts, my time spend building close links with the police?

The cars in front moved off and he put the Astra into gear. Time to call in some favours.

'Come on Adam, I helped you with the Bray press conference, it worked like a dream. And with saving that kid. Give me something back.' No reply. 'I just can't not report this, it's too big.'

'And I just can't let you Dan, no way. It's too important to the investigation. It might be all we've got.'

Another silence. They were almost at Charles Cross.

'I'm warning you', said Adam, and his voice was icy. 'If you put anything out about this, we would have to consider charging you with obstructing the investigation. It would certainly be the end of any more help we would give you.'

He felt betrayed. 'Jesus Adam, after all I've done for you.'

'For Christ's sake Dan, this is bigger than that. Can't you see it? It's bigger than your precious bloody stories. This is about catching a murderer.'

Dan indicated and pulled in to the station. His heart was thumping. One last chance.

'Ok, how long will it take you to go over the area?'

'A few hours.'

'So how about doing something tomorrow, when the search is done?'

Adam stared at him. 'You're a persistent bastard, aren't you?' he said, but his voice was warmer. 'Ok, I know you've got your job to do. Nothing for now then, but I'll try to sort something for you in the morning.'

Dan nodded. 'Thanks Adam, I appreciate that. And can we have it as…'

'Yes, ok', he cut in. 'It'll be your bloody exclusive. Call me in the morning.'

Chapter fifteen

Dan arrived at work at 8.30 the next morning. When he could get up early enough, take Rutherford for some exercise and make himself look reasonably human, he found it the best time to be in. There were only a few early journalists about, preparing and producing the breakfast TV bulletins, so the newsroom was quiet. Work could be tackled without colleagues shouting at and across you. Journalists are a rude bunch.

The canteen opened at 8.30, so he could log in to the computer, check what the freelance news wires were running and trawl through his own emails. He could spot any important stories that might dictate the destiny of his day, then shift downstairs to get some toast and sit and read the newspapers. It was a civilised way to start work. Importantly too, Lizzie came in at around 8.45, so the impression of being there before her and getting on with something useful was worth cultivating. This morning he also had a surprise for her.

From his desk he saw her striding in from the door at the far end of the newsroom. He called up the police's web site and pretended to be lost in his computer screen.

The clicking heels stopped by his side and he looked up. Perfect so far.

'Good morning', he said pleasantly.

'And good morning to you.' Her heels were relatively low today, probably only two inches. 'How are you today Mr Apprentice Detective?'

'Fine thanks', said Dan, laying his trap. 'I just thought I'd get in early to do some work on the Bray case.'

'Ah yes', said Lizzie keenly. 'I was going to ask you about that. I liked the last story we did and think we should go for another one as soon as poss.' He'd expected that. Good. 'Well, it's funny you should say that. Great minds must think alike.' She looked dubious but didn't say anything. 'I think I might have something to offer you on it today, a nice little exclusive in fact. The police have found the murder weapon, a dirty great shotgun. It's a major breakthrough for them.'

Both Lizzie's eyebrows rose. 'Sold', she said instantly. 'Very sold. Take Nigel, he's about.'

I'll have to sell it to Adam first, thought Dan, dialling his number as Lizzie bounced away.

'I can't say for definite it's the murder weapon Dan', protested Adam. 'I couldn't even say that in court. All I can say is that it's consistent with the weapon which killed Edward Bray.'

'How consistent?'

'The ballistics boys say it could have been the gun. The trouble is it's a shotgun. There are loads like it which could also have been the murder weapon. I can't prove definitively this is the one.'

'But you must think it is?'

'Between us, yes, of course I think it is. You don't find many shotguns sitting in ditches at the end of a farmer's field a few miles from the scene of a murder.'

'Ok then, that's enough for a story.' Thank God for that he thought. Selling an idea to Lizzie is tough enough. Buying it back is far worse. 'Can we see it?'

'Do you have to?'

'We can't do the story without it. It's the main shot, if you'll excuse the pun. I'll have to start my report with it.'

'I suppose so then. Are you going to come down here to film it?'

'We'll be down in 15 minutes.'

'Just one thing. What's in this for me?'

Dan knew the question was coming. 'Presumably you want anyone to come forward who may have seen someone near the ditch, behaving suspiciously, on the Monday that Edward Bray was killed?'

'Yes, of course.'

'Ok then, that's the interview with you sorted. You can say all that. It might bring someone forward.'

The report made the second slot on the lunchtime news and in South West Tonight. Annoyingly in Dan's eyes, but in fairness he supposed the council tax going up by almost 20 per cent in Devon was a more important story. The pensioners were outraged. And as Adam had said, they couldn't prove it was the murder weapon, so there was that slight element of uncertainty.

Still, it was a good scoop. It certainly justified at least some of his disappearance into the investigation and banked him some time. It should keep Lizzie off his back for a few more days. He didn't want to let go now, not when there was a new lead. He wanted to be there until the end, to see an arrest and more, he wanted to see the murderer's face. He wanted to be in court for the trial. He wanted to report on it, on what the judge said in his sentencing.

Adam held the shotgun up to the camera whilst Dan talked about the police believing it to be the murder weapon. Nigel filmed some close ups of the gun's barrel, long, dark and menacing. The light slid off it. The gun was kept encased in plastic sheeting, Dan explaining to the viewers that was to preserve any potential forensic evidence. Anyway, he thought, it looked more dramatic like that.

Adam did his appeal for public help. Then there were pictures of the ditch and field where the gun was found, followed by Dan's piece to camera, standing by the ditch and recapping on the story. A decent bit of work he thought, as he lay stretched out on his favourite sofa that evening, not bad at all. He gave Rutherford's head a rub and was rewarded with a whine, which turned into a yawn.

His mobile rang seconds after the report ended. Adam.

'Nice story, he said. 'I thought it worked well. In fact, I had the Assistant Chief Constable onto me earlier, congratulating me. He said it was a very good idea of mine to put the discovery out on TV. He said it would reassure the public we were making progress.'

Dan smiled. 'Then I shall let you take all the credit', he said. 'And did the ACC mention it might help catch the killer too?'

'I'm sure he meant that as well.'

'So where do you go from here then, now you've got the gun?'

'That's exactly why I called.' Adam sounded buoyant. 'You know I told you there were some fibres on it?'

'Yes. Any use?'

'Oh yes.' The stress on the words left no doubt. 'Yes indeed. It's our first real clue in this whole case. Fibres are great for a detective. They're a godsend. They're always falling off and sticking to people and objects. These ones had got stuck around the stock of the gun. We think it was wiped off after the shooting, but they were tiny and the killer must have been in a hurry and missed them.'

Dan could imagine Adam, one hand on the phone, the other a clenched fist, waving it triumphantly. 'They missed them! There were only a few, but enough for the forensics boys to work with. They've come back to me with a result.' A pause. A stern tone, very stern. 'And before I tell you, this is not for the TV, ok?'

'Ok.'

'Not for the TV or anyone else? I'm letting you in on this as a friend.'

A friend? 'Ok I said.'

'Promise?'

'Promise!'

Adam chuckled. 'Sorry I had to ask, but this is really sensitive stuff.' His voice changed back from light to sombre, friend to detective. 'The fibres were from the boot of a car. A BMW to be exact. In fact, to be even more exact, a BMW 318 sports coupe, manufactured between late 2002 and the end of 2003.' He whistled in admiration. 'The forensics people are bloody miracle workers. They've got a database of all this stuff and they can be that precise.'

A memory of seeing a car just like that teased Dan's brain, but he couldn't place it. He could feel the excitement at the other end of the phone and knew he was about to find out anyway.

'And do you know who's got exactly that car?'

'Who?'

'Come on, think.'

Dan thought, but couldn't bring the memory home. Adam could be almost childlike with his teasing.

'Come on, tell me!'

'Gordon Clarke.'

'Clarke?! But he's got an alibi.'

'Yes, but he's also got some explaining to do. No one else connected with the case has a car that fits the fibres. I'm going to pay him one of my little visits tomorrow morning. He doesn't know what it's about yet; he just thinks we're tying up some loose ends. Think of it as a nice Christmas surprise for him. Do you fancy coming along?'

'I'll be at Charles Cross at the usual time', said Dan, feeling a rising buzz of anticipation.

Chapter sixteen

As they drove into Ermington Business Park, all three of them stared at the green BMW parked outside Erme Internet Design. Suzanne Stewart had again insisted on driving. Dan had been forced to sit in the back, squeezed up alongside a large metal box full of copies of statements taken in the investigation. Adam had explained they might need to refer to them, depending on what Gordon Clarke said.

Ellie greeted them with the usual offers of tea or coffee and a seat to wait, but Adam wasn't in a mood to delay.

'Thank you, but no. We just need a quick word with Mr Clarke please. It's urgent.'

As if on cue, Gordon Clarke emerged from his office. Dan wondered if he'd been listening at the door. Nervously even? His prepared smile faded and the outstretched hand dropped to his side when he saw the look on Adam's face.

'How can I help you officers? Is there something wrong?' His voice wavered and Dan thought he sounded frightened. And was it his imagination, or did the man look pale?

'Can we have a chat in your office please sir?' said Adam, in a tone that said that was exactly what they were going to do.

Gordon Clarke retreated quickly behind his desk as though it offered some magical defensive barrier. He sat down heavily.

'Mr Clarke, I've got a couple more questions I need to ask you', began Adam looking him straight in the eye.

'Certainly Inspector, but I don't know how much more I can help you. I've told you everything I know.' His voice was definitely wavering now.

'Let's just go back through the Monday when Mr Bray was killed.' Adam referred to some notes he'd taken out of his pocket. 'You were away shopping for the day as I recall. In Bristol?'

'That's right. Well, not just shopping. I went for a computer fair, but it wasn't very useful, so I went shopping instead. I didn't want to waste the day, and there are such good men's clothing shops up there', he said, with a winning smile to Adam, one follower of fashion to another.

'I see', said Adam coldly. 'And you left Plymouth about 8 o'clock in the morning?'

'That's right.'

'And you didn't get back until about 7?'

'Correct.'

'And how did you get to the station Mr Clarke?'

'I got a taxi Inspector. The last time I parked my car at Plymouth station it got scratched. And it's expensive to park there too.' He patted his wallet. 'The taxi's just a few pounds more, and it means you can have a couple of glasses of wine on the train on the way home.'

Dan wondered if his answer was too fluent. It sounded rehearsed. Prepared ready to justify not driving to the station?

'And where was your car whilst you were in Bristol Mr Clarke?' continued Adam, still looking him straight in the eye.

'At home Inspector. Parked in my garage. Why?'

Adam ignored the question. 'Are you the only one who drives your car Mr Clarke?'

'Yes Inspector. Ellie's driven it a couple of times for me when she's taken me home from business receptions after I've had a drink, but that's it.'

'Does anyone else have a key to the car sir?'

'No Inspector, just me.' Dan was sure he was looking worried now. His fingers were picking nervously at a stray splinter on the edge of his desk. 'What is all this about?'

'All in good time sir', said Adam, smoothly. 'And are there any spare keys to your car?'

'Yes Inspector. There's a set at home and one in my desk here, just in case. I'm covered both ways then. A businessman can't be without his car.' He managed a weak smile.

'I see sir.'

Gordon Clarke was picking harder at the desk now. He looked at Dan and Suzanne Stewart, but both sat with their faces set. They'd been warned not to interrupt. Adam jotted down some notes. If he meant to load pressure onto his suspect it was working.

'Officers, would you mind please telling me what this is about? It's rather intimidating.'

Adam looked up slowly. 'Of course Mr Clarke. I don't know if you saw the news yesterday, but we've found what we think is the shotgun used to kill Edward Bray. Well, when I say we found it, what I mean is a farmer found it. In a ditch. Just up the road from here in fact', said Adam in a friendly way, as though the fact that the gun was found so close was a mere detail.

Dan scrutinised Gordon Clarke for any reaction, but there was none.

'Yes, I had heard Inspector. But I don't see what that has to do with me?'

'Well sir, the forensics team have been looking at the gun. And they found something interesting. There were some fibres on it. Just a few, but enough for them to identify where they came from.'

Dan thought he saw Gordon Clarke stiffen. He stopped picking at his desk.

'Yes Inspector? Will that help you find out who committed this terrible crime?'

'It might well do sir. I certainly hope so.' Adam paused, eyes boring into his suspect. 'The fibres came from the boot of a BMW, manufactured between late 2002 and the end of 2003.' He let the words linger. 'A car like yours sir', he said, tilting his head towards the yard where the BMW stood.

Gordon Clarke stared at them. His mouth opened, but he said nothing.

'Gordon Clarke, I'm arresting you on suspicion of involvement in the murder of Edward Bray. You do not have to say anything, but it may harm your defence if you fail to mention something now you later rely on in court. Do you understand?'

A silent nod, so slight it was almost imperceptible. 'That's the formal caution sir. Now, would you mind coming with us to the police station? And I'll need the keys to the car. There's a forensics team coming to have a look at it. They'll be here in a minute.' Gordon Clarke still said nothing. He looked stunned. 'I can get a warrant of course, but I didn't think you'd mind. I'm sure you wouldn't want to bother a magistrate.'

Nice bluff thought Dan, but it worked. Still open-mouthed and silent, Gordon Clarke reached into a drawer and pushed a bunch of keys across his desk.

It was the same interview room they'd used to question Tony Rye, but this time there were five people in it. Adam sat flanked by Dan and Suzanne Stewart on one side of the table, Gordon Clarke and his solicitor, Julia Francis on the other. He'd called her as soon as Adam had read him his rights, the words gushing out of him like a desperate plea for help.

She was a stern looking woman, almost matronly Dan thought, but without a nurse's tenderness. She wore a black suit, had short blonde hair and watery blue eyes which rarely blinked. Her features were sharp and her face prematurely lined. Dan guessed she was about 40 years old.

Suzanne Stewart pressed a button on the tape recorder and the familiar metallic buzz filled the room. She introduced them all. She gathered some papers and looked about to ask a question, but Julia Francis spoke first.

'Mr Clarke would like it recorded that he came here freely and willingly to help the police. He is a law-abiding citizen and a local businessman of good reputation and some prominence. He always tries to help the police whenever he can, and will gladly do so on this occasion. He does however feel he has done as much as he can in relation to the murder of Edward Bray. He has told the detectives gathered here all he knows of Mr Bray, and everything about his relationship with the deceased. He can think of nothing else which may assist the investigation. As he has already said, he was in Bristol on the day that Mr Bray was murdered. He has nothing to add to his previous comments on that matter.'

She paused and looked up from the statement. Dan thought her face might manage a cold smile, but nothing came. 'Now, if there's nothing else officers, Mr Clarke would like to be released so he can continue about his lawful business.'

She made to stand up, but Adam said 'just a moment please', and she waited. She leaned back on her plastic chair and looked at him. He did smile, but not kindly. It seemed to say 'nice try'.

'We'd like to thank Mr Clarke in turn for helping us with our inquiries', he said smoothly. 'But there are a couple of other questions we need to ask him. As a man who likes to help the police, I'm sure he'll have no objection?'

Gordon Clarke leaned over to Julia Francis and they exchanged whispers. She nodded and turned back to Adam.

'Mr Clarke is of course prepared to help you in any way he can Chief Inspector. But if I think you're asking him questions which he cannot or should not answer, it's my duty to advise him so and rest assured, I will.'

'Thank you', said Adam. 'I'm sure you will.' He straightened his tie and seemed to gather himself for the attack.

'Mr Clarke, can you explain how fibres found on the shotgun which we believe was used to murder Edward Bray match those from the boot of your car?'

'Don't answer that', cut in Julia Francis almost before the end of Adam's question. 'Chief Inspector, that's a matter for you to explain, not Mr Clarke. I've had the chance to do only a brief preliminary check, but we estimate the fibres you've found match not only Mr Clarke's car, but more than ten thousand others. If you're trying to imply they match only Mr Clarke's car then that's highly misleading and could be regarded as an attempt to entrap my client. The courts rightly take a very dim view of such underhand behaviour. I would expect better from a senior police officer.'

'It's a bit of a coincidence, isn't it, that his car should match the fibres, when he happens to work near where the gun was found and he disliked Edward Bray immensely?' said Suzanne Stewart angrily. Adam reached out a hand to her in a calming gesture.

Julia Francis looked haughtily at Suzanne as if she were an insolent schoolgirl.

'That may be your view officer, but so far you haven't produced any evidence to suggest Mr Clarke had anything whatsoever to do with the murder of Mr Bray. In fact I'd have to say your case is marked by a lack of evidence.' Her voice rose. 'From what I understand, you can't even prove the gun you have is the one that killed Mr Bray. Even if it was, the fibres you've found on it match thousands of cars currently on the roads of Britain. Are you seriously suggesting that based on that, you consider Mr Clarke a suspect? I'm afraid I'm starting to conclude this interview is a complete waste of my client's valuable time.'

She looked Suzanne up and down, as though trying to work out what depths of stupidity might give rise to such suspicion. 'Now, I ask again. Is there anything else you'd like to ask before you release Mr Clarke to go about his lawful business? If you insist on keeping him here on such embarrassingly tenuous grounds, I shall be forced to apply to a judge for his release. I very much look forward to seeing his reaction to your case. I shall also of course discuss with Mr Clarke whether an action for wrongful arrest and unlawful detention would be appropriate.'

The hint of a smile was creasing the corners of Gordon Clarke's face. He was a very different man from the one they'd arrested earlier. Adam was writing, just doodles on his notepad. Suzanne glared at Julia Francis through narrowed eyes.

'Mr Clarke', said Adam, looking up. 'The keys to your car. You have three sets I believe?'

Gordon Clarke looked sideways at his solicitor, who nodded. 'Yes', he said.

'And one you keep with you?'
'Yes.'
'Another is kept at home?'
'Yes.'
'The other at your offices in Ermington?'
'Yes.'
'And your car was in the garage at your home when you were in Bristol?'
'Yes.'
'Does the garage door have a lock?'
'Yes?'
'Do you..'

But before Adam could finish the question, Julia Francis cut in. 'Is this relevant to anything Inspector, or am I right in thinking you're just fishing rather hopelessly?'

Suzanne snorted and seemed about to say something, but Adam's arm rose calmingly again. 'I think it is relevant, Ms Francis, yes', he said patiently. 'So if Mr Clarke wouldn't mind?' She pursed her lips, nodded almost imperceptibly. 'As I was saying, Mr Clarke, do you always lock the garage door when your car is in there?'

'Not always Inspector, no. Sometimes, if I'm only popping home for a while, I leave it open.'

'But it's locked when the car's in there for a longer period?'

'Yes.'

'And would have been locked when you were in Bristol?'

'Yes.'

'Can the garage be entered from inside your house Mr Clarke?'

'Inspector, really', interjected Julia Francis, sounding exasperated. 'I'm afraid I simply cannot see this as relevant. It's starting to appear that you're hounding my client, presumably out of desperation with the lack of progress in your investigation. If this continues much longer, I will have to apply to apply to a judge for Mr Clarke's release.'

Dan thought he heard Suzanne snarl. But Adam was a model of patience. 'Just a couple more questions please, Ms Francis. I assure you they are relevant.'

'Very well then', she said sharply, 'but a few moments longer is all I'm prepared to allow. My client is a busy man.'

'Thank you. Mr Clarke, as I was saying, can you get into the garage from inside your house?'

'Yes. But the door to the garage from the house is always kept locked.'

'And does anyone have keys to the house, apart from you?'

'No.'

'And there are no spare keys to the garage anywhere, to your knowledge?'

'No.'

'And there have been no signs of any break in whatsoever, to your house, garage or car?'

'Naturally not, or I would have reported it to the police.'

'So..'

'Inspector, that really is enough.' Julia Francis cut in again, and this time her voice was cold with finality.

'I think we've established beyond doubt that no one else could have got into my client's garage and driven his car on the day that Mr Bray was tragically killed.' She stood up, Gordon Clarke also getting to his feet. 'Now, before we leave, is there anything else?'

Adam shook his head silently. He turned to Suzanne. 'What's the state of your relationship with Kate Moore, Mr Clarke?' she asked. 'Just how smitten were you? What would you do for her?'

'Don't answer that'. The same legal brick wall again. 'Officer, that has nothing to do with your case. My client's private life is just that, private. Now, I ask again, is there anything else?'

Suzanne Stewart uttered a low 'no'. A vein was throbbing angrily in her neck.

Julia Francis began walking towards the door, Gordon Clarke following.

'There is just one thing Mr Clarke, if you wouldn't mind?' asked Dan, to looks of surprise from the two detectives. He didn't have time to wonder what he was doing, it was instinct. Gordon Clarke stopped, shrugged. 'How do you tend to keep the rain off when the weather's bad sir? An umbrella? A hood on your coat?'

Julia Francis looked from Dan to Gordon Clarke who laughed, an irritating, arrogant titter.

'I'm always glad to help the police. Especially with such important matters as my wardrobe'. His tone was rich with ridicule. 'I have a couple of very fine hats I like to wear, if that helps you at all. They're not as fashionable as they once were, but I enjoy wearing them.'

'Bloody woman', growled Suzanne Stewart as they sat down in the canteen. 'I've had dealings with her before. She's one of Plymouth's worst. A nest of vipers would come off second best in a scrap with her. God knows how many bloody crooks she's got off. She's a crook herself.'

'She was only doing her job, the same as we do ours,' said Adam calmly, but Dan thought there was an edge to his words. His shoulders were sagging and he looked tired. Even the way he stirred his coffee was laboured.

'Anyway, she's got a point. We don't have a case. It's that simple. We've got a gun that we think is the murder weapon, but we can't be sure. It's got some fibres on it that come from the boot of a BMW of which there are thousands. Forensics have found nothing else in the boot of Clarke's car to suggest a shotgun's been in there. I've had Clarke's neighbours checked out and they say they don't think they saw his car on that Monday, which could mean it was in his garage, or just somewhere else. But of course, after two weeks they can't say for sure anyway. It's just not the sort of thing you remember is it? A car, or lack of it scarcely makes much impression in a street. On top of that, Clarke's got an alibi anyway. And there's no hint someone else could have been using his car on the day Bray was killed either.'

Adam pushed his chair back from the table and sighed. 'No case', he said. 'We haven't had one from the start and we still don't have one now. I hoped the fibres might be our breakthrough, but it's typical of this investigation that even they don't help us much. Luck's just not running for us with this one.'

There was a silence while the three of them stared into their drinks. Suzanne had bought a chocolate bar too, but she'd so far left it untouched.

'What do you think though?' asked Dan. 'What do you really think? Do you have a hunch about who killed Bray?' Suzanne gave him a warning look. 'This isn't to try and pin you down or anything like that', he continued. 'It's just for my own satisfaction. You don't like Gordon Clarke do you?'

Adam stirred his coffee again. 'No, I don't like him. I get the feeling he's lying to us. I've thought it from the start. I know those fibres don't prove a thing, but I still think it's a hell of a coincidence that they happen to match the car of a man who's strongly connected with the case. But that's still a long way from proving he's a murderer.'

'Proving yes, I understand that. But what about a hunch?' persisted Dan. He couldn't bear the thought of not knowing what had happened to Edward Bray and why. Even a guess would do.

'A hunch? Well, I'd say he's certainly covering something up, but I don't know if it's anything to do with the murder. And if it's just some stupid business or tax thing, or something with that secretary of his, frankly I couldn't give a damn. What do you think?'

'I get the feeling he's hiding something too', said Dan. 'Some of what he said was too rehearsed for me. It was like he was remembering a script rather than telling us what actually happened. He sounded like some politicians I've interviewed. No honesty, just a recital of some policy. I don't like him either, but as you say, that's a long way from making him a murderer.'

'I think he had something to do with it', said Suzanne abruptly. 'I've been doing this job long enough not to believe in co-incidences.'

'Fair point Suzanne, I agree', said Adam. 'And I think you're right. But it still isn't anything you could put in front of a jury.'

She nodded. 'How's the overtime budget looking?'

'It's ok. This hasn't been the most costly of inquiries. We haven't had enough leads to make it expensive. Why?'

'I was just thinking sir. Clarke's about all we've got. We haven't got much in the way of other leads to follow. So why not put a watch on him for a few days? If we look like we're leaving him alone and he has got something to hide, he might relax a bit and give something away. It must be worth a try surely? What else can we do?'

'I did consider that Suzanne. I think it's a long shot. One thing we know for sure it that this was a well planned killing. I can't imagine the murderer giving himself away now. He must realise we're struggling, particularly, if it is Clarke, after that little scene. But then again, as you say, what else have we got? Why not? Let's go for it then. We'll have a tail put on him until Monday morning and see what we come up with.'

Adam leaned back and seemed happier now he had at least some action to take. They sipped their coffees in silence, lifting them up when one of the canteen ladies came to wipe their table. She fussed around them and then spoke falteringly.

'Excuse me, I know you're very busy. I'm sorry to interrupt you, but may I just have a very quick word?' She sounded painfully nervous.

'Hello', said Adam warmly, ever the gentleman. 'It's no problem at all. In fact it's a pleasure to have a chat with one of the ladies who look after us so well here. How can we help you?'

'It was you I wanted to have a word with', she said, looking at Dan. 'You're that chap on the TV, aren't you? I recognised you straight away. I always watch South West Tonight', she said proudly. Dan nodded and put on the indulgent smile he used for talking to viewers.

'My son wants to try to get into the media, and I was wondering if you'd mind giving him some advice? He's at university in Exeter at the moment and doesn't know how to go about getting in.' Her voice was trembling. 'I'm really sorry to bother you. I bet you get people coming up to you all the time like this. I'll understand if you're too busy of course.'

'It's no trouble at all', said Dan. 'The only way I got into TV was people who worked there being kind enough to let me come in and have a look around. I never thought they'd be interested in someone like me, so your boy's got as good a chance as anyone.' He rummaged in his wallet and held out his card. 'What's your son's name?'

'Adrian', she said.

'Ask Adrian to give me a call on the mobile number on here and I'll arrange for him to come in to have a look round. Then we can see about getting him some work experience.'

The woman looked as if she'd been blessed. Not for the first time, Dan wondered about the extraordinary power of television.

'Thank you, thank you so much. Oh, thank you.' Her words tumbled out. 'He'll be so grateful. I'll get him to call. You are kind. Thank you.'

'That'll be you getting the best bits of meat at lunch', said Adam as she glided off to wipe down the other tables. Even Suzanne was smiling. That's a first, thought Dan, then felt guilty for it.

'Do you mind if I ask something?' said Suzanne. 'What was that stuff about how Clarke keeps the rain off him? That was one of the more bizarre questions I've ever heard in an interview.'

'It was just a thought', said Dan, who still wasn't sure himself.

What was it about, he wondered, aware both Adam and Suzanne were watching him. He knew it'd been an instinctive question, something that had surfaced from his sub conscious. The only thing he could think of was a quirk he'd noticed about the way his brain worked. When he had time to kill, he'd often tackle the Daily Telegraph's cryptic crossword. On a first sitting, he'd get maybe half the clues and then get stuck. But if he walked away for quarter of an hour and did something else, didn't think about it, he'd be able to come back and usually finish the puzzle.

It was something he'd never understood. All he could think was that his sub conscious mind kept working on the clues, even though he wasn't aware of it. The question about the rain had come from the same place. He suspected his brain was chewing over the case without telling him. What bothered him was that his subconscious was obviously more powerful than his conscious mind. He wasn't about to try to explain all that now.

'Have we checked if there's any CCTV footage of Clarke at the station?' Dan asked.

'Yes', said Suzanne. 'I did that when we were checking his alibi. They have a couple of cameras because of attacks on cars parked there. It's not very clear, but you can see him getting out of a taxi at about a quarter to eight.'

'How clear is it?' asked Dan, who still didn't know why it might be important but thought he might as well run with it anyway. 'Is he wearing a hat like he said? Can you see him clearly?'

Adam looked at him quizzically. 'Carry on,' he said encouragingly. 'Keep going. Some of the best detective work is done on instinct. Follow it through.'

'You can't see his face', said Suzanne. 'He's wearing a big hat with a wide brim and the collar of his coat is up. But it certainly looks like him. The build is right and it's at the right time of day. There's also a shot of him in the evening, getting into a taxi in the rank just outside the entrance. It's still raining and he's got the hat on again. The times are spot on with what he said. There's similar footage from Bristol station.' She paused. 'Are you saying it might not have been him?'

She shook her head. Adam said nothing, just looked at Dan. 'It must have been', Suzanne went on. 'We've got his debit card buying the ticket at Plymouth Station, his mobile signal traced in Bristol, his cashpoint withdrawal at the station in Bristol and the text he sent from the train too, with info on it only he could have known. His secretary told us that. What are you thinking?'

'I really don't know', said Dan, and he still didn't. 'I can't explain it. It just felt like something I needed to ask about.'

Chapter seventeen

Emma Paget flicked through the book looking for the right page. It was a big, encyclopaedia like thing, some four hundred pages in all, expensive too, but she'd bought it because she knew the answer must be in there. She was ok with computers, competent in how to use them, but no expert. She could have done with calling in someone who really knew what they were doing, but this had to be done by her alone. She didn't want to risk a confidence.

It was dark outside and the hospice was quiet. There were still patients to be cared for, but it all wound down in the evening. Most of the visiting had finished and the patients were gathered around the televisions, or playing cards in the lounge. The staff were used to seeing her here late. She'd said good evening to a couple before locking herself away in her office.

'Emails, emails', she muttered to herself as she flicked through the book. The computer's screensaver lit up her face with flying stars. She found the page and began reading. It was exactly as she feared. Deleting an email doesn't mean it's gone forever, irretrievable.

Copies remain, in hidden folders and on the hard drive. She read on, to the section about permanent deletion. That was what she needed. Her hand hovered over the mouse.

~

Edward Bray's office was dark and deserted, until a key turned in the door's lock and a light clicked on. Penelope Ramsden looked around the familiar room. It was tidy, of course it was, she still insisted on that in the same way Mr Bray had done. Mr Bray, she thought, Mr Bray.

His office felt hollow to her, unnatural. The police had been through here, checking the computer, looking for papers, documents, anything that might give a clue as to why he'd been murdered. Murdered. The word echoed in her head and she thought of the man in the paintings on her wall, so proud, strong, so full of life.

There were still traces of the silver dust they'd used to check for fingerprints. The computer had gone, they'd said they needed to test it for evidence. But his desk was still here, the ordinary wooden desk from an ordinary office supplies store, not a grand mahogany one that so many bosses would delight in. She bent down and began opening its drawers.

~

When the hell am I going to have a chance to tell him? Thought Dan. He'd forgotten about Arthur Bray in the excitement of Clarke's arrest. Now he'd been released, they were back in the Murder Room and it was preying on his mind. Especially after what happened with Arthur and Suzanne Stewart.. It had to be soon, as soon as possible now. But Adam was lost in thought, just standing there, staring at the felt boards.

He reached out and straightened the photograph of Edward Bray. 'I'm not sure you deserve it from all that I've heard' Adam said quietly. 'But I will get them, don't worry. I will get them.'

He stared at Bray's picture, the web of suspects around him. The killer was in there somewhere, he was sure of it. This was no opportunistic crime, nothing committed on the spur of the moment. It was well planned and motivated by hatred. Hate, that was the key. The fatal shot, straight into the heart said it plainly. The people circling this photograph, all had a reason to hate the man. It was just a case of working away, checking alibis, whittling down the list of suspects until he found the killer. Or was he fooling himself? Hadn't they tried to do that already? And got nowhere..

That call from Hawes hadn't helped. He'd wanted to know how the interview with Clarke had gone. Were charges imminent? No, not exactly sir, not imminent. Not likely at all in fact, not against Clarke, not against anyone.

He'd tried to dress it up as best he could, but Hawes wasn't stupid, far from it. He'd been a detective himself, knew when a case was going badly. A few more days, the Assistant Chief Constable had warned, then staff would be drifted off to work on other cases. Hawes hadn't said it, but he knew what that meant. Other cases where there's a chance of a result. The Bray investigation would be wound down. Still active of course, reviewed occasionally, but wound down. And he knew exactly what the chances of a result were then. He was running out of time.

The door swung open and a balding head poked into the room.

'Hello chief'. Jim Fowler sounded surprised. 'I didn't expect to see you here. I thought you'd be out on the case.' What case? Thought Adam. I don't have a case.. 'I was going to leave a note.'

'I'm just having a think Jim. You know Dan, don't you?' From the window Dan nodded a greeting. 'So then, no note required, how can I help you?'

Fowler slid around the door. It was a quirk of his that he always wore soft-soled shoes and moved almost silently. Creepily, a couple of the women detectives said. 'It's just a quick one chief, but I thought you'd better know, it could be important.'

Adam had almost convinced himself that money played no part in Edward Bray's murder, that it was a matter of burning hatred and cold revenge, but he managed an expectant look anyway. Always make your team feel you're interested.

'I've been working through the payments in and out of his accounts again, just like you asked after we found all that money in his house.' Adam nodded. 'And all the people and companies check out as legit. There's just the one oddity.'

'Carry on'.

'Each month chief, for the past five years at least, Edward Bray has taken out two thousand, five hundred pounds in cash on the last Friday of the month. It's happened without fail, since a few months after he took the business over. We missed it the first time because it's hidden through a couple of other linked accounts and a savings scheme.'

'Really?' Slow, thoughtful, genuine interest. 'And no hint what the money was used for?'

'None at all chief. All his bills seem to be paid through his bank account using standing orders and direct debits. His salary comes from another account. There's no obvious need for big sums in cash every month.'

Adam adjusted his tie. 'Interesting', he said, and he meant it. Perhaps money was something to do with the killing after all? That amount of cash each month was more than his own take home pay. What could Bray need it for? Was it some form of reward for himself? Some hobby, some end of month blow out on drugs or something like that? Some night or two away in London, at a fancy hotel with a couple of classy call girls?

Why did blackmail keep echoing in his mind? What if Bray was being blackmailed by someone? What if he had threatened to stop paying, call in the police and the killer couldn't risk that, had to stop him? What if the lay by meeting was a regular event to pay up? What could he be blackmailed for?

Sex was the usual answer, any detective would tell you that, some sordid sexual secret. But none of their inquiries had even hinted at a relationship, let alone anything that might leave Bray open to extortion. Then again, you never really knew what went on in people's private lives, did you? Look at his own…

Enough of that. Some business indiscretion would be another reason, maybe something illegal, perhaps some corruption, but the Eggheads had been all over the books and had found nothing. And anyway, what about all that cash they'd found in his house? What was that for? Almost a hundred thousand pounds they'd counted. Where had it come from? He shook his head in frustration. He was starting to think there was much more to Edward Bray than he'd managed to find out.

A pointed cough landed him back in the murder room. 'Is there anything else I can help you with at the moment chief?'

'Don't think so', said Adam and Jim Fowler made to slide out of the door. 'Just one thing first Jim', said Adam. 'How rich exactly was Bray?'

Fowler smiled. It was the type of question an accountant liked. 'In terms of investments, portfolio, business, property or personal wealth?'

'Just the headlines please Jim.'

'Very rich chief.' He nodded vigorously to emphasise the words. 'His properties were worth about eight or nine million. On top of that, he had a significant share portfolio, worth several hundred thousands.' He pulled at each of his fingers and Adam thought he looked like he was counting off the pounds. 'The business had about half a million pounds in its accounts. His personal account had almost exactly a million in it.' The accountant's smile grew. 'So very rich chief.'

Dan whistled from the window as the man left. 'He was doing ok for himself then.'

Adam nodded. 'Yes indeed. But I'm not sure any of that helps us in the case.'

Dan saw his opening. 'I know something that might help.' He tried not to sound nervous, but could feel a prickling sweat at the base of his back. 'Well, just a little bit.'

'What?'

'Before I tell you, I just wanted to say I've been trying to tell you for a while now, but I haven't had a chance. And..'

'Just get on with it please.' Adam sounded weary. 'I've had enough for one day.'

He told Adam about his evening visit to see Arthur Bray, how he'd been watching a film on Sky Movies, one of those you have to order, enter a personal identification number to pay for. How he often did it, had been watching one on the evening Edward had died. How he'd ordered it as he always did, as he had his tea, about 5.15.

'He didn't realise that could clear him. He's not up with all this technology stuff.'

Adam looked at him, shook his head. Dan couldn't read his expression.

'I wasn't trying to do any of my own investigating. I was just, well, worried about him after that press conference.' Still no reaction from Adam. 'He was so upset, and he had no one else to talk to. So I thought I'd pop round. That's how I found out. I'm sorry, I have been meaning to tell you, but..'

'Ok, ok.' Adam cut in, sounded irritated but not angry. 'Here's the formal reprimand. I can't be bothered to shout at you. Don't ever go off talking to anyone connected with a case again without clearing it with me first. You could scupper the entire investigation. Got that?'

'Yes'. Dan tried not to let his relief show. It hadn't been as bad as he feared.

'And in fairness, well done, good work, all that sort of thing.' Adam sounded tired, disillusioned even? 'I didn't really think he was the killer, but it's good to get him out of the equation. I wish you'd told me earlier though. It would have saved, well, some discomfort for him.'

Dan knew exactly what he meant. The gossip had been so hot around the station even he'd got to hear it. DC Reed hadn't been as discrete as Suzanne Stewart had hoped.

'I found out something else too. I'm not sure if it could help, but it's worth knowing..'

'In a mo. Just one thing first. Are you with me for the rest of the day?'

Dan checked his watch. It said 3.45, which meant it was probably about four. No calls from the newsroom and he'd filed a couple of good stories recently, so he was probably in credit with Lizzie. 'I think so. Why?'

'I really need a beer. Let's go get a couple in.'

～

An electric guitar's distorted chords and a wailing voice were escaping from The Minerva's door, so Dan and Adam looked at each other, then walked on another 30 yards down the hill to Porters Bar.

Dan was still feeling relieved. He'd half expected to be thrown off the inquiry. Maybe more than half. But then he thought what was he talking about? He wasn't on the inquiry. He was a journalist, seeing how it was done to help him understand for future stories and to produce a decent report on this one when it was over. But he knew he'd been drawn in, hopelessly so. He'd breached the rule that was drummed into journalists, just as it was with medics, or the police, or social workers, or any other profession. It was a fundamental. Don't get involved.

A bereaved and crying relative is a customer, a client, an interviewee, not a friend. A big fire is a television spectacle to be filmed, not something to be put out. A common joke between journalists and fire crews went that they were selfish for putting the blaze out before it could be filmed. So it was that a murder investigation was to be written about, reported on, not get involved in. But he felt a part of this one.

It was early evening, and apart from four young lads who looked like officer workers sitting around a table in one corner, the pub was empty.

'No Doom Bar', said a disappointed looking Adam as he studied the pumps. 'I was looking forward to that. I knew it wasn't my day.'

'Ah, but it may be yet.' Behind the bar was a welcome barrel. 'They have that rare and beautiful beast, Spingo.' He was glad of some lightness in the conversation. Adam looked lifeless, deflated.

'Spingo? It sounds like a kids' sweet.'

'Have I let you down yet? Go and sit down, master detective, and I'll get the drinks in. You look like you've had a bad day.' Adam didn't smile.

Dan paid for the beers and joined him at a table by the window. The detective's blue silk tie wasn't tight to his collar, the first time Dan had seen that happen. It was only perhaps an inch or two down, but for a man who habitually straightened his tie when times were good it was an ominous sign.

It was dark outside, on the cusp of the downward tail of the rush hour, but the roads were still busy as commuter-laden cars grumbled their way home. The odd worker strode gratefully away from their office, coats pulled up around their necks. December had brought a chill bite of wind to the clear night air.

Adam took a sip of his pint and his eyes widened. Dan smiled, felt the tension break.

'Spingo', he said, as if introducing an old friend, 'is brewed in one place, and one place only; the Blue Anchor pub in Helston, way down in west Cornwall. You do see it regularly at beer festivals, but not often in pubs. So we are indeed lucky. It's got a great taste, but is also strong and fabled to have mildly hallucinogenic properties. So take care. Cheers!'

Adam raised his glass, leaned back and took another deep draw. 'So what's the matter then?' asked Dan. 'You've been looking miserable all afternoon. Case not going well?'

Adam laughed out loud, and took another long drink of his beer.

'That's some understatement. As far as I can tell, it's not going at all. My main suspect is out of contention. Tony Rye and his affair! Most of my other possible suspects have good alibis. The only two who don't are Emma Paget and Penelope Ramsden. Paget says she was at the gym. We've checked with their reception. They've got an electronic log of who comes in, and her card was swiped at 4.17. However they don't swipe people out, so we don't know what time she left. She says about six, but no one there can confirm that. So at least she's in the frame, and we'll keep looking at her, but quite honestly, I can't see it. I can't see the hate there, or the motive.'

'That thing I was going to mention back at Charles Cross', said Dan. 'I found out why Bray saved the Hospice when I spoke to his Dad. I would have told you when we were talking about those Apple Tree poems he wrote, but you wanted to get on with interviewing Hicks and Stead. It's another insight into him. I can't see how it helps the investigation, but you'd better be the judge of that.'

Adam loosened his tie further, then unknotted it, and hung it over one of the chairs at the table. 'That's better', he said, and leaned back, stretched. 'Go on.'

'I got it wrong, well mostly wrong. When I saw those big No Smoking signs at his office I put that together with his mother dying of cancer and thought she smoked, and that was what killed her. Bray was obviously devoted to her. Remember what he told Gordon Clarke? "The one woman he'd ever been involved with he had no choice about, and she'd broken his heart", were his words I think. It seemed simple enough. That had to refer to his mum. So I thought he must have hated smoking after that.'

Adam nodded. 'Fair conclusion.' Dan took another sip of his beer, thinking over what Arthur Bray had told him.

'I was wrong. She didn't smoke, it was Arthur. He was a chain smoker until she contracted cancer. Then he gave it up, just like that. The doctors said they couldn't be sure it was his smoke that caused it, probably wasn't in fact, but he blamed himself anyway.'

Dan closed his eyes, remembering the old man, slumped in his armchair, struggling to get the words out.

'Well Edward Bray certainly did blame him', he continued. '"Not much short of murder', were the words Arthur said he used. That, incidentally, was why they used to have the blazing rows we've heard about. Mrs Bray's death was the start of the disintegration of the relationship between father and son. There are a quite a few poems about it in the folder. I've been looking through them. One goes something like this.'

"Murder isn't always simple,
A knife or a gun,
For love or hate.
Murder can be subtle,
Hidden in selfishness,
Consequences ignored,
More lethal."

'After Mrs Bray's death', said Dan, 'Arthur worked even harder to try to make it up to Edward in some way, by building up the business for him, but that only drove them further apart.'

Adam drew in a deep breath. 'And he saved the Hospice because he remembered going there as a child to see his Mum?'

Dan shook his head. 'No, I got that wrong too. It's not so simple. I think that is part of it, but Arthur Bray says it's because it was another way Edward had to get at him, to remind him of what he'd done. I'd guess it's a mix of the two reasons. Nice eh?'

A man and woman were having an argument outside in the street. Voices rose until the woman shouted 'screw you then', and stalked off in the direction of the city centre, her boots clicking on the cobbles. The man looked around him helplessly, then followed. Dan thought about Kerry and wondered how long it would be before they had a similar confrontation. That was if he chose to carry on the relationship of course. If..

'Families eh?' said Adam, with feeling. 'Families!' Dan remembered the last time they'd come close to talking about their personal lives and what had happened. He stayed silent. Adam could talk if he wanted to. He wouldn't ask.

'What about Penelope Ramsden then?'

'Whew', said Adam, after another sip of beer. It wasn't clear if he was talking about the drink or her. 'Now there's an odd one. She was at the office until five she says, although again no one can confirm that. The lads she has working there leave at 4.30. They start at half eight you see, something Bray had about beginning work early. So she could have got to the lay by. In terms of motive, well, don't think this ridiculous, but the only one I can possibly see is love.'

Dan spluttered into his drink. 'Love?!' Of all the unlikely couples he could ever imagine, Edward Bray and Penelope Ramsden..

Adam chuckled at the reaction. 'Yes, love. She's an amateur painter – not bad in fact - and there are about a dozen portraits of him in her house. There are four in the lounge alone.'

Dan shook his head. He knew he shouldn't think it, but he found the idea of such emotion in her hard to believe. And Bray an amateur poet, and her an amateur painter, and neither knowing it of the other.

'She clearly loved him, though she says she never told him so', said Adam. 'I wondered if maybe she had and he'd spurned her. That's a good motive, but I've no evidence of it whatsoever. It's just a thought, but I'm still struggling to see her with a shotgun, lying in wait in a lay by, then shooting her boss.' He shook his head too. 'But it's about all I've got at the moment.'

Dan thought back to the first day he'd met Adam Breen, smart and commanding, standing in a lay by where Edward Bray had been murdered, radiating authority and certainty that the killer would soon be caught. And now..

'You must have some other ideas, surely? Some other suspects?' He ran his finger around the rim of the pint glass. 'At the start of this you said you'd never had so many. There must be some left.'

Adam leaned further back on his chair, looked up at the ceiling and spread out his arms.

'Where?' he asked simply. 'All the obvious ones have been ruled out by their alibis. 'Rye was a hot suspect and he's out. His mistress and her neighbours confirmed he was with her. It was a source of plenty of local gossip, that little liaison. Clarke was a good suspect too, but he was in Bristol. The tail we put on him came up with nothing. Those idiots Hicks and Stead are out. Their mobile traces have come back. They were by the river, fishing I suppose, then to that shop where they broke the milk bottle, then got a bus, then went home, just as they said. They only live just around the corner from each other and the phone traces show Hicks going home, Stead stays with him for a few minutes, presumably having a chat, then Stead's trace goes back to his own place. The traces are that precise.'

Adam paused for some more beer. 'We've checked other people who didn't like Bray, but they've got alibis too. Kate Moore was at a lovely middle class couple's place, working on their staircase. They're straight as they come, impeccable alibi. I can't be bothered to list all the rest but they check out too.'

He looked out the window as a taxi pulled up, a couple of women clambered out. 'Could it be someone entirely unconnected with Bray then?' Adam went on. 'Yes, of course it could, but why? This was clearly a well-planned killing, so why would someone unconnected with him do it? We've been back through his past at length. Anything that's shown up as a possible motive we've looked at. Everything's drawn a blank.'

'What about the 999 call saying Bray's body was at the lay by?' asked Dan. 'That sounded like a good lead. You know, the one you thought was the killer, or an accomplice.'

Adam shrugged. 'It could have been them, but then again, it might not. It might just be someone innocent, who found the body, but doesn't want to get mixed up with the police. That happens all the time. Maybe a couple meeting up in the lay by for some illicit sex, something like that. It happens. If it was the killer, why call us? The only reason I can see is to make sure the time of Bray's death was clear and certain, to give someone an alibi. But as I've said, all the people we've checked have impeccable alibis anyway, and wouldn't need to have Bray's body found to establish them.'

'Well, what about a professional killing then? A contract job?'

'You're lapsing back into crime fiction Dan. Contrary to what those authors tell you, there aren't that many hit men around. I've never met one in my career and I don't know many detectives who have. We've checked over the local crims who might be up for something like that, but they've all got good alibis. There's no word of any other non-local criminals suddenly appearing in the area. We'd have been told, we've got a good network of informers. And anyway, those assassins that I have heard of don't use shotguns. The shotgun is the weapon of an amateur killer, something relatively easy to get hold of but still lethal. They're too big, too imprecise, too messy for a professional. They use handguns. I can't rule it out obviously, but I can't see it.'

Dan took a slurp of beer and considered. He wanted to come up with some great solution, but there was nothing. Of course there wasn't. That was the stuff of books, the epiphany moment. It wasn't reality. If Adam couldn't see one, how could he expect to?

'So what are you going to do then?' he asked lamely.

'What can I do? I'll keep investigating. People tend to kill for love first of all, or loss of it. That's why I thought of Penelope Ramsden. Revenge is mixed up in that, and it's the second most common motive. Then it's money. After that, you're struggling for a reason. On the money side, there's the couple of thousand he took out at the end of every month. That suggests some form of blackmail, but where? By whom? Nothing we've turned up gives any possible cause for blackmail. It could just be that he took the cash and went off for a weekend in some posh hotel, big meals, even prostitutes. And then there's all the money in his house, almost a hundred thousand pounds now we've counted it. What the hell is that about? That suggests he's got some dodgy business dealings going on, or even that he's blackmailing someone, but again we've turned up nothing that could even start to explain it. It's all a bloody mystery.'

Adam took another deep drink. 'Pah!' he spat. 'It was my bloody fault. I thought at the start this could be a fairly straightforward case, some business rivalry thing. Fatal. I must have jinxed it.'

The door opened and a couple came in, the man much older than the woman. Boss and secretary, thought Dan? She sat at a table in the furthest and darkest corner of the pub while he went to the bar and ordered the most expensive bottle of wine they had. Dan took that as confirmation.

'So what are you going to do next then?' he asked Adam.

'We'll niggle away at any leads that come up. We'll keep looking at people who might want to harm Bray. I'll keep thinking about it. But right now I don't feel much hope of cracking it. I don't think you're going to get your 'police arrest the killer' story here mate, but you might well get a 'police stumped' one.'

Adam leaned back on his chair again and stretched his arms. 'It's the lack of evidence that's the problem. I was hoping for some breakthrough, but so far there's been nothing. I hate to say it, but I'm just not hopeful of getting a result on this one. Whoever did for Mr Bray thought about it hard and planned it well, and they're running rings around us at the moment.'

Dan had never seen Adam look so dejected. The lines around his eyes and mouth, normally fine and slight had deepened. They looked etched. For a man who usually carried himself upright, his shoulders were drooping as if burdened by an invisible weight.

Dan took a swig of beer and digested the news. It felt like a personal insult. It had never occurred to him the case he had worked on may not be solved.

'Do you think you're not going to crack it? Honestly?'

'I never say never, but I'm not feeling hopeful. From the start, what we needed was a break and we've never got one. Not a sniff. It's a well thought out murder and a tough one to crack for that.'

Dan wondered what he was going to tell Lizzie. He'd anticipated a big splash of a story on the inside track on how the police caught the man who killed Edward Bray. That was how he'd won the time to follow the investigation. He couldn't imagine her being sympathetic to the police's problems. Not to mention his.

He tried not to sound desperate. 'What about that cancelled appointment in Bray's diary, the one you thought might have been the murderer?'

'Now that is curious.' Adam sat up, sounded more animated. 'I've been thinking about it a lot. It looks like the killer, or certainly an accomplice, but we haven't got anywhere with it as a lead. The name in the diary was Ed Smith. It's false. I had all the checks run, but nothing came up to match it. There are no criminals, local business people, or anyone who knew Bray of that name.'

'What do you make of it then?' asked Dan.

'Probably that whoever planned to kill Bray was going to do it earlier, but for some reason couldn't, and cancelled the meeting. I spoke to Penelope Ramsden. She vaguely remembered the caller. It was a man, and well spoken, but that's all she could give us, nothing more.'

Adam leaned forwards, as if sharing a confidence. 'He said he wanted to meet Bray to talk about a big business deal involving selling some land, and he wanted to do it at that lay by because the land was near by and you could see if from there, actually see it's potential. He wouldn't say any more. It may look suspicious to you and me. It may even have to Bray. Who knows? But maybe his curiosity and greed got the better of him and he went. And we know what happened then.'

'But why would the killer cancel an appointment?'

Adam shrugged. 'That's what I've been thinking about. If we knew that, we'd probably crack the case. It could have been something important, like not being able to get hold of the shotgun at that time. It could be something trivial, like the killer suddenly having second thoughts. I just don't know.'

Dan pondered into his pint, but could think of nothing either. Still it seemed to him a possible opening. They weren't exactly spoiled for them.

'Were any of the potential suspects doing anything interesting or unusual that day? Something that could have come up that would have forced them to cancel the appointment. I don't know what, something like a domestic or family emergency?'

Adam smiled. 'You are starting to think like a detective. I like it. We did have that checked out, but nothing showed up with any of them. Nothing at all.'

Dan felt an inexplicable excitement. 'Something had to have happened though. Something unforeseen. If this was the planned killing we're sure it was, something went wrong on that day that meant the killer called it off.'

'It wasn't that day, remember? It was the day before.'

'What?'

'According to Penelope Ramsden, it was the day before that the man rang in to cancel the meeting.'

'So it's unlikely to be a sudden emergency then', said Dan slowly, drifting in thought. 'It was something the killer knew was going to happen the next day to make the murder impossible.'

'I'm with you', said Adam, looking more interested. 'What kind of thing are you thinking?'

'I don't know. Perhaps something like a work commitment that meant the killer couldn't get away. Or had to be somewhere else.'

'Yes, but nothing like that showed up with any of the possible suspects. It might not be that at all. It could be something simple, like they got cold feet', said Adam. 'It's interesting speculation, but I'm not sure it helps us.'

The idea wasn't letting Dan go. 'I don't know. I think you're right. If we get an idea why, it might be a way into the case. What do you know the day before that might stop you doing something the next day?'

Adam shrugged. 'Too many things. I've been through all this. Ok, as you said, it might be work, or a family thing.' Dan couldn't tell if he was interested or just resigned to playing along. 'What makes you change your plans for the next day?'

'I tell you what the main one is. The weather.' Dan leaned forwards on his chair, his voice excited. 'If it's a rotten day, we sometimes put filming off until the weather improves. TV is tricky in the rain and the pictures never look as nice. And if I'm going to take Rutherford for a walk on the moor, we soon forget it if the forecast is looking horrible.'

'The weather', said Adam, who'd suddenly snapped back into the conversation. 'The weather. Now there's a thought. The weather.'

'But how would the weather affect your plan to kill someone?' asked Dan.

There was a silence as they looked at each other, minds racing.

'Do you remember when Bray was killed', said Adam, with increasing excitement. 'It was a wet and miserable day. Remember?'

'Yes, I do', said Dan who had cursed being called out in it.

'What does wet weather make you do? It makes you cover up. Use an umbrella. Put up your hood. Wear a hat. Very useful if you don't want to be recognised.'

'I've got it', said Dan. 'But that only works if the cancelled meeting was a fine day.'

'It was', said Adam. 'I know because I had a rare day off after being called out the weekend before. I took Tom to the park and we played football. It was beautiful. Shirt sleeves weather even.'

There was another silence. They were so wrapped in their thoughts that for once the beers in front of them stood untouched.

'Does it help us at all?' asked Dan, finally.

'I don't know', replied Adam. 'But at the very least it gives me a new idea to explore. And that's a bloody relief in itself.' He finished the remains of his pint. 'Another?'

'Just a half please', said Dan. 'I've got to drive home.'

'Me too', said Adam, getting up and making for the bar. 'It is good stuff, isn't it? Best thing that's happened to me today. Best discovery certainly. I've uncovered just about nothing else.'

Dan checked his phone while Adam was at the bar. He knew there were no messages, but he looked anyway. He wondered what Kerry was doing. He hadn't spoken to her for a while. Was she hurt or playing it cool? Or had she just lost interest? Got fed up with him? That was what usually happened. He normally managed to scare women away.

He knew he did it, but he'd never understood why. In the morning he always wanted to flee from any emotional entanglement, but by the evening it had become appetising again. Was it a primitive fear of the dangers and loneliness of the night and a need to have someone to share it with? And in the morning, was it the rejuvenation of sleep that made him feel strong enough to want to face the world alone, unencumbered? Whatever it was, it didn't make for good relationships.

Would she like to hear from him? She'd been very good-natured about being effectively thrown out of the flat. She'd even taken his T-shirt as a hostage for a return visit. But he had been abrupt – rude in fact - and he wondered how he'd feel if he woke up next to her tomorrow. He didn't want to suffer the urge of being desperate to escape again. He decided to leave it and not text her, for now at least.

'There you go', said Adam, delivering the two halves. Dan thought how unsatisfying they always looked compared to a full pint. 'Let's leave work behind for a bit. I'm fed up with thinking about the bloody case. How was your weekend? My detective's intuition sensed something interesting there.'

Dan managed a coy smile. 'It's funny you should say that, I was just thinking about it myself.'

'So then, what happened?'

'We went out for a walk. Up to Dartmoor, near Princetown. Very pretty it was', said Dan evasively, but with little hope of shaking Adam off his tail.

'And you're trying to tell me that's all that happened? I wish all my cases were as easy to crack as you.'

'Ok then. To cut a long story short, we ended up in her bath afterwards to warm up.'

Adam chuckled and his face lightened. 'Good stuff', he said. 'So who is the lucky lady, and what's she like?'

'She's called Kerry. She's a kind of middle manager thing for Sweb, the electricity company. She's quite pretty, at least I think so. A nice girl.'

'I take it you've heard the expression 'damned with faint praise'?', said Adam, who was chuckling harder now. 'I don't think I've ever heard a better example. 'Quite pretty'? A 'nice' girl?'

'Ah, well, you know', said Dan, who didn't know what to say. Was he that obvious? 'Yes, I like her, I wouldn't have gone out with her otherwise. Yes, she's pretty. But if you're asking do I want to try a big long-term relationship with her, I think you've already rumbled the answer is no.'

He leaned back on his chair. 'When I was in the office last week, a couple of the girls were talking about boyfriends they'd had who they weren't particularly keen on. They said they were better than being alone, and 'would do for now'. Those were their words. Mercenary eh? They called them 'practice boyfriends'. Well, I hate to say it, but I think I feel the same about Kerry. She's a decent lass. I quite like her company, but I'm not sure I'd like her around too much. It's winter, it's cold and lonely, and there's no one else about, so I quite like seeing her.' Dan noticed Adam had dissolved into silent laughter. 'Is that so wrong?' he added tetchily. 'Am I being too honest?'

Adam gathered himself with what seemed like an effort. 'No, no, no, of course not', he said, still trying to control his laughter. 'No, I think we've all done it. It was just good to re-live it.'

Dan was still looking annoyed.

'I used to get off with junior officers', said Adam, and Dan couldn't hide his surprise.

'Well, it was an easy target', he added. 'They looked up to me. They were about the only women I ever met.

This job can be a killer for the social life. It's only human to occasionally want to be with someone warm and cuddly. Don't beat yourself up about it.'

'I'm not really', said Dan, both amused and warmed by the pep talk. Adam could have been his father. 'I'm quite happy with what I'm doing. There's only the occasional tinge of guilt. What bothers me are her feelings. I think she likes me much more than I like her. I think she'd like us to be in a proper relationship, and I'm just not up for that at all.'

'When are relationships equal? One person always feels more than the other. There's always an imbalance. Look at...'

Adam stopped sharply. Dan was certain he'd been about to say 'look at me and..', but that would have been the start of an inroad to a life he wasn't sure he was ready to reveal, something he'd reacted angrily about before. It was a sacred place. Me and what, Dan wondered, me and what? The two men looked at each other, both holding their half-pint glasses. They were almost empty.

'Look at what?' said Dan gently.

Adam shook his head and took a deep breath. 'I need the loo a minute', he said. 'Wait there.'

At least the toilets were clean, thought Adam, as he stood at the urinal. Cold, but clean. His breath formed clouds, which bounced back off the white tiles. So many pubs didn't care for their toilets, so many probably believed their customers were too drunk to notice and they weren't worth spending money on. But he always remembered what a pub's loos were like.

They gave you an insight into how the rest of the place was run. Never eat in a pub with a dirty toilet.

He was trying to block out his thoughts, he knew it. He'd been about to tell Dan about Annie. He'd come so close, within a second, just a few more words and that would have been it, it would have all come out. He hadn't told anyone about it, had carried it all himself. People at work might suspect, but no one knew. No one would.

He smiled grimly. Tell someone at work, and it would be around the building within an hour, round the city in a couple and around Devon and Cornwall by the end of the day. He wasn't joking about seeing your private life written on the police station's toilet walls. He'd known it happen to other officers. The police weren't an understanding service, certainly not a caring one.

He wanted to talk to someone about it though, he knew that. He wanted to unburden himself, let it go, just have someone listen, then perhaps hear some sympathy and support. He'd surprised himself with that. He thought he was stronger.

Why hadn't he spoken to one of his friends about it? He didn't like the answer to that, but it was true nonetheless. He didn't have any friends. His job was his life. His job, and Annie and Tom. His work never allowed time for a social circle. And not many cared to mix with a policeman. His family were all he wanted anyway, he didn't need friends when he had such a wonderful wife and son. But he didn't have them any more, did he? His job had seen to that. And as for Sarah.. Now he had nothing, no family, no friends, just his work. He slapped the palm of his hand against the cold white tiles.

But he hadn't lost his family had he? Not yet, anyway. There was still hope, Annie had said, but sometimes it didn't feel like it. And there was only hope if you sort work out. Those were her words. Sort work out. But how could he do that? He was a Detective Chief Inspector and that meant working all hours. Crime didn't run to a family friendly rota. And if he left CID, wouldn't he be betraying Sarah?

So what was he going to do? He wanted to stay here in this pub tonight, drink until the alcohol numbed the pain, not go back to that cold and lonely flat to think about his life. He wanted to talk about it, talk about Annie and Tom and how much he loved them and how he wanted to be back with them. And Sarah too, and how he would always fight – however hopelessly – to make up for what happened to her.

But it wasn't easy, was it? It left you vulnerable. Did he trust that man sitting out there waiting for him? Wouldn't he just go and blab about how weird and screwed up the police really are? Wouldn't he tell his friends and other journalists about what the job really meant and what it did to the people? The people like him.

But he did want to talk. And Dan, well, he'd been decent hadn't he? Trustworthy. He was a good man, wasn't he? He hadn't let out any of the inside stuff on the case, had he? They got on well didn't they? They were becoming friends, weren't they? It had surprised him, but he knew it was true. He'd like to have a friend.

He slapped the cold wall again and walked out of the toilets.

Dan was looking out of the window as a motorist attempted to park in a space opposite the bar. The engine's over-revving penetrated the pub. Adam followed his gaze.

'Took me bloody ages to get the hang of parking too', he said, sitting down.

'One of my first distinctions at work was to demolish a wall', said Dan. 'They made the mistake of giving me a car with a tow hook on the back and my reversing was a bit too enthusiastic.'

Both men laughed, a little nervously Dan thought. The car was half up on the kerb now.

'Listen Adam', he said. 'You've helped and trusted me no end and I very much appreciate it. I know you like to keep your private life to yourself and I respect that, but if there is something you want to talk about, I can promise you it won't end up written on the toilet walls back in the station.'

The two men looked at each other. Outside, the motorist gave up the space and drove off. Another car nipped in and parked first time. Such is life, thought Dan.

'You know what I'd like?' said Adam, looking at his empty half-pint glass. 'Another pint of that, and another to follow, and probably a few more after that. How's your dog's bladder?'

One of the stranger questions I've ever been asked thought Dan. 'Pretty good.' What else could he say? He could hardly leave now. 'I'll get them in.'

Chapter eighteen

Adam began his story as soon as Dan sat back down.

'Annie and Tom live in a lovely house in Peverell. It was our house, the three of us together.' Adam stared down into his drink. 'We've been apart for four months now. I see Tom as much as I can. Annie lets me come round whenever possible. She says he misses me. And she misses me too.'

Both men lifted their beers. Dan wondered how much more he could drink and still be in a reasonable state for work tomorrow. Facing Lizzie with a hangover was neither wise nor pleasant.

'We separated because of my job. She wasn't seeing enough of me she said, and she was absolutely right. She wants us to get back together. I want us to get back together. But whenever things start getting better, another case like this comes up. My pager goes off and I have to go.'

Adam looked down accusingly at the small black box clipped to his belt, as if it was a mighty enemy.

'It's part of the job. You know that. You accept it. You know that when you join the police. Jesus, you know it even more when you join CID. It was made quite clear to me. A big incident means you go. No arguments, no delay, no exceptions, no nothing, you just go. People's lives can depend on you. And it's right; it's what you do the job for. And if we're honest, it's exciting. It's great in fact. It's dramatic and unpredictable and you feel like you're doing something that really makes a difference. I bet you feel the same about your job.'

Dan just sat there looking at Adam. He didn't need to say anything. Listening was enough. He felt he was being hit by a tide of long suppressed emotion. He managed a nod.

'It's great when you're just living for yourself. But then something changes', Adam continued. 'Just a little something to start with. You meet a woman you quite like. And you start going out together. And then you get to know her better, and you get to like her more. And then you fall in love with her. Even police officers can fall in love, did you realise that?'

His voice rose and he sounded defiant. Dan didn't know what to say, but he knew he didn't have to say anything.

'And then you know what?' he continued. 'You start to think she's more important than the job. Imagine that! More important than your job. What would the Chief Constable say? So you resent it a little when you get called out. But it's ok, because there's plenty more time together, and she's proud of you, and understanding, and she tells you to go, and not worry. So you go. And it's all ok. You solve the crime and feel good about it, and she's there for you when you finally get home.'

His voice rose, and a couple of people on nearby tables half turned.

'Then something happens which you never thought would. You decide to get married. And you're happy, so happy. You're the happiest person on earth. I know everyone says that, but I was. I can remember every second of that day. I still go back over and over it again in my mind. It was everything. Annie looked stunning, the weather was beautiful, our friends and family were all so kind and happy for us. It was just a perfect day.'

The barman collected the empty pint glasses from their table and gave a nod of respect at the number, but Adam didn't seem to notice.

'Then you buy a house, and settle into a routine and it's all lovely. You still get called out, but she's supportive. There's no trouble at all. You clear up the case and come home again. She's waiting. Wonderful. It can't get any better, but suddenly it does. She's pregnant. It's not an easy pregnancy, but we love each other through it. And then Tom's born. And I just spent that night holding him, and looking at him and Annie, and crying with happiness.'

Now Dan saw what he thought he never would when he'd first met Adam. There were tears shining in the edges of his eyes.

'And you take your son home and you watch him grow. And it's wonderful. You can actually see his little personality developing. And he was such a smiley baby. Always smiling. You don't need a TV anymore when you've got a baby. You just sit and watch him. And he grew up so fast, so very fast. But I kept getting called out to these murders, and rapes, and shit like that, and I think Annie was getting fed up with it. She didn't say anything but I could feel her resentment. I didn't feel so close to her as I did before. I felt a gap opening up. But I had to do my job. When I was called, I had to go. And do you know what really did it?'

Dan just shook his head again.

'The day Tom said his first word, I was out investigating an armed robbery in Falmouth. I didn't get home that night. Annie told me the next day. And instead of feeling excited and pleased and happy, I felt guilty. We had a big row. Can you imagine that? Your son's said his first word and you end up rowing with your wife.'

Adam's hand gripped the edge of the table. It was trembling. 'She told me that my job was coming between us. I knew that, but I'd been trying to ignore it, block it out. So I promised I'd spend more time with her and Tom. I had a word with my Superintendent and he agreed to help. It got better for a while. But then it was back to the endless call outs and more arguing with Annie. Then one day she said she'd had enough. It was my job or my family. She said she doesn't want Tom growing up not knowing when he'll see his father. She says it'd be better if he just knew he was going to see me every weekend. So I left the house, stayed in a bed and breakfast for a few days, then rented a flat just around the corner, on the edge of Peverell. That's where I've been ever since.'

A tear worked free but he caught it with a hand. 'She says she just doesn't think she can be a policeman's wife. And I don't know if I can blame her. But I know I can't leave the job. There's something else you see, something that keeps driving me. Something I've never told anyone else about. Only my family know.'

He looked Dan in the eye. 'I know I can trust you mate, but this is the big secret. If it got out, I could be forced out of the police. Ok?'

Dan nodded, didn't want to speak, break the spell.

'I got into police work for a reason, a bloody good reason. I've got a sister, a younger sister. Sarah's her name. She's just a year younger than me. Beautiful she was, long blonde hair, tall, thin. Funny, clever, kind. You'd have loved her.' Adam managed a strained smile, but it faded fast.

'We were in the sixth form together. We were both doing A levels. I was doing ok, enough to go to university. But she was brilliant. The teachers were saying straight A's for her, a place at Oxford or Cambridge if she wanted it. We were all so proud of her. And then..'

Another deep draw at his beer, then another, the pint gone. Adam pushed the empty glass across the table.

'She was attacked on the way home from a night out. Beaten and raped. Put in hospital. She survived, but after that, she was a different person. She was quiet, withdrawn, couldn't stick at her courses.' Adam gazed at the empty glass. 'She dropped out of sixth form college, spent a few months at home, then moved away. She got a job in a factory and a flat somewhere in Hull. She chose it because she'd never been there before. She wanted somewhere new, away from everything that had happened. I hardly speak to her now, a brief call at

Christmas and on her birthday and that's about it. She doesn't seem to want to know anything or anyone that might remind her of the past.'

Adam rolled his head and closed his eyes. 'That was it. A life ruined. The bloke who did it was never caught.' A deep breath. 'I joined the police to stop people like him.'

Adam wiped his face with the sleeve of his jacket and stood up. 'One more?' he asked, unsteadily. Dan checked his watch but the numbers were out of focus. Time didn't matter anyway. He needed a drink after that.

Adam returned with two more pints of Spingo.

'I think Kerry knows I'm not that keen on her', said Dan. 'But it hasn't stopped her. Annie must have known what it'd be like when she married you surely? So why do they do it then?'

'Because they always think things will change.' Adam emphasised the point by prodding the table with his finger. 'They always believe that you'll be there in the end, or you'll come to love them in your case. It's a romantic thing. They're brought up to believe in happy endings and that's what they do.'

Dan's blurred thoughts registered this as a good theory, except that he hadn't found a happy ending for himself so far. He suddenly felt lonely, very lonely. Rutherford would be waiting for him of course – wasn't that why he'd bought the dog? – but no sympathetic partner, no hug and cuddle, no cup of tea, no one to listen, no warm and understanding wife..

'I don't know if I'll ever be able to settle down happily' he said, gazing deep into the certainty of his beer. If he was honest, it wasn't always a great comfort, but what else did he have?

'When I was 21 I met the woman of my dreams. We were at University together. We were in the same year. She was a stunner, an absolute stunner. She was beautiful, clever, even perfect I'd say. Thomasin was her name. She was just an inch short of me. Five feet eleven she was, with a model's figure. She had brown bobbed hair, cut to the chin. It was all different tints; something Yeats might have called every shade of Autumn. She had these wonderful cheekbones, and brown eyes, and beautiful lips, and I just fell for her completely. But you want to know what was funny about it?' Dan considered for a second. 'Or not funny, to be more accurate?'

'What?'

'We were in the same year at college. The same year. And guess when we met?'

'When?'

He gritted his teeth. 'In the last week. In the last week of our last year. Now how about that for fate having a laugh? Not funny I'd say. Not bloody funny at all.' His head was spinning and he took a deep breath. 'We met on a bus into town on one evening in our last week. And I fell for her so badly, but we didn't have a chance. She was going to law school in Chester. I was going to journalism college in Cardiff and we didn't stand a chance. We tried to see each other for a while, but the distance and pressure got too much, and that was it. I've never stopped wondering what it would have been like if we'd met sooner. And you know what? I compare every woman to her. And none of them match up. None at all. In fact, I've given up trying. I'm resigned to being alone. I don't like it, but that's the way it is. That's partly why I got a dog. You know what I comfort myself with now? I say to myself I never want to get involved in something I wouldn't just walk away from. I can't take the emotion. I'd rather just be alone.'

Adam stared at him in silence. He looked stunned. Dan felt the same. He didn't know where all that had come from. Because Adam had unburdened himself on him? He felt a tightening of his throat, excused himself and made for the toilet. He shut a cubicle door behind him and sat on the toilet seat, breathing deeply and trying not to think of Thomasin.

When he emerged and sat back down, Adam's face was sympathetic, understanding.

'I think that's one all on the emotional outpourings', said Dan, by way of an apology.

'It must be the beer', said Adam, tapping the Spingo. 'I guess we're both just not used to having our feelings disturbed.'

'I think you may well be right'. Dan sighed. 'Anyway, you're the one with the more challenging life at the moment. So what are you going to do about Annie?'

Adam took a deep breath and let it out slowly. Dan wondered if his head was spinning too.

'I miss them terribly and I know they miss me as well. And I'm sick of living alone in a flat. But I know I can't give up my job. It's part of what makes me what I am. You can see why now. If I did give it up to be with Annie, I'd end up resenting her for it, and that would destroy us.'

'Sounds like a no win scenario.' He'd heard plenty of those before. Lived many himself. 'Any ideas how to sort it out?'

'I'm just going to have to make sure I spend more time with them. But every time I do, we get a big case and I get called out. It's like the fates conspiring against us.'

'Just like me meeting Thomasin with a week of our University lives to go.'

The two men sat and contemplated in silence. Outside a siren wailed and a police car sped by, its flashing light shifting blue shadows around the bar. Adam looked down at his pager, half expecting it to go off.

'I think I'd better be off', said Adam. 'I feel whacked.'

'Me too', agreed Dan. 'Let's get a cab.'

'Just one thing before we go', said Adam. 'If Rutherford can wait for a minute.' Dan nodded. 'Don't give up hope.'

'How do you mean?'

'Don't give up. Don't think I'm being patronising, or trying to be your Dad or any of that shit, but I've suffered a broken heart in the past. Most people have. I thought it'd never pass, but it did. What mends it is when you meet someone special.'

He caught Dan's look. 'I know it sounds like Mills and Boon crap, but it's true. They kind of, well, they make you forget and you wonder what the problem was in the first place. Annie did that for me. So don't despair. You never know what's out there waiting for you, or who, more to the point. I know it doesn't feel like it, and no one believes it when someone else tells them it, but life can get better, and it does. It will. Don't give up.'

Dan wasn't in the mood to believe it and would have been irritated to get that kind of pep talk from his friends, but from Adam it felt comforting and he appreciated it.

'I don't know what to say about the rest of the investigation', said Adam, as they climbed slowly into a black cab. 'We'll carry on with it of course, but quite honestly I haven't got a clue what to do next. I'm going to have to have a few hours to think about it and go through some of the stuff we've already dug up. It's routine and dull and I don't think there's much point you being in on it. If I were you, I'd go back to your newsroom for a couple of days, probably until the start of next week in fact. I'll give you a call if something comes up. But I think it's going to be a lot of sifting paper for now.'

The journey passed in silence until the taxi pulled up outside Adam's flat. Dan thought he was right. It looked lonely and cold. Adam put out his hand and Dan shook it.

'Thanks', said Adam. 'For your help on the investigation, the beer, and just being around. It's been, well, refreshing to have someone to talk to. It's made me feel much better.'

'Me too Adam, me too.'

Chapter nineteen

He didn't like to admit it, but life felt slow away from the Bray inquiry. He'd covered a couple of routine stories in the last few days, a big crash and traffic jam on the A38 near Exeter and the start of an attempted murder court case in Truro. Both had been straightforward, satisfactory, and dull.

The most interesting thing had been that text message from El, as cryptic as ever. 'Operation Exposure proceeding well. Results possible soon, standby. El.'

This morning he had nothing planned, so wasn't it time he rang Adam, to see if there was any update on the investigation? He knew there wouldn't be – Adam would have called – but it'd be good to talk to him anyway. They'd said they'd go for a beer at the weekend, though less of a session than the last one he hoped. He'd had to call in sick, claiming an upset stomach. He thought Lizzie had bought it, but he didn't want to have to try it on again in a hurry. Those eyes of hers saw through excuses.

He started logging in to the computer and his mobile rang. Adam.

'Hi mate'. He tried to hide his excitement. 'What's happening?'

'Same as was Dan I'm afraid, nothing to interest you.'

'Ah. Oh well, good to hear from you anyway.' The computer wouldn't take his password. Two setbacks in as many seconds. 'So no progress at all?'

'None. The investigation's being wound down. What is it, Tuesday, a week until Christmas?'

Dan checked the date on his watch. That at least was reliable. 'Yep'.

'I've got until the weekend, then my detectives start going off to work on other cases.'

Why did he suddenly feel a failure? The first case he'd worked on and it wouldn't be solved. He couldn't believe it. And how was he going to break it to Lizzie?

'We had Emma Paget come in, consumed by guilt, to confess.'

'What?' said Dan sharply.

Adam chuckled. 'Nothing exciting, calm down, I was just teasing you. She came in to confess that she'd deleted some emails from Bray. They'd been discussing re-developing part of the hospice's grounds and how much money could be raised from it. It was his idea. She didn't want the hospice directors to know and she was worried it could come out in the inquiry, so she deleted them. In her words, she was then 'consumed with guilt' about it. She came in to Charles Cross to tell me. I got the Square Eyes to have a look, just to check, and the funny thing was she hadn't deleted them at all. They were just as she said, nothing of any real interest at all. And one of the instructors remembered seeing her at the gym at the time Bray was killed. He wasn't there when we went checking last time, he's been on holiday. He remembers it well because he fancies her apparently.'

Dan felt a sudden desire to meet Emma Paget. After that row with Kerry, when she'd stormed out, accusing him of being a 'commitmentphobe', he might well be looking for a new woman. But then again, he might not be. Life alone wasn't so unappealing. It was certainly simpler. And there was Christmas to look forward to. Christmas alone..

'Penelope Ramsden's out too', continued Adam. 'I went round to check a few things with her, and to see if she could give me any more on the man who cancelled the appointment but she couldn't. I still think that was our best hope, but we've managed to get nowhere with it. Still, the visit wasn't wasted. Her neighbours confirmed she'd been home about the time Bray was killed. They'd taken some paints round that had been left with them. They were delivered to her place, but wouldn't fit through the door. Often happens apparently.' He chuckled again. Why was he so chirpy? 'I also uncovered a major crime there.'

Dan couldn't see Penelope Ramsden as a criminal. 'What?'

'She'd got a few of Bray's silver coasters on her table. I recognised them from the office. They must be a memento for her. I turned a blind eye, won't be pressing charges.'

Dan could imagine her sitting at her table, gazing at the portraits, picking up a cup of tea from one of the coasters. Touching it, remembering him..

'So that weather idea about the cancelled appointment didn't come to anything?'

'Not a thing. Same as everything else in the case. No evidence, no leads, no hope of a conviction. Nothing.'

'Adam, you sound remarkably cheerful given all that. Mind if I ask why?'

'Well, I'm annoyed about the investigation being run down, if that's what you mean. But there's nothing else I can do. The high honchos are right. I've got no more leads to follow, so what can I do? Why do I need so many staff? It's happened before. You have to be realistic. You don't always solve the crime. It's frustrating, but that's the way it is. I did my best, everyone on the team did. If there are any new developments, we'll be back onto it, but otherwise.. I learnt early not to beat myself up about it too much. I solve more than I lose.'

Dan thought back to their conversation in the pub. 'And Sarah?'

A pause, the hum of a phone line, a change in Adam's tone. 'She'll know I did all I could.'

Brave front my friend, he thought, but I know you better now. Time for a change of subject.

'You still on for that beer?'

'Yes indeed. The city should be busy, last weekend before Christmas. I'm looking forward to it.'

'Me too.'

'Dan, there is just one thing I wanted to let you know. It's only minor, but I said I'd tell you if there was anything that might be interesting.'

A Popular Murder

He picked up a pen. 'Go ahead.'

'Arthur Bray's been asking for a few days now if I can release Edward's body for burial. I was keeping hold of it on the off chance we got a breakthrough and needed to do some more tests. But as we've just about given up, I've let him have it. The funeral's this morning. You going to go?'

'No, I don't think so.' He could think of few things worse. A tiny group of people gathered to grieve for a man knowing how many others would be glad he was dead. 'I don't think it would be appropriate. But we might run some news on it.'

'Well from what we know of Edward Bray, I doubt there'll be crowds of mourners in the streets.'

'I agree', said Dan, thinking what a sad testament to a life that was.

∽

Lizzie was keen to cover the funeral – he knew she would be, she loved her death and disaster – so he called Nigel and told him to bring a black jacket and tie. Dan always kept his in the back of his car, most reporters did. You never knew when you'd suddenly be covering a disaster that could make your day's wardrobe look horribly inappropriate. He'd been caught out when the Queen Mother died, had to nip into Dingles to buy a black tie. Not cheap either, 50 pounds it'd cost him. Still, it should last for the rest of his career.

Then the nasty call, to Arthur Bray. They could film from the road without asking permission, but it was only polite and decent.

'My news editor', he said, carefully distancing himself from her decision, 'would like me to ask whether we can come along and film at the church.' Silence from the other end of the phone. 'We wouldn't want to come inside of course, that would be far too intrusive. We would just stand outside, at a discrete distance, get some pictures of yourself and the other folk arriving and leaving, and then broadcast them tonight.'

Another pause. 'Why would you want to do that Dan?' the old man asked softly. 'It's just us saying goodbye to Edward.'

A good question, he thought. Arthur Bray wasn't making this any easier.

'Arthur, as you know, we've closely followed what's happened with the search for Edward's killer. My editor thinks your son was so well known, and there's so much interest in the case, it would be important to film the funeral.' Still silence. It wasn't enough he thought, not enough. 'It closes a chapter in the story and it's a mark of respect', he added, wondering at his own flannel.

There were a few more seconds of the gentle hum of the telephone line before Arthur Bray spoke.

'Yes, I understand. I do find it difficult you know, being at the centre of so much interest. I've never known it before. I've always just lived a quiet life. This isn't easy for me.' More hum of the line. 'I take it if I said no you could just film from the street anyway?'

'Yes, we could Arthur, but I don't think we would.' He felt happier now; at least he was being honest. 'We leave that sort of thing to the tabloids. It's disrespectful and unfair. It's my duty to ask you, but if you don't want us there you have my word we'll leave you alone.'

Again nothing. Was the old man still there? 'Arthur? Arthur?'

'Yes Dan, I'm here. I was just thinking.' More silence. 'Thank you for your understanding and honesty. You really have been so kind to me.' Dan felt shameful. All he'd done was cover a damn good story. 'Yes, you can take your pictures, but please don't disturb anyone who comes along. It's just going to be me and a couple of family friends.'

'Of course Arthur.' He tried to hide his relief, at the answer and being able to end the call. 'Thank you. I hope the day goes as painlessly as possible for you.'

He sat back on his chair and stared up at the ceiling, rolling his head, trying to loosen the tension in his neck. For all his bravado, all his tough act, he found other people's grief by far the hardest part of his job. Well, he'd better get used to it. Crime reporting was full of it. And with frustrating, incomplete endings too. He thought back to the old days on Dartmoor, the simple life of filming plants and ponies. He sighed and walked down to the canteen to find Nigel.

⁓

They stood across the road from the church, a safe and respectful distance. It was a small funeral, perhaps only a dozen people in all. Dan saw Arthur Bray go in, but most of the others he didn't recognise. Penelope Ramsden was there, her sobbing clear from across the street. There was an elegant and beautiful woman – Emma Paget? – too, representing the hospice no doubt. Dirty El turned up, got out of his car, took a couple of fast snaps and was gone again. 'Tonight', was all he'd said with one of his sly winks. They got their pictures and left quickly.

~

That evening, he didn't watch South West Tonight. Filming the funeral had been bad enough. He didn't want to see it again. He timed their jog for the half hour the programme was on and got home to find a text message on his phone.

It was from Kerry, apologising and asking if she could cook for him at the weekend. He didn't know how to reply. He felt like shutting the doors and staying in alone, just him and the ever understanding Rutherford. But he'd grown to like her more than he expected and he felt guilty about that row. After all, she'd been right, hadn't she? He was a commitmentphobe. But he wasn't sure he could face her, face anyone come to that. He messaged that he was busy with work and would call her tomorrow. It sounded pathetic, unconvincing, but he hoped he'd feel better then. The winding down of the Bray inquiry, the funeral and the coming Christmas had deflated him. The swamp was sucking him down with renewed vigour.

He sat in front of the TV and drank, beer after beer, but didn't feel any better, not even slightly drunk. A bad sign. He didn't see the action on the screen; his head was full of Edward Bray, Kerry, Gordon Clarke, Adam, Alan Jones, Penelope Ramsden, Lizzie, Dirty El, Emma Paget. Who had killed Edward Bray? Why? Think, come on, think, the answer's in there somewhere. Nothing came to him.

A Popular Murder

Rutherford nuzzled his cheek, startling him. The dog could sense when he was suffering. He reached out and patted the sleek head. 'Fancy a walk my loyal and faithful friend?' Rain was beating in on the bay window, but why not? Rutherford deserved it.

He changed, put a baseball cap on to keep the rain at bay and they headed into Hartley Park. He freed the dog from his lead and he bounded off through the Chestnut trees that lined the green. From beneath his cap, he was surprised to see a couple of other dog walkers struggling through the rain.

The dog sprinted back with a large stick, skidded to a stop and Dan wrestled him for it. The wet grass meant he could pull Rutherford around, forcing him to slide over the turf despite his scrabbling claws. Dan laughed at the baffled look in the dog's eyes, but he wouldn't let go of the stick. He felt better for it, for coming out and for the entertainment of his stupid but always amusing dog.

They walked off across the park, and Dan saw a familiar shape in front of him. It was Alex, his next-door neighbour but one, his Golden Labrador Beth ambling beside him. She was one of the very few dogs Rutherford got on with and they sometimes ran together across the park. This time though Rutherford was growling and the two dogs were facing up to each other.

'Alex, hey Alex', shouted an alarmed Dan, striding over. He didn't want to have to deal with the aftermath of a dog fight. He knew who'd come off worse.

The figure turned around. It was a middle-aged woman.

'Err, sorry, I thought you were someone else', said a flustered Dan, grabbing the still growling Rutherford's collar and pulling him away. 'Come here stupid.' The dog backed off. 'I thought you were a friend of mine', he said to the woman. 'Sorry. It must be your hat and coat, I couldn't see you properly.'

She smiled, a kind smile. 'That's alright', she said. 'You startled me but I knew you couldn't be too bad or Sandy would have had you.'

Fat chance, thought Dan, but he smiled too. That was the way dog owners communicated, via their pets.

'Sorry', he said again. 'And you say sorry too', he added to Rutherford, who'd found another stick and had stopped growling.

'Goodnight', she called over her shoulder, walking away.

Dan stood watching her go, the dogs, the swamp, the rain, all forgotten as a barrage of thoughts crashed around his mind. He stood there, watching her retreating figure, the golden blur of the dog dancing around her. He'd thought she was a man. Not just any man, but a friend. The dark and the rain caused the mistake. The dark and the rain..

Even the leaking water spreading through his socks went unnoticed. Only a jab in the back of the knees from Rutherford's new stick brought him back to the park. 'Dog', he said, grabbing his collar. 'I think you might just have done something very clever indeed.' He put Rutherford's lead on and they turned back towards Hartley Avenue.

'Adam', he said urgently, into his mobile phone.

'Evening Dan. Are you ok? You sound a bit out of it.'

Dan took a breath and calmed himself.

'I think I am mate. Something strange has just happened. Very strange. I can't tell you about it now, but I will tomorrow. Are you up for another evening beer?'

'Sure.' Adam sounded unruffled by the nighttime call. 'Why not, it's Christmas. The Mannamead at 7.30?'

'Great. I'll see you there.' He wanted to blurt it all out, but knew he needed time to think. 'Adam, just one thing.'

'Yes?'

'Have you still got the number of that bloke who rang in and told us about Hicks and Stead playing their 'Kill Edward Bray' game?'

'The pub landlord? Yeah, of course. Why? What are you up to?'

'Just dig it out and ask him if they're in the pub tonight, and what they're doing will you?'

'I could do, sure, but why? What's going on?'

'I don't honestly know at the moment. I'm still trying to work it out. But you told me to follow my hunches remember?'

'Yes indeed.'

'That's exactly what I'm doing.' But he thought it was more than that, didn't he? 'It's worth a try isn't it?'

'Sure, it's easy to do. If you're convinced it's worth it?'

'I think it might be. Give it a try and I'll tell you what I'm thinking tomorrow.'

Adam knew he wasn't going to get an explanation.

'Ok mate, I'll do it now. See you tomorrow then. This had better be good.'

Chapter twenty

Dan walked into the Mannamead at seven, picked a pint of Brains SA and sat at a table in the no smoking section at the back. The signs reminded him of Edward Bray's office, appropriate, he thought. He took out the A4 piece of paper he'd brought and checked it through.

He found himself wondering if Sherlock Holmes worked like this, and chuckled at the thought, making an older couple on a neighbouring table look questioningly at him.

Adam arrived early. Dan took that as a compliment.

'You've had me wondering all day what you're up to', he said. 'I really had to concentrate on this assault case that's been dumped on me. I'm going to get the drinks and then you're going to tell me. Ok?'

'Fine by me', said Dan, who felt and looked smug. 'The SA's good', he called at the detective's back.

Adam returned with the two pints and took his coat off. Its shoulders were damp from the beginnings of a drizzle. He sat down, took a sip and looked meaningfully at Dan, then at the piece of paper on the table. 'Come on then, let's hear it.'

'Right', said Dan. 'Just before I start, remember you're the expert at this, and if there's anything I've got wrong here, just tell me. I won't be offended. I know I'm an amateur at this detective lark.'

'Just get on with it please', said Adam levelly.

'Right, well, here's the problem as I see it.' He took a drink of his SA. 'Good stuff this isn't it?' Adam's warning look prompted him back to the point.

'The problem is we have a few people with motives, but all have alibis which rule them out. And I'm going to discard the theory of someone unknown carrying out the killing because I'm sure that by now we'd have met anyone who had any dealings with Edward Bray that might have made them want to kill him. And that line of thought doesn't help us anyway, does it?' Adam nodded impatiently. 'So here's what I thought.'

He paused and smoothed out his piece of paper.

'I'm sorry if I disturbed you last night', Dan continued. 'But something strange happened to me.' He told Adam about taking Rutherford for the walk in the park.

Adam looked unimpressed. 'So?' he said. 'So what?'

'This is what.' Another drink of beer, some familiar courage. 'Well, I mistook that woman for a friend of mine. I mistook her because it was raining and she was wearing a big hat and coat.' Adam's eyes began to widen. 'It was raining and she'd dressed for it', Dan continued. 'Because that's what you do when you're out in the rain. You dress for it.' He underlined some words on the piece of paper. 'And when are weather forecasts at their most accurate? As close as possible to the time you need them for is the answer, whether it's a picnic, or getting in a harvest, or whatever it is you're planning.' He looked at Adam, who was staring down at the paper. 'In practice, that's usually the day before.'

Adam sat back on his chair and put his pint down. 'Jesus', he said quietly. 'Jesus.'

He was looking at Dan but not seeing him, lost in thoughts of the investigation. Dan sensed it and waited, scanned the other drinkers in the pub. Couples, old and young, groups of lads and women, most dressed up, a good mix, lots of laughter, all getting into the spirit of Christmas.

'I like it', said Adam at last, picking up his pint. 'I like it. I can see where you're going and I like your thinking. So whoever killed Bray needed it to be a wet day, so they could disguise themselves. Hence the cancelled appointment on the fine day. But why do they need a disguise if the only person who could recognise them is Bray himself, and he's going to end up dead?'

'They would do if Bray wasn't supposed to die.' Dan let the words linger. 'What if they didn't mean to kill him? What if they just meant to wound him, really hurt him, and it went wrong? The weather provides a reason for them to be wrapped up in clothing that means they can't be identified, and it won't look suspicious to anyone who might see them.'

Adam looked down at the paper again. 'But that shot to the heart says whoever it was did mean to kill', he said. 'And anyway, whatever the intention, it only brings us back to all the usual suspects we've looked at. Because then hate would still have to be the motive, hate and revenge. And that brings us back to our old problem. All our suspects have good alibis.'

Dan had spent most of the day thinking about his theory and couldn't see any way round that either. He'd been hoping Adam might. The two men looked at each other.

'Shit', said Dan, taking a drink of beer. 'I really thought I was on to something.'

They sat in silence, staring at the piece of paper on the table. 'I'm sorry', said Dan. 'I got all excited and took you along with it. I should have known better. The failings of the keen amateur I suppose. I'm sorry if...'

'Hang on.' Adam cut in, and his eyes were bright. 'Hang on. It doesn't work unless what you're thinking fits in with something else I've found out.'

Adam paused, smiled slowly. It was his turn to have the advantage. Dan felt a surge of irritation.

'What?' he said. 'Come on, I've done my bit.'

'Well', said Adam, leaning forwards and lowering his voice. 'Here's a thing. I did exactly what you said last night. I called the landlord of the Red Lion and asked him to keep an eye open for me. He seemed a decent sort. He was certainly keen to keep in with the police. And guess what?'

'What?'

'Hicks and Stead were in there again. And guess what else?'

'What?'

'They were celebrating. The landlord said they were quite drunk and loud and were definitely celebrating something.'

A Popular Murder

'Interesting indeed', said Dan slowly. 'I have always wondered about those two, that's why I called you. I think it must have been the story I saw, the one we covered a year or so ago, when Hicks was being evicted and told the reporter he'd like to punch Bray. That and the Kill Bray game.'

He breathed out slowly and closed his eyes, imagining his way through it. 'If they did have something to do with the murder, their celebration would tally nicely. They'd have seen the funeral on the TV and known it meant the investigation had stalled. But how does that fit in with what I was thinking about the need for a rainy day?'

Adam smiled wryly. 'Quite', he said. 'How indeed? Well try this.' His voice had lifted, full of new hope. 'There's something else the landlord told me. Something which I couldn't quite place before, but which now takes on a great deal of significance.'

'What?' asked Dan eagerly. 'What?!' he repeated as Adam's mouth relaxed into an easy smile.

'There was someone else there with them; someone the landlord had only seen in the pub a couple of times before. He said that what happened last night was a bit odd. This man came in, not long before closing, and they obviously knew each other well because Hicks and Stead were laughing and shouting, arms around him, all over him. But he was sober and was trying to get them out of the pub.'

'Who? Who was it?'

'He didn't know the man's name, so I asked for a description. And guess who it was?'

'Who? Who?! Come on, don't tease me! Who?'

Adam's smile broadened and he finished off the remains of his pint. He put the glass down and leaned back on his chair.

'None other than Gordon Clarke.'

Chapter twenty-one

'I think I've got it', said Dan, blowing on his coffee.

'So do I', said Adam. 'But as it's your first time, you start off and we'll compare notes.'

It was Thursday morning, Christmas now just five days away. Dan, Adam and Suzanne Stewart were sitting in the canteen at Charles Cross. It had been decorated in a way that said someone was making an effort, but not much. A few strands of threadbare tinsel glittered half-heartedly on the windowsills and there were a series of pictures of Santa, Rudolph, elves and Christmas stockings around the room. Crude genitals had been drawn onto some of the elves. It was scarcely brimming with festive cheer.

'I wish you two would get on with it', said Suzanne impatiently. 'You're like a pair of schoolboys.'

Dan had expected her to be hostile, angry, but Adam had told him she was a professional and if he had any help to offer in solving the case she would gladly take it. It was in all their interests. More, it was in the interests of justice he'd said, making Dan feel both proud and nervous. He was still conscious she thought he had no place here, but personal feelings had been put to one side, for now at least, and he appreciated it.

'Go on then Dan', said Adam. 'You got the break. I've told Suzanne about what we discussed last night. We've both had a chance to think it over. Let's see what we've come up with.'

'I only got the break through luck', protested Dan. 'And it was only because you released Edward Bray's body so his family could have the funeral. That set it all going. So it was down to you really. I can't claim much credit.'

'Luck's an important part of the job', said Adam. 'Come on then, what do you reckon?'

Dan sipped his coffee. He'd slept little last night as he worked over and over in his mind the events he thought had led to the killing of Edward Bray. But he didn't feel tired. He looked at the meagre decorations around him and wondered if he felt the same way now he had as a child, with his pile of presents on Christmas morning. It was a buzzing excitement of anticipation mixed with the security of knowing the mystery would soon be solved. Or at least he hoped so.

He cleared his throat and took another sip of coffee. 'This is what I think happened', he began. His voice sounded thin, nervous, and he coughed again. 'It was essentially a series of co-incidences that led to the murder of Edward Bray.'

'It wouldn't be the first time that's happened', said Adam.

'Shhhh', said Suzanne. 'Let him get on with it.'

'Thanks', said Dan. 'Well, the story starts back in Plymouth's Small Claims Court. To help the courts run efficiently, all the bankruptcy cases Edward Bray had brought were heard in one day. That was where Gordon Clarke, Andrew Hicks and James Stead met and set this whole sequence of events in motion. I imagine they sat around as the cases were heard, one after the other. They must have got talking and found a shared interest. That interest was hating Edward Bray. I suspect they even discussed what they'd like to do to him, not pretty I'm sure, and not a smart move in a courthouse. But anyway, at that time I think it was just talk. They were three angry but essentially law-abiding men and they were letting off steam. That was all. I think they supported each other that day as one by one they were bulldozed by Edward Bray's lawyers. They enjoyed each other's company and they swapped numbers and became friends. From what we now know, they were certainly thick as thieves on the night of Bray's funeral, although I'm guessing then that Clarke was trying to get them out of the pub before they said or did anything that might attract too much attention. But anyway, back in the weeks and months after they met in court, it was all innocent. I don't doubt they used to have a few beers and talk about what they'd like to do to Bray, but I think that was it. At worst it was the infamous 'Kill Edward Bray' game, but at that stage it was just talk.'

Dan paused for a sip of coffee and waved at the canteen lady who had asked him about helping her son to get into the media. She beamed back.

'Then comes the second co-incidence, and this time the most important one. Gordon Clarke is introduced to a beautiful woman who he immediately falls for. That woman is Kate Moore. He gives her his charm and chat and finds out she's also in a legal dispute with Bray. I'd say it was an extraordinary co-incidence, but given the number of people Bray took to court, it might not be that surprising. Anyway, he meets her and I think he's besotted. But as we know, she's not so keen. She says she's got too much on to think about a relationship. I think she was just being polite, giving him a brush off in the kindest way she could. But her kindness backfires spectacularly. Fatally in fact. Gordon Clarke now has another reason to hate Edward Bray. The bitterness of their past business dispute aside, he thinks if Bray's out of the way, maybe, just maybe, Kate might be more interested in him. That I think was the catalyst.'

Dan looked up from his piece of paper. How was he doing? Adam was nodding. Encouraged, he continued.

'Then he goes for one of his regular drinks with Hicks and Stead. But this time he's been thinking seriously about what he can do to get rid of Edward Bray. I don't think it's wrong to say he's a clever man. In any case, he's certainly not stupid, and he is a schemer. Just look at his array of business dealings and how, when he's been knocked down, he manages to get up again somehow. He's certainly resourceful. So he's come up with a plan. It's based on having two accomplices – he's got Hicks and Stead in mind of course – and he talks them into it. This is conjecture I know, but I wonder if he told them he was going to kill Bray. I think Hicks might have gone for a murder plan – he's certainly the tougher one - but not Stead. I wonder if he's got too much to lose. He's got a very young child remember, no more than a baby really. I think Clarke might have said he was going to put on a big hat and mask, or balaclava, and shoot Bray in the kneecaps, something like that, to teach him a lesson. That may be where the need for a rainy day comes in, but I think it becomes more important in another part of their plot. I'll give you my thoughts on that in a minute. Anyway, whether he intended to kill or maim, that's just speculation. What I am sure of is that he talked them into his plan, and from then on they were bound together in their conspiracy. So when Bray was killed, even if Hicks and Stead didn't think that was the plan, they could scarcely say anything, could they?'

Adam was nodding again, as was Suzanne. Dan took another sip of his coffee. It was almost cold.

'So how did they do it?' asked Adam.

Dan arched his back against the chair. It was aching.

'It's a clever plan, and you yourself have told me several times how well thought out you believed it was. I agree. I think it was very clever indeed. To me, it reeks of a group of people nurturing a grudge, and the pressure of it slowly building up. It's an unsettled score, unfinished business. It's like a snagged nail you eventually just have to pick, or a loose thread you have to pull. You can ignore if for so long until one day you've had enough, or – as I think went on here - something happens to make it impossible to resist any more. That something was Clarke's infatuation with Kate Moore.'

Adam looked at Dan in a way that was a curious mix of amusement, respect and impatience.

'Don't get bogged down with your prose', he said. 'You're in detective mode here, not reporter.'

'Apologies', said Dan. 'I was getting carried away. I'm still a journalist by trade, although I am enjoying the moonlighting.'

Adam said nothing. Dan looked out of the window and wondered how he was going to turn all he now knew into a TV report, which would last for probably all of two minutes. It needed a couple of hours at least.

'So, how did they do it? Well, this is what I think happened.' He closed his eyes, seeing the killing unfold in his mind. 'Clarke was the ringleader throughout all this and I think he did the killing. But he must have known his relationship, or attempted relationship with Kate Moore would come out. And that would point the finger at him. So he needed a watertight alibi. Hence his trip to Bristol.'

Suzanne Stewart was shaking her head. 'But if he was in Bristol, how could he have been the murderer?' she asked.

'Simple, but clever', said Dan, trying not to sound smug. From the look on her face he didn't think he'd succeeded. 'He didn't go to Bristol. Andrew Hicks did.'

'What?' Her face creased with scorn, the truce forgotten. 'But I checked the CCTV, and the bank records of him using the cash point at Bristol station and his mobile phone trace too. They all put him in Bristol.'

'They put his mobile and cash point card in Bristol, but not him', replied Dan as gently as he could. He didn't want to rub it in. 'He's got roughly the same build as Hicks remember. They used that. I think he gave Hicks his coat, hat, bankcard and phone, and sent him to Bristol for the day to give himself an alibi. He even wrote and stored a text on his phone for Hicks to send to his secretary on the way back, so it'd look authentic. She was taken in by it, as we know. She was sure it was him.'

Suzanne Stewart's face had turned a dull red. 'But Clarke stayed behind and I think it was him who killed Bray', continued Dan, avoiding eye contact with her. 'Hence the fibres on the shotgun matching the boot of his car.'

Suzanne Stewart was still shaking her head and looked about to say something, so he continued quickly.

'I imagine he took off in his car early in the morning – he was banking on it being something so common that none of his neighbours would notice – and parked it near where he and Stead were to go fishing. They meet up and sit by the river, get cold and wet, then go into the shop and break the milk bottle. That was deliberate so the woman would remember them. They made a big fuss to make sure of it. She said they behaved like gentlemen remember? Then Clarke gets into his car and makes it to the lay by just in time to wait for Bray. I checked the timings and it's about 6 or 7 minutes from the shop to the lay by. They knew Bray was obsessively punctual. That would have put Clarke there waiting for him by about ten past five. Perfect.'

He felt a shudder across his back as his mind replayed the murder.

'I'm guessing Clarke wore Hicks' fishing gear. You've seen the sort of thing, those big yellow, thick plastic cover all things. It's tight, has a hood and combined with the wellies they wear, it means no fibres will be left at the lay by. In the shop, he keeps the hood up so the woman can't identify him accurately. There was no CCTV there as we know, they'd checked that beforehand. The fishing gear adds to the part he's playing and it's also useful when he comes to do the shooting. Any blood or nasty stuff just wipes off. It's designed for handling fish guts after all. Stead goes home by bus, as he and Hicks would normally do. Clarke has given him Hicks' mobile, which he's been carrying, so the trace shows them going from the river to their houses. They live very close together remember? He leaves Hicks' mobile under a brick or some such thing in the back garden of Hicks' house, set on silent no doubt for extra insurance, lingers there for a minute so the trace of his own phone makes it look like they're having a chat, then goes home himself.'

Adam was still nodding. 'What about the gun?' he asked.

'Clarke wants to get rid of the gun as soon as possible, just in case someone's witnessed the shooting and the police are on the way. He can't go too far, so he dumps it in that ditch. It's deep and over-grown as we saw, and it's ideal. He'd have seen that as he drove to work. It was just his bad luck the farmer decided to do some ditch clearing when he did. Mind you, that was about the only bad luck they had, apart from the obvious one – the key one - of me walking Rutherford in the rain. That was our piece of luck.'

'It took long enough coming', grunted Adam.

Suzanne shifted in her seat, her face still angry. Dan got the message.

'Anyway, as I was saying, when he's dumped the gun he goes and sits in his car somewhere secluded until just before the right time to be getting home from Bristol. I imagine he parks somewhere near his house, probably in some anonymous street, and walk the rest of the way so no one sees his car. He's got the fishing gear in a bag. He's been wearing his usual work clothes under it and puts on a coat he's left in the car. Again he banks on no one noticing him. It's a good chance; it's a dark and wet autumn night after all. Then he sits quietly in the house in the dark until Hicks comes round in a taxi from the station. Clarke's waiting and opens the door and turns on the light. If anyone's watching, it'll look just like Clarke coming home. Hicks has Clarke's coat and hat on and it's dark.'

Dan paused and closed his eyes again, going over his thoughts.

'Hicks brings Clarke's phone with him, so the mobile trace leads to the house. Clarke's already scrubbed the fishing gear quietly in the bath in case there were any traces of Bray's blood on it. Hicks picks the fishing gear up, waits for a while to make sure no one's watching, then goes home himself. I think it was Stead who called us about the killing, from that pay as you go mobile at a prearranged time. They wouldn't want to risk any calls between any of their mobiles. They had to call us as soon as possible so that Clarke had the alibi of being on his way home from Bristol. They couldn't rely on someone finding Bray's body and calling us. It might have lain there all night. It was dark, wet and miserable and not many people are going to stop there. And in all of this, we've scarcely heard Stead's voice, have we? We've seen him and Hicks together, and Hicks has always done the talking. I can't help thinking that must be deliberate, just to minimise the slight possibility one of us could recognise it from the tape of the call. If we did, it would be game over, wouldn't it?'

Dan paused whilst Adam and Suzanne Stewart digested this.

'Why the cancelled appointment?' asked Adam. 'Why that odd question you asked Clarke about how he kept the rain off him? I've kept on wondering about that.'

'I genuinely didn't know how important that was when I asked it', said Dan. 'It was just a strange feeling, so I ran with it. We didn't have anything else at the time so why not?'

No reply. Both Adam and Suzanne Stewart were thinking their way through his ideas.

'I think the weather is the answer', Dan continued. 'For the plot to work, it had to be a rainy day. Otherwise wearing that big coat and hat would look odd. As would the fishermen in their weatherproofs. I think they had it all planned for that day of the cancelled appointment, but the forecast was for sunshine. So they had to cancel it.' He looked at them both, but they were still lost in thought. 'Even murderers can be let down by the weather it seems.'

A Popular Murder

Suzanne Stewart was twisting her silver necklace around, glaring at him. 'What about the gun?' she asked. Her face was still throbbing red and he wondered if she was taking this personally. 'You seem to have all the answers. Where did that come from?'

'I don't know', confessed Dan. 'That's the one thing I can't see. We haven't got any evidence that helps us with that. It's a standard shotgun. I guess Clarke bought it somewhere in the run up to the murder. They're not difficult to get hold of. Hicks or Stead may even have bought it for him. That's just guesswork. But I'm sure Clarke's the main mover in all this. He hatched the plot and he pulled the trigger.'

Dan leaned back on his chair, went to sip the rest of his cold coffee, thought better of it and put the cup down. He looked at Suzanne Stewart and then Adam. Both were still silent, thinking. 'The prosecution rests', he said.

Adam shook his head. 'Not quite. Now we've got to prove it, and that's going to be the hard part. I think we've got just one chance.' He stood up and stretched. 'Come on then', he said. 'Let's give it a go.'

Chapter twenty-two

From Dan's seat in the back of the Astra, the police van following them looked menacing. Inside were six members of Devon and Cornwall police's Tactical Aid Group, known throughout the force as Tag. It was a quarter to seven, an hour before dawn, and the Tag team were going to smash in the door of James Stead's house and arrest him.

'I want to frighten him', Adam had said. 'Really shake him up. It's the only chance to get him to talk.'

The briefing in the Murder Room had been simple. No resistance expected. Break down the door and take him away. He'd have a few minutes to dress, that was it.

'We've got to get Stead safely before there's any chance that Clarke or Hicks can talk to him', Adam had said. 'He's the weak link. The other two are pretty tough but I don't think he is. It's only through Stead we've got any chance of a prosecution. If Clarke or Hicks get to talk to him before we can question him, they'll drill it into him that we haven't got a case if he keeps quiet. I can't take that risk. That's why we're picking him up alone, and nice and early. I want him safely in a cell in Charles Cross before word gets out that we've arrested him. Clarke will just send that wolf of a solicitor of his to help Stead out and that's the last thing I want. We can go get Clarke and Hicks after we've talked to Stead. Hopefully by the time we do, we'll have enough to charge them all.'

'But he's got a baby in there', said Dan, who was feeling uncomfortable. 'And I think he's very much the junior partner in all this. I reckon he's been dragged along by the other two.'

He thought he heard a snort from Suzanne Stewart. 'Welcome to the harsh reality of police work Dan', said Adam. 'He's our one chance and we've got to take it. Even that tape of him calling 999 saying there's a body is inconclusive. They were a bloody clever bunch this lot. Minimal words, distorted from the mobile phone and he must have been talking through some sort of cloth, and probably with something in his mouth too. I don't doubt it was him, but in terms of proof, it's so muffled the voice experts will only give me 'an opinion that the voice could be a suspect's'. It's that distorted. Guess how much use that is in front of a jury?'

Dan didn't need to answer. 'Damned clever this lot were', spat Adam. 'And through all this, don't forget we're going to arrest a man who's part of a conspiracy to murder. That's murder Dan, the most serious crime there is. So he doesn't deserve any sympathy.'

Suzanne Stewart indicated and the car turned left, the police van still close behind them. It was another damp morning. She put the wipers onto intermittent and they squeaked across the windscreen.

'This is the endgame, the all or nothing bit'. Adam's voice rose. 'If we don't get the story out of him, that's it, case closed. We'll know who did it, how and why, but we won't be able to prove it. And that's worse than not knowing. I don't intend to let that happen. I want him shaken up, then I want to pile on the pressure. I want to let him know how long he won't be seeing his wife and baby son for as he rots in jail. Then I shall make it very clear to him how much less time he'll serve if he tells us everything and testifies in court. I hope it'll be a persuasive argument.'

Dan said nothing. Adam's intensity was unsettling. He hadn't seen his friend like this before. He thought he understood. For him, Dan, the thrill of solving the crime had kept him going. That was his moment. It had given him energy and drive. When the puzzle was finally solved, he started to relax. For Adam, this was his moment. For him, what counted was a conviction, the securing of justice. What happened over the next few hours would determine whether that would be the outcome.

The car turned left again, rumbled over some cobbles, slowed and pulled up. 'This is it sir', said Suzanne in a whisper. The tension had got to her too.

They were in an unremarkable street full of terraced houses in the Lipson area of Plymouth. Cars were parked along both sides of the road and the streetlights were on, casting an orange glow. The grey stone pavements and black slate roofs shone in the drizzle. A cat scuttled past them and disappeared into the shadows beneath a car.

They'd pulled into a side alley just around the corner from James Stead's house. The back doors of the van creaked slowly open and the Tag team clambered out. They were dressed all in black; from their boots to their trousers and hooded fleece tops, adorned with the Devon and Cornwall police crest on the chest.

'Any need for body armour sir?' whispered a tall and muscular man.

'No, I don't think so sergeant', said Adam quietly.

'Just the ram then lads', said the sergeant turning to his team. One hopped back up into the van. There was a slow scraping noise and a metallic black object, like a small pneumatic drill emerged. Two other black clad team members took it carefully into their arms. The man hopped back down from the van and quietly closed the doors.

'We're ready when you are sir', said the sergeant.

'Let's go get him', replied Adam.

They walked back round the corner into the street. One or two lights were on in the windows of the row of houses, but number 47 was in darkness. There was a black metal gate, which Adam pushed silently open. He beckoned to the Tag team. In front of him was a green wooden door, with a circular bronze handle and oblong letterbox with bronze numbers above it. From his position at the back of the group, Dan noticed the door looked freshly painted. He imagined James Stead as a devoted family man, out here one Sunday afternoon working on his house.

Adam stood aside as two of the Tag team took hold of the ram, steadied themselves and then turned to him with their unspoken question.

'Do it', said Adam, an urgent whisper.

A Popular Murder

The first swinging thrust brought a cracking of wood, the next a splintering. On the third the door flew open. Adam stepped into the hallway just as a man wearing a grey T-shirt and blue shorts came stumbling down a flight of wooden stairs.

'Hey, hey, you!' he shouted, blinking in the torchlights that shone on him. 'What the hell's going on?'

Adam waited until he was almost at the bottom of the stairs. He held up his warrant card, which the man peered uncertainly at. 'Police', said Adam in his most commanding tone. 'James Stead?' He knew it was.

'Yeah. What is this?' He looked around at the Tag team and at Adam. 'What's going on?'

From the top of the stairs came a woman's voice. She sounded frightened. 'Jim, Jim, what's happening? Jim!' A baby began wailing. Dan felt a stab of pity. He turned away.

Adam saw nothing but his suspect. He intoned the familiar words.

'James Stead, I arrest you on suspicion of involvement in the murder of Edward Bray. You do not have to say anything, but it may harm your defence if you fail to mention anything now you later rely on. Do you understand?'

A slow and silent nod. Wide, frightened eyes. From upstairs the woman began screaming, and the baby wailed ever louder.

～

'Mr Stead, I'm going to try and do you a favour', said Adam to the shape slumped over the table in the interview room. 'I think I can help you. That's if you want my help?'

James Stead had his head in his hands and said nothing. Dan thought he heard a slight catching of breath and wondered if he was crying.

'Mr Stead, if you won't talk to us, we can't help you', said Suzanne Stewart in the kindest tone Dan had heard her use. 'Mr Stead, we want to help you', she tried again. 'Mr Stead!' she repeated shrilly, but still he didn't move.

Adam and Dan exchanged glances. They'd been going on for almost an hour like this. Adam looked worried, his face tense with lines, a sheen of sweat. Dan wondered if Clarke and Hicks had been cleverer even than he'd suspected, and indoctrinated Stead not to say a word if he was questioned. He could imagine them either side of him, pounding it in. 'Stay silent and we're all safe, stay silent and we're all safe..'

'Mr Stead, we know all about it. We know what happened', said Adam, standing up and leaning over to whisper into James Stead's ear. 'Shall I tell you what happened? Shall I take you through it?' His words became harder, louder, more forceful. 'Shall I take you back through it in exactly the same way that I'll take the jury through it when you're in the dock in Plymouth Crown Court charged with murder?'

Dan thought he saw the man flinch, but there was still no reply. He stayed seated, body slumped over the table, head in hands.

'And do you know the sad thing about all this Mr Stead?' asked Suzanne, now standing on his other side. Her voice was kindly again, like a trusted aunt. They

A Popular Murder

were playing the good cop, bad cop routine Dan had seen in the films. But in the films, it worked..

'The sad thing Mr Stead', she continued slowly 'is that at this rate, you're the only one who goes to prison. Do you realise that? Just you, all alone. You're inside while those people who you think are your friends are outside laughing at you. Because we've got your voice on a tape when you called us to tell us to come and find Edward Bray's body. We've got your voice and that puts you up to your neck in the murder. We know exactly what happened with you and Gordon and Andrew. But happily for them, their voices aren't on any tape. So they walk off. They walk off whilst you go down to prison on a life sentence. A life sentence Mr Stead.' Still no reaction. 'I think patsy is the word people use for someone like you, isn't it? Someone who takes all the blame and rots in jail whilst everyone else goes off happy and free.'

She paused to stare at the man, to see what effect her words were having, but there was nothing.

'Now I won't be unfair and say that'll mean you're in jail for life', she went on, more kindly now, almost reassuring. 'Oh no, it won't be that bad. Life doesn't mean life. Not these days. You'll get out – eventually. Judges have to give what they call a minimum tariff you see. That's how long they think you should serve. You can look forward to coming out in – what should we say – 15 years time? You could see your son's 16th birthday if you're lucky. That's if you're lucky. You could stay in longer than that of course. And that's if your boy can remember who you are. And if he even wants to see you again.'

I'd have cracked by now, thought Dan. But still James Stead sat slumped with his head in his hands on the table, saying nothing.

Adam sat down at the table again. 'Mr Stead, we can help you. If you give us a full statement and agree to give evidence, we can make sure you're rewarded for it. I have to be fair and tell you that you'll still go to prison. But it's my belief you weren't the one who came up with the plot, and I can tell the judge that in your favour. I can tell him how you helped us bring the real culprits to justice and that will get you a considerable discount from your sentence.'

Still James Stead sat slumped, his head between his hands. Still he said nothing.

'Mr Stead!' shouted Adam. 'What is the matter with you? I'm trying to help you here.' He slapped the table, but got no reaction. 'Think of your wife! Think of your son! Think of 15 years in prison, you, in a tiny cell, probably with some vicious murderer and a crazy drug addict. Do you really want all that?! Mr Stead!'

Still there was no movement from James Stead. Adam reached over to the tape machine on the wall. 'Interview suspended at 10.37', he said angrily, and stabbed at a button. There was a long metallic buzz and he got up and stalked out of the door, followed by Suzanne and Dan.

~

'What is that bloody man's problem?' growled Adam as they sat in their usual seats in the canteen. He picked some semicircles of plastic from the top of his polystyrene cup and splashed hot coffee over his hand. 'Shit!' he hissed savagely, wiping it off with his immaculate handkerchief. 'I reckon we've got another hour before Clarke gets to hear about him being arrested and sends that bloody solicitor in. Then we're sunk. The whole case goes tits up then. I'm not having that. There must be some way to crack this bastard.'

He stood up and stretched. 'Jesus, it's got me bloody tense'. He looked down at them. 'Come on you two', he growled. 'Help me out here. Think of something.'

Suzanne shrugged. 'I don't know what else we can throw at him that we haven't already sir', she said. We've tried all the threats and bribes. What have we got left?'

'Nothing', said Adam bitterly. 'Nothing. Not a bloody thing. I was sure he'd crack. I thought the wife and baby stuff would do it, but not a thing. Not a bloody thing. I think those two have got to him. I think they've brainwashed him not to talk to us in any circumstances, and despite anything we say.' He paused to undo the top button of his shirt, and slide his tie down an inch. 'Clever bastards', he added.

There was a silence. Dan looked down at the floor to avoid being drawn into another waving session with the woman who'd appeared behind the canteen counter. It scarcely fitted the mood.

'It looks like all your good work and imagination is going to be wasted', said Adam, looking at Dan. 'We're going to know the answer and not be able to do a thing about it. Not a bloody thing. That is the most galling thing I have ever known. We'll know who did it, and why and how, and we can't do a thing about it. Not a bloody thing. The bastards have out thought us every step along the way. Even when we do get a break, they're ready for it and they can stop us in our bloody tracks. And we can't do a thing. Not a bloody thing. Bollocks!'

A couple of uniformed sergeants on a nearby table look round, then turned back and began gossiping quietly between themselves, still glancing over occasionally. Adam was right about how quickly word spread in a police station. Everyone knew that James Stead had been arrested and this was the moment the murder could be solved. Dan had seen it in the eyes of several officers they passed as he tailed Adam to and from the interview room. They might yet be disappointed, he thought. As will I. I was planning this as an exclusive for tonight. As will Lizzie, and she doesn't take disappointment well. He didn't want to think about that.

'Shall we try the baby line again sir?' asked Suzanne without hope in her voice.

'It's about all we've got, isn't it?' replied Adam, who was cooling to his usual calm. 'All we can do is keep trying. Have you got any ideas Dan? You haven't said a word in there.'

He didn't know what to say. Secretly he'd come to think of this as his case, him one of the detectives working on it. Not a journalist reporting it, a detective investigating it. He was proud of his vision of how the crime was committed, was convinced it was right, wanted to see the barristers go through it in court, at the trial, somehow making it all real. The thought of the case being abandoned as unsolved brought a knot of anger to his stomach and made his back ache with frustration. He desperately wanted to do something, and yet..

They were still looking at him.

'You know', he said slowly, 'you've always made me very welcome in shadowing you, but this time it doesn't feel right.' He shook his head at Adam's frown. 'It just doesn't feel right here. When I've chipped in before, it's either because you've asked me to or because it didn't feel like a critical moment in the investigation. This does. This feels like the real thing. It feels like the end of the story. You've got a man in there who you've arrested because you think he's part of a murder plot. Depending on what he says, you're going to charge him and a couple of others with the most serious crime going. It doesn't get any bigger than that.' He looked down at his coffee cup, then back up at them. 'It's bloody scary stuff. Maybe I've lost my nerve but I suppose I think it's a job best left to you professionals. After all that's happened, I am still an amateur here. That's why I haven't said anything.'

Adam leaned back on his chair and laughed. It was heartfelt, and it drained the tension from his face. He reached out and put his hand on Dan's shoulder.

'Mate', he said, his voice still ringing. 'I'd say you've been doing rather better than the so-called professionals on this one. When we get back in there, chip in whenever you feel like it. We're at the stage where we've got nothing to lose. We just need to get him talking somehow. Just a few words and I think we can get in to him. That's all we need, just a little opening and we're in there. If you've got any ideas, give it a shot. We can hardly do any worse.' He got up from his chair. 'Come on, let's get back to him. This is our last chance.'

~

James Stead lifted his head and looked at them as they walked through the door of the interview room, but then rested it back down on the table.

'Now Mr Stead', said Adam, standing beside the table. Suzanne joined him, Dan stayed by the door. 'Where were we? Ah yes, my offer to you. My kind offer. Please listen closely. This is the last time I'll make it.' Still no reaction from the slumped figure. 'If you don't talk to us, you and your friends Andrew Hicks and Gordon Clarke will today be jointly charged with the murder of Edward Bray. That's murder Mr Stead. It's not scrumping apples, or riding your bike without lights, or dropping litter. It's murder. The most serious crime there is under English law. It's so serious, there is only one sentence the law allows for murder Mr Stead. That's life in prison. It's nice and simple. If you're convicted of murder, you're sentenced to life in prison. Life in prison Mr Stead. Think about that. Your life, in prison. That is, unless you start talking to us of course.'

The figure remained slumped over the table, unmoving. Again Dan thought he heard a slight noise, perhaps a groan this time, but he couldn't be sure. He edged closer.

'So you won't be seeing that lovely son of yours grow up Mr Stead. And you won't be seeing that lovely wife either. In fact, you won't be seeing a thing apart from the inside of a prison cell. Not a thing. That is, unless you talk to us. You see, I don't think you're a killer Mr Stead. But if you don't talk to us, I'll have no choice but to charge you with murder. No choice. I won't be able to prove any different, will I? But if you talk to us, I don't think you'll end up charged with murder, and I'll do all I can to make sure you get the lightest sentence possible. How about that for a deal? It's not bad, is it? But this is the last time I'll offer it.'

Dan saw Adam glance at his watch. Their time was running short. Still there was no movement from the figure slumped over the table. Adam turned silently away in frustration, his face taut and his teeth gritted.

'Mr Stead, may I have a word please?' asked Dan, wondering what he was doing. Adam turned to him, his eyes widening. Dan gave a slight shrug and sat down at the table opposite James Stead. What the hell, he thought. Adam was right, we can't do any worse.

The man slumped over the table didn't move.

'I can see you don't want to talk to the police officers. I was wondering if you wouldn't mind having a word with me? I'm not a policeman you see. I'm a journalist, a reporter for ITV News.' There was no reaction from the figure. Was this the right thing to say? Didn't it just sound stupid? Ludicrous? Embarrassing? What was he doing?

'I work for South West Tonight, the local TV news programme.' He stopped, not knowing what to say next. 'Do you watch it?' he added lamely.

There was what sounded like a grunt from the figure. 'I'll take that as a yes then', continued Dan, trying to make his voice jolly.

'I'm here because ITV have, in their wisdom, decided to make me their Crime correspondent. I didn't ask for the job, it just got dumped on me. It was quite a change, and a surprise, but it turned out to be very interesting. Intriguing in fact.' What was he talking about? He didn't know. It was instinct again. Just talking, keeping it going, filling the air, hoping. 'I didn't know anything about how the police work, so I was sent to shadow an investigation. That's why I'm here.'

Dan was certain he heard a grunted word this time. It might even have been a 'so?' but he couldn't be sure. He looked down at the man, then up again and saw Adam nodding his head eagerly.

He still had no idea what to say, but he knew that feeling well enough from being thrust into live broadcasts and hearing the dreaded words 'fill, fill, we haven't got the next report', in his ear. Just keep talking and hope something happens. Keep talking..

'I used to be the Environment Correspondent you see', he continued. 'But ITV like to shift their correspondents around from time to time.' More jollity. 'They say it keeps us fresh. I'd say confused would be more accurate.'

'I know.'

The figure was still face down on the table and the words were mumbled, muffled, but Dan was sure James Stead had spoken.

Adam was nodding, frantically now. 'I'm sorry, did you say you know?' asked Dan.

James Stead lifted his face from the table. He had been crying. His eyes were swollen an angry red. 'Yeah', he said shakily. 'I know.'

A Popular Murder

He wiped his eyes with a sleeve. 'I liked your reports. I really liked it when you had a go at South West Water for pumping sewage out into the Sound. They deserved that. They never told us. We were fishing there and they never told us. You did.'

'I used to fish', said Dan, still not knowing what else to say, but sensing he had to keep talking. 'When I was a kid. Not in the sea like you. We lived near Bedford. You couldn't get much further from the sea. I used to go fishing in the river there, the Ouse. You could catch lovely roach and perch and chub.'

'There's great fishing in the Sound', said James Stead, his voice soft with memories. 'You catch loads of different fish. I can escape from work, and Janet and the kid.' He sounded dreamy now. Was it something he'd resigned himself to losing? 'It's best in the summer. The fishing's not as good then, but it's so warm and beautiful. I love it. I spend all my time there when I can. I love it.'

At that moment, with those words, Dan saw it, the way in to the man. They'd been hammering away at a false weakness. Like so many men, it wasn't his family that was the passion of James Stead's life. He even enjoyed escaping them. It was his hobby. It was fishing.

Adam was tapping his watch, still nodding hard. Dan understood. Their time was running out, but he wasn't ready to move on yet. It felt wrong, too soon. He'd only just got the man talking. He could easily clam up again.

'I caught a huge conger eel earlier this year', continued James Stead. 'It made the Evening Herald. Did you ever catch anything big?'

'No, not really', said Dan, his mind spinning. Was he really trying to get a man to confess to his part in a murder by talking about fish? 'I caught a fair size pike once, but I was so scared I had to scream for my uncle to help me reel it in.'

James Stead laughed. 'I felt like that with the conger', he said. 'I got it in on my own, but boy could it fight. It was vicious when I got it on the pier. I had to get my mates to help me unhook it.'

Dan saw the opening. This is the moment. Take it. Quick deep breath, calm, steady. Take it.

'Did Andrew help you?'

Stead's face clouded. 'Yeah, yeah, well, kind of.' A twitch below his eye. 'He was there, but he sort of stood back and laughed and watched me struggle. A couple of other lads helped me.'

He fell silent, bowed his head and stared down at the table. Behind him, Adam's eyes were wide, wild, and he was nodding frantically. He should chat more, thought Dan, about anything, any old flannel, loosen Stead up, not take the risk yet, but they were running out of time. Running out of time, and this was the opening, maybe their only chance. Take it.

'You don't like him much, do you?'

A silence, ticking on. Dan rolled his toes around the holes in his boots to steady himself. He thought he could hear his heart pumping. He kept his eyes on James Stead. Eventually the man lifted his head slowly and looked into Dan's eyes.

'No.' he said slowly. 'No, I don't. When I first met him, I thought he was great. He was really kind to me. But then he kept telling me what to do, him and..'

James Stead stopped, silenced by the knowledge of his error.

'Gordon Clarke?' asked Dan.

Stead nodded. 'Gordon Clarke', he said, his voice falling. He stopped again. Dan could hear Adam and Suzanne Stewart holding their breath. He thought he was too.

'You know, don't you?' The words so quiet, almost inaudible.

'Yes, we know', said Dan gently.

'I didn't kill Bray. I hated him, but I didn't kill him. I talked about killing him, but I didn't do it.'

'I know', said Dan, with genuine kindness now and a sudden ache pressing behind his eyes. 'I know you didn't. Just tell us about what happened and we'll sort it all out.'

Chapter twenty-three

Dan was sitting at his desk in the newsroom and fretting over whether he'd tried to be too clever. It wouldn't be the first time, not by any means. When would he learn?

He'd sat in the interview room for an hour while James Stead had poured out everything he knew about the murder of Edward Bray. His guesses had been right. The way he'd seen it was the way it was. Even his theory that the original idea had been to wound Bray, not kill him, was borne out by what James Stead said. Clarke was to wear a Frankenstein mask and kneecap him, that was what he'd been told. A jury would decide the truth of his story, but it might just save him from a very long time in prison. He'd left a near ecstatic Adam organising the arrest of Gordon Clarke and Andrew Hicks and returned to the newsroom.

'Any update on the Bray case?' Lizzie got her question in before he'd even had a chance to sit down. 'We're light for real news today. It's Christmas and no one's doing anything apart from enjoying themselves, the selfish lot.' A heel ground into the carpet. 'We could do with a story. It'd be nice to see some more return for letting you go off and enjoy yourself with the police.'

Dan nearly bit, but restrained himself. If only you knew, he thought. That could wait for the book he was half thinking about writing.

'I may have a pleasant surprise for you', he'd said. 'I can't confirm anything yet, but save me a space at the top of the running order and I'll get back to you later.'

Her eyebrow rose. 'Excellent', she said. 'You can call it my Christmas present. I look forward to seeing it.'

That had been at 12.30 when he'd been elated, buzzing, full of confidence the case would be quickly complete. Now it was 5.30, just an hour until they were on air and he was fretting. His back ached hard. Adam had promised to ring him as soon as there were any charges. So far he'd heard nothing. He glared accusingly at his silent phone and shook his head as Monica looked pleadingly at him from the producer's chair.

At 5.45 he was about to take the long walk over to Lizzie and make his excuses when his phone rang. Adam.

'Blimey, it's about time!' said a heartily relieved Dan. 'We've got 45 minutes to go before we're on air and I've had enough stress for one day.'

'Sorry, sorry', said Adam. He didn't sound sorry at all. 'It took a while to go through it all with them. Both have denied it, but with Stead's evidence we've got enough to convict them. I've charged them, Clarke with murder, Hicks with conspiracy to murder. Stead

A Popular Murder

gets the same charge but as I promised, I'll make sure he's treated much more leniently. He may even get off with conspiracy to wound. That depends on the advice of the Crown Prosecution Service.'

Dan wrote all this down carefully. 'How close was it?' he asked. 'Getting Stead to talk I mean.'

Adam whistled down the phone. 'Hollywood close', he said. 'Real movies stuff. That solicitor ran panting in to the station about 20 minutes after Stead had told us everything. I kept her waiting a few minutes on principle, and just long enough for Suzanne to get some revenge.'

'In what way?'

'She'd only paid for 20 minutes parking on her car. Suzanne grabbed a handy traffic warden from the canteen and he gave her a ticket.'

'Nice trick', said Dan. Suzanne Stewart had risen higher in his estimation. 'Just a couple more questions.' His eye was on the newsroom clocks. 'What about the money angle? Did anything come of that?'

'I don't think so. We checked Clarke's accounts and there's no evidence of Bray blackmailing him. I think he was murdered for love and hate, because Clarke loved Kate Moore and hated Edward Bray. They're the oldest motives going. In this case you get both.'

Dan scribbled this down too, thinking it would make a very good piece of script for the court case.

'The gun? Any news on that?'

'Stead says it was bought second hand from a shop near Exeter by Hicks. He paid cash and used some fake ID. It's not hard to do.'

'And what about all that money Bray had in his house? What do you make of that?'

There was a pause and the mobile line hummed and clicked.

'Adam?' he said. 'You still there?'

'Yes, I'm here. I really don't know about that Dan. It doesn't seem to fit into the case anywhere. I can give you my guess for what it's worth, but I've got no evidence to back it up with.'

'Go on.'

'I think he took the money out of his account at the end of the month and just hoarded most of it in his house. I can't help but wonder if he liked to get it out and look at it. Maybe for him it was a symbol that he'd made something of his life. He didn't have much else, did he?'

Monica was beckoning at him from across the newsroom, the deadline close now. He didn't have time for the growing pity he felt for Edward Bray.

'Finally Adam, about the investigation. Any official comment from the police?'

'You can say it was a long and difficult investigation and I'm proud of the hard work of my officers. That's all my officers, even the amateurs.' He chuckled. 'Perhaps you'd better not put that bit in. Are you going to stick it on the news tonight?'

'You bet', said Dan, giving a thumbs up across the room to Monica who held up both her arms as though cheering. 'It'll be a great scoop for us. I can't say they did it of course. We'll have the courtesy to wait for the jury to decide on that. But I shall say the three have been charged and what with.'

'Go for it mate. We've got a TV here at the station. I shall watch with interest. Then we'll open some of this beer the high honchos have kindly sent us.'

'Thanks mate.' Some beer later would be a very good thing indeed, he thought. Lots of it in fact. 'Right, I'd better go and write this up.'

'Just one thing Dan, before you go. Well, two, well, three in fact, but don't worry, I'll make it very quick. Firstly, thanks for all your help on this investigation. I don't know if we'd have cracked it without you.' Dan was about to plead luck, but Adam continued. 'Secondly, thanks for being a friend to me during some difficult times. I appreciate that most of all. Thirdly, if you're at a loose end over Christmas, another night on the beer would be very welcome. I'm spending a few days with Annie and Tom, but I'll be about most of the time.'

Adam sounded hopeful; the first time Dan had heard that in his voice when talking about his family.

'I'd like that Adam, thanks very much', said Dan, who had developed a curious lump in his throat. 'And thanks to you for everything too. I started this job feeling lost. Now I feel much better about it. And thanks even more for your friendship.'

'That's enough of the love in', said Adam warmly. 'I've done my bit, now go and do yours. Go tell the world about it!'

∼

The opening drumbeats of the South West Tonight title music boomed out. Dan sat in the brightly lit studio and felt the familiar surges of adrenalin pulse through him. The autocue rolled on the camera in front of the newsreader.

'We begin tonight with some breaking news. A man's been charged with the murder of the prominent local businessman, Edward Bray. Two others have been charged with conspiracy to murder him. Our Crime correspondent Dan Groves can tell us more. Dan..'

At police headquarters in Exeter, a group of senior officers gathered around the wide screen television in the press office. They'd sent beer and whisky to the detectives in Plymouth, but they were celebrating with orange juice and lemonade.

'Good result that', said Assistant Chief Constable Hawes, after South West Tonight.

'Good piece of public relations', said Deputy Chief Constable Flood. 'I'm pleased my idea to let that reporter shadow the investigation worked out. We might consider doing it again sometime. Cheers everybody!'

On his favourite great blue sofa that night, Rutherford laid out on the floor beside him, he wondered how to reply to the text from Kerry about Christmas. Her mum had shopped specially and the family would love to meet him. She'd bought smoked salmon and Cloudy Bay wine to go with it, both his favourites. She'd done her research well.

He was more than very welcome she'd said. He could go. Should go. Probably would like to go. But still her words from their last night together were nagging at him. 'I can help you. I want to help you.' He didn't like the sound of that. 'I want to help you.' He wasn't sure he wanted to be helped.

He thought about the changing fates of the people he'd met over the last few weeks and what they would be doing at Christmas. Adam would spend some time with his family. Was there a chance of a happy ending there? He hoped so. At least someone deserved one; they were so rare and precious.

James Stead, Gordon Clarke and Andrew Hicks would be in prison on remand, waiting the long months before they were put on trial. Arthur Bray would watch some films and think about what had happened between him and his only son. Tony Rye would be trying to patch up his marriage. Suzanne Stewart – with the new man? - he didn't know, wasn't sure he cared. Penelope Ramsden would no doubt spend much of the holiday in tears. He wondered who she would paint now.

He had photocopies of Edward Bray's poems to read, but he'd save them until he was feeling brighter. They weren't Christmas material. And come the spring, he thought he might plant an apple tree in the flat's garden.

There was Sunday's News of the World to look forward to. El had been in touch, had been working his dark arts. 'Had to go into a massage parlour to follow him', he'd said. 'Had to pay extra, told the girls my fantasy was being a photographer and I wanted to take some pics of them while they looked after me. Told them it was what did it for me. Got charged a hundred quid for it, but worth it. Got a few nice shots of Jones with a couple of the girls. Very lucrative. He's told the paper he was doing it for research purposes..' It was revenge, but he wasn't sure he wanted or needed it now.

As for himself, well, he'd helped to solve a murder. That was something to be proud of, although really it was only a piece of luck. He was sure Adam would have cracked it anyway, despite what he'd been kind enough to say.

He had a new job that he'd secretly begun to enjoy and he had a new friend in Adam. El wanted to know if he would be interested in drinking Christmas away with him, and some other friends had similar plans. Rutherford had turkey to look forward to, his favourite. He had an invitation from Adam, another from Mike and Jo, and another from Kerry. He had a few days off and the sales were coming up, time maybe at last to get some new boots. It wasn't bad really, was it?

He scratched the dog's ears and was rewarded with an appreciative whine and a thump of his tail on the carpet. He couldn't say he was happy. He could still feel the pull of the swamp on the edge of his consciousness, but he appreciated his fortune and he was content. For now.